Avalonian Quest

By the same author
THE TALE OF THE TUB
KING ARTHUR'S AVALON
FROM CAESAR TO ARTHUR
LAND TO THE WEST
THE LAND AND THE BOOK
GANDHI
THE QUEST FOR ARTHUR'S BRITAIN
ALL ABOUT KING ARTHUR
CAMELOT AND THE VISION OF ALBION
THE ART OF WRITING MADE SIMPLE
THE FINGER AND THE MOON
DO WHAT YOU WILL
THE VIRGIN
THE ANCIENT WISDOM
MIRACLES
A GUIDEBOOK TO ARTHURIAN BRITAIN
KINGS AND QUEENS OF EARLY BRITAIN

Geoffrey Ashe

Avalonian Quest

METHUEN · LONDON
In Association with Fontana Paperbacks

First published 1982
in association with Fontana Paperbacks
© 1982 Geoffrey Ashe
Printed in Great Britain for
Methuen London Ltd
11 New Fetter Lane, London EC4P 4EE
by Hazell Watson & Viney Ltd
Aylesbury, Bucks

British Library Cataloguing in Publication Data

Ashe, Geoffrey
  Avalonian quest.
  1. Legends—England—Glastonbury (Somerset)
  I. Title
  398.2'0942383   GR142.G5

ISBN 0 413 48800 4

Contents

Illustrations 7
Acknowledgments 8
Preface 9

Part One: **Questions**

1. The Extraordinary Place 13
2. Beginnings in Half-Light 21
3. Beginnings in Daylight 43
4. Joseph and Arthur 54
5. The Saint, the Grail and the Thorn 76
6. Resurrection? 98
7. Way-Out 112
8. A Remoter Background 131

Part Two: **Answers?**

9. The Terraced Track 153
10. A Notable Temple 168
11. Ariadne's Dance 182
12. A Point of Origin? 202
13. Sacred Mountains 222
14. Towards Sanity 245

Appendix 256
Notes 267
Bibliography 274
Index 281

Illustrations

PLATES

Between pages 96 and 97
1. Aerial view of Glastonbury
2. Glastonbury Tor, north face
3. Glastonbury Abbey: part of the ruins
4. Glastonbury Abbey: Lady Chapel

Between pages 208 and 209
5. Chalice Well
6. Vertical aerial view of Glastonbury Tor
7. Course followed by the maze on Glastonbury Tor
8. Chalice Hill and the Tor

LINE DRAWINGS

i.	Town plan of Glastonbury	page 16
ii.	Cross from reputed grave of King Arthur	69
iii.	'Cretan' maze pattern	155
iv.	Labyrinth design on Cretan coin	180
v.	Labyrinth graffito at Pompeii	
vi.	Tablet from Pylos, Greece	
vii.	Etruscan vase picture with maze spiral	
viii.	Carving on Hollywood stone, Co. Wicklow	181
ix.	Welsh *Caerdroia* pattern	
x.	Carving in Rocky Valley, near Tintagel	
xi.	Plan of 'Walls of Troy' turf maze, near Brandsby, Yorkshire	
xii.	Hopi Mother Earth symbol	193
xiii.	Spiral design from Mal'ta, Siberia	216

Acknowledgments

Acknowledgment and thanks for permission to reproduce the plates is due to Aerofilms for plates 1 and 2; the Mansell Collection for plate 3; the BBC Hulton Picture Library for plates 4 and 8; J. Arthur Dixon for plate 5; and the National Trust for plates 6 and 7. Drawing 1 and the maze outline on plate 7 were drawn by Neil Hyslop. Drawings 4, 5a, 12 and 13 are from Jill Purce, *The Mystic Spiral* (Thames and Hudson); drawing 6 is from Marija Gimbutas, *The Gods and Goddesses of Old Europe* (Thames and Hudson); drawing 7 is from Evan Hadingham, *Ancient Carvings in Britain: a Mystery* (Garnstone Press); drawings 8 and 9 are from W. H. Matthews, *Mazes and Labyrinths* (Dover Publications); and drawings 10 and 11 are from Jeff Saward, *Caer Sidi* (privately published, Benfleet, Essex).

Preface

Some time ago I wrote a book on the history and legends of Glastonbury, entitled *King Arthur's Avalon*. People have gone on reading it ever since, and that is one reason for my belief that the subject has an enduring fascination. But meanwhile, many things have happened. New thinking, new discoveries, the growth of a new kind of interest, have led me to judge that a new treatment is called for; and the decisive impulse has come from a discovery of my own, which seems to put the topic in a fresh light, and has turned up unexpected clues in such unexpected places as Arizona and Java.

This second book is in no sense a recantation. *King Arthur's Avalon* had a good deal in it that was hasty and speculative, but, looking through it again, I am surprised how well it stands up. *Avalonian Quest* does not profess to take its place altogether. I have not re-told the history of the Abbey, for instance, except in outline. But much that was a matter of guesswork when I wrote *King Arthur's Avalon* can now be given a little more solidity.

On the legends of Arthur and Joseph of Arimathea I have been lucky enough to hit on some fresh evidence. My suggestions about the former were published in *Speculum*, the journal of the Medieval Academy of America (April 1981), and in a somewhat different form in *Kings and Queens of Early Britain* (1982).

When I went to live at Glastonbury, I heard that the place was 'sleepy' and even 'dead'. That has not been my experience. Having had the privilege of being there myself, I can only say that I have never known so much activity anywhere else, or met so many people. I would

Preface

like to express my thanks to David Thackray, the National Trust archaeologist, for help and advice in my explorations of Glastonbury Tor; to Monica Sjöö, for permission to quote at length from an article of hers in *Wood and Water* (Candlemas 1981); and to Robert P. Thomas of the University of Southern Mississippi, for a most acute observation on the topic considered in the second part of the book, after I discussed this during a visiting professorship in March 1982.

PART ONE

Questions

CHAPTER ONE

The Extraordinary Place

I

Glastonbury is a small market town in central Somerset, in the west of England. Its population is seven thousand or so. Architecturally it extends over about five centuries, historically over a longer time, but no buildings of the earlier town are still standing. Fleeces and hides are the raw materials of its industry. It is divided into two Anglican parishes, St John the Baptist's and St Benedict's, with late medieval churches. Ecclesiastically it is better known for its Abbey, once the greatest in England, with a church surpassed only by old St Paul's. The scanty yet awesome ruins stand in a forty-acre rectangle which the town surrounds on all sides.

Seen from within, Glastonbury is picturesque, beautiful here and there, but scarcely exceptional. Seen from outside it is extraordinary. If you approach from Bristol or Bath over the Mendips, you have a sudden vista of low-lying country in which a single hill juts up inconsistently with a tower on top. That is Glastonbury Tor. It is not as solitary as it looks from the Mendips. The town is cradled in a hill-cluster in which the Tor, rising to 518 feet above sea-level, is the highest point. Its neighbours are all different shapes. They are the smooth-domed Chalice Hill, close beside it across a little valley; Wirral or 'Wearyall' Hill, a ridge outstretched towards Bridgwater; and Windmill Hill, its comparatively flat top built over, on the side facing Wells.

The Tor itself has survived much geological change because its upper part is of sandstone, harder than the limestone below and less subject to erosion. From some angles it appears conical, from others whalebacked. Its grassy sides are terraced, giving a vague impression of a

Mexican pyramid. The tower at the apex is all that now remains of a church dedicated to St Michael the Archangel. Like the Abbey which lies beneath (invisible from the summit, however, because Chalice Hill gets in the way), this is a recognized historic site. The Tor belongs to the National Trust, the Abbey to the Church of England, in the shape of the Diocese of Bath and Wells.

Around Glastonbury, and between it and the Bristol Channel, is a wide expanse of moor. Much was formerly under water, much was impenetrable swamp. The hill-cluster, towering sharply above the levels, has the air of an island and in past times was not very far from being so. Hence in part its romantic name the 'Isle of Avalon', and also another name, said to have been bestowed by the Celtic Britons – 'Ynys-witrin', the Isle of Glass. The latter has caused etymological distress, because 'Glastonbury' itself, in its shorter form 'Glaston', looks as if it should obligingly mean 'the Glass Town' but doesn't.

The flat region towards the sea was reclaimed for human use during the Middle Ages and after. To the north-west there was still an extensive body of water as late as the eighteenth century, called Meare Pool. Henry Fielding, born at nearby Sharpham, may have had it in mind in a topographical passage of *Tom Jones*. A spell of heavy rain even now can turn the fields below Glastonbury into small lakes. The whole area is traversed by drainage channels. Some are known by the old local name of 'rhynes'. At Sedgemoor ten miles away, in 1685, the Duke of Monmouth's rebel army came to grief beside one such channel. The story recalls *Macbeth*. A fortune-teller, it is said, had told Monmouth that he need fear nothing till he came to the Rhine. He assumed that this meant the river in Germany, and found out about rhynes too late.

Ghosts of his men still wander. Glastonbury itself is surprisingly short of ghosts, but it more than compensates their absence in other ways. Centuries ago it was a national shrine and place of pilgrimage. While its Abbey is a wreck, its legends survive. Two are particularly famous. One tells how Joseph of Arimathea, the rich man who laid the body of Christ in the tomb, sailed to Britain with several com-

The Extraordinary Place

panions and built its first church at Glastonbury. He brought the Holy Grail, which was afterwards lost, and searched for by King Arthur's knights. The other legend concerns Arthur himself, making out Glastonbury to be the Avalon where he was taken wounded after his last battle. In the reign of Richard I (it is alleged) the monks of the Abbey found his grave in their own graveyard.

For many years nothing seemed to be left of this haunted and haunting antiquity but dead stone. Yet in modern times, and at a sharper tempo during the past quarter-century, the ancient life has stirred again. Glastonbury has experienced rebirth as a Christian centre. It has begun to draw visitors from all over the world. And it has also witnessed spirit communications, pop-mystical festivals, UFO sightings, proclamations of an Aquarian New Age by latter-day prophets. A resurgent mystique has made it, for many, an 'alternative' spiritual capital claimed not only by Christians but by a medley of neo-mystics, even by feminist Goddess-worshippers. Its aura glows brightly for thousands in America, who, in the manner of William Blake, look to a spiritual resurrection spreading from Albion. As a place attracting cranks and gurus and visionaries, as well as seekers of a saner and wiser kind, Glastonbury is the Los Angeles of England.

2

Where has all this come from, turning a small country town into a totally anomalous place, like no other town of its kind and in every other respect most unlike Los Angeles? What is the mystique rooted in? To consider the problems attentively is to realize that plain answers are hard to come by.

Common sense would urge that the Avalonian phenomenon, past and present, is an edifice of delusion. Critical scholarship has assaulted the legends – the two best-known, and others also – and tried to discredit them. Rationality of course dismisses the visions and dreams and supernatural influences. Yet in one case after another the attack has

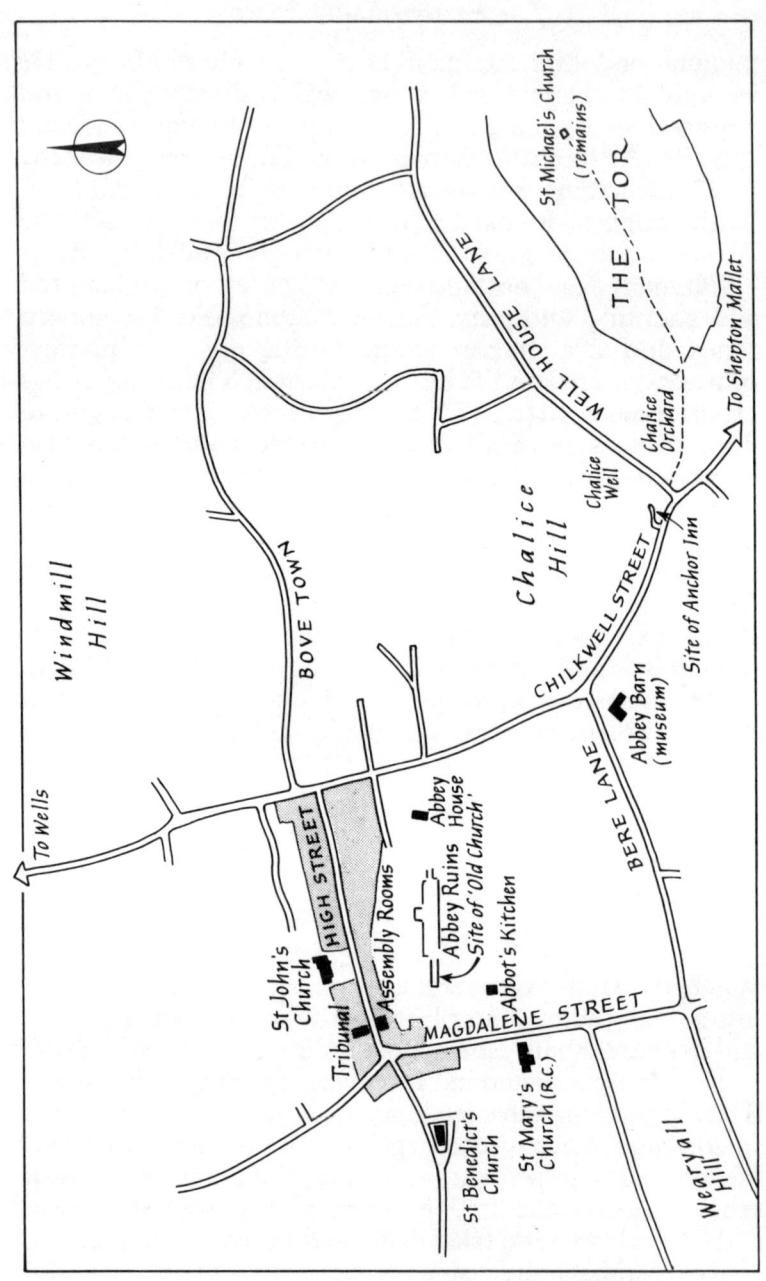

i. Town plan of Glastonbury (simplified)

The Extraordinary Place

turned out to be inconclusive. The destruction of the legends has often been almost final, but less often quite so; awkward, intractable little facts persist in spoiling the argument. Visions, dreams and influences have dissolved in nonsense; yet repeatedly some grotesque exception, something that swims against the rational stream, gives an onlooker pause.

All of which will become apparent. It might be suggested at the outset that this ambiguity, this difficulty of being clear-cut, is a main reason for the growth of far-fetched beliefs and eccentric enthusiasms. At Glastonbury it is oddly hard to close *any* door, and I am not speaking of feelings but of the results of sober investigation. That alone, however, could not account for the positive peculiar spell, the Strong Magic. Plenty of places have a misty legendary past. There are not so many places of which you can say what Aelred Watkin, the learned headmaster of Downside, once said to me: 'You have only to tell some crazy tale at Glastonbury and in ten years' time it'll be an ancient Somerset legend.' There are not so many places of which you can say (well, almost) what Calvin said of the Book of Revelation: that a man who gets involved with it is either mad when he starts or mad when he's finished.

Sometimes the madness can be a benign sort, even a holy sort, and not lead astray. But the spell of Glastonbury is by no means agreeably romantic. Outsiders are apt to come expecting meditative peace, and encounter what may be called bad vibes. I have known visitors, sound in wind and limb, who were literally incapable of climbing the Tor. Nor do such vibes confine their effects to visitors. They work subtly and subconsciously in the life of the place. Parish clergy, and layfolk engaged in civic projects, meet with complications and enmities going beyond what is typical of small towns. Some of the recent activities, despite much spiritual talk, have turned uncommonly sour and even sinister.

Tom Graves, a local printer and author who experiments with dowsing, claims that people go insane here through misuse of terrestrial forces. I am not sure what these forces are, but support for Tom's mode of thinking has come from a more publicized author, Fay Weldon. Her novel *Puffball*, published in 1980 and received with acclaim, is about the subjection of a town couple – chiefly the wife – to rural sub-witchcraft. The main action takes place within sight of Glastonbury Tor. Much is made of inscrutable Nature. But the Tor is a presence that is far more specific, and threads of its insidious power are woven into the equivocal happenings.

This novel, it should be stressed, is the work of an author who is decidedly not ensnared or committed. Fay Weldon lived for three years where her characters do, more or less, but had no trouble in breaking away and leaving. Her story is sophisticated and embodies a good deal of scientific knowledge. Yet when interviewed for the *Observer* (17 February 1980) she said:

> In all the occult traditions there are certain nexuses of spiritual power, like Glastonbury Tor: and if you live within sight of one, as we did, you do get the sense of things being worked out, of battles being waged. The power is there, and I am quite sure it exists. When I first went to Arthur's Grave, I saw it as nothing but a tourist trap. But then I went again one evening, and it *was* nuministic – it was transmitting – there was this odd, still feeling of something going on. A brooding power, not evil in itself, but indifferent, and certainly unhelpful.

And 'power' of this kind can cause harm through those who attempt to use it.

> People get into the magic of the countryside, and try to harness the indifference to their own ends.

With sombre results, such as she has imagined in the novel.

Supernatural or not, Glastonbury's more disquieting aspects are well known to breed credulity, fantasy, wishful thinking. What is not so often noticed is that the effect cuts both ways. Supposedly responsible scholars are liable to be as gravely unsettled as anybody else the moment they touch Glastonbury. With them it is an 'anti' unbalance instead of

The Extraordinary Place

a 'pro' unbalance. Confronted with this place, and its history and legends, they seem more disposed to exorcize than to search for truth. Tempers are lost, objectivity gives way to emotion. The mass of academic vagaries – suppression, misrepresentation, false logic, baseless conjecture stated as fact because anything is better than conceding substance to the legends – has to be seen to be believed. I have no wish to make such an accusation against scholars in general. But it applies quite widely enough to make one wonder what on earth is the matter. The Glastonbury Madness is no sparer of persons or professions.

For the present, let us acknowledge the facts while trying to remain on a human level. Is the spell merely a product of modern fancy, plus over-reaction against it? Or does the experiencing of Glastonbury as special have real antecedents in its past? Never mind, for the present, how these have worked through into the minds of people today. Are they there at all?

It is sometimes asserted that the spell, or magic, or special character, is felt only by outsiders – consciously felt, at any rate. Natives of the town know nothing of it and care nothing. To a certain extent that is true. It is also understandable. Even apart from a perfectly natural lack of interest, human beings who have adapted to the environment where they live and work are less likely to notice anything special than those who come from elsewhere and take the shock. But in any case the statement needs to be qualified, and the qualification supplies a clue.

Some of those who belong to the neighbourhood do value their mythos and have a disarming faith in their favourite legends. This is especially the case with the deeply rooted, who see all others as foreigners. I could instance Miss Edith Rice, a very distinguished local lady, three times mayor; or Mr Ray Burrows, an expert on the Somerset dialect. I have observed also that some who deny in plain terms admit backhandedly. An art dealer, who told me she couldn't see that Glastonbury was special, went on to a panegyric of its wonderful 'eccentrics' which implied, in effect, that it was. A foreigner may encounter reserve, and an air of hard-headed unbelief and indifference. But this may be a reaction against the tactlessness, idiocy and worse of the neo-mystics who have beset the town. With trust, people who seem unresponsive are apt to open up more.

Now the strongest of the quiet local convictions is that Glastonbury was the first British home of Christianity. That is the belief which has so long found expression in the story of Joseph of Arimathea. Ray Burrows said to me: 'One sign of being accepted here is that you get a nickname. Mine is "Bugs".' (He uses it as a pen-name.) 'Well, we don't say Joseph of Arimathea, we say Joe 'mathea. He's one of us.' Local tradition, moreover, is selective. Not only is it concerned with the Christian foundation, it is much less concerned with anything else. King Arthur is shadowy, and modern speculations hardly impinge at all.

This instinct or intuition is sound as far as it goes. It fastens on an aspect of Glastonbury which does set it apart. The Joseph legend reflects a historic quality which the place possesses, which other Christian sites do not, and which would still be a fact if all the legends were exploded. It has been, in the past, *a place of great beginnings*. Popular belief sees it as the scene of one, the Christian beginning. Popular belief, while on the right track, is too cautious. It has actually been the scene of four. Initiatives which we would expect to find happening in London, or some other major centre, have happened in this out-of-the-way spot. To pass them in review is to move towards an appraisal of what is here, whether one detects a unique, spirit-rousing *genius loci* at work, or puts everything down to chance.

CHAPTER TWO

Beginnings in Half-Light

I

The first of the great beginnings is that event so lovingly looked back on, the dayspring of Christianity in Britain. It can be given a valid meaning in terms of history. The further question is whether the known beginning has a prior, more radical one behind it.

Glastonbury Abbey grew from an ancient monastic settlement. Historians who dismiss Joseph of Arimathea are willing to accept that this was the first British Christian community. The late Professor R. F. Treharne wrote a book called *The Glastonbury Legends* which is the best-known attempt to annihilate them. Yet Treharne has this to say:

> One fact is clear: when the English [i.e., the conquering Saxons] arrived at Glastonbury soon after 658 they found a great and famous Celtic monastery already established and flourishing there, a monastery already venerated as the holiest place in Britain, with a primacy in time springing from great antiquity stretching back to a lost origin before firm history begins in this part of the land. No other house in Britain, either then or at any later time, claimed such a primacy or sought to wrest from Glastonbury the proud boast of being the first and the oldest religious house in Britain.

History can shed a little indirect light on the early community. The Church had an organized official status in Roman Britain from an early date in the fourth century, when Constantine the Great decided to favour Christianity and to make it, in effect, the state religion of the Empire.

Avalonian Quest

Roman Britain had at least three bishoprics, London being the chief. However, the number of Christians was probably very small. The bishoprics were part of the imperial system rather than native growths, and, being in the east of the country, they were blotted out by the first waves of heathen Anglo-Saxons in the fifth century and have no relevance to anything afterwards. But meanwhile the rest of Britain had begun to develop a Christianity with deeper roots and broader support. Outstanding individuals such as St Patrick had already made their mark. At Glastonbury, it is very likely indeed that the first native Christian institution took shape – the pioneer monastery – or at any rate, the first that survived. Whatever may have happened elsewhere, this was the place where (to use the vernacular) Britain's Christianity took off and stayed airborne. It is the only Christian site with unbroken continuity from Celtic Britain into Anglo-Saxon England, and through the ensuing centuries. The reason why there was no break, as there was in cities such as London, is that by the time the Saxons reached central Somerset they had been converted themselves, and took over Glastonbury without destruction or disruption. It was the recognized senior establishment, on what came to be known as the 'holiest earth' in all the land.

Its seniority and sanctity do not imply a wide-ranging influence. Archaeology suggests (as the legends themselves do) that this was not a mission centre and that the conversion of Somerset, though pre-Saxon, was late. But there the community was, in its almost-insular fastness among lagoons and marshes. It began as a group of monks living as hermits, each in his wattle cell, and meeting for worship in a church. Thus far the description would fit any early Celtic community. But Glastonbury had one unparalleled feature, which was to be the inspiration and focus of its provocative legend-weaving: the community church itself.

It comes into view in Saxon charters and the hagiographic 'Lives' of Welsh saints. We glimpse it as it stood in the enlarged monastery of later times, and continued to stand till 1184, when it was burnt down. The shell of the Lady Chapel marks the site. It was sixty feet by twenty-six, a simple rustic building of wattle-work. Timber reinforce-

Beginnings in Half-Light

ments and a lead roof are spoken of, but as additions to the original structure. It was dedicated to the Virgin Mary. And even at an early period it was called the Old Church.

A hyper-critical scholarship has claimed that it was only called so to distinguish it when another was built nearby, and that it was not regarded as 'old' in the sense of 'ancient'. For this notion I know of no evidence whatever. The manifest explanation is that it dated from time immemorial, and no one knew how it had got there. This is borne out by the absence of any early statement naming a founder. A series of saints, kings and pilgrims, before and after the Saxon advent, reputedly visited the spot; not one of them, however much his biographers sought to glorify him, ever got the credit for building the church. Always it was said to have been there when they came. Even the earliest hermits were not its builders. They had gathered at Glastonbury because of it.

It was the Old Church that impelled enquiring minds to probe backward in time, past the monastery, into the historic unknown. How *had* it got there? The earliest speculation in writing is also the wildest. It occurs in a life of St Dunstan, Glastonbury's greatest abbot, composed about the year 1000.

> There is on the confines of western Britain a certain royal island, called in the ancient speech Glastonia. . . . In it the earliest neophytes of the Catholic rule, God guiding them, found a church, not built by art of man, they say, but prepared by God himself for the salvation of mankind, which church the heavenly Builder himself declared – by many miracles and many mysteries of healing – he had consecrated to himself and to holy Mary, Mother of God.

However, the fancy of a wholly miraculous foundation gave way to attempts at history. The key figure here is William of Malmesbury. He was an Anglo-Norman cleric, author of a book on *The Acts of the Kings of the English*. Finished about 1125, it was the first work of historical scholarship to appear in England after the Norman Conquest. In it William mentioned Glastonbury, and said it had been founded by King Ine of the West Saxons early in the eighth century. Readers pointed out that this was an error and Glastonbury was older. He therefore went to the Abbey, stayed there for a time, and examined its records. The result of his studies was a small book *De Antiquitate Glastoniensis Ecclesiae*, 'On the Antiquity of the Church at Glastonbury', written about 1130.

Unfortunately we have no copy of his original. The surviving version is a later edition compiled at the Abbey in the 1240s. Lengthy passages have been added, improving the story all too colourfully. But William's authentic text can be retrieved, because he copied the substance of it into a revised version of his *Acts of the Kings*, thereby correcting the mistake which had started it all. By picking the Glastonbury matter out of this, we can establish what he really learned at the Abbey.

Describing the Old Church as he saw it himself, crammed with tombs and much embellished, he says:

> This church is certainly the oldest I am acquainted with in England, and from this circumstance derives its name. In it are preserved the mortal remains of many saints. ... The very floor, inlaid with polished stones, and the sides of the altar, and even the altar itself, above and beneath, are laden with the multitude of relics. Moreover, in the pavement may be remarked on every side stones designedly interlaid in triangles and squares, and sealed with lead, under which if I believe some holy secret to be contained, I do no injustice to religion.

He goes on to tell of the immense reverence in which the Old Church was held by the country people, of the custom of swearing by it as the most solemn oath, and of the belief that those buried in it were 'awaiting the day of resurrection' under the special protection of the Mother of God.

Still – how old, actually, was the Old Church? William tried to relate it to what was believed about the first Christians in Britain.

Here the documents failed him as they fail us. The

Beginnings in Half-Light

earliest sure reference to Christianity in the British Isles is by Tertullian around AD 200. While he gives no details, he speaks of Christians beyond the Roman frontier, presumably in Scotland or Ireland; and if so, there were surely some in Roman territory before that, in the country now called England, or Wales. The first relevant author among the Britons themselves is much later than Tertullian. He is a sixth-century monk named Gildas who wrote a book on *The Ruin and Conquest of Britain*. It is mainly a diatribe against most of his fellow-countrymen for sins alleged to have caused the Anglo-Saxon invasion, the 'ruin and conquest' of the title. However, he gives a few historical facts, and he seems to think 'the holy precepts of Christ' reached Britain during the time of Boudicca's rising or the repression following it – that is, between AD 60 and, say, 65. His grounds for thinking so are unknown. Other early authors, notably the great Jarrow scholar Bede, tell an inflated tale about a British king named Lucius who was baptized, with his subjects, under the auspices of Pope Eleutherius (174–89). This probably has its source in a misunderstanding, though 'Lucius' might have been a tribal chief, or a Briton of royal descent holding some post under the Roman government.

William of Malmesbury is inclined to connect the Old Church with this tale of a second-century papal mission. It was built, he suggests, by the missionaries. But he acknowledges that it may be even older.

> There are documents of no small credit, which have been discovered in certain places to the following effect: 'No other hands than those of the disciples of Christ erected the church of Glastonbury.' Nor is it dissonant from probability; for if Philip, the Apostle, preached to the Gauls, as Freculfus relates in the fourth chapter of his second book, it may be believed that he planted the word on this side of the Channel also.

William does not specify the documents, and he goes on to disclaim any desire to 'balk the expectations of readers by vain imaginations'. Clearly he learned some tradition about a Christian advent in the first century, the apostolic era. It may have been related to the tradition Gildas seems to have known, about 'the holy precepts of Christ' reaching Britain in the 60s. William was conscientious, and doubtless anxious to please his hosts at the Abbey. So, in his book, he mentions the first century as possible. But he prefers the second, and leaves the alleged disciples of Christ in anonymous haze. Names begin to appear only later, in the partly spurious edition of *De Antiquitate* composed after his death.

Nebulous as it all sounds, Dr Robert Dunning, the Somerset county historian, has stated bluntly that despite what he regards as the proved falsity of the legends, 'Glastonbury remains the cradle of Christianity in Britain, a faith brought from the Celtic world via Brittany to the very heart of Somerset.' Professor Treharne, also, allows plausibility to an extremely early Christian presence.

> Scholars in recent years have familiarized us with the idea that Christianity may first have reached these islands, not by the easy and obvious short sea-route to Dover and London, but, like so many earlier cultures and some religions of the pre-historic age, in the little boats of traders and adventurers braving the stormy western approaches between the Armorican and the Cornish coasts. We cannot prove it, and probably we never shall: but if we accept this idea as a possibility, is there anything incredible in the thought that, coming from the south-west, and along the south coast of the Bristol Channel, it was under Glastonbury Tor that Christianity found its first secure shelter and abiding-place in our remote land?

The specific reason for hazarding such a guess is that around the beginning of the Christian era, when the water-level was higher, this was an important inhabited area. Boats docked alongside Wearyall Hill, where traces of a Roman wharf have been found. During the last century or two BC and the first AD, two 'lake-villages' of Celtic Britons, at nearby Godney and Meare, were centres of what is known as the La Tène culture.

Beginnings in Half-Light

They stood among the lagoons and marshes, on patches of ground artificially built up with logs to make them safe from flooding. Godney was about a mile from the Isle of Avalon, Meare about four miles. The rich haul from their excavation is displayed in the town museum. Among the proofs of skill and sophistication – bronze mirrors, needles, safety-pins; looms and spoked cartwheels; decorative terracotta bowls; jewellery – are evidences of widespread trade and of influence from overseas. The mirrors and pottery designs are of southern inspiration. Tin came from Cornwall, iron from the Forest of Dean, amber from the remote Baltic. Glastonbury wares have been found in Wales, northern Ireland, Brittany. The villages flourished for some decades into the Christian era, being finally overrun by Celts of another strain, the cruder and more efficient Belgae. The village of Godney (the one commonly known as the 'Glastonbury lake-village') ceased to exist, probably towards the time of the Roman invasion. The one at Meare survived longer in a muted style.

Hence, this area was known overseas. Voyagers from far afield had motives for coming to it. A contemporary date for the Old Church, as such, would admittedly be out of the question. Apart from any problems of durability there were no churches anywhere as early as this. Even a mission would be improbable. But a visit, perhaps a stay, by someone who happened to be a Christian, is not too absurd to contemplate.

Where does Joseph of Arimathea come in? Not yet.

2

Historically, the Christian 'great beginning' is the beginning of the community. Its members may have gathered because of memories of earlier residents, or beliefs about a cross-marked grave. They may even have gathered around a building; the Old Church in some form may have preceded them. But setting the clouded dawn aside, and reverting to the institution, can we pin down a date for that?

Avalonian Quest

The newly Christianized West Saxons arrived in 658 or thereabouts. Even the toughest scepticism has never been able to put the foundation later. In the Saxon era, documentation by chronicle and charter starts to cohere. If Glastonbury had been Saxon it would have been recorded as such, with a Saxon king or saint named as the founder. It is not. What the record tells us is that the newcomers found the British community already in being and, it seems, already old. There is no sign that they heard any clear account of its origins. These were therefore beyond living memory, and probably beyond the memory of anyone the oldest monks could have spoken with.

William of Malmesbury quotes a charter dated 601 in which a British regional king endowed the Old Church with 'the land of Ynys-witrin'. 'Ynys-witrin', it will be recalled, is supposed to have been an old name for the 'island' of Glastonbury. The abbot's name is given as Worgret. It looks authentically Celtic, being perhaps the same as 'Wurgeat', which is documented in Wales. ('Worgret' occurs as a Dorset place-name and is there thought to be derived from an Old English word for 'gallows', but an abbot would hardly have been called 'gallows'.) The date 601 cannot be trusted, and has been challenged as spurious on the ground that it is given as AD, and AD dating was not employed in Britain so early. An older style of dating might, of course, have been adapted by a copyist. Despite this difficulty about the charter, it would be unreasonable to deny that the monastery was there at the time it is ascribed to.

Nothing, however, points to any particular foundation date. We are back in a stretch of British history where trustworthy documentation scarcely exists for anything, over most of the country, and it is futile to demand it. A sentence of Gildas (to be scrutinized presently for another reason) suggests that the monastery was known to him, and had an honoured status, in the year when he wrote – during the 540s. This is in keeping with the judgement of Professor David Knowles, the historian of monasticism in England, who puts its foundation date in the first half of the sixth century. However, his date would apply to the formally-

Beginnings in Half-Light

organized religious house. The original hermits were very possibly on the spot long before. Even the late Professor Finberg, whose anti-Glastonbury animus could carry him to the point of sheer *reductio ad absurdum,* had to undermine his own attempted dismissal of the whole early history by admitting the likelihood that 'there were solitaries living in hermitages amid the Somersetshire marshes before any monastery was founded at Glastonbury'.

A backward limit would be the late fourth century, because the monastic mode of life, even in its simplest form, only reached north-west Europe then through the agency of St Martin of Tours. The earliest person in Britain known to have been a monk is a certain Constans, who gave it up in 407 to join his father Constantine in a *coup d'état.* There is nothing to show where his community was, and it may even have been in Gaul. At Glastonbury we might hope for clues from archaeology. Archaeology is not very helpful. It attests the wattle cells of the early monks, and a Celtic-looking boundary ditch. But in this ill-defined phase the chief form of dating evidence is imported pottery, and none has come to light in the Abbey.

With the Old Church, therefore, and the British monks who lived beside it, we simply do not know. A tradition of priority which no one else ever disputed is the only datum. In recent years, however, a new possibility has opened up: that the Isle of Avalon had another Christian settlement, which was at least as early as the one on the Abbey site, and dropped out of the record because of some consolidation which left it deserted.

All attempts to argue that nothing could be proved at Glastonbury before the Saxon advent collapsed in 1964–6 when Philip Rahtz excavated the summit of the Tor, which is a small plateau. He uncovered traces of buildings much older than the present tower, and some were certainly pre-Saxon by a wide margin, with pottery dating. Occupation refuse scattered among them included numerous bones of cattle, sheep and pigs. The occupants were meat-eaters. On the assumption that Celtic monks abstained from meat, Dr Rahtz judged that the Tor complex belonged to layfolk and was probably a fort. However, his reason has turned out to be inconclusive. A religious settlement is now thought to be more likely, at least by some.

The Tor findings have given new weight to a curious medley of clues hinting at Christians on its lower slope also. One is in the legendary 'Life' of St Collen, an early Welsh hermit. He is said to have lived in a cell which was on the Tor, but inferentially not at the top, because he had to climb to get up there. His story is important for the light it sheds on ancient beliefs about the Tor itself, and we shall be looking at it again and considering what happened to him. For the moment it is simply his location that matters.

Two medieval Arthurian romances suggest a lingering tradition of holy men in the same area, in the days when the romancers suppose Arthur to have lived – the late fifth century, or the early sixth. The more intriguing passage is in a story of the Grail quest, *Perlesvaus,* best known in translation from the French as *The High History of the Holy Graal.* It was composed early in the thirteenth century and purports to be based on a Glastonbury manuscript. The author uses the name Avalon, and in one episode he tells of Sir Lancelot visiting the place.

Lancelot has been riding all day. Towards evening he is in a great valley that stretches away into the distance. Looking up to his right, he sees, on the 'mountain' beside the valley, a new chapel – or to be precise (as another episode shows) an old one rebuilt. It stands in a graveyard and there are three other religious edifices nearby, each with an orchard. Forest is round about, and 'in the heights of the forest before the chapel' is a spring, from which a stream runs down into the valley. Lancelot goes up to the chapel. The last part of the climb is steep and he dismounts to lead his horse. Three hermits come out of the chapel and meet him.

The description cannot be fitted to the Abbey. Yet, on his own showing, the author was there. Why should he get it wrong? The explanation would seem to be his hearing or reading that in Arthur's time Avalon harboured a community in another place. In terms of the Tor instead of the Abbey, his account makes fair sense.

Owing to the swamps and lakes, a horseman approaching

Beginnings in Half-Light

Glastonbury in the putative reign of Arthur would have had to come from the east, by what is now the A361, the Shepton Mallet road. Lancelot is pictured riding in from that direction and skirting the Tor on its southern side. To his left he would see the distant Polden Hills, to the right the much closer line formed by the Tor, Chalice Hill and the ridge of Wearyall. As he drew near he would not follow the modern road. He would descend to the old road, Cinnamon Lane, which is lower down near the old water-line. From this level the hills far ahead past Wearyall strengthen the impression of a long, broad valley, while the near range on the right, beginning with the Tor, looks surprisingly 'mountainous' and would have looked even more so when there were no fields or buildings, and forest grew on it. The spring which feeds what is now called Chalice Well would have appeared, from Cinnamon Lane, to be 'in the heights of the forest'. If you follow the lane as it swings north towards the modern road, part of the Tor's lower slope forms an apparent top near Chalice Well, in the area now called Chalice Orchard. A chapel sited there would be naturally spoken of as 'on the mountain', and the last part of the climb to it would be as steep as the author indicates.

This then is where he locates the buildings. His fullness of detail pretty well rules out guesswork or hearsay. He was there as he says. None of the details can be seen from the Abbey; it takes a longish, purposeful walk to establish them. They would fit a settlement in or near Chalice Orchard. And St Collen's cell could have been in roughly the same area.

The other Arthurian text is more familiar: the last part of Malory's version, the version that underlies many later treatments, including Tennyson's *Idylls*, T. H. White's *The Once and Future King*, the musical *Camelot* and the film *Excalibur*. After the battle which puts an end to the Round Table, Sir Bedivere rides all night and discovers a hermit – actually an ex-archbishop – who has just dug what appears to be a grave for Arthur. A chapel and hermitage lie 'betwixt two holts hoar' (wooded hills), and the place is said to be 'beside Glastonbury'. Bedivere remains there as a hermit himself with the archbishop. Later Lancelot

Avalonian Quest

comes there. The chapel and hermitage are now said to be 'betwixt two cliffs'. Lancelot also stays, and he and Bedivere are joined by other survivors. While the description is unlikely to reflect any first-hand knowledge, Malory has in mind a small valley beside Glastonbury but not in it. He does not even mention the Abbey, and could be read as implying that there was no monastery on its site in Arthur's time. Lancelot and his comrades do not enter the Abbey as monks, nor does the archbishop, though it would have been only a little distance away if it existed, and the proper retreat for a cleric of his rank.

Malory could be using some report of the small valley between the Tor and Chalice Hill. It is just below the spot defined in *Perlesvaus*, so close that a single community could have included both places, with the Chalice Well spring as its main source of water. There was formerly a sheltered recess on the Tor side of the valley, with trees and another spring, which was lost to view during the nineteenth century inside a structure built by the waterworks company. One point of minor yet perceptible interest is that an inn which used to be at the end of the valley was called Anchor Inn. A ship's anchor would make no sense here. A tradition of hermits – anchorites – would.

A folk-belief along these lines is attested by the memoirs of William Weston, a Jesuit who travelled through the West Country in 1586. He stayed near Glastonbury with an old man who was a former Abbey servant. His host told him of making private pilgrimages to some ruins 'on a high hill' which were said to have housed the first Glastonbury Christians. Weston, writing from memory after an arduous mission, is confused about distances, but he apparently means the Tor. As for the ruins, the obvious supposition is that the old man climbed to the church of St Michael on the summit. But he was over eighty, and he climbed on his knees. Ruins on a part of the hill nearer the base would qualify better. Weston's exact phrase is 'old foundations and broken fragments of masonry'. By 1586 there may have been merely a few odds and ends of stone, which were later carried off as building materials, and lost to posterity. Still, some 'broken fragments' might yet be unearthed. If they

Beginnings in Half-Light

were anywhere near Chalice Orchard, in the area which the *Perlesvaus* author indicates, that would be very interesting indeed.

3

The second of Glastonbury's beginnings was pointed out by Joseph Armitage Robinson, who was dean of Wells, and an authority on Somerset history. Like Treharne he was no believer in the legends. Indeed the standard would-be refutation, first published in 1926, is his work. But he saw the significance of an event in the community's life which can be proved: its adoption by Cenwalh, king of Wessex.

This was a consequence of a long delay in the Saxons' conquest of south-west Britain. An upsurge of British resistance had held back the growth of the Teutonic settlements for fully half a century. Bards ascribed it to the leadership of Arthur. By way of preface to Cenwalh, it may be as well to assess that notion. Ideas about Arthur may have played a part at Glastonbury during the phase Cenwalh inaugurated. They certainly did play a part in the lore of the medieval Abbey.

The origins of the Arthurian Legend lie in the same broad sweep of time as the origins of the community. It is very poorly recorded, largely owing to the Saxons themselves and their associates the Angles. These peoples first achieved a regular footing in Britain as auxiliary troops, recruited from abroad after Britain ceased to be part of the Roman Empire. They were barbarians hired to defend the country against other barbarians, chiefly Picts. The arrangement was in keeping with late Roman policy. The Britons' Welsh descendants attributed it to a king called Vortigern, and made him a national villain. His villainy was in retrospect. If the scheme had worked they would doubtless have praised him for it. But the settlers (led, reputedly, by Hengist and Horsa in Kent) made ever heavier demands on their employers. Meanwhile thousands of their kinsfolk swarmed in unauthorized. Somewhere about the middle of the fifth century the entire horde broke loose and surged across Britain plundering. After some nightmare years they withdrew to their allotted space near the North Sea and the Britons enjoyed a respite in which they could re-group and organize counter-thrusts. It was a false dawn, and decades of see-sawing conflict were to follow before the position was even temporarily stabilized. But out of this period there emerged a legend of British resurgence and even triumph. Arthur was the symbolic hero, the architect of victory, the champion of a Christian people against the heathen.

Who he was if he was anybody, and how it happened, are questions which have caused endless debate. I think a provisional answer can now be given. It makes little difference to Glastonbury whether this is right or wrong, but it may be worth saying – or rather, repeating – what I suspect to be right.*

'Arthur', actually the Roman 'Artorius', was the name or nickname of the last man who had any serious claim to paramountcy over the Britons, before the ex-Roman territory fell apart under barbarian pressure. He is documented abroad as 'the king of the Britons', and as 'Riothamus', which Latinizes a British form and means the Supreme King or High King. This is a title used like a name, a more frequent practice than is commonly realized. ('Augustus' was used similarly by the first Roman emperor; and so was 'Genghis Khan' – meaning simply Supreme Ruler – by a Mongolian chieftain whose personal name was Temujin.) Continental records that bring the Briton into brief view trace a campaign he fought in Gaul during the last agonies of the Roman Empire in the west. No early writing in Britain mentions this, though it does presently become part of the Arthurian Legend. However, an obscure Breton history (long neglected, for reasons I will not

---

* The ensuing paragraphs are a bare summary of a tentative solution based on research undertaken in 1980. I published the main argument, with full references and justification for the statements made here, in the quarterly *Speculum* (April 1981, pages 301–23, 'A Certain Very Ancient Book'). I have also presented it in various academic lectures, and enlarged on it in *Kings and Queens of Early Britain* (1982), chapters 6 and 7.

Beginnings in Half-Light

go into) apparently refers to the same king and his activities, and calls him Arthur.

In Britain, before his venture overseas, he probably fought scattered actions against the Angles, Saxons and Picts in the free-for-all raiding of the 450s and 60s. During the ensuing lull he probably started the refortification of Cadbury Castle, twelve miles from Glastonbury towards Dorset. Cadbury is an Iron Age hill-fort with massive earthwork defences. John Leland, in the reign of Henry VIII, quotes local lore affirming that it was Camelot and that Arthur 'much resorted to it'. The Camelot of romance is a dream-city which could never have existed, but a Camelot in the sense of Arthur's headquarters would be feasible. Excavations directed by Leslie Alcock in 1966–70 showed that the hill was uninhabited in the Roman period, or nearly so, but was afterwards refortified with a huge drystone rampart surrounding an eighteen-acre enclosure. Remains of a gatehouse and a hall were also discovered. Other hill-forts are known to have been reoccupied and refurbished, but nothing like the Cadbury-Camelot citadel has been found anywhere else. The dating evidence – chiefly imported pottery, as on the Tor – points to the later fifth century or the sixth, and would just allow a beginning in the 460s.

Another British leader in this phase was Ambrosius. Gildas mentions him as a commander, and his name reappears in later writers. He may have been a general in the High King's service, possibly a co-ruler or regent. In the late 460s he seems to have taken the offensive and tried to contain the Anglo-Saxons in their enclaves. Meanwhile the High King himself went on the foreign expedition that brings him into provable history. Anthemius, one of the last western emperors, asked for British aid in holding back the Goths who were threatening to conquer Gaul. Doubtless he offered a subsidy from the Roman treasury. Arthur-Riothamus, as we may call him, crossed the Channel with an army. After sundry manoeuvres he was betrayed and defeated near Châteauroux, and escaped into the nearby territory of the Burdungians, where he disappears from view. This happened late in 469 or early in 470.

Avalonian Quest

With Arthur-Riothamus gone, Britain began dissolving into regional kingdoms. Angles and Saxons entered the island at new points and pressed forward from their existing settlements. Ambrosius may have continued in command for a while. There is evidence, however, for a body of veterans known as 'Arthur's Men', who recruited new members and helped British regional rulers against the barbarians for three or four decades longer. Arthur's Men may have played a crucial role in a major victory at Mount Badon, sometimes identified with one of the hills around Bath, sometimes with a hill-fort near Swindon, sometimes with other 'mounts'. Wherever it occurred, Badon was won about 500 and was the main reason for the half-century pause.

The result was a bardic warrior-saga of 'Arthur and his men' in which the career of the High King became ill-defined. The saga included not only his real exploits but battles fought after his going, and spread the 'Arthurian' period over a much longer time than one man's credible *floruit*. It may have absorbed traditions of other heroes. Possibly, indeed, there was a second British leader called Arthur, and the legendary king is a fusion of the two, Arthur-Riothamus and this successor; but I do not think he is necessary to explain all the facts.

A Welsh monk, Nennius, preserves a list of twelve victories probably taken from a poem in Arthur's praise. It makes him the Britons' war-leader, *dux bellorum* in Nennius' Latin. Several of the battles are acceptable as Arthur-Riothamus'. But Badon is the climax, and here Arthur is introduced as a larger-than-life hero slaying 960 foes single-handed: his connection with that victory is clearly involved in a process of legend-making. A Welsh chronicle, the *Annales Cambriae*, also mentions Badon and adds another battle, the tragic Camlann, at which he is alleged to have fallen. This is dated impossibly late – 539 – and no amount of conjecture can reasonably push it back into workable history. But it may have been an internal clash in which a last remnant of Arthur's Men broke up. Or the leader who fell may have been the hypothetical second man so called.

Beginnings in Half-Light

Other traditions of Arthur, as a warrior with a royal title regarded as rather dubious or of limited scope, were handed down at the monastery of Llancarfan in Glamorgan and worked into legends of the Welsh saints. The Welsh remembered little or nothing about the continental campaign, though there may be a faint echo of it in *Culhwch and Olwen*, a tale in the collection called the *Mabinogion*. The Bretons, however, whose ancestors were Britons who had emigrated in the Arthurian period, remembered it better. His departure with no recorded death led to assertions on both sides of the Channel that his grave was a mystery, and indeed that he was not dead at all and would come back as a Celtic Messiah. The idea of the Return of Arthur may have started among the Bretons and spread to Cornwall, with the Welsh taking it up later. As a supernaturalized figure he attracted pre-Christian myth, even becoming a sort of retroactive god.

Modern conjecture about him has tended to fasten on Nennius' phrase *dux bellorum*, or the two brief notices of battles in the *Annales Cambriae*, and to picture him in a purely military role. Although this is not a total mistake, it seems to lead into the early layer of heroic legend rather than to historical truth. But anyway, we may now leave him for the moment, and revert to the period when his Britons were still keeping the heathen at arm's length. It was chiefly then that an inviolate British west built on the remnants of imperial Christianity. The Glastonbury community reflected a gradual new Christian structuring, centred on monasteries, because the urban life of Roman Britain was far gone in decay; and the long lull after Badon enabled it to flourish, together with several others, the most successful being in Wales.

Then the Anglo-Saxons went through a change themselves. At first, faced by widespread enmity from the people whose land they were occupying, they had exterminated or enslaved or ignored. There may have been much more coexistence than chroniclers on both sides imply, but no British institution, certainly no Christian one, survived on a joint basis or was adapted into a Saxon form. So far as we know, the Church expired as an organization. After the pause, however, when a renewed advance was nearing its limits, a series of papal and Celtic missions took effect. Once again: by the time the West Saxons occupied central Somerset they were Christians themselves. That is why Glastonbury was never eclipsed, and why there was continuity here from Celtic Britain to Anglo-Saxon England in a specific body.

Because of this we can recognize – surprisingly – a Glastonian beginning for the State as well as the Church. This was the first place where Saxons and Britons explicitly renounced conflict and mutual avoidance, and started constructive co-operation. Until Cenwalh's troops arrived Glastonbury belonged to the British kingdom of Dumnonia or Dyfneint, which extended from Somerset to the Cornish extremity ('Devon' is derived from 'Dyfneint'). For some time, however, the Saxons had been encroaching on Somerset, and in 658, or whenever the precise date was, Cenwalh defeated the Britons and occupied what is now the central part of the county.

But his dynasty had learnt to respect Dumnonia, as a genuine kingdom with an identity of its own. So indeed it was; it did not finally succumb for almost another two centuries. Cenwalh had suffered at the hands of the still-pagan Mercians in the Midlands, and his own Christianity was due to a personal conversion. At Glastonbury he did not destroy or disperse the British monastery with its Old Church. He took it over in peace and endowed it. Presently we begin to get authentic charters, testifying to a recognized tract of monastic land, which came to be known as Glastonbury's 'Twelve Hides'. The hide as a measure of area varied widely. In the West Country it was generally fifty or sixty acres.

Cenwalh and his successors, notably Ine in the early eighth century, made Glastonbury their chief holy place and – in Armitage Robinson's words – a temple of reconciliation. Their patronage may have been extended, in the same spirit, to other non-Saxon houses, though these were more recent and never developed anything like the Glastonian continuity. The process went beyond British-Saxon partnership. Within Glastonbury's precinct, Englishmen (as Anglo-Saxons were soon, in effect, becoming) mingled

Beginnings in Half-Light

with Celts who continued to join the community, including Irish. In their united work and study, it may be claimed, the United Kingdom had its symbolic birth long before its political realization. The descendants of these same Wessex rulers became the first sovereigns of all England. The House of Windsor traces its ancestry to them.

4

Glastonbury's Irish were increasingly active. They ran the monastic school for centuries, and were responsible for the first steps in legend-making we can be sure about. They asserted that several of the saints of their own country had come to the place, had lived there, had even been buried there. In a general way, pre-Saxon visits by Celts from overseas were perfectly believable and may well have happened. Missionaries and scholars did travel to and fro between Ireland and western Britain. But the Irish at Glastonbury boldly tried to annex individuals, and used them to fill the early void with great names.

One was St Patrick himself. Admittedly Ireland's apostle was a Briton by birth, and might have gone back to his native land. There is no actual reason to suppose that he did. The Irish, however, said he did. The story which took shape was that he formed Glastonbury's hermits into a regular community about 460, and that his tomb was in the Old Church. This became a treasured belief of the monks. William of Malmesbury was prepared to accept that there was something in it. After he had come and gone, the Abbey produced a charter which Patrick was alleged to have drawn up, naming the hermits. The document was a fake, its only point of interest being a reference to an oratory on top of the Tor when Patrick arrived – not history, but perhaps a further hint at a tradition of early Christians settled thereabouts.

Another saint claimed by the Irish was Beon, said to have been a hermit at Meare in St Patrick's time, and to have made a causeway through the marshes by which he walked to the Old Church. On one of his walks his way was blocked by a demon whom he thrashed with his stick. Whoever Beon really was – and he may, alas, have been a Saxon of later date – he was identified with St Benen or Benignus, a disciple of Patrick. The parish church now known as St Benedict's was dedicated at first to Benignus, and that dedication lasted till the middle of the seventeenth century. Its present name is two steps removed from the original saint.

The Irish also claimed St Brigit, the foundress in Ireland of the religious life for women. She lived about the close of the fifth century. Historically her main connection is with Kildare. One result of the Irish glorification of Glastonbury was a belief that she came to Beckery, near the tip of Wearyall Hill, and settled there. 'Beckery' is said to be derived from the Irish *Bec-Eriu* meaning 'Little Ireland'. It occurs as a name of islands off Ireland itself. The etymology has been challenged, but the Brigit story was probably meant to supply a pedigree for an Irish group that built a chapel at Beckery. Excavations by Philip Rahtz in 1967–8 uncovered the remains of the chapel, and a cemetery, with dating material pointing to the eighth century when the Glastonbury Irish were growing important. That is far too late for St Brigit. But the medieval Abbey stuck to the tale and displayed relics – her necklace, her wallet, her distaff.

Irish legend-making led to claims which were still more far-fetched. Even the great Columba, founder of Iona, was said to have come to Glastonbury. Such flights of fancy were not taken very seriously. But St Patrick's tomb in the Old Church carried more conviction than might have been expected. It drew Irish pilgrims in substantial numbers. From the ninth century on, writers who took the normal view – that Patrick was buried in the land he had evangelized – found the belief in the Glastonbury tomb so firmly entrenched that they could not ignore it, and felt obliged to explain that it was the tomb of Patrick Senior, another man of the same name. Two of them, in commentaries on an early ninth-century calendar of saints, speak of Patrick Senior's resting-place as 'Glastonbury of the Gaels, that is a monastery in the south of England', adding that

Beginnings in Half-Light

'the Scots used to dwell there' as at a holy place of their own. 'Scot' in those days confusingly meant 'Irishman'; Caledonia's colonization from Ireland had not yet altered its name to Scotland. The second commentator says the Irish first frequented Glastonbury as pilgrims.

The vigour of Anglo-Irish collaboration, and the lavish patronage of a series of kings, gave Glastonbury a potent gravitational pull. It was on the way to the medieval grandeur which brought it the sobriquet of *Roma Secunda,* the Second Rome. There were subtler factors at work in this than mere growth. Legendary invention and forged credentials were widespread medieval abuses, but here they reflected the special character of the community, and prepared the way for unique developments.

Glastonbury was a crucible of cultural fusion. It was part of the Anglo-Saxon ecclesiastical system, yet it kept its Celtic element, and Celtic Christianity had a quality of its own. This is not easy to define with precision, and is often blown up into a delusion that Celtic Christians were separatists, even proto-Protestants. In fact their faith was Catholic and they never repudiated Roman supremacy in principle. But the Celtic Church, for well over a hundred years, had only tenuous links with the centre. It developed practices of its own. When Rome reasserted itself in the British Isles, matters which sound like administrative details, such as the method of fixing Easter, became rallying cries in disputes which raged for decades before harmony was attained. A sense of insular 'otherness' lingered on.

Beyond this there was a difference of attitude to the pre-Christian order, and the old gods and myths. Christians in the Mediterranean world had been persecuted by pagan Roman authorities, and had built their faith, to a large extent, on the memory and cult of the martyrs. In retrospect the old gods were unreservedly evil, devils in disguise. The distinction between the old order and the new was black and white. The Church in the British Isles had no comparable background. Persecution had been slight in Britain, and non-existent in Ireland, which was outside the Empire. While clerics might denounce paganism in the same strain as their continental colleagues, Celtic Christians in general had much less against it. The mythology of the Welsh and Irish domesticated a number of the ex-deities, turning them into monarchs, heroes, magicians. King Lear may once have been a god. King Lud, the founder of London, certainly was.

Even some of the saints trailed pagan conceptions after them, with only a minimal disguise. Saints of course took the place of gods in other parts of Christendom, but among the Celts, the boundary-lines and contrasts between the old and new worlds were less distinct. St Brigit herself had attributes of an Irish goddess of the same name. Her feast was on 1 February, which was the date of the goddess's fire-festival, and in her convent at Kildare the nuns tended an ever-burning fire for many centuries after her death. Early Irish poets hymn her as 'mother of the King of Heaven', 'mother of the Great King's Son', even in plain terms 'mother of Jesus', implying that she was Mary reincarnate; and she remains traditionally 'the Mary of the Gael'. She is also spoken of as a priest or bishop – this in a Church which never ordained women. Druidism, which did ordain women, and may have taught a form of reincarnation, is very probably in the background.

The Irish presence at Glastonbury meant that Celtic myth could hover in its Christian air, and that any pre-Christian local lore could enter legend more easily than it could at most places in England. That is a fact to bear in mind when trying to penetrate such arcana as the Grail stories.

CHAPTER THREE

Beginnings in Daylight

I

It was a king of Cenwalh's West Saxon line who set in motion the third Glastonian beginning.

In the ninth century, England was beset by a fresh horde of invaders, the Danes. Alfred the Great, who was king of Wessex himself, was the last standard-bearer of resistance. When the Danes were triumphant almost everywhere else, he was still holding out in Somerset. The anecdote of the burnt cakes belongs to this nadir of his reign. His guerrilla base at Athelney was among the marshes twelve miles south-west of Glastonbury. From there, in 878, he moved forward and turned the tide of warfare. After him his son and daughter, and then his grandson Athelstan, pressed the counter-attack. Since the other English kingdoms had been wiped out by the Danes, the advance of Wessex meant that Wessex simply expanded till it covered everything. Athelstan was king of all England, and crushed the last opposition at Brunanburh in 937. England's large population of Danish settlers acknowledged his supremacy.

The Danes had never been such total destroyers as chronicle and poetry have suggested. But one effect they certainly had, the ruin of religious communities and therefore, in that age, the near-ruin of learning and education. During the few years when Alfred reigned in peace, he tried bravely to repair some of the damage, founding a school and commissioning translations of classic works. Athelstan too made small attempts at restoration. But the monasteries were virtually gone. Glastonbury came to the fore as the only major survivor.

It owed its escape, as in the past, to its situation. The Danes had never captured it. They had raided it and departed. Continuity was tenuous but real. When Athelstan was king a few resident scholars, chiefly Irishmen, were still keeping it alive. One relic of this phase is a fine manuscript *Life of St Cuthbert*, now in the library of Corpus Christi, Cambridge. Recovery came through its ablest abbot, St Dunstan, a man of multiple genius appearing at the right moment.

His family was related to the West Saxon royal house. He was born about 909 at Baltonsborough south-east of the Tor, and went to school at the attenuated monastery. Its rebirth became the dream of his life. An uncle who rose to be archbishop of Canterbury introduced him to Athelstan's court. For some years Dunstan was more or less a royal ward, and used his opportunities to get hold of books, learn music, and study such science as the age knew. As a result he was accused of sorcery and expelled. He went home and took monastic vows. Athelstan's young successor Edmund recalled him and made him his chief adviser. In 943 another vendetta by trouble-makers led to another estrangement. When the court was at Cheddar, Dunstan was on the verge of leaving it and going abroad with some ambassadors whom the king was receiving. Edmund, however, was saved from death in a hunting accident by what he regarded as divine intervention, and decided that he had wronged Dunstan and was being given a chance to make amends. He did so by appointing him to the vacant abbacy of Glastonbury.

Dunstan at once began its re-creation as a Benedictine abbey, on the grand continental scale. That implied a wide-ranging programme – education, the copying of books, farming, public works, charity in a very broad sense. One priority of course was new building. Two hundred years before, King Ine had added a bigger church to the east of the old one. Dunstan remodelled and enlarged it, with side aisles and a tower. (William of Malmesbury did not much care for the result. 'A basilica was produced', he says, 'of great extent in both directions; wherein if aught be lacking in seemliness and beauty there is, at any rate, no want of necessary room.') The living quarters were also rebuilt. The graveyard, which was south of the Old Church, posed a special and unusual problem. After three or four or five centuries – who knows? – it was so densely packed with burials that it would hold no more. Dunstan solved the problem by piling a fresh layer of earth on top. His added stratum gave the cemetery a second storey, held in place by a surrounding wall. It was to play a part in an unforeseen argument.

As his new creation expanded, the Abbot walked about everywhere with a cross-handled staff, inspecting and advising. He rose at dawn and spent hours editing manuscripts in the writing-room. He encouraged crafts, notably the making of glass. Archaeologists have discovered his furnace near the cloister, a pit lined with pieces of Roman tile, and have identified a broken bead, a fragment of window-glass, a piece of a green bowl. Outside the Abbey, Dunstan's brother Wulfric managed the monastic estate. A start was made on the first major reclamation and drainage of the low-lying country towards the sea. It was still swampy, with a permanent lake at Meare, the one that remained as Meare Pool till the eighteenth century. The whole area was subject to flooding when the thirty-five-foot tides of the Bristol Channel joined forces with rivers swollen by rain. Dunstan had embankments thrown up to confine the nearby River Brue, and launched similar projects which his successors carried on, till a system of sea-walls and drainage ditches made the levels down to the coast fit for farming.

Under his headship the Abbey attracted many 'men of high birth and eager spirit'. But he was looking beyond, and planning that the house should be a fountainhead of renewal for England, with the Benedictine Order restoring civilized ways. His outgoing and almost missionary programme was continental rather than English. It gathered momentum because he had contacts overseas. The rebirth was not a chance happening which would have happened then in any case; it required the right man as well as an adequate base of operations. Not only was Glastonbury the one major community, its abbot was possibly the one Englishman with the will and ability to do what Dunstan did. Somehow, the two had come together at the right moment.

To lead his enterprise the Abbot picked on a monk named Aethelwold, a friend of some years' standing. Aethelwold was a musician and a gardener. Dunstan, it is said, had a dream in which he saw a magnificent tree, with branches spreading all over Britain carrying monks' cowls instead of fruit. At the top was a larger cowl which was Aethelwold's. Encouraged in his choice, he sent his friend to restore the monastery of Abingdon which the Danes had wrecked. Aethelwold moved on to become bishop of Winchester, leaving Abingdon in the charge of another Glastonbury monk, and himself sponsored abbeys at Ely and Peterborough. The branching-out continued. Glastonbury remained the visible parent stem; Professor Knowles, in *The Monastic Order in England*, makes Dunstan's appointment to its abbacy his point of departure. The whole movement took a Benedictine course, laying a basis for medieval culture.

Dunstan became archbishop of Canterbury and, in effect, prime minister. But he kept in touch with his Abbey. A volume belonging to him, known as the Bosworth Psalter, was probably written there. It mentions several saints whose names shed light on the beliefs which had taken root. Two Patricks are recognized, one of them the apostle of Ireland, the other the 'Patrick Senior' who seems to have been postulated to account for the Glastonbury tomb. Perhaps the monk who compiled the Psalter had private doubts about the claim to the greater Patrick. The Psalter also names Brigit and Gildas. Inclusion of Gildas may reflect a notion that that cantankerous Briton had some Glastonian connection. The notion appears explicitly later, and has a share in the legend-making.

2

Glastonbury's fourth beginning was the beginning of one of the richest imaginative adventures of the Middle Ages, Arthurian romance. While Arthur was not invented here, the Abbey was implicated in the events which led to his

Beginnings in Daylight

apotheosis. We cannot be sure what order these happened in, or who influenced whom, or to what extent. The outcome, however, is plain enough.

William of Malmesbury, writing his *Acts of the Kings of the English,* felt bound to ask how the English – that is, the Anglo-Saxons – had come to Britain in the first place. Like his search for the origins of Glastonbury, the question drove him to plunge into a distant past. His work at the Abbey increased public awareness of this past and public knowledge of it, or, at any rate, knowledge of what had been handed down about it. Reading Gildas, together with Bede and Welsh writers, he pieced together an account of what followed Britain's turning-adrift from the Roman Empire. After the story of Vortigern, and the story of his barbarian auxiliaries who got out of hand, William goes on:

> The strength of the Britons grew faint, their diminished hopes went backwards; and straightway they would have come to ruin, had not Ambrosius, the sole survivor of the Romans, who was monarch of the realm after Vortigern, repressed the overweening barbarians through the distinguished achievement of the warlike Arthur. This is that Arthur of whom the trifling of the Britons talks such nonsense even today; a man clearly worthy not to be dreamed of in fallacious fables, but to be proclaimed in veracious histories, as one who long sustained his tottering country, and gave the shattered minds of his fellow-citizens an edge for war. Finally, at the siege of Mount Badon, relying upon the image of the mother of the Lord which he had sewn upon his armour, he made head single-handed against nine hundred of the enemy and routed them with incredible slaughter.

By the 'Britons' who talk nonsense about Arthur, William almost certainly means the Bretons. They were well known to be descended from Britons who had crossed the Channel in the fifth and sixth centuries. French authors attest the vigour of their Arthurian tradition. Elsewhere in his book William remarks in passing that the grave of Arthur is 'nowhere beheld', and ancient songs therefore

Avalonian Quest

prophesy his return. William accepts Arthur's reality, but, lacking solid information, draws on the Welsh bardic matter stressing his role as a warrior and commander-in-chief, with Ambrosius rather than himself as the political head.

Beside gathering data on Arthur, William noted a belief that Gildas belonged for a time to the Glastonbury community. This was now taken up by Caradoc, a historian at Llancarfan, the Glamorgan monastery where scraps of Arthuriana were preserved. In the early 1130s Caradoc wrote a 'Life' of Gildas including a Glastonbury episode bringing Arthur in. Caradoc's tale accepts Arthur's kingship, as some others told at Llancarfan did, though he is inconsistent about the scope of the title and its legality in his eyes. When Gildas is at Glastonbury in this account, another, minor king named Melwas is ruling over the Summer Land, i.e., Somerset. The monastery is therefore in his domain. He carries off Arthur's wife 'Guennuvar' and keeps her at Glastonbury. Arthur brings up troops from Cornwall and Devon to recover her. His advance is slow because of the watery surroundings. Before serious fighting breaks out, Gildas and the abbot mediate, and the dispute is settled by negotiation. Melwas restores the lady, and makes his peace with Arthur in the 'temple of holy Mary', meaning the Old Church.

William and Caradoc together had lit the fuse, but the Arthurian explosion came from another quarter. It came from an author who professed not to be composing fiction, but to be acting in the spirit of William's remark that Arthur deserved to be 'proclaimed in veracious histories'. He was an author of richer imagination and less scrupulosity – Geoffrey of Monmouth.

Geoffrey was a minor cleric. He may have been Welsh, he may have been a Breton born in Wales. Many Bretons returned to the island of their ancestors in the wake of the Norman conqueror. After attracting attention with some 'prophecies of Merlin', he published, about 1136, a *History of the Kings of Britain* which became one of the great books of the Middle Ages. Traces of its influence extend to Shakespeare and beyond.

Beginnings in Daylight

Beginning with a wandering Trojan named Brutus, said to have been the first king of Britain, Geoffrey runs through seventy-six monarchs who reigned before Julius Caesar's invasion. They are all fictitious, though a few are not actually his inventions, and belong to earlier Welsh legend. Moving into historical times, he gives a garbled account of Britain during the Roman period. Next comes Vortigern, the evil genius of post-Roman Britain, who betrays his country to Hengist and Horsa and the Saxons (the word 'Saxon' being used for the whole Teutonic medley).

The *History* rises to its climax in the reign of King Arthur. Conceived at Tintagel through Merlin's magic, Arthur succeeds to the crown at fifteen. Battles with the barbarians in Lincolnshire and Scotland build up to a victory at Bath (Geoffrey's interpretation of Badon) which reduces the surviving Saxons to virtual nullity. Arthur then conquers Ireland, Iceland, and – after a twelve-year peace – Norway and Denmark. Next he makes a successful foray into Gaul. He holds court splendidly at Caerleon. A Roman demand for tribute and submission draws him into a major Gallic campaign. He sweeps all before him and enters Burgundy, but the wicked Modred, left at home as deputy-ruler, rebels against him. He returns to Britain and fights the traitor by the River Camel in Cornwall. Modred is slain, but Arthur, grievously wounded, has to be removed to the Isle of Avalon for his wounds to be attended to. After that, the Britons decline and the Saxons conquer what is now England.

Geoffrey's story of Arthur introduces some of the famous characters – not only Merlin and Modred, but Guinevere, Gawain, Kay and Bedivere. Arthur presides over an order of knighthood, though not yet a Round Table. The story formed the pseudo-historical framework into which the subsequent romances were fitted. While Geoffrey's book, throughout, is mainly a flight of fancy, he can be detected using and torturing bits of Welsh legend, bits of Roman history, bits of authentic matter about the Saxon conquest. In his preface, however, he makes a claim which transcends all that. He says he found his material in 'a certain very ancient book written in the

British language', given him by Walter, archdeacon of Oxford. 'British' probably means 'Breton', as in William of Malmesbury. Geoffrey's implication is that William's dismissal of Breton 'nonsense' was a mistake. He, Geoffrey, has got hold of it in a written form and found it acceptable.

Some copies of his *History* have a note at the end in which he names and cautions other historians.

> The task of describing the [Welsh] kings . . . I leave to my contemporary Caradoc of Llancarfan. The kings of the Saxons I leave to William of Malmesbury and Henry of Huntingdon. I recommend these last to say nothing at all about the kings of the Britons, seeing that they do not have in their possession the book in the British language which Walter, Archdeacon of Oxford, brought from *Britannia* [presumably Brittany, though some think it could be Wales].

Did the book exist? It could hardly have supplied Geoffrey with the whole fabric of his *History,* as he pretends, but it could have supplied a part. His only specific statement about it is that it gave him information on the disaster which ended Arthur's career. Hence, it was probably a source for his Arthur story if it was a source for anything. Until lately, expert opinion generally maintained that it was a pure invention. But the facts which seem to have emerged about Arthurian origins suggest that Geoffrey did read some lost Breton history which included a narrative of the High King's march through Gaul in 469–70, and gave his personal name as Arthur, as one known Breton text apparently does. Details of this affair can be disinterred from the fantasy.

The creation of Arthur as we know him was, in the end, ironic. William of Malmesbury, the careful historian, picked up Welsh Arthurian fragments and did what he could with them in the paragraph quoted. But the status of the characters was confused. Ambrosius had become a king, though there is no early evidence that he was. Arthur's name survived almost wholly in the warrior-saga and extravagant fairy-tales based on it, like *Culhwch and*

Beginnings in Daylight

Olwen. The saga included a piece of bardic fancy transmitted by Nennius about his incredible prowess at Badon, where he was seemingly present in spirit rather than in the flesh. This was the best that Wales could offer.

In Brittany, along with fairy-tales, a record of the High King's Gallic campaign was preserved. William accepted the warrior tradition as modern historians have tended to do, and brushed the Bretons aside. He was wrong. Geoffrey discovered some version of their history, took it seriously, and was, however crazily, right. He restored Arthur to a firm kingship, credited him with battles in Britain as a matter of course, but also added the Gallic war. He exaggerated, he distorted, he got the dates in a tangle, he even altered the enemy for the king's greater glory. But he kept just enough details to show what events his imagination was working on.

His account of Arthur's betrayal and passing is a skilful fiction that blends traditions. After the real betrayal Arthur-Riothamus vanished, so far as the record goes, in Burgundy. Geoffrey brings Arthur to Burgundy, but then takes him back to Britain so that he can fall at the Camel, supposedly the Camlann of Welsh story-tellers. Then Arthur departs to Avalon – the apple-island, as the name is usually taken to mean. Geoffrey is not here referring to Glastonbury, though, of course, apples grow there in plenty. Rather he has in mind an 'otherworld' place in Celtic mythology, a place of wonder-working and healing and immortality, called in Welsh 'Ynys Avallach'... which may mean either 'isle of apples' or 'isle of Avallach', a mythical king. The equation of Glastonbury with this island is a problem we shall have to face, but not yet. Geoffrey gives the familiar spelling or nearly so. In the Latin of his *History* Avallach becomes, as would not be expected, *Insula Avallonis*. Geoffrey has been influenced by a real place-name in Burgundy, Avallon, which certainly has the 'apple' meaning. Probably Avallon was mentioned in whatever version of Arthur-Riothamus' Burgundian passing fell into his hands.

After the *History* had supplied the framework, a colossal literary growth followed. It was fuelled by rediscovery. For hundreds of years, Anglo-Saxon conquest had virtually effaced the traditions of Arthur and his companions wherever it extended. Memories survived on the Celtic fringe, not in England. But with the circulation of Geoffrey's *History* and adaptations of it, King Arthur became popular with the Anglo-Normans and their court. He was transformed into a national rather than a regional figure. Meanwhile Breton minstrels were spreading his renown through France. The result was that a mass of Celtic legend flowed back from Wales and Cornwall and Brittany into England and France, the whole territory where educated people spoke French. It embraced much more besides strictly Arthurian matter, including tales from Ireland. Storytellers drew on it for the great new cycle of romance. Fresh themes took shape, fresh characters entered literature: the Round Table, the royal city of Camelot, the Grail; Lancelot, Galahad, Tristan and Iseult. The extent of the Celtic inspiration is a matter of debate, its presence is not.

Glastonbury had a continuing role in this. In coming to terms with much that is undoubtedly legend, one fact is worth remembering. So far as Arthur was a real person, the fifth-century High King, we must associate him mainly with southern Britain and with the south-west rather than the south-east. Only there could an army have been recruited and transported to Gaul, in pursuance of an agreement with an emperor. There too, and within sight of the Tor, was Cadbury-Camelot. At Glastonbury Arthur was not an out-of-place figure or a manifest import from somewhere else. He may truly have gone there, as Caradoc would like to think, if hardly as Caradoc alleges. Or at any rate, stories of him may have been told there early. That has its relevance to the next phase.

The case of Cadbury, indeed, suggests that there actually was an Arthur tradition in Somerset, strong enough to linger on locally after the Saxon occupation, as very few did. When Leland wrote about Cadbury in 1542, he quoted village lore to the effect that it was Camelot. Sceptics have cast contempt on the village lore and implied that Leland merely guessed. But – let it be said again – excavation revealed that the hill *was* converted into a stronghold, of

Beginnings in Daylight

vast size and only most imperfectly paralleled anywhere else, in more or less the right period. Even a modern archaeologist could not have predicted the 'Arthurian' rampart under the grass, without going below the surface. It really is beyond serious credence that Leland, or his informants, picked on the best-qualified hill in England (so far as anyone knows at present) by sheer luck. A valid local tradition that 'King Arthur lived on the hill', or something of that kind, is a great deal more likely.

It might be argued that local Arthurian fancies were generated by the nearness of Glastonbury itself with its legends, and perhaps by the neighbouring place-name 'Camel'. Even so the incredibly good guess – by the villagers or by Leland himself – would remain. But furthermore, Arthurian fancies are found up and down Britain, and far more plentifully in Cornwall and parts of Wales, yet nowhere else have they picked on a hill-fort as Camelot, much less on a hill-fort which has turned out to be . . . what Cadbury is. It is only here that the thing has happened.

At Glastonbury, old British stories may have faded out as the English grew more dominant and the Celtic presence was diluted. The absence of such stories in early writings does not prove that they were never current there, earlier still. They could have been preserved orally, and if they were not, they could still have been spread to Celtic lands – by way of Llancarfan, for instance – and handed down as others were: those that were rediscovered in the twelfth century and drawn into Arthurian literature. A Glastonbury tale which appears first in writing during that century, or even later, was not necessarily invented then. It could have been brought into England with the rest, returning after a spell of exile.

CHAPTER FOUR

Joseph and Arthur

I

So to the two most famous legends: the one which says that the first Christians at Glastonbury were led by Joseph of Arimathea; and the one which says that King Arthur, far from becoming immortal, died like anyone else and was buried in the Abbey. They need to be seen (as they too seldom are) against the historic background that precedes their visible début. It should be clear by now that although they appear late in the surviving records they cannot be treated as sudden, arbitrary fictions. Nor can they be assessed rightly in isolation, as if there were no special quality or aptitude in the place where they were told.

With the Joseph legend, the basic fact is the Old Church. Modern discussions not centred on that reality are out of focus. As we saw, when genuine charters and history begin, it seems to have been standing already from time immemorial. At some stage its lead and timber reinforcements came to be ascribed to the Roman missionary Paulinus, in the seventh century, but with the unwavering implication that the building itself pre-dated him. The latter belief was embodied in the notion of a miraculous foundation, before any Christian advent at all. That story was non-committal as to when the miracle happened, and was supplanted by the more mundane yet glorious claim which William of Malmesbury heard – that the Old Church was built by human hands, but in the dawning of Christianity in Britain: perhaps by second-century missionaries, perhaps as far back as the apostolic age and by men who had known the Lord. The latter assertion was almost bound, sooner or later, to attract a name from the New Testament, and Joseph was the man whom the monks produced.

Joseph and Arthur

The obvious comment is that there is no need to wonder about traditions or sources. They simply wanted to have a scriptural founder, and, for some unknown but purely fanciful reason, picked on Joseph.

But why him? I asked that question some decades ago and it has remained oddly disconcerting. Christian legends brought much greater disciples to England's shores, including St Paul, even St Peter himself. They and others were available and would have been far more impressive. Joseph is a minor character, who appears in the Gospels only in connection with Christ's burial. He is cautious, afraid to confess his faith openly. The apocryphal *Acts of Pilate*, which form part of a pseudo-Gospel ascribed to Nicodemus, give a tale of his imprisonment by the Jews and release by the risen Lord; but even this does not take him outside his home country. One or two non-Glastonian legends that involve him in missions are of doubtful date, and never bring him into the right part of the world, or into the company of anybody who goes to Britain. He is a strange person to choose as the leader of a pilgrimage to the remotest west, devised to glorify an abbey.

Official scholarship has an answer, though it is not always affirmed as dogmatically as it used to be. Its originator was Armitage Robinson, the dean of Wells who wrote so perceptively about King Cenwalh. He expounded it in *Two Glastonbury Legends*, published in 1926. In 1976, as a public-relations exercise for a book touching on Glastonbury, the substance of it was trailed through the press as if it were a new and conclusive revelation. Actually it is a theory only; it has been current, now, for well over fifty years; and in all that time (so far as I know) nothing has been found to confirm it and several things have been found to call it in question.

The fact on which it depends is that we get nothing in writing about a named founder of Glastonbury till very late. Into that context of prolonged anonymity Joseph, it is assumed, could be slipped without trouble by a stroke of the pen, with no rival to oust. And that was how it happened. He makes his entry as the founder – and this is true, no one disputes it – in the revised edition of William of

Malmesbury's *De Antiquitate,* composed at the Abbey in the 1240s. William spoke merely of the belief that the Old Church was built by disciples of Christ. His reviser-interpolator makes it specific, expanding his suggestion about Philip. The pious verbosity would prove that the passage was not William's, on grounds of style alone.

> St Philip . . . coming into the country of the Franks to preach, converted many to the Faith and baptized them. Working to spread Christ's word, he chose twelve from among his disciples, and sent them into Britain. Their leader, it is said, was Philip's dearest friend, Joseph of Arimathea, who buried the Lord.
>
> Coming therefore into Britain 63 years from the Incarnation of the Lord, and 15 from the Assumption of Blessed Mary, they began faithfully to preach the Faith of Christ. But the barbaric king and his people, hearing such novel and unaccustomed things, absolutely refused to consent to their preaching, neither did he wish to change the traditions of his ancestors, yet, because they came from far, and merely required a modest competence for their life, at their request he granted them a certain island, surrounded by woods, thickets and marshes, called by its inhabitants Ynys-witrin. . . .
>
> Thereupon the said twelve saints residing in this desert, were in a very short time warned by a vision of the angel Gabriel to build a church in honour of the Holy Mother of God and Virgin Mary in a place shown to them from heaven, and they, quick to obey the divine precepts, completed a certain chapel according to what had been shown them. . . .
>
> And as it was the first in the kingdom, God's Son distinguished it with greater dignity by dedicating it in honour of his Mother. . . .
>
> The said saints continued to live in the same hermitage for many years, and were at last liberated from the prison of the flesh. The place then began to be a covert for wild beasts – the spot which had before been the habitation of saints – until the Blessed Virgin was pleased to recall her house of prayer to the memory of the faithful.

Joseph and Arthur

The 'recalling' is ascribed to Faganus and Deruvianus, leaders of the mission to the British king Lucius in the second century. They came to Ynys-witrin, discovered the deserted Old Church, and appointed members of their party to stay there and restore it to use. With these the community began, being later reorganized by St Patrick.

Jejune as it is, the passage has a point of interest, the date AD 63. As a rule Joseph is pictured as elderly at the time of the Crucifixion. Hence, a date thirty-odd years later would be a curious choice for anyone writing pure fiction with only a conventional image of him. Alternatively, if the date was pre-assigned by some legend of Philip's mission to Gaul, the choice of Joseph is even odder. The Holy Grail stories take up the apocryphal tale of his imprisonment, and say he was kept miraculously alive for a long period, but they stretch it too far: he is not set free till AD 70. William's interpolator cannot have been thinking of that. But this date agrees with Gildas' apparent belief that Christians came to Britain during the time of Boudicca's rising, or very soon after. The key may lie in the indication in Gildas' book that he knew the Glastonbury community. His belief could reflect an early version of the story of the first Christians on the site, which he heard there, and which gave a date c. 63; the date then somehow drifted on into the Middle Ages.

To revert, however, to the academic view. It denies that the passage quoted is a written version of a pre-existing tradition. If such a tradition had been current much earlier (it is argued) William would have heard it and named Joseph in his authentic text, and he does not; it is only the interpolator who does, many years after. What we have here is a literary annexation. Between William's time and the 1240s, the Joseph of British legend did indeed appear on the scene, but he appeared in the Grail romances, which were part of the Arthurian cycle. They depicted the Grail as a miraculous vessel from the table of the Last Supper, and made Joseph responsible for its coming to Britain. None of the romances portrayed him as founding Glastonbury.

The argument – sometimes implied rather than stated –

is that the monks of the 1240s adopted him because their recent predecessors had laid claim to Arthur himself, by the faked discovery of his grave. Joseph enabled them to improve on that claim by making out that their founder, the chief of the 'disciples of Christ' who built their church, was an Arthurian character. He was a disciple of Christ and the Grail stories had brought him to Britain. Therefore the Abbey annexed him. He was a secondary fraud, following the primary fraud of Arthur's grave.

Academic criticism does not always put it precisely thus, but always, in principle, it binds the themes together. Though Arthur comes after Joseph in date, the king has to be considered before the disciple. We must grasp, first, what the monks professed to have done when they announced his exhumation; then, what weight should be given to the case against them; then, what the facts are likely to have been; and finally, what the ambience was in which these legends evolved. Only with the Arthur story fairly assessed can we examine the logic which is said to have led on to the Joseph story, and either accept it as the explanation of him or look for some alternative.

3

It was in 1191 that the monks said they had found King Arthur's grave. They had found it in their own burial plot south of the Lady Chapel, which had replaced the Old Church, destroyed by fire seven years before. The Glastonbury hill-cluster was thus proved to be the real Isle of Avalon, Arthur's last earthly destination. These statements challenged the belief that the king's end was unknown, his grave a mystery, his Avalon unlocatable.

Several medieval authors give accounts of the find. The fullest are two by the Welshman Gerald de Barri, otherwise Giraldus Cambrensis. In an age of growing Arthurian credulity, Gerald was a sceptic, not afraid of poking fun at Geoffrey of Monmouth. He tells an anecdote of another Welshman who was possessed by evil spirits. When the

Gospel of St John was laid on his chest the spirits fled, but when Geoffrey's *History* was substituted, they came back in greater force. Hence Gerald would have been unlikely to believe a report which was favourable rather than unfavourable to Geoffrey's fantasies, unless he had followed it up himself and seen reason to accept it.

So indeed he seems to have done, soon after the announcement. If the details given by him and others are put together, they amount to a circumstantial report. In substance it is this. Henry II picked up a hint from a Welsh or possibly Breton bard, indicating that Arthur was buried in the graveyard of Glastonbury Abbey between two pyramids. The word 'pyramid' is used here in an early sense, to mean an obelisk or tapering pillar. The pyramids were the headless shafts of what were originally two Saxon memorial crosses with inscriptions on them. These were real and William of Malmesbury describes them. The bardic hint was passed on to the abbot. He took no action, but later, when a monk died who had expressed a wish to be buried in that place, the community carried out a full-scale excavation.

This happened in 1190 or very early the following year. For convenience we may stick to 1191, when, it seems, the results were publicized. The area was hung round with curtains to screen it from sightseers. Seven feet down the diggers came to a large stone and, on its underside, a leaden cross with a Latin inscription in crude lettering, meaning 'Here lies buried the renowned King Arthur in the Isle of Avalon.' Nine feet farther down – the great depth is stressed – they uncovered a coffin made of a hollowed-out oak log. Inside it were the bones of a man. His skull bore the marks of ten blows, one of them, above the left ear, so damaging as to suggest that the impact which made it had been the cause of his death. The man had been big. His skull was well above average size, and a shin-bone was longer by three fingers' breadths than the shin of the tallest monk. Towards the foot of the coffin were a number of smaller bones, and a lock of yellow hair which crumbled to dust when someone tried to lift it. These were the remains of Guinevere.

We can pursue the history of these bones. They were

deposited in two painted chests, and reverently stored. When a new Abbey church was built, the one that now fragmentarily fills such a huge space, a black marble tomb was constructed in a place of honour before the high altar. On 12 April 1278, Edward I made a state visit with his queen Eleanor. The monks opened the two chests and showed their contents to the royal couple. After a short exhibition outside the gate, they wrapped all the bones in precious cloths and returned them to the chests, which were immured in the marble tomb while Edward and Eleanor looked on. There they stayed till the pillage of the Abbey after the Dissolution. Today a notice marks the spot. Nothing marks the more interesting spot where the exhumation occurred.

The Middle Ages saw one or two outgrowths from Arthur's association with Glastonbury. He was said to have seen a vision of the Virgin at Beckery – a story adapted from one of the Grail episodes. Also, the bridge over the Brue near the end of Wearyall Hill was called Pomparles, the Bridge Perilous. This is claimed as the place (one of at least five places) where Sir Bedivere cast Excalibur into the mere. In Arthur's time there would at least have been a mere to cast it into.

On all this affair the modern orthodoxy, beginning with Armitage Robinson, was set forth most fully by Professor Treharne in *The Glastonbury Legends*, already quoted. What is alleged is that the monks invented Glastonbury's connection with Arthur and faked his grave as the most spectacular possible proof. The precise extent of their fraud has never been agreed, but the essential case has remained unaltered.

Two issues have to be faced: not only the actual force of the argument, but also – unfortunately – the way it is presented. The latter must affect one's assessment of the former. Treharne's book has much good sense in it about the historical setting, but this throws the character of the rest into sharp and significant relief. Whenever he tackles the actual legends, especially the Arthurian one, something goes eloquently wrong. I am sorry to have to say this about an author who is no longer alive; an author, moreover, who comments generously on one of my own ideas. But there are things about this argument which have never been brought into the open, and adequate discussion demands that they should be. I follow Treharne's version simply as being the most thorough and the best known. Others are not substantially different.

We are told or led to understand that Arthur was never associated with Glastonbury before. Perhaps he went there, Treharne concedes, but that is irrelevant. No one put it on record that he did, no one gives any hint at a tradition to that effect. 'The legend linking him with the Abbey springs entirely from the "discovery" of 1191.' Treharne, like all spokesmen of the orthodox view, stresses the fire of 1184. The Old Church was the most grievous casualty, but not the only one. Most of the rest of the Abbey burned down as well. Henry II helped to meet the cost of rebuilding, and several of the nobility followed his lead. The Lady Chapel, on the Old Church's site, was completed about 1189. In that year Henry died. His successor Richard I needed money for crusading. No more royal grants came in, and few other donations.

As to what happened next, here is Treharne, verbatim.

> In this crisis some unknown monk must have come forward with a suggestion which marks him out as a genius who would have made his fortune in a modern advertising agency. By a brilliant stroke of imagination he proposed a superb advertising stunt – 'Find Arthur's tomb!' To an age which read far more avidly of King Arthur and his Queen, his knights of the Round Table and of their treacherous foes, than it read of the whole calendar of saints, the impact of such a discovery would be tremendous, the appeal irresistible. In the golden age of forgery, here was the master-forgery of all! Perfectly timed and staged, on any grounds other than those of morality and religion it deserved to succeed, and succeed it did, and has gone on succeeding down to our day.

The chief motive, then, was fund-raising. A secondary motive which is sometimes proposed is the wish to please those who ruled in England, by proving that Arthur was dead and would not return, thus discouraging the troublesome Welsh who looked for him as a Celtic Messiah.

Such is the academic account, as it has been copied with slight variations from book to book, and given out as if it were fact. In reality it is pure speculation. One must decide for oneself whether Treharne's tone is that of dispassionate scholarship. Certainly his 'must have' is a danger signal to anyone acquainted with historical writing, and in any less congenial context the scholars who accept this theory would be quick to pounce. The account omits and falsifies such facts as there are, and is open to several objections which are never faced.

What about the assertion that the grave was faked with the prime purpose of raising money? Medieval monks were perfectly capable of this. But there is not, in fact, any record of the Abbey exploiting it as charged. If the monks' intention was to appeal for funds by saying 'Support our shrine of King Arthur', why do we never catch them doing it? The notion hangs on a conjecture without evidence. Much the same applies to the political motive. Did the kings of England ever use the grave to demoralize the Welsh? It does not appear so. Some of them showed an interest in Glastonbury, and that was understandable. Though Richard I gave the Abbey no money, he presented Tancred of Sicily, in 1191, with a sword which he pretended was Arthur's; the coincidence of date is so close as to suggest that he took a hint from the Abbey's announcement. Edward I strengthened his claim to the Arthurian succession by paying his state visit in 1278. A similar visit was paid in 1331 by Edward III. But while these sovereigns approved the Abbey's archaeological feat, nothing can be inferred about its being contrived for their benefit. So far as the record shows, the monks never used Arthur's grave to attract funds. They never sought royal favour by brandishing his dead bones in Celtic faces. And Treharne does not even try to show that they did. 'Must have' is the sole argument here, and so far as silence carries weight, silence rebuts it.

What about the presupposition? Is it still true that whatever the motive, the grave was a palpable invention because Arthur was not connected with Glastonbury before? The trump card is the testimony of William of Malmesbury. Writing a lifetime earlier, he says, as a Welsh poet does, that Arthur's grave is unknown. Seemingly his researches at Glastonbury did not lead him to change his opinion. If the grave was supposed to be in the Abbey cemetery, it would surely not have been forgotten. Someone would have told him when he was there. Hence it is inferred that the story of Arthur's burial was concocted later, and the story of Henry II and the bard was concocted with it, to explain the previous silence by making out that the grave was a well-kept secret hitherto withheld from the Abbey. And – the argument goes on – there is no other relevant matter before 1191.

But there is. Arthur *was* connected with Glastonbury. The earlier story is the one in the 'Life' of Gildas by Caradoc of Llancarfan, composed not much after 1130. This of course is legend, not history. It is the first known version of the theme of Guinevere's abduction, which recurs with variations in medieval romance. We might say that Arthur's queen was abduction-prone. The point, however, is that Caradoc does bring Arthur to Glastonbury, and to the Old Church, within a few paces of the grave-site. Treharne refers to Caradoc twice in a different connection. In his bibliography he lists a book which gives the whole passage, and another which sums it up. Yet he never mentions it. What is a reader to conclude?

As for the grave itself, it does appear that the Abbey knew nothing of it in William's time. But the inference that because there was no tradition of it at Glastonbury, there was no tradition of it anywhere, does not follow at all. It is special pleading, in defiance of the whole twelfth-century trend. So far as we know, Arthurian traditions – except possibly at Cadbury – were nowhere current in the main body of English territory for hundreds of years. Yet some, perhaps many, had started there. The silence means only that the Anglo-Saxons did not preserve them, since they concerned aliens and enemies. They survived outside, in Wales and Cornwall and Brittany. From 1125 onwards they were drifting back with the general drift of Celtic storytelling, and going into the Arthurian cycle with the rest.

Some of these traditions had historical content, some concerned particular places. Here and there the departure and return can be glimpsed, if not traced in detail. There is little doubt that Amesbury (for example) was a place of some significance while it was still in the Britons' hands. It was once 'Ambresbyrig', and the 'Ambr' of this name was very possibly Arthur's colleague Ambrosius. During the time following the Saxon conquest, no one on the spot and no one in England gives the least sign of knowing anything relevant about it, even though the dedication of its church to the Breton saint Melor suggests informative contacts. But after five and three-quarter centuries Geoffrey of Monmouth reasserts its pre-Saxon importance, and in a somewhat confused way, showing that he is drawing on tradition and not spinning a fiction out of present knowledge. Amesbury is still very properly an 'Arthurian' town in Malory. Much the same seems to have happened at Bamburgh. The British fort Din Guayrdi, which stood there before, was forgotten in England but remembered in Wales, and it re-surfaced in romance as Lancelot's castle Joyous Gard.

At Glastonbury, the continuity of the community from Briton to Saxon might have been expected to safeguard pre-Saxon traditions. But not necessarily about Arthur. The English prevalence from the tenth century on would have been quite enough to blot out any memories of a man whom the English cared to know nothing of. Ideas about his burial could have returned in the twelfth century embedded in a mass of repatriated material. That is more or less what is implied in the account of Henry II learning the secret from a bard, whether Welsh or Breton, and informing Glastonbury Abbey. (Professor Loomis, very much a Glastonian sceptic, nevertheless allows the possibility of the bard in his *Arthurian Literature in the Middle Ages*: see page 67 of that work.)

Such a view is supported by another silence. After the Abbey made its announcement, no one challenged it. Other such claims were hotly contested. When Glastonbury professed to have the bones of St Dunstan, Canterbury retorted that Glastonbury was lying, because Canterbury had them. With the Arthurian Legend, the major sites tend to suffer from multiplicity. We have several Badons, several Camlanns, and so forth. But as Treharne himself says, 'No other place in all Britain but Glastonbury has ever claimed to be the "Isle of Avalon".' No rival grave of Arthur ever seriously competed. At this point the fraud theory recoils on itself. If Arthur's grave was such an immense asset to its possessors, why did no city or other abbey put in its own claim, or at least raise a sceptical voice in envy? Why did the Welsh allow English monks to get away with a monstrous falsehood? The impression must surely be that a belief on the subject was already established, though not publicized. Once the secret had leaked out from its Celtic hiding-place, once the Abbey had produced even a semblance of confirmation, those who knew the Arthurian traditions knew that there could be no denial.

3

To say so is not to say that the belief was true, only that it was prior to the excavation. The monks were working on data of some sort, as they affirmed; or at least, the arguments purporting to show that they were not are so ill-founded as to create a presumption in their favour. What they really found is another question.

Critics in the past have insinuated that they found nothing. Perhaps they did not even dig. They forged the cross with the magic name on it, and they brought bones from some genuine grave to put on show. The detail about the site being curtained off has been invoked as suspicious. However, none of this will hold water. Modern archaeologists do not actually carry curtains about, but they do keep the public at a distance, and store their finds in huts out of sight. The theory of total fiction is now defunct, and it has been so for practical purposes since someone pointed out that the description of the grave is not what monks in 1191 would, or could, have invented. They had not the knowledge to invent anything so plausibly primitive. Pure imagination, in those days, would probably have conjured up a stone sarcophagus, and hardly a crude object like a hollowed-out log.

Conceding that the monks did dig, and did produce human remains, Treharne has this to offer:

> What, then, were the Glastonbury skeletons? Had the monks, by an amazing stroke of luck, perhaps while digging a grave for one of their community, accidentally unearthed a genuine Celtic burial in its original site? Or had they, as seems much more likely, salted the mine in preparation for the 'discovery'? Had the clever publicity-agent of the chapter suggested to the new Abbot, Henry de Sully, that it would be a good idea to transplant into the Abbey graveyard, behind the secrecy of screened excavations, the remains of some prodigious but nameless Celtic chieftain and his wife, buried, more than 1000 years earlier, in one of the dug-out canoes which used to rock gently by the wooden landing-stage at the causeway of the prehistoric lake-village in the swamp below the Tor?

To which flight of fancy Leslie Alcock, the director of excavations at Cadbury, retorted:

> Historians have gone to considerable lengths to add colour to the hypothesis of a forgery, even suggesting that the monks had dug up elsewhere a Celtic chieftain and his wife, buried over a thousand years earlier in a tree-trunk canoe or coffin, in order to 'salt' the grave. The only comment needed here is that no modern archaeologist would know where to dig up such a burial.

Attention must next be paid to another archaeologist, C. A. Ralegh Radford, and his work on the Abbey site. In 1957 he put forward an argument showing how the grave could have been, not merely authentically early, but authentically Arthur's . . . with or without Guinevere. He noted the puzzling detail that the stone and cross were found neither near the surface nor near the log-coffin, but about half-way down. This could be explained by a fact of the Abbey's history – the reconstruction of the graveyard by Dunstan, who created fresh burial room in the cemetery by covering it with a new layer of earth. Subsequent burials were in a second stratum above the pre-Dunstan ones. An original 'Arthur' grave would have been below, in the old layer. Before Dunstan it could have been marked by a rough memorial stone, on what was then the surface.

When Dunstan was abbot, monks of Celtic origin might still have preserved some lingering tradition of Arthur, and wished to commemorate him before the banking-up blotted everything out. So, perhaps, the inscribed cross was placed beside the stone, which was then tipped over on top of it and buried under Dunstan's new layer. Nothing was now to be seen, and with the increasing dominance of the English and then the Normans, Arthur was forgotten. But in 1191 the monks dug down through Dunstan's stratum, and came to the stone and cross. Then they dug down farther, through the older burial levels, and came to the hollowed-out log with the bones in it.

A few years after proposing this reconstruction, Radford carried out excavations himself. Forty feet south of the Lady Chapel, well below the present surface, he found that a large object had once been uprooted and removed. This would have been the shaft of one of the so-called pyramids, the former Saxon crosses. Fifteen feet farther south were the buried remains of a very old mausoleum – that is, a receptacle for the bones of specially honoured persons – which the second cross would once have surmounted.

Arthur's grave was said to have been between the crosses. Between them, sure enough, irregularities in the soil showed that a big hole had been dug and filled again. The refill included chips of the Doulting stone used in building the Lady Chapel. Large quantities of these chips would not have been left lying about indefinitely after the chapel was finished. Hence, the hole was the one made by the monks looking for Arthur. The traces of it went down through what was left of the Dunstan stratum and deeper. At the

Avalonian Quest

bottom were stone slabs such as would have lined early burials. These had been disarranged. Radford's work, therefore, confirmed that the monks had dug where they said, that they got down to a layer of ancient graves, and that they disturbed this, presumably while shifting the coffin. The descriptions given by Gerald and others may be exaggerated and over-colourful, but probably they are not far out.

Once again we must compare the statement of official orthodoxy with the facts. Radford explained his reconstruction in 1957. He excavated in 1962, and announced the results in sufficient detail. Treharne's book, published in 1967, never mentions him at all. And without here naming names, it is fair to add that several presumably responsible authors after him have repeated the 'fraud' dogma in the same uncritical style, and said not a word about Radford's interpretation of the site, or his work on it. Once more, what is a reader to conclude? Excusably, considering how the hostile case has been put, the united front of scholars supporting it has shown signs of cracking. Leslie Alcock is not disposed to accept it. Jean Markale, Professor of Celtic History at the Sorbonne, has observed that while the Glastonbury interment of Arthur cannot be proved, 'stranger things have been known to happen', and that his link with the place is rather favoured than otherwise by such evidence as there is.

The hollowed-out log has been held to prove that the grave was not Arthur's, on the ground that he would have had Christian burial, and the log savours of pagan customs. That is inconclusive. The question narrows down to the interpretation of the lead cross. Versions of the wording do not quite tally. However, faulty copying and reproduction from memory were so common in the Middle Ages as to be almost normal. They are not extinct even now.

Gerald says the inscription mentioned Guinevere as well as Arthur. Others omit her. But we can be pretty sure about the main portion of it, because the cross, unlike most of the Abbey's relics, was not lost at the Dissolution. John Leland published a transcript from it in 1544. William Camden published a drawing in 1607. The Latin ran:

Joseph and Arthur

HIC IACET SEPULTUS INCLITUS
REX ARTURIUS IN INSULA AVALONIA

To repeat the translation: 'Here lies buried the renowned King Arthur in the Isle of Avalon.' Camden's drawing is of one side only. If there was anything about Guinevere, it may have been on the other side.

ii. Cross from reputed grave
of King Arthur

The clumsy lettering is not in the style of the late twelfth century. If this inscription is a fake, it is far better than most medieval fakes. Opinions differ as to what date it does suggest. Radford and Alcock say it is most like lettering of the tenth and eleventh centuries, and is consistent with the cross having been made in Dunstan's time. According to another authority, Professor Kenneth Jackson, it could be much earlier; even as early as the sixth century.

For Treharne the proof of forgery based on twelfth-century legends is that Arthur is called a king when he was not. Oddly, Treharne kills his own proof a few pages later by admitting that perhaps, after all, he was. The proof fails in any case. Arthur's non-kingship is only an inference, drawn by modern historians as by William of Malmesbury, from the Welsh texts which speak of him as a warrior and war-leader with no mention of a title. The reappraisal of Breton matter has indicated another tradition which did make him royal, and went back to an original who was the Britons' High King.

A more forceful argument is the dubiousness of the final phrase, 'in the Isle of Avalon'. Gerald accepts 'Avalon' as an old name of Glastonbury, but it cannot be documented before 1191, when the exhumation 'proved' it; and would a genuine epitaph-writer, without proof in mind, have put the place-name in his inscription? Arguably the cross was forged with an eye on the words of Geoffrey of Monmouth about the Passing: 'Arthur himself, our renowned king, was mortally wounded and was carried off to the Isle of Avalon.' The cross calls Arthur 'renowned', *inclitus,* and that is the word Geoffrey uses.

So the fraud hypothesis may stand up after a fashion, but to cover the facts it would need to be drastically re-stated. The starting-point would have to be that the graveyard did contain British burials long antedating the Saxon arrival. With the growth of Arthurian story-telling along the Celtic fringe, a notion arose that Arthur himself was buried there. It could have been prompted by Llancarfan legends which introduced Arthur and located him in Somerset, as one or two did. The notion fastened on the tall Saxon crosses in the graveyard as landmarks – those crosses of which the broken shafts became 'pyramids' – and on an old monumental stone between them. Such stones remain to this day in Wales and Cornwall.

In the absence of English interest in Arthur, the belief about his burial was forgotten at Glastonbury itself, and stayed forgotten till some decades after the Norman Conquest. Then Geoffrey of Monmouth and the romancers

Joseph and Arthur

transformed him into a hero of literature. The Celtic traditions which were repatriated to England included some of those associating Arthur with Somerset, among them the one about the grave. This last may indeed have come because of a bard's disclosure to Henry II or some courtier of his. In 1191 the monks of the Abbey resolved to test it. They dug between the pyramids, struck the now-buried stone, and went on down below it to one of the earliest and deepest pre-Saxon burials. Doubtless for reasons of prestige, they decided that the bones should be Arthur's. A forger of rare skill faked the cross, copying archaic letters from old coins or charters, and drawing on Geoffrey for the wording. Henceforth Glastonbury was Avalon, for those who allowed Avalon a place on the map at all.

This is workable, yet not satisfying. First, it takes no account of the level at which the cross was reported, which fits in so strangely with the history of the site and its modifications. Secondly, it evades the issue of the forgery's competence, which, in the Middle Ages, would be startling. Thirdly, it evades another issue which the inscription raises, and which has never been squarely faced hitherto: the eccentric spelling of both the names.

'Arturius' in Camden's drawing is supported by Leland's transcript, and by an early writer, Ralph of Coggeshall. Gerald dissents, but as his own two versions are different from each other, he is evidently writing from memory rather than first hand and 'Arturius' must be taken as the correct form. It is one of several Latinizations, or rather re-Latinizations, which the name 'Arthur' underwent. None of them ever got back to its true Roman original, 'Artorius'. Geoffrey of Monmouth has 'Arturus' in his *History* and 'Arcturus', once, in a poem he composed later. Twelfth-century authors mostly copy his 'Arturus', and that is what we would expect to find in the hypothetical forgery based on him. But we do not.

A Glastonbury forger would have known William of Malmesbury. William, however, has 'Artur'. In the cruder Latin of Nennius and the *Annales Cambriae*, the name is baldly 'Arthur'. The Welsh Saints' Lives also have 'Arthur', and the expansions 'Arthurus' and 'Arthurius', and – as in Geoffrey – 'Arturus'. With so many variants we

Avalonian Quest

ought surely to find 'Arturius' somewhere. Yet up to 1191 the British leader is never once designated thus. The form is so abnormal that Gerald's memory seems to have rejected it in favour of the 'Arthurus' and 'Arthurius' of his fellow-Welsh.

For a forger to invent 'Arturius' and refer to the king thus, when neither Geoffrey nor anyone else had done so, would be an odd method of authentication. The same applies, if less cogently, to the second of the two names. Geoffrey calls Avalon 'Insula Avallonis'. The cross calls it 'Insula Avalonia'. Whoever made it was not copying from Geoffrey, or from any other known precursor.

As to 'Arturius', the truth is that a single text does give it, but in an unlooked-for setting. The Arthur concerned is not the king but a sixth-century prince of Argyll who is believed to have been named after him. He is called 'Arturius' in a book on St Columba composed about 690 by the abbot of Iona, Adomnan, an Irishman born in Donegal. This is the earliest documented Latin form of the name. British materials on the greater Arthur are all later and all employ other spellings. 'Arturius' comes first, and then, at some stage after the seventh century, is supplanted. In other words the spelling on the cross is known only as an extremely early one.

The fact that this form of 'Arthur' is an Irishman's suggests another interpretation of the data. Glastonbury's Irish were active during the eighth and ninth centuries and part of the tenth. They might have favoured 'Arturius' even if the Welsh used a different spelling. Also they were responsible for a famous grave which undoubtedly was spurious, St Patrick's.

Perhaps then we should emend the scenario. The graveyard contained a pre-Saxon burial marked by a memorial stone. The inscription was indistinct, or had a few letters which could be read as hinting at 'Arthur'. An Irish monk who had heard tales of the king decided that this must be his grave, and resolved to improve it. He made the cross, giving the name the Latin form known to Irishmen, and inserted it beneath the stone. Later came Dunstan's remodelling of the cemetery, and the burial of stone and cross. With the dwindling of the community's Celtic element, the grave was forgotten, but a tradition of it lingered in some other place where stories of Arthur did, and returned in the twelfth century to inspire the digging-up and the identification of Glastonbury with Avalon.

The 'Avalon' part itself, in view of the spelling, is troublesome whatever we do. But the Irish theory does not involve assuming that Glastonbury was really called so before there is any evidence that it was. What is envisaged is a scholar's *jeu d'esprit*, which may have influenced other scholars but need not imply anything further. The new clues to Arthurian origins show how the mind of the Irishman might have worked. If the original Arthur was the British High King who departed in the direction of the Burgundian Avallon, a vague rumour of a place so called as his last destination could have been present in his saga at any stage. The Irishman could have put 'Insula Avalonia' on the cross to suggest that the 'island' of Glastonbury was Arthur's true apple-place. Apples have been growing there for a long time.

It may be so. It is no more than a guess. However, to recall Arthur-Riothamus is to raise the final question. Whose grave, actually, was it?

If the king who departed into Burgundy is the original Arthur-figure, and the only one, his burial in Somerset seems unlikely. Still, there is no telling. He could have returned quietly to Britain, perhaps disabled and excluded from power, and spent his last years in retirement at his Cadbury fort, obscurely enough to make no difference to the doubts and legend-weaving about his end. Or if he did die overseas, his remains could have been brought back to his own country, and unobtrusively re-interred in the holy place. 'Translating' the relics of saints was a normal practice, though it would be more plausible in this case if there were any sign that Arthur was so regarded. While Nennius and the *Annales* speak of his carrying Christian emblems into battle, other Welsh clerical tradition is unfriendly to him.

Of course possibilities can be multiplied. If the Irishman, or anyone else, set the process in motion by his reading of a few doubtful letters on the memorial stone, there need not have been any real connection with Arthur at all. Or the misread letters might have been on the 'pyramids'. Gerald and Ralph of Coggeshall both seem to think that the worn writing on them was relevant though it was no longer legible. By the twelfth century it certainly was not, except in fragments. William of Malmesbury could read a few names, but nothing that suggested 'Arthur' to him. If there had been anything suggesting that name in 1191, even to the most wishful eye, it would have been pointed out to Gerald as evidence. But perhaps there was, long before. Nor would it have had to be very close. A stone still exists in Cornwall, near Slaughter Bridge on the River Camel, which was long held to support what Geoffrey says about Arthur fighting his last battle by that river. The reason was that it had a worn inscription with letters which could be misread . . . not even as ARTHUR, but as ATRY!

Yet again, some belief might have taken shape because the occupant of the grave had Arthurian associations. He could have been another man of the same name, like the hypothetical Patrick Senior. Or he could have been the last commander of the apparent armed force called Arthur's Men, using Cadbury as a base, and perishing in a Camlann on the banks of the nearby Cam. The commander of Arthur's Men could easily have been equated with Arthur.

All such speculations are pure guesswork, and the woman's bones, if they existed, are of no help in giving substance to any. The essential point is not that the grave was or was not genuine, but that the snap dismissal, the dogma of a total fraud in 1191, has been crumbling for years and now plainly does not work; and the best proof is that it can only be given the appearance of working by suppressions, tactical silences, and the pretence that theories are facts. One of its advocates has insisted in the press that legends must be 'looked at critically'. True, and that applies to twentieth-century academic legends as well as twelfth-century monastic ones.

The context of Arthur's grave is not crude fakery or arbitrary invention out of the blue, but a complex situation with many unknowns, a mystery. There was, so to speak, 'something there' before anybody made open claims about it. And certainly there was an ancient grave. In view of the crowding of the cemetery at the pre-Dunstan level, it was not remarkable that the monks should hit on a burial of some kind; but the details imply a rather special one, and archaeology confirms them, so far as they can be confirmed.

At present we cannot tell whether the grave's connection with Arthur had any basis in fact. It may have, it may not. Further discoveries are not beyond hoping for. In the eighteenth century the lead cross was in the possession of Chancellor Hughes in Wells, and it might yet be found. What is sure is that the 1191 episode must be viewed in the broad Arthurian setting. The background was not the Abbey's need for money, or its inmates' penchant for fabrication, real though these were. It was the revival in England of the lore of a Britain which preceded the English. At Glastonbury a piece of that Britain had survived, if forgetfully, without a break. It was only to be expected that some of the lore should find its way home.*

---

* In April 1982, publicity was given to a claim by a Mr Derek Mahoney that he had found the lead cross. I was consulted about it (see e.g., the *Western Daily Press*, 2 and 3 April 1982) and pursued some enquiries. As a result it appeared almost certain that this was a false alarm.

CHAPTER FIVE

The Saint, the Grail and the Thorn

I

We can now rejoin Joseph. To recapitulate, the approved view is that after the monks of 1191 had made Glastonbury Arthurian by contriving the grave, their successors in the 1240s made it more so by lifting Joseph out of Grail romance as their founder, even though the Grail stories gave no warrant for this. In Treharne's succinct words, 'The Saint was dragged in the wake of the Hero: Arthur had come to Glastonbury, so Joseph of Arimathea must come too, bringing with him the Holy Grail.' The flaws which have emerged in the first part of the case manifestly weaken the second. As it has been put hitherto, in a context of pure and sustained monastic fraud, it is a lost cause. But it could still survive after a fashion, in the sense that real traditions bringing Arthur to Glastonbury inspired the making-up of a bogus one bringing Joseph.

There is, however, a noteworthy minority view at this point. As to Joseph's adoption, via the revised *De Antiquitate*, academic opinion is agreed. But the late Roger Sherman Loomis, the principal recent Arthurian scholar to tackle the subject, was not content with the Hero dragging in the Saint. He argued that the romances did more than supply a character. The monks read one of them, the *Estoire del Saint Graal*, and took it seriously. Its story of Joseph coming to Britain with the Grail was a threat to the dominance of their own story about 'disciples of Christ' building the Old Church. It challenged their priority. They met the challenge by a conflation, making out that the chief of the 'disciples of Christ' actually *was* Joseph, and thereby safeguarding Glastonbury's claims.

Professor Loomis is worth quoting. All the rest of his

The Saint, the Grail and the Thorn

book *The Grail* is quite temperate and objective in tone, whether or not one agrees with him. But as soon as he gets to the fatal topic, everything alters. The chapter is entitled 'Glastonbury, School of Forgery and Isle of Avalon'. Here, compressed, is his account of the monks' encounter with crisis.

> We may imagine the surprise and bewilderment of these tonsured worthies when, say about 1240, a manuscript of the *Estoire del Saint Graal* came into their hands, and they read an elaborately detailed rival account of the evangelization of Britain. . . .
>
> The situation was embarrassing for the monks of Glastonbury. Should this pious narrative be denounced as a fraud? Or should the long-standing claim of their own house to being the site of the earliest Christian sanctuary in Britain, built by a band of missionaries from Gaul, be abandoned as apocryphal? Or should both be accepted and, if possible, reconciled? It was the third course of action which was adopted, presumably after heated debate.

This completely imaginary scene is presented, like the 'stunt' of Treharne's imaginary publicity-agent, as a fact. It is a little odd to find Loomis, nine pages later, dismissing the suggestions of dissentients whom he cannot refute as 'amusing speculations'.

Even if correct, the theory that Joseph was taken from Grail romance fails to answer the question 'Why Joseph?' It merely pushes it further back. Nothing in his scriptural role gave him any fitness as Grail-bringer, nor did the apocryphal legend about him in the *Acts of Pilate*. Scholars have hazarded explanations for this bizarre choice of hero, based on verbal misunderstanding (Loomis proposed a sort of French pun which has appealed to few), or on recondite notions about the symbolism of Catholic ritual. These have not carried conviction or established any consensus. But the issue of the Grail must be faced, both because of its bearing on the Joseph theme, and for larger reasons which will become plain. It is a riddle of daunting complexity, and the answer, probably, is that there is no single answer.

The Grail is never conceived as a holy relic like other relics. As a matter of fact, in an age when relics were proliferating, it is curious how little we hear of the tableware of the Last Supper. We would expect to find the cup and dish used by Christ duplicated in churches all over Christendom, but we do not. The claims are very few and very uncertain. It is almost as if there actually were some mystery, some legend of a disappearance. But this cannot be documented, and in any case, the Grail of romance does not begin as an object from the Last Supper.

Behind the romancers' images are pre-Christian Celtic myths about wonder-working vessels – horns of plenty, cauldrons of inspiration – with traces of sexual symbolism and fertility magic. Some of the myths which are drawn in seem to have been concerned with the sources of life, physical and spiritual. Their survival was helped by the special quality of Celtic Christianity, its readiness to adapt rather than anathematize. A tenth-century Welsh poem, *The Spoils of Annwn,* gives an obscure early version of the mystic quest. Annwn is an Otherworld or Underworld, a place of water-crossings and islands and uncanny fortresses, where Arthur and his men go on a perilous voyage seeking a talismanic cauldron.

The earliest extant Grail story proper was started in the 1180s by Chrétien de Troyes, the major pioneer of Arthurian romance, and continued by others. Here the Grail is more as we are inclined to picture it, but it appears in a puzzling, disturbing fairy-tale setting. Its nature is never clearly explained, and the Christian element is slight. Themes begin to show themselves which are plainly carrying on Celtic mythology. A Waste Land will become fertile again if a knight asks a ritual question. The question may heal a mysterious wounded king. There are reminiscences here of the old notion of divine kingship, of the magical bond between the king and the land. The Grail itself is a source of literal nourishment. That aspect persists even in later, spiritualized versions. When it hovers in the air over Arthur's assembled knights, they enjoy a supernatural banquet.

The Saint, the Grail and the Thorn

It is first an explicit Christian object, and holy, in a narrative poem entitled *Joseph d'Arimathie* by Robert de Boron, composed towards the end of the twelfth century. Robert was a Burgundian, and Boron is a village near Montbéliard just south of Belfort. Grail literature in general belongs chiefly to France, in its formative phases. Robert makes the Grail a vessel, apparently a 'chalice', used by Christ at the Last Supper. In his poem Joseph acquires it afterwards and collects some of the Saviour's blood in it. He is imprisoned as in the *Acts of Pilate*. Christ appears to him and teaches him secret words which are the key to the mysteries of the Grail. Joseph is miraculously sustained in the dungeon for forty-two years. Then the Roman commander Vespasian, who has become friendly to Christianity, comes to Jerusalem and executes a number of Jews in somewhat belated punishment for the Crucifixion. Learning where Joseph was imprisoned, he finds him still alive and releases him. (This is largely based on other apocryphal writings, which distort the historical facts of Vespasian's campaign to suppress the Jewish rebellion, and the fall of Jerusalem in AD 70.)

Joseph, with a party of relatives and other Christians, leaves for a foreign land which is not definitely located. He takes the Grail, and divine guidance is conveyed to him through it. After various events it is made manifest that some of the party are to go away to a distant country in the west. The poet's final intentions are unclear, partly because the narrative itself is confused, partly because he planned further episodes which remained unwritten. But one thing does emerge: that the westward voyagers, with the Grail in their custody, establish themselves in the 'Vales of Avaron'. Robert certainly means 'Avalon' – he has a couple of word-plays which put it beyond doubt. He is referring to the low-lying country of central Somerset where Glastonbury is. Celtic myth might have supplied him with an 'Isle' of Avalon which was other than this, but it could not have supplied 'Vales'; only Somerset could do that; and when he wrote, the name had just been firmly planted there by the announcement of Arthur's grave.

The *Estoire del Saint Graal*, which Loomis makes so much of, is a long prose romance enormously expanding the story. Written in France fairly early in the thirteenth century, it brings Joseph to Britain in person, crediting him with a successful mission and enlarging on his experiences with the Grail – which is described as a dish, not a chalice. Loomis maintains (and here, since he is not dealing with Glastonbury, he inspires more confidence) that Robert and the author of the *Estoire* both drew on a lost earlier work, which effected the union of the Celtic Grail theme with legends of early Christianity and the career of Joseph. The *Estoire* goes on to sketch the history of the Grail and a succession of Grail-keepers, most of the way to Arthur's time. By then, its location had become mysterious. Other romancers describe the quest for it by Arthur's knights – a long, dangerous, labyrinthine quest with a logic which never fully surfaces.

Different authors wrote with different interests, perhaps not really understanding their own materials, and the various versions are hopelessly at odds. The German *Parzival* follows a line of its own. In the French mainstream, it will be recalled, *Perlesvaus* includes a visit to Glastonbury by Lancelot. As a rule, however, the geography is unreal. Centrally important is the Catholic doctrine that Christ, at the Last Supper, instituted a sacrament by which the bread and wine of the Mass are changed into his body and blood, a physical presence of himself under the veil of appearances. The Holy Grail, as a vessel which he used when he did so (though there is no unanimity as to which one), prefigures those to be found on the Church's altars. According to the writers who give it this Christian meaning, it was a more-than-material, shape-shifting thing with wondrous properties, the vehicle of a greater sacrament revealed only to initiates. In these romances the 'life' of the ancient magic becomes Eternal Life. The vessel is a link between earth and heaven, a source of miracles and visions. The supreme vision is achieved only by the pure Galahad after much wandering. It is an insight into the mystery of the nature of God, and especially the Incarnation, God-become-Man in Christ. Probably it is much the same experience as Dante imagines at the close of the *Divine Comedy*.

The Saint, the Grail and the Thorn

But although the pagan imagery was absorbed, revalued and turned to orthodox ends, the stories retained too much that was ecclesiastically suspect: the weird beings in the castle where, sometimes, the Grail was housed; the cryptic ceremony of the encounter; the theme of an individual quest, rather than a sharing in the life of the Church; the atmosphere of initiation and secret knowledge. Some of the romancers yielded to medieval norms and toned down the legend into allegory, making it more coherent while losing mystery. But none of this was approved in clerical quarters.

At Glastonbury, while Joseph was accepted, the Grail was not. Here Treharne is quite wrong, though he corrects himself later. Towards the end of its career the Abbey claimed to possess dozens of sacred objects, possible and impossible – a sliver from Aaron's rod, a thread from Mary's robe, one of the stones Jesus refused to turn to bread, and many more. But it did not claim that it possessed, or ever had possessed, any vessel from the Last Supper. The full-blown account of Joseph which it eventually built up could not quite ignore the Grail, and incorporated bits of the *Estoire* and *Perlesvaus*. However, it replaced the marvellous object itself with two 'cruets' containing drops of the blood and sweat of Christ. Joseph was said to have brought these to Britain and to have had them buried with him. They were innocuous holy relics. He can be seen with them in a fifteenth-century stained glass window in Langport parish church.

2

While Joseph makes his first plain Glastonian appearance in the 1240s, it can be said of this, as of Arthur's exhumation, that something was astir before. The notion that there was no earlier link between the Grail theme and Glastonbury is demonstrably false. There was.

Robert de Boron's 'Vales of Avaron' is proof in itself. Loomis admits it, and calls the phrase 'perplexing' and 'disconcerting'. He suggests that the story about disciples of Christ building the Old Church was transmitted via the 'monastic grapevine' to the author of the lost book Christianizing the Grail. The author identified his characters with these disciples, and accordingly made them go to Somerset. Robert took up the motif. Coming from someone who insists that the influence went the other way, with Glastonbury doing the borrowing, this seems a considerable concession.

Worse is to follow. *Perlesvaus,* written a decade or two later than Robert's *Joseph,* has a colophon at the end in which the author says:

> The Latin text from which this story was set down in the vernacular was taken from the Isle of Avalon, from a holy religious house which stands at the edge of the Lands of Adventure; there lie King Arthur and the queen, by the testimony of the worthy religious men who dwell there, and who have the whole story, true from the beginning to the end.

The allusion to the tomb of Arthur and Guinevere makes it certain that the author means Glastonbury Abbey. His statement that it owned a book which gave him 'the whole story' is unlikely to be true, but clearly there was a reason why he should think of such a thing and see it as plausible. Scholars have argued that he cannot have had first-hand knowledge of Glastonbury because his description is wrong. That, however, is only because the scholars never came to Glastonbury and took a good look. The topography of that visit of Lancelot shows not only that the author was there, but that he very probably learned traditions, written or oral, about the early Christian settlement. Loomis, in *The Grail,* mentions the colophon twice without making the slightest attempt to explain it. His only resources are to call the author a liar and insinuate that he was mad.

Joseph of Arimathea is mentioned at the beginning of *Perlesvaus* as the Grail's first custodian, and a document could scarcely have been said to give the *whole* story if it

The Saint, the Grail and the Thorn

did not include him. The *Estoire del Saint Graal*, the very book from which Glastonbury is said to have annexed Joseph, has a more explicit phrase which suggests the opposite of that. It says Joseph was buried at 'the Abbey of Glays in Scotland'. 'Scotland' looks adverse to Glastonbury, but in fact, deviously and surprisingly, favours it. The reason lies in the old meaning of 'Scots' – namely, 'Irish'. Documents of the ninth and tenth centuries refer to an area settled by Irish in the West Country as 'Scotland', and, as already noted, to Glastonbury itself as Glastonbury of the Gaels where the Scots used to dwell. The romancer's phrase may go back to a belief, handed down and borne overseas with its meaning lost, that Joseph was buried 'in the monastery at Glaston, the Scots' holy place', or something to that effect. Loomis does not mention the phrase. It is surely very interesting that the Vales of Avaron and the Abbey of Glays occur in precisely those two romances which he says have a common source behind them, the lost original Joseph-and-Grail text. With one of the phrases, he admits the 'monastic grapevine' from Glastonbury. With the other, it seems at least equally probable.

It could still be argued that Joseph himself was not part of the package, that he was thought of on the continent and involved afterwards with the Glastonbury stories, as Loomis contends. But a major difficulty stands in the way. The Joseph of the Abbey's story cannot be simply the Grail-bringer transplanted, because they are incompatible. He comes to Britain in AD 63. The Joseph of the romances could not have done so; he is in prison in Jerusalem for more than forty years after the Crucifixion, only being freed at the time of Vespasian's advent and the fall of the city, which happened in 70. Nor is 63 a mere random or unconsidered figure. It is so blatantly at odds with the conventional view of Joseph's age that it is unlikely to be pure fancy. Something is behind it, and the 'something' cannot be Grail romance.

The date is peculiarly interesting. In the first place, once again, it agrees with what Gildas seems to think about Christians arriving during or soon after Boudicca's rising.

This in turn, because of his apparent acquaintance with Glastonbury, could be an echo of things already said there in the sixth century. In the second place, the date fits in very well with two entirely separate facts.

The Cadbury excavation disclosed an unexpected phase in the history of that astonishing hill. It was in full British control long after the Romans overran this part of the country. They finally stormed it and evicted the survivors. This action is now assumed to have been a sideshow of Boudicca. Some minor British ruler was maintaining a shadowy independence, Hereward-the-Wake style, in the hills and marshes of Somerset at just about the time when Joseph is said to have arrived, and at just about the time when the tale calls for an independent 'king' there to be his host. An independent 'king' (however petty) actually was there, or near enough. Boudicca was crushed in 61, but the Somerset rebel may have outlasted her a little, and in any case a discrepancy of a year or two is within a normal margin of error for early chronicles. If 63 is a guess it is a fantastically good guess – the more so as the known records of Boudicca's revolt nowhere mention this offshoot in Somerset; no one suspected it till the Cadbury evidence came to light.

Moreover, the guess might have to be better still. The 'king' who allows Joseph's party to settle on the island is said to have been named Arviragus. That name appears in an early marginal note to *De Antiquitate* and looks as if it was taken from Geoffrey of Monmouth's pseudo-history. However, the ultimate source for it is the Roman satirist Juvenal. He mentions Arviragus as a British chief who would have been remembered as having caused trouble during the early decades of the Roman occupation. Juvenal knows hardly anything about him and gives no clue to his whereabouts. But he could, just possibly, be the Somerset rebel, in the right place and circumstances in 63.

It seems settled that nothing in the Grail matter convincingly answers the question 'Why Joseph?'. It may now appear that the right place to look for clues could be the Abbey after all. Not only is the date 63 irreconcilable with the romances, it occurs solely with Joseph; the two are linked; and the hints that it is embedded in historical tradi-

The Saint, the Grail and the Thorn

tions once current in Somerset suggests that he is too, in his origins.

There is another, very different Glastonian issue: whether any of the mythical material in the Grail stories was centred at Glastonbury before the romancers worked on it. This would give an early connection by a different route, whether or not, in the upshot, it helped to account for Joseph. Some have drawn inferences from *The Spoils of Annwn*, where a Glass Castle is mentioned, and one investigator, Geoffrey Russell, has gone much further. These ideas must wait for a while. However, one Glastonbury text speaks of pagan matters in conjunction with Joseph himself. It is an oracular outpouring called the Prophecy of Melkin, preserved in a fourteenth-century chronicle of the Abbey, by a monk known as John of Glastonbury.

The bard Melkin or Maelgwn is supposed to have been St David's uncle and to have lived before Merlin. If he existed, in the fifth or sixth century, his prophecy would doubtless have been in the Celtic British language. John gives it in an eccentric Latin. Its real age and provenance are uncertain. So is its meaning. The following attempt in English is tentative.

> Avalon's island avid for the death of pagans, foremost in the world for the entombment of all of them, has been enriched with seers speaking by orbs of prophecy and shall in future be adorned with men who praise the Most High. Abbadaré, mighty in Saphat, noblest of pagans, has fallen asleep there with a hundred and four thousands. Among whom Joseph in marble, of Arimathea by name, has found everlasting rest; and he lies on a forked line, next the south corner of an oratory fashioned of wattles, for the adoring of a mighty Virgin by the aforesaid scryers inhabiting the place, thirteen in number. For Joseph has in his sarcophagus with him two cruets, white and silver, filled with blood and sweat of the Prophet Jesus. When his sarcophagus shall be found complete and intact, in future days, it shall be seen and open to all the world. Thenceforth neither water nor the dew of

heaven shall fail the dwellers in that most noble isle. A long time before the Day of Judgment in Josaphat these things shall be open and declared to the living.

The phrase about 'orbs of prophecy' is difficult and may refer to spheres in the sky, with an astrological sense. But the word is *sperula*, which means a very small sphere, not a star or planet. Medieval writers use it occasionally to mean a crystal ball or scrying-glass. Hence the word 'scryer', farther on.

We might suspect that part of this is a re-working of genuinely old matter, though it can only be part. On the one hand the 'cruets' belong (so far as anyone knows) to the late medieval legend which substituted cruets for the ambiguous Grail. On the other, the cryptic talk of a pre-Christian burial ground introduces a topic not found anywhere else in the Abbey's chronicles. The number of worshippers at the oratory, thirteen, contradicts what is said about the original Glastonbury group in other places. Thirteen is magical in pagan Welsh lore. To some it might even suggest a coven, and the allusions to scrying – or astrology – hint at a conversion of resident sages or wizards. The water to be released by finding the grave is a Waste Land touch recalling a primitive element in the Grail stories. Joseph's grave never has been found ... or faked. A search by John Blome in 1345 was fruitless. Considering how watery Glastonbury is anyhow, Melkin seems to promise a superfluous gift. After heavy rain, the torrents that pour down the lane between the Tor and Chalice Hill have provoked the comment: 'They must have found that grave.'

Nothing like Melkin's Prophecy, in its fullness, could be extracted from the Grail stories. A recent explorer of the Abbey's history, James P. Carley, has analysed it and detected alchemic images. He also suggests that the secret hinted at by William of Malmesbury, concealed in the floor design of the Old Church, was alchemic in nature. Another recent author, John Matthews, sees alchemic concepts in the Grail stories themselves. All this is far too complicated to pursue here. But the possibility of something pre-

The Saint, the Grail and the Thorn

Christian or non-Christian in the Isle of Avalon, dimly recalled in folklore which influenced the legends, should not be overlooked.*

3

When all known facts are taken into account, Joseph's British connection has an air of being 'given' without explanation, of being prior to any known version – whether in romance or in Abbey materials. Robert de Boron, introducing him as the Grail's custodian, has evident difficulty in getting a vessel from the Last Supper into such unlikely hands. He has to go through unwarranted falsifications of scripture to do it. Plainly, when he wrote, Joseph's role as a disciple associated with Britain was already established, and he – or the author he followed – had to make the best of it. The *De Antiquitate* interpolator brings in the mysterious 63 in defiance of the romancers.

The foremost authority on the legend is Professor Valerie Lagorio. She has shown that the *Estoire del Saint Graal* resembles legendary 'Lives' of the British saints, in content and handling. It is certainly *as if* Joseph once figured in some piece of Welsh hagiography, which brought him to Somerset, in circumstances having some hazy relation to the realities of the year 63. Speculation reaching far back was customary with the Welsh. The pedigrees of their princes include characters from Roman history, and occasionally from the Bible itself and the Christian apocrypha. A Joseph legend would have been in the same style as another one – which cannot be proved medieval, but quite well may be – ascribing the first Christian influences on the Britons to the family of the captive king Caratacus, who was in Rome at a time allowing any accompanying relatives to be converted by Paul. Joseph,

---

* I examined 'Melkin' at greater length in a local magazine, *Torc* (No. 14, Autumn 1974). But I feel the discussion ranged too far afield to justify reproducing it.

unknown or forgotten at the Abbey when William of Malmesbury was there, could have entered England afterwards with the rest of the matter that went into the Arthurian cycle, and found his way along Loomis's 'monastic grapevine' to France. In other words the belief about him could belong in the same well-proven context of British rediscovery as the belief about Arthur's grave.

This does not imply the extreme opposite view, that Grail romance itself is a product of clerical propaganda, engineered by a Glastonbury which had discovered or rediscovered Joseph. One school of thought did go to such extremes; Loomis's anti-Glastonbury case consists, to a large extent, in setting up this theory as an Aunt Sally and knocking it over. Certainly it does not work. No Abbey matter of relevant date mentions the Grail, or the romance characters other than Joseph himself. The romances were written in France, show little knowledge of Britain, and, as we have seen, refer to Glastonbury only briefly and obscurely.

But they do refer to it. Somehow it was 'given'. Joseph's connection with a British holy place would have been a bit of wandering lore – fairly old, if the phrase about Scotland is anything to go by – which the Grail's unknown Christianizer picked up and used, to give the Grail the desired meaning, and explain how it had come to Britain. If he took the point about the date 63 he cared nothing for it. He was writing fiction. The Roman capture of Jerusalem in 70 made a more dramatic occasion, and he may (absurdly) have identified Joseph with the Jewish historian Josephus, who actually was imprisoned, and released by Vespasian, about that time.

The who-copied-whom question is surely almost settled by this alone. A romancer borrowing from Glastonbury would have had every reason to change 63 to 70. He could thereby relate his fiction to a real event of historic and religious significance, however garbled. A Glastonbury monk borrowing from Grail romance would have had no cogent reason to change 70 to 63. It would have meant losing the great occasion, without making Joseph's age much more plausible – and in any case, why 63 particularly? We might suspect apocryphal Christian writings, but we can search them in vain for a reason for this date, and in any case Glastonbury did not bring them into the story at first, though it did later when the need for fuller detail was felt.

At the Abbey, whenever the Joseph story got there, it may not at first have been taken very seriously. That is the impression given by its later career when its presence is documented. Even those who insist that Arthur was only a fund-raising figment have never asserted that Joseph was. The Abbey had little to say about him for many years. Its chronicles simply noted him and passed on. In the late twelfth century and the early thirteenth, the story could have been current orally without being written down. The spurious charter of St Patrick, concocted at the Abbey during this period, mentions the Old Church's reputed builders in the apostolic era and still gives no names.

Joseph's eventual insertion in *De Antiquitate* was simply an attempt to give substance to the idea of an early Christian advent, centred, as ever, on the church. It was in much the same class as the false charters which were composed at medieval monasteries – Glastonbury itself being a major instance – to support claims to customary rights, properties, and so on. A charter may represent King X as having conferred them. Often such documents are not bogus as a modern forgery is bogus. They express what their authors believed, more or less sincerely, to be the case. Something had come down to the community in oral tradition or local custom. Its members decided that the origin had been ... whatever they made it in the charter. And sometimes, in principle, they were right.

The transmission of Joseph via historical legend, rather than literary legend, needs to be considered in the context of that odd plausibility pointed out by Treharne. In the saint's developed story he is said to have arrived by water and come ashore at Wirral or Wearyall Hill – the latter, popular form of the name being explained as meaning that he and his much-travelled companions were 'weary all'. The traces of a Roman wharf show that when the water-level was higher, this actually was a place where boats docked; while the finds at the lake-villages extend into the apostolic age and prove the proximity of centres of population with sea-going contacts. Nor is this all that can be said. Glastonbury's monks were not archaeologists. They knew nothing of the wharf or the lake-villages. If they merely made up their tale of 'disciples of Christ' coming to Somerset, with no basis in tradition of any kind, it was an extraordinarily lucky shot. We are not dealing here with a stock claim made by monasteries up and down England. The Glastonbury story stood alone or virtually so, singling out a place where a ship-borne advent from overseas, at the time asserted, was fairly credible. A tradition that reflected the circumstances making it so – a tradition that gave a footing for Joseph – might well appeal as a better explanation than pure fiction. The case is not as remarkable as the local lore of Cadbury-Camelot, but it is in the same class.

With Joseph himself, the year 63 is a little late for the lake-villages. Meare, however, was not actually defunct, and traders might have got into a habit of frequenting the area. In any case that date, if merely plucked out of the air, would require still another amazing guess – a guess hitting on that brief local independence in the 60s, perhaps also on Arviragus. Here at least the possibility of knowledge rather than guesswork can be proved by a parallel. There is a recognized instance of a fact about first-century Britain being preserved in Wales, though undocumented anywhere else, and rediscovered in the twelfth century. Tasciovanus, the father of Cunobelinus (Cymbeline), reigned in south-east Britain from about 20 BC to AD 5. We know him from his coins, but not from Roman historians, who never mention him. No historian does. Yet his name, mangled but recognizable, appears centuries later in Welsh genealogies. Then Geoffrey of Monmouth takes him up and makes him a king of Britain, Tenvantius, still correctly Cymbeline's father. For various reasons the name has changed vastly in its long-drawn transmission, but its changes can be traced. Tenvantius is Tasciovanus, remembered in Wales and in Wales only, and restored by Geoffrey to readers outside.

So behind the known legend, an item of Welsh hagiography, using historical traditions about Somerset, would be a credible thing. As for the nagging question 'Why Joseph?', the utmost that can be said is that speculation related to Glastonbury holds out a better prospect than speculation about the Grail matter. Professor Lagorio allows a 'very remote possibility' that the story of Joseph's coming took shape because, in substance, it was true. He did come. It sounds extremely far-fetched, because, though the setting existed, and voyagers might have made their way to Somerset from a variety of motives, it is hard to see why a wealthy Palestinian Jew should have come so far. There is no serious evidence for the mission of St Philip in Gaul which Joseph is supposed to have accompanied. A favourite theory, that he had an interest in the Cornish tin trade, is shaky because the Cornish tin trade was in decline, depressed by Spanish competition.

But he might have been involved in trade of some other kind, and used his knowledge of Britain to find a haven of retirement when persecution broke out. Or, to propose another scenario – twenty years after the Crucifixion, Roman conquest was opening up southern Britain to officials, merchants and assorted entrepreneurs from every part of the Empire. Joseph might have seen business chances, even apart from any religious motive: the exploitation of Mendip lead, for instance. He could still have been alive and active in the 50s and 60s. The assumption that he was already old in the time of Christ has no real scriptural basis. He had reserved a tomb for himself, but he might have done it during an illness.

Besides Professor Lagorio's 'remote possibility', at least three others have been aired. The first invokes one of the few non-British stories of Joseph which can be proved early enough to have had an influence. This is a Georgian legend in an eighth-century manuscript, telling how he went with St Philip to Lydda, now Lod in Israel. They consecrated a church to the Blessed Virgin and Joseph remained in charge of it. Here we find him as a companion of Philip, as he is in *De Antiquitate*, and the Old Church's Mary dedication might have inspired someone to transplant the tale to Britain. A second possibility is that some later Joseph's epitaph, at Glastonbury or near enough to be relevant, was misconstrued. In a church at Marseilles, the memorial of a fifth-century bishop named Lazarus gave rise to the Provençal legend that the Lazarus whom Christ raised from the dead came to Marseilles, there suffering his second and final death. This legend brought in other characters, including Lazarus' reputed sister Mary Magdalene, and eventually, with the growing fame of Glastonbury, Joseph himself.

Lastly, even Treharne was willing to entertain a suggestion of my own: that the ruins of a large house of the Roman period – perhaps actually belonging to an early Christian, drawn by the same inducements applicable to Joseph – prompted a belief that the first Glastonbury Christian was a man of substance; and Joseph was the only one whom the Gospels supplied. Roman pottery shards and coins in the Abbey have been held to hint at the existence of a villa. They were in clay imported to level up the floors of the medieval church and cloister, and since this would not have been brought from far away, it is possible that the villa was in the area of the present High Street.

No such theory can account for more than a bare belief that Joseph came to Glastonbury and had something to do with its Christian origins. If the Welsh hagiographic legend existed, it may have said little more. The Grail romancers adapted Joseph to non-Glastonian interests. He was slow to become a popular saint. English ecclesiastics invoked his name to prove the seniority of the English Church, pushing the date of his arrival in Britain farther back. But at Glastonbury itself, though the undercroft of the Lady Chapel housed a shrine for him, it belonged only to the last decades of the Abbey's life. Moreover, Joseph is unlucky in the day of his commemoration. It is 17 March, St Patrick's day, so that he is overshadowed and forgotten.

The Saint, the Grail and the Thorn

4

Several accretions to the saga are post-medieval. This is the case with the Holy Thorn. Its story tells how, when Joseph landed on Wearyall Hill, he drove his staff into the ground and it came to life and blossomed. From this miraculous stem sprang a tree that flourished ever after, blossoming at Christmas. The tree which the miracle purports to explain did once grow on the hill, somewhere, though it may not have stood where a stone slab professes to mark the spot. It was tall and double-trunked, and it blossomed approximately as stated.

The first documentary allusion does not attribute it to Joseph. This is in a doggerel pilgrimage guide printed as late as 1520, and says simply:

> Three hawthorns also that groweth in Werall
> Do burge and bear green leaves at Christmas,
> As fresh as other in May.

While there were already several trees, the parent had an unrivalled dignity. In Elizabethan and early Stuart days it became famous. Many people, including James I and his wife, treasured cuttings from it. Others regarded it as a focus of superstition, and it met its destruction at the hands of Puritans, first incompletely, then finally during the Civil War. By then its offspring grown from transplanted shoots were spread about the neighbourhood and perhaps farther afield. Various seventeenth-century authors refer to the Thorn. One even invokes its blossoming on 25 December as proof that England kept Christmas on the right day. The so-called 25 December of the continental reformed calendar, since it did not coincide with the Thorn's performance, was wrong; and so presumably was the reformed calendar.

Joseph is named at last in 1677, though still only as having planted the original tree. His miraculous staff makes its belated appearance in 1716, as an alleged folklore item retailed to an antiquary, Charles Eyston, by a local innkeeper. The fancy is far from being unique. Blossoming rods occur in the legends and iconography of other saints, including the greater St Joseph, husband of the Virgin. The primary inspiration may be Numbers 17:8, where the rod of Aaron blossoms and bears ripe almonds.

Glastonbury's Thorn is *Crataegus oxyacantha praecox*. When England finally adopted the reformed calendar, in 1752, none of the trees made the adjustment. However, they still break out in tiny white blossoms during late December or early January, dependent on the weather. There are many of them, not solely at Glastonbury. All are probably descendants of the patriarch on Wearyall Hill. The best local specimen is in front of the parish church of St John the Baptist. A sprig of its winter blossom is sent annually to the reigning sovereign.

The Thorn may be no more than a freak variant of the common hawthorn or applewort. Remarkably enough, however, the trees which most resemble it are found not far from the Holy Land. This has been acknowledged for some time and was amusingly proved at Washington, DC. There, a Thorn grows in the grounds of the Episcopalian cathedral. Somebody once cut off a piece of it, took this to the US Department of Agriculture, and asked a tree expert where it came from. The expert examined it and said 'Syria'. If there is anything in this, it suggests that the parent Thorn may have been brought back from the Middle East by a pilgrim or crusader.

Post-medieval legend-making has also produced fresh notions about the Grail. A misconception that it was a literal relic, the cup of the Last Supper conveyed to Britain by Joseph, has led to guesses as to its whereabouts and produced at least one popular candidate. The plain statement that Joseph brought the Grail to Glastonbury seems never to have been made in the Middle Ages. However close one or two romancers come to it, none says it outright, and the Abbey has him bring the cruets instead. I am not sure that anybody does make the plain statement before Tennyson. The Holy Grail episode in his *Idylls of the King* introduces the ex-quester Percivale in retirement from the court at a monastery. One of his brethren asks him about the Grail.

The Saint, the Grail and the Thorn

'What is it?
The phantom of a cup that comes and goes?'
'Nay, monk! What phantom?' answer'd Percivale.
'The cup, the cup itself, from which Our Lord
Drank at the last sad supper with his own.
This, from the blessed land of Aromat –
After the day of darkness, when the dead
Went wandering o'er Moriah – the good saint
Arimathaean Joseph, journeying brought
To Glastonbury, where the winter thorn
Blossoms at Christmas, mindful of the Lord.
And there awhile it bode; and if a man
Could touch or see it, he was heal'd at once,
By faith, of all his ills. But then the times
Grew to such evil that the holy cup
Was caught away to Heaven, and disappear'd.'

Its disappearance, of course, was not final. It 'came and went' elusively and a few saw it.

In the aftermath of Tennyson's vogue, a solid, physical Grail began to be rumoured. It was an old cracked cup or bowl made of olive wood which had been preserved for centuries at the mansion of Nanteos, three miles inland from Aberystwyth. The house stood on the site of a previous one, the home of the Powell family. Powells still lived here and had the cup in their possession. It was credited with healing powers. Water which had been poured from it was given to sufferers from various ailments.

At some point a report started circulating to the effect that this was the cup of the Last Supper. It was given a history. Joseph had carried it to Britain and it was kept at Glastonbury. When the Abbey was dissolved by Henry VIII, seven of the monks made their way to Strata Florida Abbey in Wales, taking it with them. Strata Florida succumbed also and some of the inmates, including the fugitives from Glastonbury, found haven with the Powells. The last of the seven handed over the cup to the head of the family, telling him of its wonder-working properties.

However, the story of the cup's coming from Strata Florida cannot be traced back further than 1878, and the

Avalonian Quest

full-fledged version asserting its identity and Glastonian origin is first on record about 1903. Among a number of objections, the most obvious is that the long list of the Abbey's relics, which John of Glastonbury sets down in his chronicle, does not include the cup. For some years, nevertheless, it went on being exhibited, and the sick went on drinking its healing water. At last the influx of visitors asking to see it became troublesome. For a time it was stowed away in a bank vault in Aberystwyth. The family that now owns it moved away in 1967 and lives in England, at an address which is not publicized, with the cup (or rather the last fragments of the cup) in its keeping.

One further belief is famous, beloved, and impossible to trace to its source. It avers that Joseph was Mary's uncle, therefore close to the Holy Family, and that he visited Britain long before the Gospel events, bringing the young Jesus with him. In the background of this tale we may suspect the medieval legend of the divine foundation and consecration of the Old Church. Taken literally, it could imply that Christ built it with his own hands while in Britain, before his public ministry. Those who favour this tale explain Joseph's early British voyaging by his hypothetical business interests, and claim that tin workers used to say 'Joseph was in the tin trade' as a good-luck charm on the job, as if folk-memory retained some recollection of him.

Part of the belief is that 'Christ walked in Priddy', a village on the Mendips. Sceptics maintain that the whole notion began with a children's play, written in Victorian days by the village schoolmistress: an innocent piece of fantasy which, like other pieces of fantasy, became an ancient Somerset legend. However, William Blake's lines –

> And did those feet in ancient time
> Walk upon England's mountains green? –

might be held to imply a previous version. No one knows. What is morally certain is that if the belief had existed in the Middle Ages, as an authentic local folk-tale, Glaston-

1. Aerial view of Glastonbury with the Abbey ruins in the foreground.

2. Glastonbury Tor, north face, showing the tower of St Michael's church and the terraces.

3. Glastonbury Abbey: part of the ruins.

4. Glastonbury Abbey: Lady Chapel, on the site of the Old Church. Inside, below ground level, is the chapel of Joseph of Arimathea.

The Saint, the Grail and the Thorn

bury's monks would have exploited such a stupendous distinction. They never even hint at it.

To revert to the two great themes, Joseph's coming to Glastonbury and Arthur's grave – how should we regard them?

Romantics who accept these things uncritically are mistaken. Opponents who dismiss them as pure invention are also mistaken. We must face the hard necessity of learning to take legends seriously without taking them literally. Or at least, without insisting on taking them literally. It is just possible that Joseph did come to Britain. It is slightly more than just possible that the bones in the grave were Arthur's. Both those statements now have reputable academic support. But the truth in any case is that the beliefs grew round something, in a context of abiding realities.

A subtle process runs through the centuries, transmitting, disinterring, editing, blending – not out of emptiness. The Christian advent in 63 and the royal interment both make sense as part of the Celtic matter which helped to form the Arthurian cycle. These two themes came to Glastonbury and took root. They were very probably returning to their first home; after all, it was Glastonbury they both concerned. Whether they were or not, their taking root presupposed the uniqueness of the place. Nobody maintained, and I do not think anybody could have maintained, that Joseph laid the foundation-stone of Worcester Cathedral or that Arthur was buried at Windsor.

CHAPTER SIX

Resurrection?

I

After the famous legends comes the story of Glastonbury's splendour, desolation and modern revival.

Throughout the high Middle Ages the Abbey was growing in wealth and power. It surmounted its financial crisis to become the greatest religious house in England, or, at any rate, an approximate equal-first with Westminster, and even Westminster could not compete with its special character as a national shrine. For almost three and a half centuries the builders and sculptors were adding to its enormous fabric. Today a model is all that shows what it was like at the end, with a church surpassing any other in England except St Paul's. Within its precinct the Benedictine life flourished – the liturgy, the works of education and charity, the crafts and music, the development of the library. Outside, the ancient 'Twelve Hides' of land were enlarged by bequests, donations and purchases, till the saying went that if the Abbot of Glastonbury married the Abbess of Shaftesbury, they would have more land than the King of England. The monks and their tenants continued to drain the marshes, bring waterlogged acres into cultivation, and maintain sea-walls that kept the Bristol Channel out.

To a modern eye, the Abbey during its last phase would not suggest a quiet contemplative community so much as a campus. It was a scene of varied and bustling activity. The Abbot was not only head of the house, he was the overlord and chief justice of the whole area, with a seat *ex officio* in the House of Lords. His many visitors were attended to in a separate dining hall with a separate kitchen, the Abbot's Kitchen, still more or less intact today.

Resurrection?

Hundreds of boys studied at the school. Clerks, bailiffs and other staff administered the Abbey's estates and dealt with its tenants, the farmers and craftsmen of central Somerset. The poor gathered at the gate for alms, and on major holy days the pilgrims poured into the great church, or descended the steps of the Lady Chapel to pray at St Joseph's altar below. The pilgrimage guide which was printed in 1520 listed miraculous cures said to have been worked at the shrine.

By then the neighbourhood had several Abbey-created buildings which still exist, chiefly because, in one way or another, they have continued to be used. Besides the two parish churches, there was the Abbot's court-house in the High Street; it was called the Tribunal and today it houses the town museum with the lake-village material. A few doors away was a pilgrims' hostel which is now the George and Pilgrims Hotel. A chapel in Bove Town, between Chalice Hill and Windmill Hill, has survived by being converted into a cottage. The Abbey Barn, on the road to the Tor, went on for many years in its intended role and is now a museum of Somerset rural life. Out at Meare, where the last of the waters lingered, there was a house for fishermen who supplied the monastic table. That too is standing, preserved as a structure only, not a dwelling.

The long history moved towards its close in the 1530s. While the Abbey was still rich in cash, plate and other movables, its huge domain was ceasing to be viable as a corporate entity. A rapid inflation was under way, and the Abbey drew most of its income from rents which had been fixed long before and were no longer economic. That, plus the decline of the religious orders in quality and usefulness, made Glastonbury vulnerable – as indeed nearly all the monastic houses were. In most of England, including Somerset, Henry VIII met with no great obstacles when he dissolved them. The buildings, goods and lands were seized by the Crown. The monks were pensioned off, or transferred to posts in the new national Church which the king had founded.

Glastonbury was almost the last to fall. When Henry's commissioners closed in at last, they carried out the business with exceptional savagery. Perhaps the king felt a special need to annihilate a national shrine which did not fit into his national Church. The aged Abbot, Richard Whiting, was convicted on vague charges of treason and hanged on the Tor on 15 November 1539, together with two of his monks, John Thorne and Roger James. Thorne was the maker of a famous chair which is now in the Bishop's Palace at Wells, and sold in replica to visitors to Glastonbury. The name he had taken in religion was Arthur. It is usual to take a saint's name. Here, possibly, Arthur counted as a saint.

The Abbot's corpse was dismembered, and the portions were displayed in Wells, Bath, Ilchester and Bridgwater, to show what could happen to those whom Henry regarded as his enemies. The commissioners proceeded to sell off most of the Abbey lands. A local man, John Horner, was active in assisting them and received the manor of Mells as his reward: hence the rhyme about Little Jack Horner, the title-deeds of Mells being the plum. As for the Abbey itself, it was rifled and vandalized. Lead torn from the roof was melted by burning the carved woodwork. Windows were smashed, bells broken up, books sold for what the parchment would fetch.

For some years the Abbey stayed in the Crown's hands. Under Edward VI the Duke of Somerset, known as the Lord Protector, took it over and tried to install a colony of Calvinist Flemish weavers. The arrangement foundered on their exorbitant demands, and when Mary became queen they feared persecution and went away. Meanwhile the Crown had resumed control. During Mary's reign, talk of a return by a few of the monks likewise came to nothing. In 1559 Elizabeth I granted the Abbey with its remaining lands to Sir Peter Carew. Thereafter it stayed in private possession till the twentieth century. It passed through various changes of ownership, and the lands were whittled away further.

One or two Elizabethans of note turned their gaze in this direction. John Dee, the royal astrologer and one of the arch-polymaths of his time, claimed that he had a book discovered in the ruins which contained the secret of turn-

Resurrection?

ing base metal into gold. He also had a quantity of red powder, apparently from the same cache, which was the Philosopher's Stone and would actually do it. In 1582 Dee transmuted part of a warming-pan. The book may have been an alchemical text ascribed to that earlier polymath St Dunstan. The powder is more cryptic. Something may be inferred from the fact that Dee died poor.

The poet Michael Drayton wrote a cycle *Polyolbion* which was a sort of versified gazetteer of the kingdom. In the course of it he addressed himself to the desolate Abbey:

O who thy ruin sees, whom wonder doth not fill
With our great fathers' pomp, devotion, and their skill?
Thou more than mortal power (this judgment rightly
   weighed)
Then present to assist, at that foundation laid,
On whom for this sad waste should justice lay the crime?
Is there a power in fate, or doth it yield to time?
Or was their error such, that thou couldst not protect
Those buildings which thy hand did, with their zeal, erect?
To whom didst thou commit that monument to keep,
That suffereth, with their dead, their memory to sleep,
When not great Arthur's tomb, nor holy Joseph's grave,
From sacrilege had power their sacred bones to save;
He, who that God in Man to his sepulchre brought,
Or he which for the Faith twelve holy battles fought –
What? Did so many kings do honour to that place,
For Avarice at last so vilely to deface?

Avarice did not end with Henry VIII. The main destruction, in fact, was not due to him or his commissioners but to the succession of private owners. They were not interested in Gothic architecture, but they were interested in saleable stone. The Abbey became a quarry. One occupant, impatient with ordinary demolition, blew up part of it with a bomb. The stones were sold to the highest bidders. Bits of the Abbey were built into many cottages round about, and, it is said, went into the substratum of the Wells road. Within the precinct, the Abbot's Kitchen escaped by becoming a Quaker meeting-house. So did a chapel of St

Patrick, which was attached to some almshouses built for widows of the parish by Richard Bere, the last abbot before Whiting, and continued to be used because the almshouses did. Everything else suffered, in varying degrees. This did not happen without qualms. A market house built of stones from the Abbey, across Magdalene Street facing the gate, fell into disuse because farmers thought it unlucky.

2

The modern revival is important, not only in itself, but as a stimulus to fresh thinking. Some of the revivalists claim to have shed light on problems which orthodox investigators have failed to solve – for instance, Glastonbury's origins. By a tortuous trial-and-error process, I believe light has been shed. But to reach any truth it is necessary to hack a path through a tangle of illusions. When the truth is attained, its implications about the past, the present, and any potential future, may turn out to be unexpected.

It is not clear when or how the notion of a rebirth, of a further and perhaps a greater beginning, started to stir in human imaginations. According to one account, rebirth has been part of the mythos all along, or nearly so. The last of the Glastonbury monks, Austin Ringwode, is supposed to have lived in a cottage near the Abbey till 1587. His neighbours believed him to have a prophetic gift. On his deathbed he spoke his final prophecy: 'The Abbey will one day be repaired and rebuilt for the like worship which has ceased; and then peace and plenty will for a long time abound.'

He may have done so. It appears, however, that the story cannot be traced back further than a nineteenth-century magazine article. Perhaps it came from some forgotten historical novel and was taken as fact. But even its invention would have been a symptom of an awakening of interest, and this was certainly under way in the Victorian era. The wave which then began to gather momentum remained Christian and Arthurian. The second wave, giving Glas-

Resurrection?

tonbury the reputation it has for many today, followed some decades later.

The major impulse in the first came from Tennyson. He took his position as Poet Laureate very seriously, and wrote the *Idylls* with the real monarchy in mind. His conscientious research tours in the West Country included Glastonbury. One result was the passage already quoted from the Holy Grail episode. The monk there addressed by Percivale answers:

> 'From our old books I know
> That Joseph came of old to Glastonbury,
> And there the heathen prince, Arviragus,
> Gave him an isle of marsh whereon to build;
> And there he built with wattles from the marsh
> A little lonely church.'

Tennyson struggled in the poem to express a sense of the Unseen which he believed to be valid, yet dangerous for the ordinary Christian. The knights' quest of the Grail is a desertion of the duties of normal life. The best and holiest never come back, and the Round Table degenerates. King Arthur sums up:

> 'Was I too dark a prophet when I said
> To those who went upon the Holy Quest,
> That most of them would follow wandering fires,
> Lost in a quagmire? – lost to me and gone,
> And left me gazing at a barren board,
> And a lean Order – scarce return'd a tithe –
> And out of those to whom the vision came
> My greatest hardly will believe he saw;
> Another hath beheld it afar off,
> And leaving human wrongs to right themselves,
> Cares but to pass into the silent life.
> And one hath had the vision face to face,
> And now his chair desires him here in vain,
> However they may crown him otherwhere.'

The idea of something strange, disturbing, subversive of a

good citizen's orthodoxy, was in keeping with the Grail's equivocal origins. Consciously, however, Tennyson is more likely to have had in mind a contemporary issue, the renewed energy of the Catholic Church in England. The conversion of Newman and Manning had given fresh prestige to the Roman claims and all that went with them, including the dedicated religious life and the ideal of sainthood. To Victorian Anglicanism, these were 'wandering fires' which seduced Christians from their responsibilities into a pursuit of self-centred, falsely spiritual goals. Tennyson shows that attitude in Arthur's dismissal of Percivale, who did enter a monastery, and is regarded by the king as having left human wrongs to right themselves.

Ironically, one of the most gifted visitors whom the *Idylls* drew to Glastonbury was Gerard Manley Hopkins. He made it his first port of call on a walking tour, towards the end of his time at Oxford, and moved decisively towards his own conversion soon afterwards. This was not a frequent response. Some Anglicans, focusing on Glastonbury itself rather than the Grail, saw nothing subversive about it and drew it into anti-Roman polemic by another route. Their case was that the Church of England was heir to an old British Church which was distinctive and independent. Legends of visits to Britain by early Christians were brought out and refurbished, and Glastonbury supplied a highly valued exhibit, Joseph of Arimathea. It was easy to contend that he came to Britain before St Peter founded the Church in Rome. Supposedly it followed that the British Church was senior and independent of Rome, owing no allegiance to Peter's papal successors. Doubtless the Abbey had been Roman, but that was a perversion, a deviation from the character of the first community, which was the one that counted.

This mode of thinking had its ancestry far back, in a book by Archbishop Parker published in 1572. One Victorian exponent was R. W. Morgan in 1861, whose *St Paul in Britain*, reprinted, still circulates. The most complete statement of the Glastonian groundwork came much later, in two credulous books by the Reverend Lionel Smithett Lewis, vicar of St John's in the High Street. Published in

Resurrection?

1922 and 1927, both were popular and have remained so. Readers today are probably more interested in the vicar's ardent account of the legends than in the view of their implications which underlies it. However, an anti-Roman construction of Glastonbury is still favoured by the intensely Protestant British-Israelites, who have a centre in the town. All that is proper to say here is that it is grounded on misconceptions. If Joseph came to Britain at all, it makes no difference to the Petrine claim whether he got here before or after St Peter got to Rome. The idea of an 'old British Church', fundamentally un-Roman, is not supported by any document . . . except one, which is forged.

In 1888 a first step was taken towards Glastonbury's renewal as a Christian centre. It was taken by Catholics, in successful defiance of the belief that they had no business there. A religious order bought the property at the corner of Chilkwell Street and Well House Lane, at the foot of the Tor, and built a school for its novices by the semi-derelict Anchor Inn.

Meanwhile the Abbey ruins had come into the possession of the Austin family. In 1907 Stanley Austin put them up for auction, with Abbey House, the residence at the eastern end. He had given eight months' notice of his intention, and Dr George Kennion, the bishop of Bath and Wells, had used that period to collect pledges of funds with a view to Anglican acquisition. The need for a new owner with large resources was apparent. Only prompt action could save the fragments that were left. The two remaining piers of the central tower were close to collapse, the Lady Chapel was crumbling, debris lay everywhere.

On 6 June 1907 the auction took place in the Abbey grounds. Some Catholic interest was shown, but everyone was outbid by Ernest Jardine, a Nottingham manufacturer. The other serious contender was a wealthy American woman with plans for either transplanting the ruins to America, or donating the site to the English Benedictines. However, she was too late for the sale. According to local tradition she missed a rail connection at Evercreech. By the time she arrived, Jardine had bought the Abbey for £30,000, and he refused to re-sell when she offered him more. The truth was that he was already pledged to re-sell, to the Church of England. The £30,000 was his own, but he was bidding, in effect, on Dr Kennion's behalf. Thus far Dr Kennion had raised only half the sum. Insinuating the papist threat, the bishop launched an appeal to raise the rest of it. Edward VII, Queen Alexandra, and the Prince of Wales (afterwards George V) subscribed. The amount was made up and the Church of England took over from Jardine in October 1908. In the following June the deeds were handed to the archbishop of Canterbury at a ceremony attended by the Prince. Ownership henceforth was vested in the Bath and Wells Diocesan Trust. It still is. Abbey House, the residence, is an Anglican retreat house.

The Trust undertook emergency repairs, putting in new stonework which can still be distinguished. A proposal for excavations, from the Somerset Archaeological and Natural History Society, had already been acceded to. Even under such auspices Glastonbury managed to be offbeat and peculiar, foreshadowing much that was to follow. The director of excavations was Frederick Bligh Bond, a Bristol architect who approached the Abbey in a possessive spirit. He carried out some competent seasons of work, recovering the plan of the great church, and proving the existence of the Edgar Chapel at its eastern extremity. This made its total length more than 580 feet, establishing it as the largest church in England after old St Paul's. Presently, though, he began to cause disquiet. In 1916 he gave a lecture suggesting that medieval church architects used a system of sacred geometry. He did so in the presence of that eminent historian Armitage Robinson, who was also dean of Wells, with responsibility for the Abbey. Dr Robinson disapproved.

A couple of years later, in *The Gate of Remembrance*, Bond made a catastrophic disclosure. He had been conducting his programme of excavation by spiritualistic methods, tapping the discarnate memories of the monks, with the aid of a friend who had a talent for automatic writing. In 1922 the dean felt obliged to dismiss him. Bond went to America, returned, and died in 1945, having meanwhile published further mediumistic matter about the Abbey's history.

Resurrection?

Frederick Bligh Bond was a difficult and obsessed person. His 'scripts' do not carry conviction for a moment, as authentic utterances of medieval monks. The antagonisms he aroused were made worse by the malice of a wife from whom he had separated. His removal ended all excavation for some years. Dr Radford did not appear upon the scene till the fifties. The Bond technique for exploring Glastonbury's past had its imitators. Other mediums produced 'annals' of their own, and even stranger things, such as a publication called *Winds of Truth* ascribed to the Archangel Michael.

Such were the beginnings of the revival, in its Christian aspect. The Arthurian aspect entered with the composer Rutland Boughton, best known for his opera *The Immortal Hour*. He envisaged Glastonbury as an English Bayreuth with himself as Wagner, putting on an Arthurian equivalent of *The Ring*. In 1913 he proposed the foundation of a National Theatre of Music and Drama there, with backing from Bernard Shaw, Elgar, Sir Henry Wood and Sir Thomas Beecham. The First World War put a stop to his scheme, but during the 1920s he founded a school at Glastonbury, and created a festival of music and drama using the town's Assembly Rooms. It was the precursor of all the more famous festivals at Malvern, Bath and elsewhere.

Those who remember the festival recall, as its conspicuous feature, the amazing effects which Rutland Boughton achieved with scanty resources. The support of Shaw and other celebrities was unswerving. But personal factors worked against him. First, he was a Communist. In 1926 a production of his nativity play *Bethlehem*, presenting Christ as a miner's child and Herod as a cartoon capitalist, angered the festival directors. His cycle of music-dramas on the Arthurian Legend ended uniquely with a peasants' revolt. Secondly, he had an unbridled sexual life, and the scandalized townspeople withdrew their children from his school. And finally it must be confessed that although his enthusiasm and charm were infectious, he was not a great enough composer for sustained major works. *The Immortal Hour* was a success, the Arthurian operas were not. There is no question here of genius suppressed by political prejudice. A 1961 revival of *The Queen of*

Cornwall, based on Hardy's handling of the Tristan legend, was tepidly acclaimed, and, alas, deserved it.

Laurence Housman took the festival over and kept it alive a little longer. Inevitably it faded out, yet a certain afterglow has never quite died. Modest festivals based on local talent were staged in 1963 and '64, and again in '78, '79 and '80. The latter series was centred on the Assembly Rooms, decayed but partly repaired. The festival of 1978 marked Rutland Boughton's centenary and included a concert of his music, which proved that it could still please in selection.

His original festival supplied hints for John Cowper Powys's vast novel *A Glastonbury Romance*, published in 1933, and described by Colin Wilson as 'possibly the greatest novel of the twentieth century, and one of the great mystical masterpieces of all time'. It had a powerful influence on another literary Wilson – Angus. The story revolves around the mythology of the Grail and has much to say about its pre-Christian antecedents, real and imagined. However, it still lies more or less within the Christian-Arthurian pattern, though looking constantly beyond it.

Within that pattern there have been other developments. An Anglican pilgrimage began in 1924 and is now a major annual event, drawing pilgrims from most of England, to the number of seven or eight thousand. Parts of the Abbey have been restored in a modest way for interdenominational use. The Abbey is also used each summer as an open-air theatre for plays about the legends and history, and other themes in keeping. They are directed by Kenneth Janes, a native of the town, who is Professor of Drama at Barnard College, Columbia University.

The Catholic novitiate by the Tor moved away, but a small Catholic church was opened in Magdalene Street in 1941, with the convent of a teaching order beside it. The church (which the Reverend L. S. Lewis called 'the hideous little chapel of the Italian mission') has a restored shrine of Our Lady of Glastonbury, and a fine modern tapestry combining history and legend, including what I believe to be the only portrayal of the Grail in a church.

Resurrection?

There is an annual Catholic pilgrimage as well as the Anglican. In 1979 it was attended by Cardinal Hume.

3

These initiatives and others have all enjoyed a degree of success. None has produced anything spectacular. Rutland Boughton might have done it, for good or ill, if he had been another Wagner. He was not. As for Austin Ringwode's alleged prophecy of a restoration of the Abbey as such, that has never shown any sign of being fulfilled, and it would now raise manifest difficulties. On the one hand, not enough is left to repair. On the other, if a new group of Benedictines were to take possession, they could hardly pull down the sanctified remnants and build on the site. They would have to go somewhere else.

At the Christian-Arthurian level, one senses a persisting impulse, a stubborn conviction in many minds. Glastonbury is felt to be not only unique but (so to speak) live, despite the desolation. Its story cannot be finished. Something important has yet to happen. That conviction has survived much disappointment and inspired the gradual, disjointed renewal. It has not, in a larger sense, been justified. Within the Christian-Arthurian scheme the shape of the important 'something' has yet to emerge.

It might be argued that this idea of a rebirth is simply a variant of the prophecy of Arthur's return. The dream of a long-lost glory or promise, which is not truly lost and may be recovered for a fresh start, seems to be deeply rooted in human nature. Arthur's return to reinstate a golden age, with intervening corruption swept away, is the British form of an archetypal myth. The motif can be seen at work, ostensibly demythologized, in a wide range of historic movements: for example, in the claim of the Reformation to be bringing back the pure primitive Church; in the appeal of French revolutionaries to Rousseau's natural humanity, spoilt by evil institutions, and to be put right again by good ones; in Mahatma Gandhi's vision of resurrecting a pre-industrial India of village communes. The same pattern of recovering what was lost long ago – 'apocalyptic nostalgia', it has been called – can be seen in other movements besides these. In Britain the myth of an Arthurian glory, which will blaze out again when the king returns, has hovered for centuries. Henry VII exploited his Welsh ancestry to claim that he was fulfilling the prophecy, since the Tudor monarchy was the old British one restored. Spenser applied the same notion to Elizabeth I in *The Faerie Queene*.

Today, it may be presumed, no one believes that Arthur is asleep in a cave and will wake up. (For one thing, he is asleep in fully a dozen caves, real and fictitious.) Therefore the dream has to be translated into a belief which can be held. Tudor propaganda tried it, but mystical monarchy went out of favour with the Stuarts, for the moment at least. Perhaps, for some, the prophecy of Arthur has transferred itself to Glastonbury as the holy place which is reputedly his. This too passed away, but this too is only sleeping, and here a reawakening can be seriously imagined, as it cannot be with an individual. That can hardly be the whole truth, but it could be part of the truth.

Not to be overlooked, as proof of the myth's abiding power, is the Arthurian literary revival. It has taken an interesting course. T. H. White's *The Once and Future King*, and John Steinbeck's posthumous re-telling of Malory, both carried on from the medieval romance-Arthur. So have films such as *Excalibur* (though *Excalibur* had more originality than it was given credit for). But much of the new writing has bypassed the medieval matter in varying degrees, and tried to evoke Arthurian Britain more or less as it might have been. We have had novels by Henry Treece, Rosemary Sutcliff, Mary Stewart, Douglas Carmichael, Catherine Christian, Robert Nye, Peter Vansittart, Victor Canning; plays by R. C. Sherriff and John Arden; and the astonishing poems *The Sleeping Lord* by David Jones, and *Artorius* by John Heath-Stubbs.

Glastonbury is not central to any of these. But persons deeply concerned with it have been in the background, directly or indirectly advising. A potent stimulus came

Resurrection?

from the excavation of Cadbury-Camelot. Some critics objected that the archaeological 'quest for Arthur's Britain' was either irrelevant or destructive. It has turned out to be neither. It has enriched the mythos, and inspired new creation.

CHAPTER SEVEN

Way-Out

I

The Glastonbury mystique of the later twentieth century is something else again. It has two main features. In the first place, modern mystics shift the focus away from the Abbey. Usually they look towards the Tor and its neighbourhood, with a stress on its vibes. Secondly, they reach out behind Christianity into an ambience of a different, supposedly senior kind. They see the Christian-Arthurian mythos as a growth out of some prior scheme of things, and perhaps partially a falsification.

Neither of these statements should be taken in a rigid sense. Some introduce the Abbey into their theories. But they embed it in concepts lying outside its history, outside its character as normally understood. They do not think of it as a Benedictine foundation, but as a design. Its groundplan is more important than its inmates. As for Christianity, the neo-mystics seldom declare themselves against it. But they tend to sidestep the issue by calling it a 'belief-system', one among many, and regarding it as a sort of crutch, which the faithful use but the enlightened can dispense with. Those among them who do profess it give it esoteric interpretations, which are supposed to fit it into a framework of older mysteries. The apt word here is 'Gnosticism'. Several of the most vocal neo-mystics have frankly professed or favoured that ancient heresy. One popular doctrine is reincarnation, which is more believed in than not.

Much of this is brought together in two symposia: *Glastonbury, a Study in Patterns* (1969), edited by Mary Williams and sponsored by RILKO, the Research into Lost Knowledge Organization; and *Glastonbury: Ancient*

Way-Out

Avalon, New Jerusalem (1977), edited by Anthony Roberts. The seeds were planted during the inter-war period, partly by the revelations of Frederick Bligh Bond, partly by Powys's *Glastonbury Romance*, and partly by the work of a third remarkable person, Dion Fortune.

Her real name was Violet Firth. Born in 1891, she was the daughter of a hotel proprietor in Llandudno. Her mother was a Christian Scientist. Violet became a psychologist and one of the first in England to absorb Freud and Jung. She developed an interest in occultism as Jung did, but whereas Jung studied it for its psychological bearings, Violet pressed on and practised it. She joined the magical Order of the Golden Dawn, which had once counted W. B. Yeats among its members. 'Dion Fortune' was her pseudonym in the Order. She broke away – members of such bodies frequently do – and founded her own group, the Society of the Inner Light.

Glastonbury had no special interest for her former colleagues, but she regarded it as a great energy-centre of the western world, a spiritual volcano which had erupted in past ages and would again. In the 1920s, when Rutland Boughton was running his festival, she moved in and finally settled on the Tor's lower slope, at a spot with a dramatic view up to the summit, and a year-round spectacle of sunrise and moonrise on the shoulder of the hill. The property overlooked the old Anchor Inn and was then known as Anchor Orchard. Re-naming it Chalice Orchard with the Grail in mind, she put up a bungalow, several chalets, and a temple, and conducted the place as an esoteric hostel with support from her husband, a Dr Evans. She died of leukaemia in 1946 and is buried in the town cemetery.

Dion Fortune was a prolific author and, at her best, more lucid and rational than most of her kind. A traumatic experience in youth led her to become an expert on what she called psychic self-defence. Her study *The Mystical Qabalah* presents an ingenious system spun out of Jewish tradition. She put this forward as a western alternative to the Wisdom of the East, too often cultivated by ill-advised and ill-informed seekers. Her work includes occultish short stories and novels, of a type destined to be more fashionable in the seventies. Also she wrote *Avalon of the Heart* (1934). The book is interesting for its glimpses of Glastonbury in the Rutland Boughton phase, and it set the tone for a great deal of later speculation.

A reader of her books may be repelled by stretches of fantasy and unreason, yet also struck by the keenness of the occasional insight. She foreshadowed the interests of generations after her. She was ahead of her time, for instance, in raising the issue of female spirituality which American feminists began airing about 1975, in protest against 'patriarchal' religion. That theme is explored in two linked novels, *The Sea Priestess* and *Moon Magic*, the first of which has an easily recognized Somerset locale. An enchantress who figures in both is said to be based on Mrs Tranchell-Hayes, an erudite occultist and member of the Golden Dawn, who was, to a certain extent, Dion Fortune's teacher. More of these insights and foreshadowings will become apparent in their place.

Avalon of the Heart closes with an extraordinary passage, in which Dion Fortune welcomes the return of the Catholic Church to Glastonbury.

> Every summer at midsummer's day a high cross of larch-poles stands on the Tor behind us, gaunt against the sky; and a long procession winds up, monks and nuns and Children of Mary, and the sound of singing comes to us, and a man's voice preaching fervently.
>
> If any place could become the English Lourdes it is our Avalon. Glastonbury has done her fair share of stoning the prophets, but I fancy the Holy Roman Church is made of sterner stuff than Bligh Bond with his other-world visions and Rutland Boughton with his dream of beauty; and I, for one, hope she will make good her footing, and, impenitent heathen though I am, that I shall hear her Angelus from my high veranda.

Some light is shed on the seeming self-contradiction by a speech of the enchantress in *Moon Magic*, when she is discussing sexual matters with her male magical partner.

Way-Out

'Wherever a goddess is worshipped, it is the moon-forces that are worked with, and they are important. It is the lack of them that is throwing our modern civilization so badly off its balance. The Catholics compensate in part with the adoration of the Virgin – Stella Maris, Star of the Sea – what is she but Venus Anadyomene – Venus born of the foam? And who is Regina Coeli if She is not the Moon? If you want to understand paganism, study Catholicism, its lineal descendant. "Plus ça change, plus c'est la même chose."'

In other words Catholicism is the means by which the old gods and goddesses have survived, and it is valid as such. That idea had a special aptitude to its Celtic form, and to the Grail legend, whether or not Dion Fortune realized it. But to work the idea out, and embrace its consequences, would have demanded a seriousness of thought and a reverence for fact which few of the subsequent neo-mystics were capable of. They read *Avalon of the Heart* for anything but its conclusion, and found plenty of other motifs to take hold of – lost Atlantis, Druids, vanished megaliths on the Tor, miraculous healing, revelations by dowsing. Dion Fortune's hint towards a Christian-pagan rapprochement remained neglected. Some of her Avalonian lore was wise, and today some of it has come through to a semi-vindication, but it has to be sifted for, and very differently stated.

2

In the twentieth century Druids have been popular. It is quite credible, of course, that those priest-magicians of the Celts did set foot on the Isle of Avalon, if only because of the lake-villages nearby. But as a rule the Druidism supposed to have flourished here is a romanticized version, having little in common with the real thing.

Below Stone Down, an eastward extension of the hill-cluster, are two massive oak trees beside a lane. These have

Avalonian Quest

been dubbed 'Druid oaks'. Their popular names are Gog and Magog. They are the sole survivors of a row, the rest of which was cut down about 1906. The oak was sacred in Druid eyes, and Gog and Magog are impressive, but they can hardly be as old as that.

Societies which profess to revive Druidic wisdom make much of Caesar's statement that the Druids had colleges in Britain. They maintain that Glastonbury was the seat of one of these. The Order of Bards, Ovates and Druids used to hold a May ceremony on the Tor, presided over by their chief, the late Ross Nichols. They cherished a theory about a ritual chamber inside the hill. According to some, it was reached by a tunnel running inwards from the old waterworks property next door to Chalice Orchard, Dion Fortune's home. The tunnel exists, but it is a brick-lined 'heading', in hydraulic parlance, drilled by the Bristol Waterworks Company in 1873 to tap underground springs. It runs along for about fifty feet and ends in a larger space where water seeps in. The Nichols group no longer comes to Glastonbury, but another, the Golden Section Order, has taken its place and holds May ceremonies of its own.

Romanticized Druidism has played a major role in the mythology of Chalice Well. This, in essence, is a natural spring between the Tor and Chalice Hill. It is at the top end of a strip of land running up the little valley from the place where the Anchor Inn used to be. Today the spring rises inside a stone well-shaft nine feet deep. Its flow is abundant, about 25,000 gallons a day. Allegedly it has never dried up even in the longest droughts. The water has an iron impregnation that gives a reddish or orange tinge to stones over which it flows. Despite the iron it is clear and drinkable, with a pleasant tang. Similar water comes through in at least two other places in the neighbourhood, but far less copiously. The source is unknown and doubtless a long way off, in the Mendips or even Wales.

Archaeology points to frequentation of this area during the Roman period and farther back. In *Perlesvaus*, as remarked, the account of Lancelot's visit to Avalon apparently refers to the spring, though purely as such, with no hint of holiness. It never had any Christian sanctity of the kind that would have made it 'Saint So-and-So's Well'. About 1200, the monks enclosed it in stonework and piped the water downhill into their precinct. It still makes the same journey.

The earliest documents call it Chalk Well, variously spelt, the word 'chalk' being employed in an old sense to mean 'limestone'. This name survives in neighbouring Chilkwell Street. 'Chalice' is a fairly recent modification. Old maps show that the water's reddish tint inspired an alternative name, the Blood Spring or Blood Well. In 1750, Matthew Chancellor of North Wootton was impelled by a dream to drink a quarter of a pint of it on seven successive Sunday mornings. He then announced that it had cured an asthma of thirty years' standing. For a year or so Glastonbury became a spa with thousands of visitors. A pool and a pump room were built. This phase may account for a strange underground chamber that opens out of the main well-shaft. It is five-sided and may have been a sedimentation tank, to keep the supply clean for bathers and drinkers. After reputed cures of assorted ills, including blindness, deafness and ulcers, one of the visitors drank too much and died. The town's career as a spa came to an end.

In 1888 the Catholic order that bought the Anchor Inn property acquired the Well with it. When the order departed, about twenty years later, the buildings and the long garden with the Well at the upper end came into the possession of Alice Buckton. She formed a craft centre and put on concerts and plays, including one of her own, *Eagerheart*, which was much admired. In 1919 the Well was given a lid decorated with wrought-iron symbols designed by Bligh Bond. Powys put the place in his Glastonbury novel, as a scene of faith-healing.

Afterwards the main building became a school. However, the entire property was bought in 1958 by the Chalice Well Trust, in which the guiding spirit was Major Wellesley Tudor Pole. The Trust acquired the inn, the school, a row of cottages, and the garden running up to the Well. It sponsored Philip Rahtz's Tor excavation, when the digging team was housed in the school building. This, together with the inn, was torn down after Tudor Pole's death, and the garden was remodelled. Chalice Well is open to the public, and managed by custodians responsible to the trustees. Its main support comes from a body of Companions and Associates. Most of them regard it as, in some sense, a holy and spiritual spot.

Its modern cultus was foreshadowed by Dion Fortune, who wrote of 'the wonderful holy well of St Joseph and Merlin and the Graal', and said that when it was drained for cleaning, you could 'climb down a ladder into its mysterious depths and stand where the living sacrifices of the Druids must have stood'. The stonework, she conjectured, was not due to medieval monks but to far earlier builders, 'probably of the same race who handled the mighty masses of Stonehenge and Avebury'. At least until recently, the cultus has based itself on ideas such as these. The Well, it is asserted, was a centre of Druid ritual; Joseph of Arimathea lived near it; the Grail is or was at the bottom (hence the colour of the water and, despite etymology, the name 'Chalice'). A bowl, found in obscure circumstances, is credited with a most unlikely antiquity. Miracles of healing are claimed. Spiritual presences are discerned in the garden. Lines of mystic force emanate from the Well itself.

A sort of Christianity is bound up with this. Some of the Companions belong to the Church of England, and recall that when L. S. Lewis was vicar he used to conduct services in the garden. But Chalice Well Christianity is not Christian in any normal sense. Its adherents use phrases with a Gnostic ring, such as 'the Christ Power', and are apt to think (in effect) that Christianity is a form of Druidism. They have never produced any authentically old traditions to sustain their opinions about the Well. The memoirs of the Jesuit Weston show that the man he met in 1586 thought Joseph had lived somewhere up the Tor, but that can hardly count.

Behind it all, nevertheless, two good guesses may be acknowledged. There is the evidence for an early belief, perhaps a true belief, that a Christian settlement existed in the Tor area earlier still. This can be made to extend to the valley near the Well, though nothing suggests that the Well was the settlement's *raison d'être* or had any mystic importance for it. The nature of the hit scored by the other guess will emerge in due course. As for the rest, it would be churlish to deny that faith-healing and visions have occurred here. But the emphasis on the Well itself, as the energy-source and focus of some ancient cult, seems to be misguided.

3

Enthusiasts for Chalice Well tend to be enthusiasts for the Glastonbury Zodiac theory. This was expounded in the inter-war period by Katharine Maltwood, and has since been developed – exuberantly – by Mary Caine, by the late Barbara Crump, and by members of the aforesaid RILKO. It declares that Glastonbury lies within a circle roughly ten miles across which is a gigantic diagram of the signs of the Zodiac. The figures are formed by features of the landscape, and are in the same relative positions as the constellations are in the sky. The humped ridge of Wearyall Hill is one of the Fishes. Part of the Tor is part of Aquarius. The Lion is out towards Somerton. The Scorpion straggles uncertainly over the Fosse Way. The Virgin (who, for some reason, is in an advanced stage of pregnancy) is mapped out by field-boundaries and a river around Babcary. And so on.

Mrs Maltwood called this system the Temple of the Stars. She found the first hints for it in *Perlesvaus*, the romance supposed to be founded on a Glastonbury source-document. Episodes with animals in them referred, she claimed, to the zodiacal signs in the landscape. As to the way the signs came to be there, she ascribed their making to Sumerians from the Middle East in 2700 BC, 'Somerset' being derived from 'Sumer'. Other exponents, with an echo of one of Dion Fortune's interests, have looked back to Atlantis. Anyhow the Zodiac is agreed to be very old. Mrs Maltwood thought it was the true original Round Table, and in Mary Caine's hands it becomes the source of

Avalonian Quest

the Arthur mythology, the Grail mythology, and a great deal more besides. Her discourse on its multiple meanings is a lively exercise in the association of words, ideas, images. But if we insist on asking whether it actually, physically exists, the obstacles to belief are apparent.

At ground level, so to speak, one glaring objection is that it brings in too many types of feature. If the figures were outlined entirely by contours, or entirely by water-courses, they might carry conviction. But Zodiac-finders make use of anything and everything – hills, streams, woods, ditches, hedges, roads. In central Somerset, as the Ordnance Survey shows, this freedom opens up too many possibilities. Moreover, some of the features are quite recent, and could not have been anticipated four or five thousand years ago. A recognized post-Maltwood retort is to invoke superhuman powers or Earth Forces. These powers, it is claimed, have a tendency to create zodiacs because zodiacs correspond to a pattern which is inherent in nature. Human behaviour in such matters as road-building is subtly moulded by their requirements. A natural comment is that if such mighty entities are at work, they ought to be equal to forming a zodiac correctly; whereas four of the twelve figures are wrong – we are asked to accept a ship instead of a crab, a dove instead of a pair of scales, a unicorn instead of a goat, a phoenix instead of a water-carrier.

Another stumbling-block is that the figures can only be seen from a great height, we are told: even as much as 20,000 feet. What then was their relevance to prehistoric people who could not fly? Believers have no single answer. One has spoken of hang-gliding. Others have suggested that the Zodiac was meant to be seen by gods, or UFO-voyagers. It has also been suggested that there was once a 'canopy' of ice crystals in the upper atmosphere, which would have acted as a vast mirror, reflecting the figures for the benefit of those below.

However, the real question is the fundamental one. All objections would have to give way if it could be proved that the figures are there at all. But are they? The vaunted argument that they coincide with the star map is worthless if they are not there, if they are merely products of wishful thinking. They are supposed to be obvious in aerial photographs. I have studied those photographs; I know what I am meant to see; I honestly try to see; and I simply do not. I doubt if anybody, confronted with the same photographs, would trace the figures unguided.

In April 1977 I wrote to the *Central Somerset Gazette* proposing a test.

> Let the Zodiac's advocates choose the aerial pictures which they judge to be best. Let these given out, unmarked and unidentified, to a sample of (say) a hundred people who do not know what they represent, have not heard the Zodiac theory, have not been prompted, and cannot communicate with each other. They should be asked to study the pictures carefully and report in writing on what shapes, if any, they see in them. This is a type of test well established in psychology, and not hard to run.
>
> If the Zodiac figures are so plainly there, a significant number of these innocent-eyed test subjects ought to see them, in whole or in part, and report accordingly. Should they do so, the theory will be proved, whatever interpretations may follow. . . .
>
> I would immensely welcome such a test myself. Are the Zodiac's advocates prepared to try it – of course with proper control and supervision?

I have repeated that proposal in print, in another place. It has never been taken up. As a footnote, it is worth observing that Zodiac-finders do not themselves agree on these 'obvious' figures. More than one has been re-drawn.

If the matter cannot be resolved by inspection, the believers' only hope lies in argument. They complain of the unwillingness of archaeologists to do anything about 'proving' the Zodiac. The truth is that it could not even be investigated archaeologically, let alone proved. So far as I can judge, it could only be proved in two ways. If it could be shown that zodiacs exactly like it are traceable in other landscapes, the odds against chance duplication would be so heavy as to amount to a proof of planning. If an early

Avalonian Quest

document or inscription were found with a detailed chart of it, that would prove an awareness independent of Mrs Maltwood's, and the unlikelihood of the same complex illusion occurring twice would again be tantamount to proof.

As to the first possibility, other zodiacs have been asserted (whence the notion of superhuman zodiac-creating forces), but even with the vast licence which seekers allow themselves, they have nowhere managed to construct one that is sufficiently like. As to the second, there is certainly nothing, so far, of a pictorial nature. A question not wholly settled is whether there is any indication at all that a Glastonbury Zodiac was thought of before Mrs Maltwood. The hints at it which she detected in *Perlesvaus* would never be taken in that sense by an unprompted reader. An alleged reference by John Dee has not survived scrutiny. However, one pre-Maltwood text is not quite so easily dismissed. I discovered this myself. None of the Zodiac enthusiasts ever noticed it.

Appropriately enough, it occurs in the prophecies of Nostradamus (book VI, no. 22).

Dedans la terre du grand temple celique
Nepveu à Londres par paix faincte meutri.

In the land of the great heavenly temple
A nephew at London is murdered through a false peace.

The reference to London proves that 'the land of the great heavenly temple' is England. Since the temple is unique and distinctive, it cannot be a church. Stonehenge was barely known in Nostradamus' time, the sixteenth century, and the only current idea about it was that it was a royal monument. Therefore, hardly Stonehenge. A believer in the Zodiac could fairly claim that the phrase means the Temple of the Stars, and challenge a sceptic to suggest a better candidate.

If we accept that precognition can ever happen, the second line gives an extra thrust to the words. To call the murder victim a nephew indicates that it was his uncle who

Way-Out

murdered him. In 1685, after the collapse of the Monmouth rebellion, the defeated Duke was brought to London and put to death by James II. James was his uncle, and in the eyes of Monmouth's supporters, who regarded him as the rightful king, the killing of the nephew was murder rather than execution. It was the principal step in the making of a 'peace' or pacification which was false, because the cruelty of James's agents left a bitterness which helped to dethrone him three years later. And the thought of this affair might well call to mind a 'heavenly temple' in Somerset, because Somerset was the heart of the rebellion. Monmouth's army twice camped at Glastonbury, and the fatal battlefield of Sedgemoor is not far off.

I scarcely know what to make of Nostradamus. Conceivably he picked up some notion about Glastonbury from his fellow-astrologer Dee, who was in France when the prophecies were being composed, and who notoriously had such notions, even if they did not extend to a Zodiac. Whatever the inspiration of the phrase I cannot believe that the Zodiac is 'there' as, say, Stonehenge is there. Yet many people, looking at aerial photographs or even a map, do see it. The phenomenon is akin to the Rorschach ink-blot test, or to seeing pictures in the fire. It is a fact and must be admitted.

There are reasons to be wary of the psychological doctrines of Jung. Still, perhaps they can help here. One of his favourite concepts is the mandala. 'Mandala' is a Sanskrit word meaning a circle, not simply in the geometrical sense, but in the sense of a sacred diagram. The motif is familiar in Tibetan Buddhism. Kipling introduced the Buddhist Wheel of Life in *Kim*. Jung's interest in mandalas grew from his clinical experience. He sometimes asked his patients to draw, entirely at will. They produced pictures and designs in immense variety. But he noticed a tendency to enclose a drawing in a perimeter, real or imagined, and to give it a certain balance around a centre. He also noticed that some of his patients' dreams had the same kind of imagery. They would dream of a lake with an island in the middle, or a formal garden surrounding a fountain, or people circling inside an enclosure or making their way

Avalonian Quest

deviously to the summit of a hill. The central point might be reached or it might not. In both the drawings and the dreams, everything was related to it by symmetry and orientation.

Jung claimed that Buddhist mandalas show the same type of imagery and inner relationships. In his view all such formations are projections of the Unconscious. The picture as a whole symbolizes the psyche, and the centre is what Jung called the Self, meaning its inmost nature – the true goal of the individual's quest in life, the key to vocation and psychological wholeness.

On this showing, the Glastonbury Zodiac might be explained psychologically. It is a magic circle, a stylized mandala which the Unconscious of some – but only some – takes hold of and projects on the landscape. As a result the landscape, for them, is charged with occult energies. I once heard a Zodiac lecturer exhort every member of his audience to 'go to your own sign and walk over it with bare feet, or at any rate, with thin-soled shoes'. The solemnity of that advice may draw a smile from those who don't see. But the fact that many sincerely do is part of the Avalonian spell.

4

Glastonbury has also been drawn into the ley-line theory. This was invented by a flour miller, Alfred Watkins, whose observations in the course of his business journeys convinced him that prehistoric sites were not scattered at random. He found many of them to lie along straight lines, and suggested that they were sited as markers, helping travellers to pick out cross-country routes. In 1925 he published *The Old Straight Track*. It inspired a school of ley hunters who went about looking for the sort of alignments he claimed existed.

The theory was revived in the 1960s by John Michell and others. Like the Zodiac theory, it has grown more mystical over the years. Dion Fortune foreshadowed that development as she foreshadowed others, in her novel *The Goat-Foot God*. Watkins's mundane idea of landmarks went out of favour. For a while it was fashionable to talk about *Feng Shui*, a Chinese landscape-magic invoked in the siting of buildings, but that analogy ceased to be favoured when it was realized that in *Feng Shui*, straight lines were anathema. Today the leys are regarded, somewhat cryptically, as lines of terrestrial force.

Glastonbury is not central to the scheme. However, it is said to be a place where several of the lines intersect. This proves its ancient significance as a power-point. Much the same query arises here as with the Zodiac. Arguments from the intersection are worthless if the lines do not exist to begin with, and the major objection is like one of the objections to the Zodiac figures. Possibilities are multiplied much too far. A straight line connecting, say, five megaliths might be interesting. But the ley hunter is allowed to count no fewer than seventeen types of feature as prehistoric sites. The features are widely different, and may be of widely different dates. They include mounds, stones, castles, beacons, wells, fords, trees, ponds, and so forth, some of the classes being divided into several sub-classes. They also include churches, on the ground that as churches were sometimes built on pre-Christian sacred sites, it follows that any pre-Reformation church is evidence for such a site. It isn't. The modern speculative approach admits at least three further types of evidence: dowsing, UFO-sightings and ghost stories. With such a plethora, devoid of any real coherence, it is not remarkable that a few sites should line up. It would not be remarkable if it were more than a few.

Paul Devereux and Ian Thomson, the authors of *The Ley Hunter's Companion* (1979), give forty-one specimen leys. Each connects five or more sites. They are presumably the best the authors could offer when they wrote the book. In nearly every case the straight line joins up several different types of feature. Almost the only examples where one type predominates are alignments of churches. In the absence of proof as to what was on these sites before, they carry no weight.

But while the ley theory is most decidedly Not Proven, it must be conceded that one of the few lines which do impress passes through Glastonbury. John Michell drew attention to it and called it the St Michael Line. It joins up St Michael's Mount off Marazion in Cornwall; St Michael's Church, Brentor; St Michael's Church, Burrowbridge Mump; St Michael's Church, Othery; St Michael's Church, Glastonbury Tor; and Stoke St Michael. Moreover, the line passes on through Avebury and Bury St Edmunds. The repetition of the same dedication makes this church alignment far more interesting than most, and St Michael is weightier evidence than usual for a pre-Christian site. The fact that the line also traverses such a great prehistoric monument as Avebury is striking. Since it is not perfect, ley-line purists call it a 'corridor'. But on a map of moderate scale it looks good, as a few moments with a ruler will demonstrate, and its length puts it in a special class.

Somewhat akin to the ley theory are the further ideas of John Michell, who, in *City of Revelation*, tried to fit the ground-plan of Glastonbury Abbey into a scheme of sacred geometry and numerology. Such concepts may have played a part in medieval church architecture, and Bligh Bond was already talking about them in 1916. But Michell's attempt to prove an elaborate system involving even Stonehenge suffers from much the same shortcoming as the Zodiac and the ley-lines. There are too many possibilities, too many variables. If you try hard enough, with enough ingenuity, you can prove a great deal. The competing 'solutions' of the most famous of all numerological riddles, the Number of the Beast (Revelation 13:18), should stand as a warning.

5

Since the 1960s the loudest prophesyings about a rebirth, and the most flamboyant projects with that in view, have come from devotees of fringe theories rather than Christians. Their speculative flights have ranged far and wide.

Way-Out

In 1964 a Bristol engineer, Graham Friese-Greene, published a grandiose scheme for an Avalonian university. It was to be a colossal circular structure out on the moors, supported by metal piles going down to the bedrock. Mr Friese-Greene did not say so, but it was apparently modelled on cities on the planet Venus described by George Adamski, who professed to have gone there aboard a flying saucer.

In 1971 came the discovery of Glastonbury by what was called, for a time, the Alternative Society. This was promoted chiefly by Muz Murray, the editor of a magazine, *Gandalf's Garden*. The Glastonbury Fayre, a pop-mystical festival on a farm near Pilton, attracted thousands of junior seekers. I think this is the best way to refer to them. Local citizens dubbed them 'hippies' and generally disliked them. Hotels and cafés in the town displayed 'No Hippies' signs for a full decade afterwards. However, it was a decade of cooling-off, and the event was repeated in 1979 and 1981 with much less disturbance. The generation who made the place an alternative spiritual capital believed in all sorts of things. Chalice Well, the Zodiac and ley-lines were taken for granted. UFOs were sighted almost as a routine matter. Angels and demons were confronted around the Tor. The Second Coming of Christ (hardly the Christ of orthodoxy) was expected to happen on the summit. Vigils there at the summer solstice, from a variety of motives, became a regular occurrence.

For some years after the original Fayre, a number of the so-called hippies lived in the neighbourhood. They had a café and meeting-room of their own, called themselves the New Glastonbury Community, and brought out a magazine called *Torc*. That phase ended about 1975. By then, however, some of the same impulses were finding expression in a less anarchic form.

It was the beginning of the vogue of the New Age or Aquarian Age, publicized by such events as the Festival for Mind and Body at Olympia, which Bernard Levin extolled in *The Times*. The New Age dawned in an explosion of astrology and parapsychology and psychometry and healing and vegetarianism and meditation and yoga and

Avalonian Quest

consciousness-raising and . . . one pauses for breath. To a large extent it is still with us. As G. K. Chesterton foretold long ago, 'When people cease to believe in God, they won't believe in nothing, they will believe in everything.' Amid the welter of general 'believing in everything', it has always been possible to discern a fund of goodwill, originality, hope. Some of this has channelled new energies into Glastonbury. A leading light in the whole movement has been Sir George Trevelyan, founder of the Wrekin Trust, an exploratory educational body. In 1979 he and I organized a midsummer conference which filled Glastonbury Town Hall. It was repeated two years later.

From the mixed results achieved by would-be revivalists, Christian and otherwise, one conclusion emerges plainly. Trouble and disappointment have followed, again and again, from approaching Glastonbury in a spirit which does not fit a place with so potent a mystique of its own. Too many have tried to force some preconceived idea on it, to use it as a base for pre-packaged teachings, to 'lay their own trips on it' – in fact to exploit the mystique. Dion Fortune was wiser than most of the esoteric set. Yet even she settled in Glastonbury because, as a spiritual power-centre, it was a good place to expound her own teachings and to attract like-minded persons. Other intending gurus have done much the same in recent years, and withdrawn or changed course. The interesting thing is that there seems to be some quality in the place which defeats or diverts them. A kindred delusion has been that Glastonbury can be fitted into some broader neo-religious or neo-mystical pattern. The New Age community at Findhorn in Scotland has persistently tried to annex it to its own doctrines, and treat it as one centre among many in a worldwide Network of Light: this, it must be said, in near-ignorance of its history and in total ignorance of Catholic Christianity.

One sad effect of all the incursions, from the 1920s on, was a split between the townspeople and the assorted zealots, project-mongers and professed light-bearers. Rutland Boughton with his festival had a personal talent for stirring up hostility. But Dion Fortune voiced a more pervasively provocative state of mind. In 1934, referring to the defunct festival phase, she wrote:

> We used to say that there dwelt in Glastonbury the Glastonburians and the Avalonians; the Glastonburians were those who only knew the place as a market town and a tourist centre, and the Avalonians were those who were in touch with its spiritual life.
>
> I believe that I am the last of the Avalonians, of those who were drawn to Glastonbury as a centre of ever-renewed spiritual and artistic inspiration.

She was not the last. The continued drawing of her distinction between enlightened newcomers and local peasants estranged the local peasants, making division real and self-perpetuating. That is one reason why some Glastonbury people seem blind to their heritage when they are not. They are reluctant to open up to the cranks who beset them, and to any outsider who may appear like a crank.

Gradually, however, the atmosphere has improved and the barriers have lowered. Several resident mystics have shown a new and welcome civic constructiveness, opening shops and guest-houses, helping at the Tourist Information Centre, joining the Conservation Society, working to restore the Assembly Rooms, taking an interest in the conversion of the Abbey Barn into a rural museum. Something of the change was reflected in a small book published in 1979 entitled simply *Glastonbury*, by Michael Mathias, assistant editor of the local paper, and Derek Hector, a photographer.

Meanwhile more of the mystics have tended to realize that Glastonbury cannot be used or dictated to. From their point of view, the only right attitude is a receptive one, with a willingness to learn and (if there is anything truly at work here) to let it unfold. A real rebirth might take various forms. It might involve a project or movement. But it might be no more than a Glastonian impulse inspiring some individual, some genius who would go on from the experience to bring humanity a fresh hope and vision. Who can tell?

However, one feature of the neo-mysticism must be reverted to. Nearly always it involves that view of Glastonbury as a major pre-Christian holy place. The Christian history and legends are rooted in a higher magic which was present before. Druids may be mentioned, but even they are apt to be seen as late comers. That is a vital part of the Zodiac theory, and it is implied in the ley-line theory too, because the leys are supposed to be much older than Christianity. We may dismiss these theories, and others, as flights of fancy which have confused the issues. But their inventors and advocates have really been trying to rationalize a feeling, an intuition, a sense of ancient mystery; and that must not be dismissed, because it calls for explanation, even if it is a total delusion.

Other great Christian centres do not inspire it. Whatever legends may have gathered around them, whatever claims may have been made for them, whatever older associations they may have, they convey no comparable hint of a special, different, senior vitality. They have not attracted themes like the Grail, drawing in non-Christian and unorthodox matter, rejected by the Church. They have no similar aura of influences which are not 'good' in the Christian sense, and are perhaps grounded, as Fay Weldon felt, in non-human and perilous things.

Nor do any of them show how the Avalonian leap could have been made from past literature and folklore to present imaginings. Santiago de Compostela has Christian legends not unlike Glastonbury's, about the coming of St James, yet no one has been impelled to trace out a Santiago Zodiac imprinted on Spain before his arrival. Critics may go on as long as they please about monastic fabrication and medieval romance. When they have done all they can, the reasons for the mystique in its latter-day forms simply slip through their fingers. Debates over who-forged-what-and-why in the Middle Ages have no relevance for the spell Glastonbury exerts over people whose chief interests are not in the medieval tales anyway.

CHAPTER EIGHT

A Remoter Background

I

E. A. Freeman, a nineteenth-century historian by no means given to Celtic romanticism, wrote a very wise thing.

> We need not believe that the Glastonbury legends are records of facts; but the existence of those legends is a very great fact.

That was true when he wrote, and it is true *a fortiori* today. There has to be something behind all the rampant growth. There have to be reasons. Much can be explained by the age and continuity of the community, the cultural fusion which it fostered, the undoubted inventive talents of its inmates. Much, but not everything, and certainly not the modern developments. When all the nonsense, both 'pro' and 'anti', has been discounted, the spell remains a reality. It is useless for opponents to say, 'Well, *I've* never felt anything.' I have never, myself, seen a vision or had a spiritual experience. But I can accept realities.

The spell could be interpreted in various ways. It might be the result of a long, cumulative process of mass suggestion, to be explained without mystery if we had the clue ... which we have not. It might be due to some obscure natural cause, such as a relation between the landscape and the human psyche. The sheer strangeness of Glastonbury was the first thing that ever struck me about it. When I wrote *King Arthur's Avalon* I began by enlarging on the eye-cheating perspectives, the sudden appearances and vanishings of the Tor, the inconsistency of the hills and the plain.

Avalonian Quest

Jolted out of routine by such bizarre practical jokes, the mind responds by contributing more to the moment than its usual share. Subconsciously prompted, it interprets the landscape into something truly alien to common experience. The irrational scene loosens the grip of the Ordinary and gives scope to the Fantastic. Just by a matter of an inch, it jars open the magic casements.

That leaves it a question where the Fantastic comes from. Let us at least respect the person who thinks the spell has its basis in an actual paranormal or supernatural order; in a presence of gods, spirits or angels. Let us accept, further, that it may be due not to any one cause but to a combination.

On a more down-to-earth level, Glastonbury has one very peculiar quality. With the various legends and theories, iconoclasm does succeed, most of the way. They do not survive critical scrutiny intact or anything like it. While some can be believed, if one wishes, belief must rest on faith without evidence. Yet in nearly every case, the would-be-rational alternative story has a breaking point. It confronts awkward, gritty facts which it cannot handle or exorcize.

Take – once again – the general idea of a first-century Christian advent. It has no documentary support. Yet the discovery of the Celtic lake-villages has shown that this was a place where first-century voyagers might have come; and the medieval monks knew nothing about the villages, and could not have based their assertions on them. If they merely guessed, they guessed credibly against long odds. Again, with the specific version that names Joseph of Arimathea, it is superficially easy to explain as a mere borrowing from Grail romance. Yet what are we to make of those hints at a Glastonbury story in the romances themselves, including the reference to 'Avaron' which defeated Loomis, and the reference to 'Scotland' which looks so wrong, yet as an authentic, not-understood tradition, is so right? And isn't it very odd that the Cadbury excavation should have supplied – totally unexpectedly – an indepen-

A Remoter Background

dent local chief about 63 to be Joseph's host; while Juvenal allows the possibility that his name was Arviragus?

Again, Arthur's grave is suspect in the last degree, and the notion of a fraud in 1191 seems logical. Yet Caradoc's tale of Melwas and the queen proves that Arthur was connected with Glastonbury before; archaeology proves that the monks dug down to early burials, and that their account of their finds is unlikely to have been invented; and textual comparison proves that the spelling 'Arturius' on the cross was used in the seventh century but cannot be paralleled after that.

It is much the same with the more recent aspects. The linking of the Thorn with Joseph is a post-medieval fable. Yet the Thorn is unique among English trees, and when we look round for trees which it resembles, we find them in (of all places) the Holy Land, or near it. Most of the Chalice Well mythos is groundless. Yet the water does have a reddish tinge suggesting blood, and while not absolutely unique in this immediate area, it is unlike other water in central Somerset generally and flows from a different, unknown source.

As for the Zodiac theory, the ley theory and the sacred-geometry theory, they are not sustained by any good evidence. Yet their dismissal as pure imagination stumbles over three facts, one for each. Even with the Zodiac, there is the phrase in Nostradamus. Only once in his 942 quatrains does he mention a 'great heavenly temple', and he mentions it in lines which make (for him) unusually good sense and locate it in England . . . also giving what looks like a prevision of the Duke of Monmouth. Even with the ley theory, one of the few leys which are truly impressive passes through Glastonbury. And even with the geometry, it will be recalled, William of Malmesbury hints at a holy secret (*arcanum sacrum*) enciphered in the triangles and squares of the Old Church's pavement. Whatever he means, few medieval churches are referred to in such terms by a contemporary.

Each of these items that defy the would-be-rational case might be accidental. But Glastonbury seems extraordinarily accident-prone. Why such a convergence, such a concentration? Why does the case get tripped up on every major issue, not so badly that it has to be dropped, but badly enough to drive its spokesmen into such uncharacteristic antics? It is all very well to minimize and explain away, but when this has to be done over and over again (and we have not reached the end by any means), it yields diminishing returns. Here we have an explanation for at least one form of the Glastonbury Madness, the unbalance of scholars. The normal and commendable wish to probe legends and expose their origins is so vexatiously thwarted. Repeatedly the fraud or delusion seems obvious, repeatedly it refuses to be pinned down. When Glastonbury is tamed at one point it bursts out at another.

If one were disposed to believe in a superhuman power at work, a presiding *genius loci*, it would surely have to be pictured as having an aspect somewhat as Fay Weldon imagined: an aspect neither humanly good nor evil, but unsettling and ironic, and rooted in a pagan world. This would be wholly in accord with other forms of the Glastonbury Madness. Whether a disturbing, pre-Christian presence can be taken seriously must remain a matter of choice. Setting that notion aside, I believe we must still move in the direction it points.

The deeper questions have not been answered. We do not know why all this has happened. We have no reason for the series of Glastonbury beginnings. We can partly trace the unfolding of a great history and mythology, yet neither accounts for the Avalonian phenomenon of recent years. But the recurrent feature of the latter opens up a new vista. The neo-mystics do not seek to extend the Christian mythology, or to write new chapters in the Christian history. Instead they profess to find older realities which precede and cause the rest. Their theories have that in common. Not unlike some of the Abbey's own fabulists, they are trying to give substance to an intuition. Most of the notions they have evolved to do this may be discounted. The intuition itself is worth examining. It may be sound; there may be subtle clues in the literature or the landscape which the theorists have absorbed at unconscious levels.

A Remoter Background

Are they right, on the main issue? Were the pioneer Christians taking over ground already sacred or magical, a prehistoric sanctuary? If so, what was the relationship between that sacredness, that magic, and the shape of the later history?

2

Ralegh Radford, who found the site of Arthur's grave, also hazarded some ideas about pre-Christian Glastonbury. He argued that the Tor with its neighbour hills once composed a Celtic *temenos*, holy ground. Chalice Well would have been a spring associated with a temple or shrine, and the limit of the *temenos* was the earthwork called Ponter's Ball, a bank which crosses the Shepton Mallet road two miles to the east. Ponter's Ball is not a military barrier. It would be too easy to outflank. But it might have marked the line where one kind of territory stopped and another started.

Any such argument depends largely on the changes in the water-level. It implies that there was a phase when the only approach by land was along the strip which Ponter's Ball cuts across. This would not have been the case in the more distant past. Five thousand years ago, all this area was dry. Excavations in the moors have revealed the remains of what are said to be the oldest roads in the world, some dating from 3200 BC. That is still another peculiar Glastonbury fact, which Mrs Maltwood could have invoked in support of her Sumerians. Plainly it says something about this region's importance even before the Celts, who did not enter Britain till much later. But the immediate point is that in the more distant past, with access by land on all sides, a bank two miles from Glastonbury and less than a mile long would have been nonsensical as a boundary.

Radford's theory might begin to apply in the last centuries BC, when water partly covered the moors, and the lake-villages were built on their artificial islets. Encroachment continued for another four or five centuries, till Glastonbury was almost encircled with water and marsh.

Avalonian Quest

In that period the only reliable approach would indeed have been from the Shepton Mallet direction as in *Perlesvaus*. The Celtic name 'Ynys-witrin', Island of Glass, and the equation with Avalon, both show awareness of that phase of near-insularity, whether or not they belong to it. Monastic land-reclamation and drainage did not efface memories of the older times, as Caradoc proves by saying that the swampy terrain hindered Arthur from bringing up his army. When he wrote, heavy rain and flooding could still go far towards restoring the Arthurian state of affairs.

The Celts held islands and hills in awe, as dwelling-places of spirits and otherworldly beings. This almost insular hill-cluster, surmounted by the strange cone of the Tor, could well have acquired a special numen. Its sanctity and uncanniness would have been enhanced if, as has been conjectured, it was used as a place of burial. No lake-village burial has ever been found, and the Prophecy of Melkin may embalm a folk-memory of a pagan cemetery, as it may embalm other folk-memories. Glastonbury could have been an abode of shades. But suggestions like these can never get beyond plausibility if no hard evidence is forthcoming. Moreover, excavation of Ponter's Ball has cast doubt on its being early enough.

Can anything be squeezed out of the names this place has had? The question is tangled, not to say nightmarish. 'Glastonbury' is Anglo-Saxon. The first and essential part is believed to go back to a Celtic *glasto* meaning 'woad'. This was a 'place where woad grew', and the British name for it would have been something like 'Glastonia'. Thence the Saxons derived the word 'Glaestingas' for the people who lived there, and dubbed it 'Glaestinga ieg', the Glaestingas' island. Later they changed the 'island' part to 'byrig', the familiar term for a defended place and later almost any town or inhabited spot; and in due course 'Glaestingabyrig' became 'Glastonbury'.

One or two medieval writers, supposing the first part to be a personal name, talk about a founder named Glast or Glasteing who came there in pursuit of an errant sow. Some modern etymologists approve of Glast if not the sow, but it seems more likely that he is either fictitious or wrongly

A Remoter Background

transferred from another legend. A more portentous misunderstanding was that the 'glas' syllable meant literally 'glass'. This mistake is said to account for 'Ynys-witrin'. We have a problem here, because the misunderstanding could not have arisen before 658 when the Saxons brought their language to central Somerset; whereas, it will be remembered, William of Malmesbury quotes a charter mentioning Ynys-witrin with the date 601. There is very possibly something wrong with the charter, yet, by a weird and truly Glastonian coincidence, a separate 'Ynys-witrin' could have been derived from another word meaning 'woad' – a Latin word, *vitrum* – and been separately misunderstood as 'glass'. H. P. R. Finberg, an eminent professor of local history, tried to get rid of the problem by inventing another Ynys-witrin in Cornwall for the charter to apply to: a further instance of the flights of imagination which Glastonbury inspires in otherwise sober scholars.

Whatever the etymological muddles, Glastonbury was regarded, certainly by the twelfth century and perhaps before, as a 'glass' island . . . and glass had otherworldly, magical connotations. These might never have entered the picture, if the name had been all that was involved, but something in the character of the place drew them in. Chrétien de Troyes, the romancer, adapts Caradoc's tale of Melwas and introduces a mysterious Ile de Voirre or Glass Island in the king's realm. The realm also contains the town of Bade or Bath. Chrétien's mythified Glass Island, in a mythified West Country, has features in common with the mythical Elysian Avalon. Though Chrétien himself seems to distinguish the two places, such hovering fancies in other quarters could have helped to clinch Glastonbury's Avalon identification.

3

Chrétien, of course, underlines the problem. He is a creative writer, and literary rehandling has obscured the origins. These things are circumstantial and atmospheric.

They amount to a case for a vague otherworldly aura. It supplied a soil for legends to grow in. It gave an added dimension to verbal accidents. It made the 'glass' theme and the 'Avalon' theme congenial. But while the aura may have been real, nothing in the effects can lead us back to the cause. There is no sure inference to any beliefs or practices which created the aura in the first place.

However, not every path is blocked. Two sets of clues are non-literary enough to be interesting. They point to two aspects of Glastonbury in Celtic or pre-Celtic paganism. Either could have inspired religious awe, either could have left an aura lingering, both together would have been potent indeed. One set of clues points to an Underworld aspect, the other to a Goddess aspect.

Among the relics of Welsh hagiography is a 'Life' of St Collen, the saint after whom Llangollen is named. He probably flourished in the sixth century, and, as already noted, he is said to have spent some time at Glastonbury. The 'Life' is written down in a manuscript of the time of Henry VIII. When I first drew attention to it as a key document, I was reproved for citing such a late item. But manuscripts can be copied from very much older manuscripts, and I have since been gratified to see scholars pushing this 'Life' backwards through the centuries, and citing it as evidence. My point was, and is, that no matter what its date, its account of the saint's adventure is a folklore item of immemorial age and owes nothing to medieval romance – or Abbey legends.

Collen, the author tells us, lived as a hermit on the lower slope of the Tor. One day he heard two men talking outside his cell. They said the hill was the home of Gwyn ap Nudd, king of the fairy-folk and lord of Annwn: Annwn being that Celtic Otherworld in the 'quest' poem ancestral to the Grail quest, sometimes pictured as subterranean. Collen told the men that Gwyn and his fairy-folk were demons. They replied that he would have to answer for that insult. Soon a messenger summoned Collen to climb the Tor and meet Gwyn at the top. After several refusals and repetitions, the saint took some holy water and made his way up. Passing through a magical entrance, he found himself in a splendid

A Remoter Background

palace, with King Gwyn seated on a golden chair. Gwyn offered food, but Collen knew the peril in that. Then Gwyn invited him to admire his retainers' red and blue liveries. Collen replied: 'Their dress is good of its kind. But the red is the red of fire, and the blue is the blue of cold.' He scattered his holy water around him. The palace and its occupants vanished, and he was outside, alone on the hill.

Gwyn, lord of Annwn, is an important figure in Welsh mythology. His father Nudd is the British god Nodens, who had a temple at Lydney in the Forest of Dean. He himself is a leader of the Wild Hunt, careering through the clouds with a pack of unearthly hounds, summoning souls of the dead. Other heroes are spoken of as Wild Huntsmen, including Arthur; this is one of the clear cases of Arthur attracting pagan motifs. Annwn itself may have been – among other things – a Celtic Hades, a dwelling-place of shades. That is uncertain. What is certain is that this tale bypasses all the medieval Glastonbury literature, which gives no hint of it and could never have suggested it. What is virtually certain is that it supplies a glimpse of truly ancient beliefs about the Tor being a hollow hill, a point of contact with a pre-Christian Underworld.

Several other facts point to some such idea surviving into Christian times. The site of the Old Church and its adjacent cells is one of the few places where the Tor would have been completely invisible, because Chalice Hill is in the way. Was that one reason for the choice – that a barrier stood between the hermits and the eerie abode of Gwyn? Today, from the same spot, you can look towards the Tor's summit and see the tower of St Michael's church just sticking up. But that too could be significant. Michael, the Archangel, was the conqueror of the infernal powers and therefore a proper person to hold them down. Perhaps the suppression was not entirely effective. A previous church of St Michael on the same high place collapsed in an earthquake. Considering how few buildings in England ever have, this must be reckoned as yet another Glastonian grotesquerie.

William Weston, the Jesuit, says in 1586 that the old man who used to scale the Tor on his knees claimed to hear 'the groanings, sighs and wailing voices of people in distress, so that he thought it must be a kind of approach or vestibule for souls passing into the pains of Purgatory.' Although he thus gave the phenomena a Christian gloss, he carried a cross as a 'protection against the molestation of spirits'. In his house, he kept a lamp always burning in a window that faced the hill.

To this day there is a stubborn local legend that the Tor has a chamber inside it. Usually the chamber is said to be below the summit, perhaps a considerable distance below. People are alleged to have found a way in and come out mad. In one version it has a well in it, sinking far down into the depths of the hill. Neo-Druids and kindred modern mystics have taken up the idea, with some loss of credit due to the unfortunate notion about the tunnel from the water-works property. In most of the Tor, geology would rule out a natural chamber, because it would cave in. There might be potentialities near the top. An artificial chamber, suitably walled and roofed, could have been constructed anywhere. We shall return to this. For the moment, the folk-belief in an interior space, with something rather alarming about it, is the essential datum.

Glastonbury's Underworld aspect has an air of authenticity. It persists through the centuries in different guises, and, indeed, has helped to breed a whole family of stories about underground tunnels – one connecting the cellar of the George and Pilgrims with the Abbey; one running from the crypt of the Lady Chapel all the way to Street, the neighbouring town across the Brue; at least two more in the Abbey precinct; another going from the Abbey to the top of the Tor; and two starting from the Abbey Barn. Some of these are probably exaggerations of old drains and cellar-ages. However, the one going to the Tor is supposed by some to connect up inside it with other tunnels, and dowsers who have explored the hill talk of a network of hidden waterways. It may be that none of this is more than psychological, but the potency of the Tor is marked.

A Remoter Background

4

The chief clue of the second sort lies in a detail of the Christian history which is often ignored, the dedication of the Old Church. It was dedicated to Mary, the mother of Christ. At least, that was so in 1184 when it burned down, and for some centuries before. If it was hers from its foundation, that is a fact of profound import.

Was it? We can forget the inserted story in *De Antiquitate*, claiming that Joseph and his companions built it themselves 'in honour of the holy Mother of God'. The cult of the Virgin was unknown among Christians till three centuries later. But two other legendary allusions are likely to have a touch of truth in them.

William of Malmesbury, in his genuine text, says St David came to Glastonbury. The Old Church was already there, and he proposed to dedicate it. However, Christ appeared to him in a dream and asked about his intentions. When he explained, the Lord replied that he had already dedicated the church himself in his mother's honour, and the ceremony should not be profaned by the human repetition which David intended. As proof that the vision was genuine, Christ touched the palm of his hand inflicting a small wound, and foretold that when David said Mass in the morning, the wound would heal as he spoke the words 'through him and with him and in him'. David woke. The wound was real and it disappeared as promised.

St David may have visited Glastonbury, but the rest of the story is fictitious. Its interest lies in its implications. It looks like an attempt to show, in defiance of record and credibility, that the church's dedication did go back to its fabulous origin. It had always been Mary's in heaven, so to speak. The idea of the divine dedication is already present in the story of the church being 'not built by art of man' which was current at the end of the tenth century. It may or may not have been connected with a legend of St David then, but when it is, it becomes self-stultifying – at least in terms of tangible fact. David's plan implies that the church had *not* hitherto been Mary's on the earthly level.

Hovering somewhere is a tradition taking the dedication back to the sixth century when David lived, and then tailing off. This had to be squared with a desire to believe that it was not merely earlier but very much earlier, and the story of the prior dedication by Christ was made to bridge the preceding centuries.

The other allusion is incidental. It comes in Caradoc of Llancarfan's 'Life' of Gildas, where he tells his tale of Melwas' abduction of Arthur's wife. The treaty that restores peace is negotiated by Gildas and the abbot. Arthur and Melwas end their quarrel in the Old Church, and Caradoc calls it 'the temple of holy Mary'. Here, of course, we confront an Arthur who has long since become legendary, with a life prolonged beyond its true span. The only firm clue to the supposed date comes from Gildas, who belongs to the sixth century. This second legend is not too far from agreeing with the first. St David, in reality, flourished somewhat later than Gildas. But the story of his visit to Glastonbury is related to a mistaken biographical shift which made them roughly contemporary.

Gildas himself may give us more, and this is not legend. In his book on the self-inflicted woes of Britain he denounces the sins of a king named Constantine who ruled in Dumnonia, which then included central Somerset. Constantine, it seems, murdered two young princes after swearing not to harm them. He killed them in a church, disguised as an abbot, in their mother's presence. According to Gildas the crime took place in the year in which he wrote his book, that is, somewhere about the 540s.

This is the passage glanced at once or twice before. Gildas is as irritatingly unclear as he is in most of his book, but *prima facie* he is likely to be referring to Glastonbury. The scene is apparently a monastic church, and in the 540s there were very few monasteries in Constantine's kingdom. If Gildas does not mean Glastonbury it is hard to see what he does mean. But his sentence takes the matter further. He says Constantine's victims were off their guard because they trusted in his oath and in the protection of 'the choirs of saints and the Mother'. The Latin draws a distinction. For the mother of the princes, Gildas uses the familiar

A Remoter Background

word *mater*. The Mother in whom the princes trusted is the *genetrix*. This is the word used for the Blessed Virgin by the Welsh monk Nennius, when he speaks of an image which Arthur is said to have carried into battle. It is also the word used by St Dunstan's early biographer, when he speaks of the Old Church's miraculous foundation and dedication.*

Gildas, then, is accusing Constantine of committing murder in a monastic church where the Virgin was venerated and, presumably, enshrined. It is only at Glastonbury that we have any evidence for such a church in Dumnonia so early. Either Gildas is giving contemporary testimony to the Old Church's existence with its dedication in the 540s, or he is saying something impenetrably cryptic. The former reading makes enough sense to carry weight.

On these three counts the Marian status of the Old Church seems to have been a fact as early as the first half of the sixth century. If it was not, and the church was rededicated much later, we would have to ask when. It ought to show in the records, and it does not. Now this conclusion is more remarkable than it looks. The dedication is a total anomaly, with no parallel this side of the Alps. Nothing in what is known of Celtic Christianity would account for it. Nearly all Mary dedications in Britain belong to the vast medieval wave of devotion which produced the cathedrals of Chartres, Reims, Amiens and many other cities, the 'palaces of the Queen of Heaven'. That was the second wave. The first rose in the fifth century, receiving its main impulse from the Council of Ephesus in 431,

---

* Some have argued that Gildas here means 'Mother Church'. For this figurative mother, however, the natural word (which Gildas himself employs) was *mater*, meaning the woman who loves, nurtures, cares for her children. To use *genetrix*, meaning the woman who gives birth, would have been eccentric. In Christian Latin up to AD 600, *mater* was in fact normal for Mother Church; *genetrix*, when used in a special religious sense, stood for the Mother of God from the early fifth century onward. A modern translator, who has tried to construe Gildas's *genetrix* without bringing in Mary, complains that the passage is 'difficult to follow' and guesses at a textual error for which there is no evidence at all. When Mary is admitted, the difficulty dissolves. The words are as straightforward as Gildas' words ever are.

which authorized the title 'Mother of God'. It was an eastern phenomenon which spread westward to Italy but had little impact beyond. Glastonbury, it seems, is the only British Marian site which belongs to that first wave.

A simple explanation offers itself and is probably wrong. It was the members of religious communities, male and female, who led the way in promoting Marian devotion. Glastonbury was a religious community. Therefore its members followed the Mediterranean lead. The trouble is that other Celtic communities did not. As the sixth century advanced, dozens of them sprang up in Britain, and Ireland also. None took the same path.

Glastonbury supplied some concrete and special motive for doing what Britons did not do anywhere else. If the reason lay in a reputed apparition or miracle, it would scarcely have been forgotten. A credible answer may begin to take shape if we compare the first Marian wave with the second. The second, medieval wave rose in a long-established Christendom. The first, the wave which reached Glastonbury, rose in a Roman Empire where paganism still lingered and many temples of the old gods, though little frequented, were still standing. Holy places of the old order sometimes became holy places of the new, not from Christian sympathy with the old, but because an ancient and habitual popular cultus demanded an adequate replacement. In this phase there were several instances of Mary's enthronement as successor to a goddess, whose more benign attributes she might assume.

At Ephesus the famous temple of Artemis, 'Diana of the Ephesians', survived into the fifth century. But the citizens were transferring their allegiance from Virgin Huntress to Virgin Mother, and the Council which was held in their city set the seal on the change. Another virgin, Zeus' daughter Athene, handed over to her supplanter in her own town of Athens, and in Syracuse and other venerable places. Nor was virginity in a goddess essential. Shrines of Aphrodite in Cyprus turned into shrines of Mary, hailed here as *Panaghia Aphroditessa*. In Rome, one Marian church adjoined the former temple of Isis; another, Santa Maria in Aracoeli, took the place of the temple of the

A Remoter Background

Phoenician Tanit; and the splendid Santa Maria Maggiore, on the Esquiline hill, succeeded to the temple of the Great Mother Cybele. In the context of what had been happening in the Empire, the Glastonbury dedication might lead us to wonder about a previous cult of female divinity – the transition being all the easier in the Celtic setting, where substitution was less sharp, and Brigit the saint (for instance) could still, in her fashion, be Brigit the goddess.

Once that idea is stated, several facts can be seen to fit in with it. Curiously, even the landscape does. One of Powys's characters in *A Glastonbury Romance* says 'Glastonbury is a woman.' I am not sure what Powys meant, but some years ago I realized what he may have meant. Looked at from a vantage-point near Butleigh, the hill-profile vaguely evokes a recumbent female figure. A well-defined head is lacking, but the Tor forms a prominent left breast, Chalice Hill a pregnant belly, Wearyall Hill an outstretched leg. The figure is silhouetted and incomplete. It is no use searching on the far side for a right breast or leg. Nevertheless, if you circle clockwise round Wearyall Hill, and turn towards the town keeping the image in mind, all the growth of housing and industry cannot quite disguise what you see: that the Old Church's site among the Abbey ruins lies in the sexual area of the figure.

If this titaness were to stand up, she would be about two miles high. She is not a product of myth-conditioned imagination; not entirely, anyhow. A few miles away is the Navy's air base at Yeovilton, where helicopter pilots are trained, and pilots flying over this way have been known to call the tower on the Tor 'the nipple'. One of Fay Weldon's characters says likewise. In view of certain theories about Silbury, where a pregnant goddess has also been alleged, let me disavow any notion that the hill-profile is artificial. It is not. But such a shape occurring in nature could have suggested a goddess showing herself by moulding the landscape; it could have made this a proper place for a shrine of female divinity; and the siting of the church is, at least, uncannily apt.

Chalice Well, which was proposed by Radford as the sacred spring of a pagan sanctuary, is also apt. This is the second good guess of its devotees, though their specific ideas about its pre-Christian sacredness are wide of any probable mark. Among the Celts, springs and streams often had tutelary spirits who were female beings with healing powers. With the Well, the water's reddish tinge has been cited as an extra pointer to such an indweller, because of menstrual mythology. The Well is misplaced anatomically for that. Perhaps such exactitude was not vital to early myth-making. It is an odd irony that when the monks channelled the water for their own use, they piped it down to the place that is anatomically correct. However, it would be rash to detect occult influences in the practicality of a Benedictine house.

The legends of Avalon and the Grail have distinct feminine motifs, hinting at antecedents in the pre-Christian background. We cannot be sure how early these motifs were connected with Glastonbury, or, in some cases, whether they ever were. Still, even a late linkage might be taken as implying affinity. Something favoured it in the character of the place. They are worth a mention. One of them is worth more than a mention, because it shows how a feminine cult, preserved in myth after its replacement in religion, might have contributed to the Avalon theme itself.

Geoffrey of Monmouth's Isle of Avalon, *Insula Avallonis*, is his re-spelt version of the Welsh Ynys Avallach. In his *History* it has no location. He says that Arthur's sword was forged there, and that Arthur was taken there after his last battle. In a poem which he wrote later, *The Life of Merlin*, he introduces the bard Taliesin telling more. Taliesin says that the 'Isle of Apples' is known as Fortunate because of its natural plenty and idyllic climate. Its inhabitants live for a hundred years. It is ruled by nine sisters. Their chief is Morgen, a healer and enchantress who can fly through the air and change her shape. Taliesin tells how he accompanied Arthur on his last voyage, and Morgen welcomed the wounded king, had him laid out on a golden couch, and promised to cure him if he stayed on her island.

In the person of 'Morgen' Avalon has a presiding spirit. Geoffrey did not invent her. His poem shows many traces of further research which he did after the *History*. Morgen is the lady who passes into Arthurian romance as Morgan le Fay. Confusingly, her father is named Avallach, a fact which puts a query over the 'apple' derivation. However that may be, Gerald de Barri – Giraldus Cambrensis – gives a summary of the tale in one of his accounts of the exhumation of Arthur, written about 1193.

> The place which is now called Glaston was in ancient times called the Isle of Avalon.... Morgan, a noble matron and the ruler and lady of those parts, who was, moreover, kin by blood to King Arthur, carried him away after the battle of Camlann to the island that is now called Glaston, that she might heal his wounds.

Here Geoffrey's mythology is swept away and she is firmly located at a Glastonbury which is also Avalon.

Her character afterwards undergoes an unhappy change. Celtic Christians could allow virtue to a figure out of their pagan past, and felt no qualms in accepting her magic as benign. Medieval Christians were less easy-going. Non-Christian magic like Morgan's had to be suspect. Romancers explained her closeness to Arthur by making her his half-sister, but she became less and less a healing enchantress, more and more a malignant witch.

Gerald is uneasily aware of her origins. He cannot deny the Morgan who is lady of Avalon, but he accounts for her by reducing her to a human being, and scoffs at Breton fantasies in which she was an 'imaginary goddess'. A goddess she undoubtedly was, once, and she is so referred to by three other medieval authors.

In Geoffrey's poem her island community of nine women, and her magical powers, recall communities that really existed in the Celtic world. The Roman geographer Pomponius Mela, in the first century AD, speaks of a group of nine virgin priestesses on the Ile de Sein, off the coast of what is now Brittany. They cured the sick, and could reputedly take on animal shape, foretell the future, and control the weather. Morgan herself can be traced to her divine origins by way of Welsh matter in which she is called

Modron instead. She is Matrona, a Celtic goddess, who gave her name to the River Marne. 'Modron' is simply 'the Mother'. The variant 'Morgan' is due to her fusion in Welsh mythology with an Irish deity, the Morrigan, who became an aspect of herself. At Glastonbury, the dedication of the Old Church, and the domestication of the goddess as Morgan, could both point backwards in very different ways to a cult of this Celtic Mother. It might even have had something to do with Glastonbury's acceptance as her island, her Avalon.

Kindred feminine motifs come to the surface in the Grail stories. There is, of course, a female symbolism in any wonder-working vessel. The Celtic ones underlying the Grail include a cauldron that belonged to the goddess Ceridwen, and the cauldron in the *Spoils of Annwn* poem. The latter is watched over by nine maidens who are evidently akin to the sisterhoods of Avalon and the Breton island. The Grail itself is tended and carried by women, in brazen defiance of the ecclesiastical norms of the Middle Ages. Again, one or two of the romances have a strong Marian element in their imagery, symbolism and inspiration. Galahad achieves the ultimate vision at a ceremony called 'the Mass of the Glorious Mother of God'. While the nature of the vision is only hinted at, it seems to be like the mystical experience which closes the *Divine Comedy*, and that is granted through Mary's intercession.

How far any of these things may be related to Glastonbury is a hard question. They could reflect some sort of Glastonian lore drawn into the romances through the Grail's connection with the place, as attested by Robert de Boron and the author of *Perlesvaus*. Just such an ancestry has even been claimed for the tale of the abduction of Arthur's queen. Guinevere goes on being abducted, with variations, throughout the age of medieval romance-making; but the Caradoc version where Melwas takes her to Glastonbury is the prototype. Some have expounded her in this setting as a Celtic Persephone, carried off by the lord of a Celtic Hades. If so, she would be in the same class as other royal figures of Welsh legend who undoubtedly are ancient deities reduced to more or less human stature.

A Remoter Background

Caradoc mentions the 'glass' explanation of the place-name, thereby giving an otherworldly touch.

In the upshot we have a second possible aspect of pre-Christian Glastonbury, more elusive and more intriguing: a Goddess aspect. Goddess and Underworld together, preserved in legends with support from the hill-on-island topography, would account for much. But when this is said, it is not apparent that we can say any more. There is no direct evidence for either in the sense of inscriptions, temple ruins, or anything similarly solid. If we push the clues to the limit, we still never get a coherent picture, or glimpse the outline of a known, unifying myth. The aspects fail to coalesce.

True, the cauldron kept by nine maidens is housed in Annwn, and St Collen goes into Annwn by way of the Tor. But there is no meaningful overlap. He does not see the cauldron or meet the maidens. Annwn in itself is too hazy a conception, and it was certainly never localized in the Tor exclusively. The theory that Caradoc's Guinevere is a sort of Persephone, imprisoned in Annwn as a sort of Hades, might bring Goddess and Underworld together if it could be accepted. I am dubious. On the face of it, we cannot get beyond these two aspects, we cannot arrive at any logic which makes them better than conjectural. They simply float about.

Perhaps they were real, but were never linked. Perhaps Glastonbury had two pre-Christian phases – corresponding, let us say, to the La Tène Celts and their supplanters the Belgic Celts – with two different kinds of numinosity, Goddess-centred in one phase, Underworld-centred in the other. If that were so it would be futile to look for a unifying factor, and absurd to carry guesswork further, with so many unknowns. Now, however, we come to a physical fact which puts the whole issue in a fresh light; though the quest which it inaugurates is no easy one.

PART TWO

Answers?

CHAPTER NINE

The Terraced Track

I

Visitors often ask whether the Tor is artificial. This in fact is the most frequent visitors' question of all, and it is easy to see why. The impression of the Tor's artificiality is due partly to its rising so oddly above the surrounding flatland, but more to the terraces running along its sides, one above another. Its well-known resemblance to a stepped Mexican pyramid does not impress itself on the eye because it is pyramidal – though, viewed end-on, it can appear so – but because it is stepped. The terraces are clearest on what may be called by approximation the north face. About noon, in fine weather, the sun picks them out in light and shadow. They can also be distinguished from the rest of the hillside by differences in the colour of grass.

The only firm evidence as to their age is a picture in William Dugdale's *Monasticon*, which shows them as already existing in 1654. Though worn and weathered, the terraces are still traceable over long stretches, all the way round and most of the way up. To the visitors' recurrent question, the answer is that the Tor is a natural hill, but one that shows signs of having been artificially shaped. The hill exists because of its erosion-resistant top. For the terraces there is no such easy explanation, geological or otherwise. But proper study of them has long been prevented by a dogged delusion that there is.

In *King Arthur's Avalon* I mentioned a theory which invoked the ever-popular Druids, and a belief that they held the hill in awe as an abode of the dead.

It has been suggested that the terraces . . . are the remains of a spiral pathway by which they scaled it in procession, blessing or cursing the shades which had passed below.

I am not sure who first made that suggestion. However, Dion Fortune put something like it in *Avalon of the Heart*.

> Those who have seen the famous Glastonbury Tor, about which so many legends gather, are always perplexed as to whether it is natural or artificial. Its pyramidal form, set in the centre of a great plain, is almost too good to be true – too appropriate to be the unaided work of Nature. Viewed from near at hand, a terraced track can clearly be seen winding in three tiers round the cone of the Tor, and this is indisputably the work of man. Who were they who worshipped in high places and climbed to them by a processional route?

It is strange that Dion Fortune saw only three 'tiers', since, on the north side, there are obviously more than three. She may have been doubtful about the upper ones because of a broad area on the southern side where they vanish. This blank zone is certainly adverse to the idea of a simple spiral, winding all the way from the base to the summit. But in 1966 a new possibility began opening up. Geoffrey Russell, a visitor from County Cork, hit on the idea that the terraces were the remains of a prehistoric maze: not in the modern sense of a puzzle, but in the older sense of a long, twisting, devious approach to a centre, sometimes called a 'meander'. A design in Chartres Cathedral is a frequently cited instance. A maze like this is 'unicursal' in contrast with the branching-out puzzle type as at Hampton Court, which is 'multicursal'.

Russell developed and published his idea. On this showing, the Tor track is vastly more complex than Dion Fortune thought. It goes round not merely three times but seven. Its course is not a simple spiral, but an adaptation, stretched out to fit the hill, of a backtracking spiral which appears in antiquity in widely separated places. The backtracking explains why it is absent from a part of the hill which a simple spiral could hardly avoid traversing.

The Terraced Track

One of the strong features of Russell's case is that the pattern – unlike the Glastonbury Zodiac – does indisputably occur elsewhere. His septenary maze shows very plainly on Cretan coins which recall the legend of the Labyrinth housing the Minotaur. Hence it may be called for convenience the 'Cretan' spiral. That does not imply any assumption of Cretan influence, and indeed it is so widespread as to make Cretan influence unlikely. The pattern or its mirror-image is found also in Greece, Italy, Wales, Cornwall, Yorkshire, Ireland, and (as will emerge) in another locale which is much more surprising. It is older than any other comparable design, and there seems to be no parallel for its far-flung recurrence.

In its usual diagrammatic form the track of the maze cannot execute seven full circuits, but it has seven clear back-and-forth circlings. If a mark is made on the peri-

iii. 'Cretan' maze pattern

Avalonian Quest

meter across from the entrance, the point of a pencil tracing the maze will pass it seven times.

To justify studying this maze-family in detail, the case for the Tor maze must be examined first. If that, in the end, cannot be sustained, the others are beside the point. If it can, they are apposite. But it is interesting at the outset that they exist, with magical or symbolic importance. The huge specimen on the Tor, if real, would doubtless have been threaded on foot as a ritual.

Unlike the fringe theories, this one has attracted some academic support. Only a little. Most archaeologists have ignored it. But Philip Rahtz, who carried out the Tor excavations in 1964–6, wrote: 'The argument is complex, but it is worth consideration.' And elsewhere: 'If the maze theory were demonstrated to be true, it would clearly be of the greatest relevance to the origins of Glastonbury as a religious centre.' Rahtz's view was that the maze, if real, might have been made in the second or third millennium BC, the era of the great ritual works such as Stonehenge, Avebury and Silbury, with which a labyrinthine Tor would have to be ranked. He allowed, however, that it could have continued in ritual use long after, perhaps by British Celts of the pre-Roman Iron Age.

Use by the Celts must be assumed if Russell's interpretation is to stand up. He linked the maze with the quest of the Grail. He pointed out that the Welsh poem *The Spoils of Annwn*, which introduces a cauldron ancestral to the Grail, also mentions a place known as Caer Sidi. This he construed to mean the 'turning' or spiral castle. Caer Sidi in the poem is a point of contact with Annwn and, conceivably, the place where its cauldron is watched over by the nine maidens. There is a difficulty here, because the same poem mentions a Caer Wydr or Glass Castle, and Glastonbury, Ynys-witrin, ought to be Caer Wydr rather than Caer Sidi. At any rate, Russell maintained that the story of the quest, with its long wandering pursuit of a mysterious goal, went back to ceremonial maze-threading by pre-Christian Celts. They walked round and round and round, from the base of the Tor – Caer Sidi – to a centre (presumably) at the top. The end of the journey would have been a ritual involving, maybe, a symbolic vessel. The Annwn connection would fit in with the belief attested in the Collen legend, that the Tor contained an entrance to it.

Russell laid too much stress on such speculations, and, for that reason, met with less acceptance than he deserved. He involved the maze not only in mythological guesswork, but in Jung's theories about mandalas. Whatever the value of all this, it did not belong in an argument he should have addressed, primarily, to archaeologists. He was not helped by some of those whom he did persuade, such as Oliver L. Reiser, a retired professor of philosophy, whose sketch of the theory in his book *This Holyest Erthe* includes the following:

> One wonders: is it possible that the labyrinth will turn out to be the morphogenetic field pattern for the embryogenesis of the *World Sensorium*?

Further, though Russell had the hill surveyed, it seems that he never attempted to prove his maze by the most elementary method of all. He never threaded it. If the discoverer himself could not or would not do this, the scepticism of others may be pardoned.

2

My own belief, for some years, was that Russell's case was credible but nothing more could be done about it. I never scrutinized the Tor with the maze in mind, nor did I try to follow its course. I assumed that it could be 'reconstructed', convincingly or otherwise, by anyone who cared to do so . . . and that was all.

A fresh impulse came in June 1979. At that time I was helping to prepare the Glastonbury midsummer conference sponsored by the Wrekin Trust. Its membership would be coming from all over Britain. I produced a programme mentioning the hypothetical maze, and offering to form a guided party to thread it, if enough people showed interest. Three days before the conference, it struck me that I had only a nebulous notion of how the track was supposed to run. I knew the pattern, but I did not know how Russell applied it to the Tor. He had never made that clear enough, or if he had, I had missed it.

I therefore spent a long hot afternoon trudging round the hill, trying to decide which terraces corresponded to which maze-circuits, and how they joined up and doubled back. I managed to work it out after a fashion, and wrote some instructions. Partly because the weather changed, I was fortunately not called upon to shepherd a party through. A few enthusiasts asked for copies of the instruction sheet. None of them ever reported back to me. Perhaps none of them ever made the attempt. I now think this first interpretation was incorrect for part of the way. But the result was good enough to be encouraging. I wanted to settle the question, so far as it could be settled, and to do it by the down-to-earth method which Russell rejected – simply trying to thread the maze. Later that summer I revisited the terraces many times to see if the route could be made precise. At last I concluded that it could, with only minor and explicable breaks. My views appeared in a booklet *The Glastonbury Tor Maze*, which was brought out by a local publishing venture associated with a bookshop.

The main opposition, it must be repeated, does not come from any counter-argument but from the dogma that the whole system has an obvious commonsense explanation. From this it is thought to follow that the maze need not be discussed at all, being merely a superfluous fantasy. I have been sternly told that 'Somerset archaeologists agree that the terraces are such-and-such', though it was plain from what the archaeologists said that they had never even properly looked, and had merely adopted a hearsay 'obvious explanation'. I am cautious of such dicta, being not unmindful of another controversial site, where all theorists were crushed by archaeologists with an 'obvious explanation', and then re-crushed a few years later with another 'obvious explanation' which was quite different from the first. The case of the Tor is similar, only more so, and the answer is simple. No such explanation exists. Or

The Terraced Track

rather several purportedly do, and since they contradict each other, none of them can fairly be called obvious. The net effect of stating them all together is to prove that the system is a genuine problem. Nor is their mutual cancellation the only trouble. Each runs into difficulties of its own, and all run into difficulties when we come to what is disclosed by actual maze-threading.

The one favoured by the National Trust, which owns the Tor, is that the terraces are early agricultural workings – strip-lynchets, shelves for vineyards. Even potato-growing has been proposed. The object of working a hillside on such a vast scale, and with such an expenditure of labour, would have been to make maximum use of high ground when the country below was water-logged. That motive would rule out potatoes as the whole explanation, since they were not introduced into England till after the draining of the marshes.

It must be acknowledged that parts of the system have been put to agricultural use. A tithe map dated 1844 marks an area near the eastern end as 'Tor Linches'. Such use may also account for some apparent confusion in a small portion of the north face. But there is no evidence for agricultural use of the whole system or anything like it. Much less is there evidence that the system was created by or for agricultural work. It is most improbable. Plenty of hills have strip-lynchets on them, including one near the Tor, but it would be hard to find a comparable hill which has them all the way round and virtually all the way up. A vertical aerial photograph (Plate 6) shows the difference. The notion that cultivators wanted to use every scrap of ground is refuted by the absence of any such system on Chalice Hill next door, which is a far more natural and credible place for these activities.

Another explanation is that the terraces are paths worn in the hillside by grazing animals. In the newsletter of the Glastonbury Conservation Society (January 1981), Mr R. D. Reid quoted this as the opinion of nineteenth-century farmers. In the following issue (April 1981), Mr Derek J. Lawrence called it 'an insult to commonsense'. He was right. Sheep and cattle do use the terraces, as places to walk and rest, but they did not make them. Paths really worn by animals can be seen on parts of the Tor itself and on Chalice Hill opposite. They are far narrower, closer together, and more numerous. Animals could trample a hillside for centuries without making terraces like those on the Tor. Animals *have* trampled countless other hillsides for centuries without doing so.

A further suggestion is that the terraces were made by humans to provide a footing for themselves and their beasts, with some purely mundane purpose in mind, such as getting horse-drawn carts up the hill. This seems to be refuted by the course they follow. They weave up and down most impractically, and the transitions from level to level are too steep for the imagined ascent.

Finally, two theories assert that the terraces are natural after all. Geologists have argued for freak erosion of strata of differing hardness. A seismologist has invoked the thirteenth-century earthquake which destroyed the previous church on the summit. Both ideas are open to verification and, so far as I know, it is completely lacking.

Besides the mutual contradiction, which explodes the notion of a plain answer making further enquiry otiose, all these theories have a further weakness. Whatever cause may be offered, it is no good pretending that its action on the Tor has been normal or commonplace. It has produced a very strange, very unfamiliar effect. Isolated hills terraced to this extent, apparent pyramids with an air of design, are not often found; at any rate in Britain. What are the chances that this rare, perhaps unparalleled instance should have occurred, simply by accident, at Glastonbury of all places?

3*

The maze theory requires that there should once have been seven paths going round the Tor, all running along continuous terraces, with connections between them running

---

* Most of this section is adapted from my booklet. Any reader who finds it opaque without first-hand knowledge of the Tor is welcome to skim or skip.

The Terraced Track

generally up and down. Weathering, trampling, and shiftings of soil and strata have made parts of the scheme a matter of conjecture. Yet certainly terraces can be distinguished at seven different levels, and while they are not now continuous, they are more nearly so than a casual glance might suggest. Effects of light and shadow, variations at ground level, make it difficult to take in the whole system at any one time or from any one angle. Sometimes a path is hard to discern for a person trying to walk along it, yet is easily followed with the eye from a distance. Sometimes a terrace is almost invisible from a distance, yet clearly defined when looked at from above or below. Scrutiny in a combination of ways shows how much of the system is, arguably, there. Aerial photography confirms that impression.

Even where a presumed terrace has vanished, a vestigial path usually survives. The whole plan can be reconstructed in such a manner that a maze-threader is hardly ever improvising a route through featureless grass. There is nearly always a visible way of some sort. The few total gaps are at the lowest level, where farming activity can be seen to have altered the surface, and at the highest, where the effects of steepness may be presumed to have done likewise over the centuries.

For discussion in detail, some terms need to be agreed on. The seven paths – sometimes with well-defined strips of terrace to run along, sometimes not – may be numbered as Paths I, II, III, IV, V, VI and VII, starting from the lowest and outermost which goes round the base, and ending with the one nearest the summit. The same Roman numerals may apply to the terraces on which they run, where identifiable. The paths are at right angles to the two principal routes up the Tor; or to be more precise, they would be if the Tor were circular, as the maze is in Cretan and other contexts, but its elongation causes distortion.

The ascent routes need to be defined also. One of them is reached from Well House Lane near the Chilkwell Street end. After a steep stretch of surfaced footpath between hedges, a climber enters the Tor field and passes up through it, to a metal gate or stile in the Tor's boundary

Avalonian Quest

fence; then, just above, starts the ascent of the Tor proper close to a bench. This may be called Ascent Route A. The climb is long, but much of it is gradual, along a ridge. In 1980 a flight of steps was made flanking the steepest part. The other upward route is at the far end of the Tor. Again the climber goes through a field and boundary gate, and then begins the ascent, which is shorter and steeper. This may be called Ascent Route B. Steps have been made in this area also. Neither A nor B is a single, clear-cut, narrow way. Both are fairly broad corridors within which the line of ascent can vary.

A walker who goes up Ascent Route A, and turns left to circle the Tor clockwise, passes along the north face to Ascent Route B. At Ascent Route B the walker can swing round to the right and continue along the south face, returning to Ascent Route A. The boundary fence around the base of the Tor delimits the territory within which walking must be confined. Along most of its length, it separates the National Trust land from fields and other properties to which the public has no access.

Suppose we study what happens during that sweep along the north face from Ascent Route A. As we trace the paths, following their terraces wherever these can be made out, they undulate a good deal. But the trend is upward, with a net increase in altitude as they approach the far end and Ascent Route B. If we now retrace our steps to Ascent Route A, and go counter-clockwise along the south face instead, a difference is apparent. The terraces are more nearly horizontal. They come round to Ascent Route B lower down.

And there, at the far end, is a significant feature. The terraces which have come round from the north face make a downturn towards the numerically matching ones from the south face. From a vantage-point on the higher part of Ascent Route B, it is possible to look down and see four of them doing it: the terrace carrying Path III round the north side descending – apparently – to meet III on the south; IV descending to meet IV; V to meet V; VI to meet VI. So likewise in photographs taken from a distance, such as the one by David Gentleman which is used as a National Trust

The Terraced Track

poster. Inspection on the spot suggests that the other terraces, when intact, would have done the same. All the Ascent Route B area has been obscured by tree growth, human activity and soil movement. Nevertheless the downturn is manifest, and suggests a planned linkage completing the circuits.

Today, Terrace V coming round from the south goes a shade too far. Its descending equivalent from the north face would not meet it squarely, but intersect it obliquely some yards along. In fact, V extends far enough to cut across IV in its downward curve. This is the one area where the maze interpretation looks awkward. However, it is also the one area where we can be sure, from the 1844 tithe map, that stretches of terrace were put to agricultural use. Moreover V at this point differs from every other stretch of terrace in having a row of trees planted along it. The single flaw in the system, therefore, can be neatly and fairly accounted for as an extension due to later work.

Study of the ground, and comparison of photographs of the two faces of the Tor, put these connections beyond serious doubt. Because of them, the system can be viewed as a continuous whole, as the maze theory requires. It encircles the Tor with a kink at Ascent Route B. When it is viewed thus, the kink makes sense as a downward adjustment, after the net rise along the north face.

The kink, of course, is a further objection to the 'obvious' explanations. Despite all havoc around Ascent Route B, the downturn of the terraces coming round from the north face can still be made out. Why should erosion or earthquake have produced it? Why should farmers or vine-cultivators have bothered to make it, especially as, to connect V, VI and (perhaps) VII on the north with V, VI and VII on the south, the slope has to be steep and adverse to agriculture? Archaeologists, by the way, do not appear to have even noticed the kink. When I mentioned it to one, who had good reasons for knowing, he said innocently: 'But don't the terraces just go straight on round?' 'No,' I replied, and drew his attention to a photograph which I am morally certain he had seen before.

The air of design becomes more striking when we look

across at the north face from the upper part of Well House Lane, and ask why the gradual rise, necessitating a drop at the end, should have occurred. The contours supply the answer. If maze-cutters had started from Ascent Route A and worked along the north face, they could only have minimized the trend upwards by swerving out into territory which now lies in fields below the Tor. There the slope is much gentler. They would have had to cut immensely wide terraces for the lower paths, or at least make the paths wander outwards and far apart. Hence, they would have been impelled to stay within the steeper area (that is, today, inside the Tor's boundary fence) and allow the contours to carry them upwards. Which is what we do find.

It looks as if maze-cutters on the south face may have confronted the same problem – as if, indeed, it may have been their experience which determined what was done on the north. As we go counter-clockwise from Ascent Route A, Terrace I, carrying the lowest path, actually does have to spread out to a disproportionate width, while II also spreads as it proceeds. A correction then seems to be made at a place due south of the tower, where there is now a small wood. Terrace I turns inwards so abruptly that it looks as if it were running on from II. Terrace II, though broken up today by the wood and by human activity in the area, can soon be found reappearing at a higher level, and seemingly nudging III a little upwards as well. This creates another, comparatively minor kink in the system, affecting the lower south-face terraces only. It still does not bring them far enough up to meet the corresponding north-face ones at the end, so the major kink at Ascent Route B remains necessary for them as for the others.

A modern result of the system's being lower on the south face than on the north is regrettable. Over a fair distance between the wood south of the tower and Ascent Route B, despite the upward correction at the former place, Terrace I remains so far down that it runs through fields outside the boundary fence, and has been partly effaced by farming. Terrace II above it, after its brief phase of confusion in the wood, runs close to the fence partly inside and partly outside. Along this stretch a present-day maze-threader, de-

The Terraced Track

barred from the fields, can only approximate by keeping close to the fence on the inside. However, the detour is slight.

Since terraces run on just seven levels on both faces, yet at such differing elevations, theories about strip-lynchets and geological accidents are all the more implausible. If the paths are reconstructed in keeping with the maze theory, all the existing terraces are used, none are left out. The only qualification is that the south-west part of the Tor has ledges which might be called ghost-terraces. There is one on the right of the bench where Ascent Route A begins its main climb. This very soon blends into I and presents no problem. More troublesome are two running alongside III and just above it, which go a long way before they blend into it, so that III, for a time, is triple. The terrace and its ghosts are much closer together than the true terraces in this part of the Tor, but they confuse. They could represent three attempts at the same path. At any rate, the ghosts vanish. It is impossible to find more than seven levels on the south face as a whole, as it also is on the north.

We might wonder why a ritual or magical scheme, if it existed, should have had to be as complex as Russell argued. The seeming importance of the Cretan pattern, to be considered presently, is not a sufficient reason to jump to conclusions about its likelihood here. Constant use of Ascent Route A has obscured whatever vertical links may have carried maze-threaders from one level to the next. So, might not the paths have formed concentric rings round the hill, with no links at all? Or might they not have been joined across Ascent Route A so as to form a simple spiral, beginning with Path I at the bottom and winding upwards steadily, rather than the Cretan in-out-in-out-in pattern (on the Tor, up-down-up-down-up)?

In practice, neither scheme would work. Paths I, II and III, on both faces, meet Ascent Route A at levels where they could credibly be joined across it. But the higher paths do not. A simple spiral would break at the completion of its third circuit, in a dead end at the foot of the ridge; and farther up, the spacing of the paths on the south face is utterly wrong. The blank patch of hillside is a fatal obstacle.

Concentric rings or the simple spiral can be contrived with the three lower paths, but not above, where any attempt to make joins across the ridge would require hopelessly artificial contortions. Dion Fortune, looking for the simple spiral, was right not to carry it above the first three. By stopping there she perforce left the upper terraces unaccounted for. The Cretan scheme handles them all, and very well, by making the paths connect on the ridge in another way.

One final point. Ascent Route A has two large embedded stones. The lower, with a slightly smaller companion possibly split off from it, is behind the bench at the perimeter. The other is some distance uphill. On the theory of concentric rings, neither stone has any significance. On the theory of a simple spiral, the lower stone might serve as a starting-point, but would be a poor one – it ought to be lower still, and to the left – while the upper would again have no significance. On the Cretan theory, both make sense as markers. The lower stone marks the point of entry into the system. The upper marks the point where a maze-threader must begin circling. The instruction would be to start at the lower stone, climb Ascent Route A as far as the upper stone, and turn left. From one to the other the distance can be reckoned as seventy paces, bringing in the key number seven again; but that is not a notion to insist on. What is more interesting is that the starter stone by the bench is individually marked on the 1/2500 Ordnance Survey map as 'Living Rock'. Some of the neo-mystics, before there was any question of its role in the maze, singled it out as a 'broken fragment of an old megalith' and claimed that they could pick up a sort of electric current from it.

Full directions for threading the maze are given in the Appendix. It is worth mentioning that maze-explorers who have used these directions have succeeded in getting through with no prompting from me.

Despite all the hints at a design, nothing here is certain as yet. The proved possibility of threading the maze – or at any rate, making a good approximation – does not prove it to be real. Too much remains a matter of inference and gap-bridging. In particular, the linkages between levels are

The Terraced Track

blotted out, or rather blurred into an amorphous corridor along the much-trodden Ascent Route A. But given the complexity of this Cretan spiral, it is fair to ask whether even the possibility of it is likely to have taken shape on the hill by chance, and in such a way that all its relevant features are used, including even the two stones. A natural supplementary question amounts to an *a fortiori* version of one already put. What is the likelihood that all this should have happened by chance at Glastonbury, at a place so utterly and disconcertingly apt? Anyone who doubts the force of that argument should try proving the possibility on another hill.

Final proof could come only from archaeology. A promising approach might be to explore the entrance area, and also make a cutting from top to bottom across several of the terraces towards the eastern end of the north face, where they are narrow and well-defined. Traces of structures at the entrance; traces of a buried pavement, or other surfacing, on the terraces; fragments of tools employed in shaping them; objects dropped anywhere – all such things would be clues to the frequentation of the Tor. Any that were datable might have a story to tell.

CHAPTER TEN

A Notable Temple

I

Meanwhile we have the judgement of Professor Rahtz: 'If the maze theory were demonstrated to be true, it would clearly be of the greatest relevance to the origins of Glastonbury as a religious centre.' Even these interim findings are the first real evidence in support of the belief that the Isle of Avalon was a major sacred site before Christianity. Moreover, the maze fits in with a number of the clues to its early history and prehistory.

Thus Chalice Well, Radford's hypothetical sacred spring, is in the little valley below the maze entrance. Given a great sanctuary on the Tor, the Well could hardly have avoided being associated with it. The tinted water would have flowed down the valley as it still does, though now through decorous channels. Pilgrims to the maze would have arrived first at the stream, and doubtless walked the few yards to its source, as a natural resting-place before the long climb and ritual circling.

Again, if the maze existed, a certain awe might have lingered at its approaches in Christian times. The entrance and the adjacent terraces would have remained visible, even if trees grew to obscure them. Immediately below is the very area where convergent clues hint at an early Christian use, as if it were out of the ordinary. There are those allusions – perhaps only legendary, yet still thought-provoking – to a chapel, cells, hermits, on the slope and in the valley. St Collen would perhaps have lived hereabouts. His eerie summons up the Tor, into Gwyn's palace, could be an echo of folklore about the enchanted ground of the maze; folklore which perhaps survived into the sixteenth century, to inspire Weston's friend with his dread of the

A Notable Temple

'molestation of spirits' as he approached the high place.

Collen recalls a broader issue. So indeed does the Well. The saint's legend suggests that ancient Glastonbury had an Underworld aspect. The Well, if more doubtfully, suggests a Goddess aspect. Would the maze be in harmony with either?

With the first, certainly. Spirals and mazes in general seem to have had numinous Underworld links in very early times. The motif occurs in various places and is not confined to any one ancient culture. Western Europe's Palaeolithic cave-paintings may supply the key to its ancestry. Those wonderful figures of animals, and possibly gods, are not painted in the caverns where people lived or even close to them. They are not works of art to be looked at. They are religious or magical, and the subterranean gallery is a shrine, aloof from the everyday world and the profanation of casual glances. In several cases, furthermore, the paintings are not only away from the inhabited area, they are hard to reach at all, far down in the dark through tricky, dangerous passages. Nature provided a kind of subterranean maze, and the painters regarded the place it led to as suitable. Tortuous and difficult access, and the numinous Underworld, went together.

With the rise of civilization much the same idea recurs. As a human product the maze is involved with religious mysteries, and we get distinct signs that it had its beginnings in inwardness and depth rather than outwardness and height. Babylonian writings connect mazes with the 'bowels of the earth', and with the coiling intestines of animals slain by augurers – that is, with organs hidden from normal view. In countries with caves, something like the Palaeolithic theme reappears. Enquirers at the oracle of the Greek god Trophonius had to grope their way in through a complication of spikes and railings, and when they had done so they found themselves in a cave, allegedly an antechamber of the infernal regions. Robert Graves cites two definitions of the word 'labyrinth' as meaning primarily 'a mountain cave' and 'a subterranean cave'.

A persistent if erroneous theory avers that the Cretan Labyrinth itself should be identified with a complex of underground passages at Gortyna, on the side of Mount Ida. This is mentioned by Roman authors and described by travellers in the eighteenth and nineteenth centuries. The Labyrinth at least has cavernous associations in Virgil. He says its architect, Daedalus, flew to Cumae in Italy and built an oracular temple, with golden reliefs on the gate depicting the Minotaur and the Labyrinth itself; and there dwelt the Cumaean Sibyl, who uttered her prophesyings in a cave. When Aeneas, leader of the migrant Trojans, came to consult her, he asked to be allowed to meet his dead father in the Underworld, and she guided him down to it through another cave. In Virgil we are dealing with civilized poetry remote from prehistoric myth, yet associations of the same kind are suggested by the elaborate spiral carvings at Newgrange in Ireland and other ancient passage graves.

The Tor maze, if it exists, tends upwards and not downwards. Starting from the base, it could hardly do otherwise. But it could have had its point – or part of its point – in the Tor being a hollow hill, a portal into the Underworld, as the Collen legend asserts. Moreover it has a puzzling feature which Russell noticed, and my own investigations confirmed.

The path making the final circuit, numbered V in the descriptive scheme, appears to break off without quite finishing its course. It ought to twist inwards and upwards to the summit. But while its terrace runs some distance along the south face, just as it should, it suddenly vanishes in a confused area full of nettles and bushes. Beyond and above are signs of a landslip. The topsoil has gone, leaving a large patch of sandy surface exposed. Farther on again, where the terrace might be expected to continue, it does not. After a piece of very steep hillside there are doubtful traces of a vestigial path going on to the ridge, where a maze-threader could turn right, and complete the journey by climbing to the top. But this is faint in the last degree, with nothing like the clarity of the preceding terrace.

Close to the patch of sandy surface is a tree with a big round stone beside it. That stone could be a marker, as the two on the first ascent may be. Does the visible maze-spiral

A Notable Temple

end here, at this third stone, without making its final twist at all? The idea has a certain allure. Apart from the apparent markers on the ascent, this is the only large stone anywhere on the Tor. If it were a third marker, the maze would use all the stones as it uses all the terraces. But the implication would be that the ritual centre was not on the top but underground, and the final approach to it was by a tunnel now blocked, leading inwards from the neighbourhood of the stone. This would be the chamber so persistently asserted by local legend.

If it did not exist literally it might still have existed ritually and mythically. A maze-threader, at the stone, might have been subjected to some experience induced by drugs or hypnosis, and completed the journey by penetrating the heart of the hill in spirit. Celtic legend recognized caves which were not there in the normal way, and were only entered under special, magical conditions. This applies to several of the caves where Arthur and his knights lie asleep. As a matter of fact, the 'Life' of St Collen gives a curious hint. Speaking of his retreat on the Tor, the author says he 'made himself a cell under a rock in a secret place out of the way'. This was where he received his summons into the Underworld. A hermitage on the easy slope nearer the valley and the water supply would seem more likely, and the 'rock' and the secrecy may be mere flourishes by a writer with no real knowledge of the Tor. But could he be drawing on some tradition about a journey which was made in spirit from the nook in the hillside by the round stone?

To revert, however, to mazes and spirals in general. They are relevant to the Underworld aspect but not so plainly to the Goddess aspect. Meanders, rough spirals, and linear designs of various sorts are incised on the bodies of prehistoric goddess figurines from south-east Europe. The specific Tor maze-spiral on Cretan coins recalls the former power of the Great Mother in Minoan Crete. However, the coins come too long after her heyday to prove a connection with her. While, as we shall see, that is not the whole story, there is no immediate logical leap from Crete to Britain. The coins cannot say anything about Matrona

Avalonian Quest

or Modron, the Mother who (in Celtic or earlier guise) is the deity we might wish to find at Glastonbury.

Yet something else may. At this point we confront a surprising fact. It could be that the Tor maze is mentioned by a classical author. It could be that it resolves a much-discussed problem in his text, and clears away some mistaken fancies which have grown round it.

2

This author is known to us indirectly through the work of a later one, Diodorus Siculus. Diodorus was a contemporary of Julius Caesar. Born in Sicily, he travelled widely and settled in Rome, where he put together what he called the *Historical Library*. It was a compilation of world history, real and legendary, in forty books. In book II, chapter 47, he records an account of a northern island and its people, which he says is taken from 'Hecataeus and certain others'. Since he fails to specify the others, it is assumed that he means chiefly Hecataeus. Two Greek authors had that name. Hecataeus of Miletus lived in the sixth century BC, Hecataeus of Abdera in the fourth. Diodorus' is the latter. His writings are lost. The long excerpt gives a tantalizing glimpse of them.

It begins:

> In the region beyond the land of the Celts there lies in the ocean an island no smaller than Sicily. This island, the account continues, is situated in the north and is inhabited by the Hyperboreans, who are called by that name because their home is beyond the point whence the north wind [Boreas] blows. ... The following legend is told concerning them: Leto [the mother of Apollo] was born on this island, and for that reason Apollo is honoured among them above all other gods. ... And there is also on the island both a magnificent sacred precinct of Apollo and a notable temple which is adorned with many votive offerings and is spherical in shape.

A Notable Temple

Furthermore, a city is there which is sacred to this god, and the majority of its inhabitants are players on the cithara.

There is much more, but this will do for the moment.

The 'land of the Celts' then comprised a large tract of Europe from the Bay of Biscay across Germany. However, those who have discussed the passage agree that the island, however mythicized, must be Britain. Diodorus lived when Britain was no longer so mysterious, but here he is transcribing what he found in his source-book, without comment. Hecataeus – as we may say for convenience, even if 'certain others' have a share – can hardly be writing from first-hand knowledge. He mixes myth with information. The name 'Hyperboreans' which he gives to the Britons (or some of them) raises strange issues, as we shall see. But attention has fastened on his 'notable temple' which is 'spherical in shape'. Modern writers have claimed, and even taken for granted, that he is talking about Stonehenge. The Greek word translated 'spherical' is assumed to mean 'round' or 'circular'. Thus, for instance, Ward Rutherford in his book *The Druids*: 'He [Hecataeus] tells us that the island housed a vast temple in circular form, which can only be Stonehenge.' Gerald S. Hawkins, in *Stonehenge Decoded*, tries to effect the same identification by a less obvious route. He argues that 'spherical' means 'related to the celestial spheres'. The temple, on this reading, was designed and laid out for astronomical purposes.

One way or another, the assumption that this thing is Stonehenge is very natural. I once acquiesced in it myself. But I had not looked up the word in a Greek lexicon, and I now query whether the advocates of Stonehenge ever did. The word is *sphairoeides* (σφαιρέιδης). Liddell and Scott, the supreme authorities on classical Greek, give only one rendering besides 'spherical' itself, namely, 'globular'. They quote a phrase in Xenophon where the word is applied to a round knob on the end of a lance. But they do not allow that it can ever mean 'circular' – that is, round in two dimensions – or 'related to spheres', either. Therefore Stonehenge is ruled out. So are all other megalithic circles.

How can we make sense of this word? Should we try? Perhaps the temple is entirely imaginary. Yet further on are details suggesting that Hecataeus' story has substance in it, and if it has, the temple ought at least to be taken seriously.

> They say also that the moon, as viewed from this island, appears to be but a little distance from the earth and to have upon it prominences, like those of the earth, which are visible to the eye. The account is also given that the god [Apollo] visits the island every nineteen years, the period in which the return of the stars to the same place in the heavens is accomplished; and for this reason the nineteen-year period is called by the Greeks the 'year of Meton'.

The first sentence, about the lunar mountains, is quite unlike myth or fable and hard to interpret. One might be led to wonder whether the Britons invented telescopes! But the second sentence puts us on firmer ground. The nineteen-year cycle is a fact of astronomy. Nineteen solar years are almost exactly equivalent to 235 lunar months, so this period brings the celestial bodies round into the same relationship. The cycle was known to the Babylonians and Greeks. On the advice of the astronomer Meton (hence Hecataeus' mention of him) it was used to regulate the Athenian calendar between 338 and 290 BC.

More to the point, it was known also to the Druids. That is the implication of a bronze plate called the Coligny Calendar, found near Bourg-en-Bresse in the department of Ain. In Hecataeus' time the first wave of Celtic settlers had been in Britain for well over a century, perhaps nearer two. Hence, his statement makes good sense: he is talking about a calendric myth of the Druids in Britain. No known classical author speaks of the Druids as familiar with the nineteen-year cycle. Hecataeus is neither guessing nor copying from someone else. He has British information of some kind. That being so, it is reasonable to try to explain his temple as something other than fiction.

In that period a globe-shaped building would be out of the question. The word might perhaps refer to a spherical

A Notable Temple

chamber inside a more conventional structure. We could picture a small, steep-sided amphitheatre with a domed roof on top, the building as a whole looking like a modern observatory. But that too would have been unparalleled then, and incredible in Britain. Britons might have made an amphitheatre by digging a pit, but there is no evidence that they would have been equal to a dome.

If Hecataeus is speaking of any real thing at all, the word *sphairoeides* must be wrong. A scribe wrote it mistakenly for another word. Manuscripts of Diodorus show no disagreement at this point, so the slip was probably in the copy he read, and he simply reproduced it. Before printing, the question of misprints does not arise. But errors could creep in for a variety of reasons, such as damage, poor legibility, the wandering of the copyist's thoughts, or faulty hearing when one scribe was writing from another's dictation.

We need a Greek adjective which could have become *sphairoeides* through a plausible error. There was one, *speiroeides* (σπειροέιδης). In Greek the difference is a matter of only two letters, φα or πε. The error would have been especially easy if someone was reading a manuscript aloud to the scribe making the copy. One word might well have been mis-heard as the other, the more so because in classical Greek the letter φ, 'phi', was an aspirated *p* and had not become phonetically the same as *f*. English has much the same double sound when a word ending *p* is combined with a word beginning *h*, as in the once familiar 'top-hole' for 'excellent'. Thus Hecataeus' actual adjective for the temple may have been *speiroeides*. What does it mean? It means 'coiled' or 'spiral'. The temple 'spherical in shape' would, correctly, be 'coiled in shape' or 'spiral in shape'. So the reference could be to the sacred hill-maze of Glastonbury with its complex coiling terraces, still in use, as Rahtz conjectured, long after its likely date of construction.

As for the gods, the context might be read as implying that the temple was Apollo's as the 'precinct' and 'city' were. Strictly, however, Hecataeus does not say so. Elsewhere he speaks of the precinct and the city as governed by the same family, but not the temple, which seems to be distinct. When he mentions it in the first passage quoted, he has just explained that Britain was the birthplace of Leto, Apollo's mother. The cult of Apollo was sometimes linked with hers. Homer, in the *Iliad* (V.445-8), tells how the god rescued the wounded Aeneas during a battle, and carried him to his temple in the Trojan citadel. Apollo shared this with his mother and also with his twin sister. 'In the spacious sanctuary, Leto and Artemis the Archeress not only healed him [that is, Aeneas] but made him more splendid than ever.' At the British temple, the Celtic god whom Hecataeus calls Apollo may have been worshipped jointly with the goddess whom he calls Leto. Or the temple may have belonged to the mother alone, a Celtic version, perhaps, of an earlier goddess for whom it was created; Hecataeus seems to regard 'Leto' as the authentic Briton.

Before asking who the British Apollo and Leto were, it is worth glancing at a theory which has had weighty support. It suggests that 'Apollo' is derived from a word in an ancient language ancestral both to Greek and to the Celtic family, and that this word meant 'apple'. Hence Apollo is the apple-god, and the name 'Avalon', the place of apples, may go back to the cult of a god identified with him. The prior Welsh form 'Avallach' is equivocal. The enchanted island may be the apple-island, or it may be the island of a hero or god called Avallach. While the 'apple' etymology of the Greek name is now out of favour, it is an intriguing fancy that some learned Briton hit on it and thought it was right, so that traditions of a deity equated with the apple-god produced the name 'Avallach'.

However, this has nothing to do with Hecataeus. Who is Apollo in the setting of early Celtic Britain? Stonehenge's advocates have tried to enlist him in their cause. They point out that Stonehenge has a solar orientation. Therefore, they contend, it had something to do with sun-worship, and a Greek would naturally have thought of Apollo because Apollo was a sun-god. The trouble is that in the mainstream of Greek mythology, Apollo was not a sun-god. He was a complex deity with a medley of interests, the most important of them being music, poetry, medicine and inspiration. His solar aspect came late. Hecataeus may have been aware of it, but he would scarcely have called a British

A Notable Temple

sun-god Apollo for no other reason than his being a sun-god.

As it happens, we know which god of Celtic Britain was held to be the same as Apollo, or, at least, was worshipped as a Celtic aspect of him. The evidence is much later than Hecataeus, but nothing earlier calls it in question. He was Maponos or Maponus, the 'Divine Youth'. Four inscriptions of the Roman period prove the identity. The chief reason seems to have been musical. On an altar at Hexham, Maponus is equated with 'Apollo the Harper'. Hecataeus shows the same notion at work. In Apollo's sacred city, he says, most of the inhabitants play on the cithara and sing hymns to him. When the god makes his visit every nineteen years he plays on the instrument himself.

The inscriptions are in northern England. Maponus' northern cult is also attested by the village Lochmaben and a stone called Clochmabenstane, both in Dumfries-shire. However, he was not confined to the north. Traces of him are found in Gaul, and he is semi-humanized as a hero, Mabon, in the legends of Wales. His cult in the south of Britain would be perfectly credible.

If the British Apollo is Maponus, the British Leto is Maponus' mother. We know who she was as well. She was Matrona, and in the Welsh legends where Maponus becomes Mabon, his mother becomes Modron. Here she is, then – that very Modron who is also Morgan, the lady of Avalon, the healing enchantress who receives the wounded Arthur in her apple-island ... just as the healer Leto receives the wounded Aeneas. True, the 'Avallach' conjecture would run into an obstacle here, because when Avallach is spoken of as a person he is Morgan's father, not her son as the Apollo connection would require. But changing mythologies do change divine relationships, splitting up and re-combining.

Hecataeus' Apollo and Leto are thus, very probably, the Celtic deities Maponus and Matrona, the latter in his eyes being the genuinely British figure with a local association. If the temple is the sacred hill with its maze-path, the notion of a cult of the Mother there is in keeping with what he says. She, under whatever name, would have come first,

Avalonian Quest

and her son, 'Apollo', would have grown to overshadow her, though not necessarily to the point of ousting her. Chalice Well would have remained a healing spring of Modron the Celtic 'Mother', or Morgan or whatever we care to call her, the goddess in her later guise. The spring would have served pilgrims going to the spiral sanctuary above.

The maze, then, shows signs of linking up with the possible pre-Christian aspects of Glastonbury, the Underworld aspect and the Goddess aspect. As yet cohesion is lacking. The Underworld link, thus far, is only by way of the connotations of mazes in general. The Goddess link, thus far, is only by way of a certain reading of Hecataeus, which is alluring because it leads to the right goddess. It remains true that nothing in mythology seems to draw the aspects together.

Virgil might appear to offer a hint. When he tells of the oracle at Cumae, with its golden relief of the Labyrinth and its Underworld-wise Sibyl, he also makes it clear that the god of the temple was Apollo. This might take us further if Hecataeus' British god actually were Apollo. It would give the same grouping of themes – maze, Underworld, Apollo – and thence Apollo's mother. But the only British Apollo whom we know anything about, the god whom Hecataeus may be supposed to have in mind, is not the classical one. He is a lesser Celtic deity who was worshipped as an aspect of him. There is no sign that Apollo-Maponus had anything to do with oracles or the Underworld.

However, all these arguments omit an important factor. None takes any account of the special character of the spiral. The Tor maze, if real, is not just any 'coiled' track. It follows a highly specific course, the Cretan with its septenary wanderings. The next step is to survey the known cases of that particular maze and see what light they may shed.

In substance this is the same thing attempted by some of the neo-mystics: interpreting Glastonbury by relating it to symbols or myths or systems outside it. If Glastonbury has a Zodiac, the widespread conception of the zodiac in

A Notable Temple

general, and the astrological doctrines based on it, ought to tell us something about Glastonbury. If the Tor is a nodal point in a scheme of ley-lines, the meaning of ley-lines, whatever it may be, should illuminate the Tor. If the Abbey is laid out by sacred geometry, the same technique elsewhere (as revealed in megaliths or the Bible, for instance) should show the builders' intentions. The idea is sound. It is only the application that fails, because one part of the equation is missing in each case. Without good evidence for the Zodiac at Glastonbury, other zodiacs of whatever kind are irrelevant. Without good evidence that ley-lines exist, the alleged Tor node is meaningless. Without good evidence that sacred geometry was practised, at least in John Michell's sense, anything read into the measurements of the Abbey is arbitrary.

But the maze theory does, provisionally, supply both sides of the equation. The pattern fits the Tor well enough to evoke a strong probability, and it is found, beyond any question, in other places. Therefore its meaning in other places may help to elucidate the Tor.

iv. Labyrinth design on Cretan coin (this arrangement inverts the lettering)

v. Labyrinth graffito at Pompeii

vi. Tablet from Pylos, Greece

vii. Etruscan vase picture with maze spiral and 'Game of Troy' figures

viii. Carving on Hollywood stone, Co. Wicklow, Ireland (the maze is the dark line)

ix. Welsh *Caerdroia* pattern

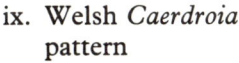

x. Carving in Rocky Valley, near Tintagel, Cornwall

xi. Plan of 'Walls of Troy' turf maze near Brandsby, Yorkshire

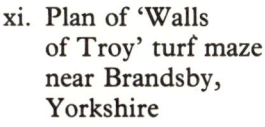

CHAPTER ELEVEN

Ariadne's Dance

I

Once again, to call this maze 'Cretan' is not to assume that anything in Crete was the model, or that similar mazes in other countries must be copies. Crete in fact does not supply the earliest instances. The coins bearing this pattern, in either a round or a square form, belong to the last two or three centuries BC. Their interest, and the justification for the 'Cretan' label, lies in their link with the far older Labyrinth story and the hint of an underlying tradition. They were minted at Cnossus, the erstwhile Minoan capital where the Labyrinth was supposed to be. A tablet found there, dating from more than a thousand years earlier, has a 'Linear B' inscription in which the word 'labyrinth' occurs. Coins issued at the same place in the intervening centuries also have linear designs on them, together with bulls' heads, and even the Minotaur himself.

More evidence comes from a graffito at Pompeii. On a crimson-painted pillar in a building called the House of Lucretius, the same essential pattern is crudely but correctly scratched in a square form, with the words 'LABYRINTHUS HIC HABITAT MINOTAURUS'; 'the Labyrinth, here lives the Minotaur' – perhaps a rude reference to the owner of the house. It seems that in the classical world, where the tale of the Labyrinth was familiar, this was a standard way of representing it.

Which, of course, is perplexing. Daedalus is said to have planned the Minotaur's home as a maze in the modern sense, a puzzle. It was multicursal, with branching paths and blind alleys. Only a series of correct choices led to the monster's lair. When Theseus undertook to slay him, he had little hope of finding the way unaided, or getting out once he was inside. Help came from King Minos' daughter Ariadne. With Daedalus' connivance she taught Theseus the secret, and gave him a thread to pay out as he walked and follow as he returned. But if the spiral gives us the plan, Ariadne was superfluous; there was no puzzle.

The truth behind this confusion is that the Labyrinth legend, as we now know it, actually is confused. It is a literary composite with an alien factor. Some of the linear motifs on the coins show Egyptian influence. Several tombs of pharaohs really were built with indirect approaches and multiple entries. Classical authors describe a true Egyptian labyrinth of gigantic size to the east of Lake Moeris. This existed, and its ground-plan was partly recovered in 1888 by the archaeologist Flinders Petrie. It was a temple-complex in the Fayyum, built in the nineteenth century BC for Amenemhet III. It covered an area of about 1000 feet by 800, and its numerous corridors and chambers were bewildering and probably meant to be.

At some period a notion took shape in classical minds that the Cretan Labyrinth was a building imitated from this Egyptian structure. Apollodorus, in the second century BC, says Daedalus made the Cretan one like the Egyptian though only one-hundredth the size. That would work out at about 100 feet by 80, not as big as the maze at Hampton Court. Apollodorus may have had an exaggerated idea of the Egyptian prototype. Diodorus (the same who preserves Hecataeus' report on Britain), and the more important Pliny, both accept his description. Excavation has given it no real support. The palace of Cnossus may have been hard to find one's way about in, and folk-memories of the Minoan bull-cult may have conjured up a ritual area with the Minotaur as an inmate. One wall has a linear design on it, which could have supplied a hint for the design on some of the coins. However, the Labyrinth in the sense of a building made to baffle is the result of grafting Egyptian concepts on a more authentic Cretan tradition. This tradition can still be traced in the literary versions, and here the spiral belongs.

Homer reveals what Daedalus was originally believed to

have done. He is describing pictures worked by Hephaestus on a new shield for Achilles (*Iliad* XVIII.590ff):

> The god depicted a dancing-floor like the one that Daedalus designed in the spacious town of Cnossus for Ariadne of the lovely locks. Youths and marriageable maidens were dancing on it with their hands on one another's wrists.... Here they ran lightly round, circling as smoothly on their accomplished feet as the wheel of a potter... and there they ran in lines to meet each other.

Even when the Labyrinth is turned by legend-makers into a building, housing the Minotaur, some of those who tell the tale have not lost sight of its origins. They try to combine discrepant ideas about it. Daedalus, they say, invented a dance giving the secret of the route, and he or Ariadne taught it to Theseus. On the way home from Crete, Theseus put in at the island of Delos with Greek prisoners whom he had freed, and they held festivities. They performed Daedalus' dance, and he instituted it on Delos as a ritual. It came to be called the *Geranos* or Crane Dance.

A Crane Dance was regularly performed well within historical times. Plutarch, in the first century AD, says it is still a Delian custom. He describes it as 'an imitation of the circling passages in the Labyrinth, consisting of certain rhythmic involutions and evolutions', a phrase which would fit the Cretan spiral. The second-century satirist Lucian, in a treatise *On Dancing*, mentions dances called 'The Labyrinth', 'Ariadne' and 'Daedalus'. People in Delos, and Crete itself, were still dancing them when Lucian lived.

Quite possibly they were all the same, or much the same, and we are merely getting different names for them. More than possibly the maze-spiral on the coins portrays the course followed by Labyrinth-dancers from time immemorial, circling in to a centre and out again – either traversing a marked floor as Homer perhaps implies, or, a more tricky exercise, reproducing a known pattern. Apparently the dances were performed without change from the Minoan age to the classical age. If they were, the

Ariadne's Dance

accuracy of the spirals on the coins, as a record of the true Labyrinth, would be no problem despite the long interval.

A few years ago the Labyrinth dance was revived as a May ceremony at Glastonbury, by one of the neo-Druid groups. Adopting the square form of the Cretan pattern, as in the Pompeian graffito, they laid it out with string and pegs in a field, and capered through. At the first attempt they did not bring enough string, so the maze was too small and entangled the participants' feet, but later the rite was carried out with precision.

As to the more distant background of dances like this, we can only guess. It has been claimed that the file of dancers, following a sinuous path, once imitated the coilings of snakes in motion: gods in serpentine form. This would be in accord with the Underworld affiliations of mazes, since snakes are chthonic creatures that emerge from holes in the ground. One theory maintains that all the serpents of mythology go back to a Sumerian primal serpent named Zu, who lived in the waters under the earth.

The curious 'doublethink', by which the Cretan Labyrinth is both unicursal and multicursal, is very persistent. The Roman poet Ovid compares its complexities to the windings and retrogressions of the River Maeander in Asia Minor – the river from which the word 'meander' is derived. In his *Metamorphoses* (VIII.155ff) he describes the execution of Minos' edict that the Minotaur must be concealed from the world:

> Daedalus, a man very famed for his skill in architecture, plans the work . . . and leads the eyes into mazy wanderings, by the intricacy of its various passages. No otherwise than as the limpid Maeander sports in the Phrygian fields, and flows backwards and forwards with its varying course, and, meeting itself, beholds its waters that are to follow, and fatigues its wandering current, now pointing to its source, and now to the open sea: just so Daedalus fills innumerable paths with windings, and scarcely can he himself return to the entrance, so great are the intricacies of the place.

The image is obscure. If Ovid means that the 'innumerable paths' branched out from each other, why does he not say so? Why make the river his simile? How could mere 'windings' create a problem? A maze-threader would only need to keep walking.

A reason for the ambiguity may be that the old dance-spiral was too stubborn an influence. If the dance was originally in the open, without guidance, that would indeed have been exacting. The movements in and out, back and forth, in the company of other dancers easily capable of getting mixed up, would have called for skill and self-possession. Once the scheme was laid out in a marked track, or in the plan of a building, that difficulty would have vanished. The Labyrinth legend would then have called for a new form of perplexity – the multicursal. But the notion of perplexity through mere convolution was so deep-rooted that it was hard to forget. The magic of Daedalus' septenary pattern was too ancient and potent.

Its age and potency may appear from some of its occurrences in non-Cretan settings. The square form of it has been discovered on a tablet from Pylos in western Greece, which may be as early as 1200 BC. This is an isolated case and its meaning is unknown. But the maze-dance itself is said to have been performed in Italy, where the Pompeian graffito shows awareness of the pattern, and at Troy. For whatever reason it is associated with Troy as well as Crete. In the Trojan connection horsemen are involved, as if the Trojans had a ritual equestrian exercise in which the same path was followed. It may have begun as a feature of some Trojan cult paying semi-divine honours to Theseus' son Hippolytus. His name means 'horse-stampede'. According to legend he was dragged to death, after an upset in his chariot, by the horses that drew it. His father Theseus could be the link between Troy and Crete. It is intriguing to find the association as late as 1418, when the Seigneur de Caumont, writing of a visit to Crete, speaks of Daedalus' Labyrinth as 'today popularly called the city of Troy'.

On an Etruscan vase found at Tragliatella in Italy are a number of incised figures including two armed riders, with emblematic birds on their shields. Behind them is a circular

Ariadne's Dance

representation of the spiral, exactly as on the Cretan coins except that it is a mirror-image. Inside its perimeter is the word TRUIA, Troy. The date of the vase is uncertain. It may be as early as the seventh century BC.

The nature of what is going on comes into the open in Virgil's *Aeneid* (V.545–603). Virgil calls the horseback manoeuvre the *Lusus Trojae* or Game of Troy. He describes an imagined performance by actual Trojans, sons of Aeneas' settlers in Italy, from whom the founders of Rome were believed to be descended. The exercise forms the set-piece conclusion to funeral games honouring the memory of Aeneas' father. It is carried out by thirty-nine boys – three troops of twelve each, plus their troop-leaders, one of whom, Aeneas' son Ascanius, has overall charge. The account as a whole suggests a complex series of figures, with the troops dividing and reuniting in various ways, and fighting mock-skirmishes. But at one point Virgil speaks plainly of their 'riding right and left in intertwining circles', and indicates the origin of the pattern:

> They say that once upon a time the Labyrinth in mountainous Crete contained a path, twining between walls which barred the view, with a treacherous uncertainty in its thousand ways, so that its baffling plan, which none might master and none retrace, would foil the trail of any guiding clues. By just such a course the sons of the Trojans knotted their paths.

This reference to the Labyrinth comes earlier in the epic than the passage already mentioned, about the temple at Cumae. There, the reader may be assumed to know about it, and Virgil simply recalls it as 'the Cretan building in all its elaboration, with the wandering track which might not be unravelled'. He slips into the same ambiguity as Ovid. The Labyrinth has only one track, however long and contorted . . . yet people lose themselves in it.

Virgil goes on to say that in later life Ascanius taught the Game of Troy to the citizens of Alba Longa, and it passed down to the Romans. Thus he accounts for a ceremony which was still a Roman institution in the first century AD.

Nero took part in it as a boy, and it is portrayed on a medal which he issued. By that time, however, it seems to have become a more spectacular cavalry display.

2

Italy supplies another instance of the spiral which may be ultimately Cretan-derived. On the rock of Naquane at Val Camonica, near Lake Garda, is a pocked line which reproduces it for most of its course, though it goes a little wrong at the centre. Beside this design is a not-quite-human figure, perhaps the Minotaur in person. That is as far as the spiral seems to go by the Italian route. But it appears, and more impressively, in the British Isles, quite apart from anything which may or may not be on the Tor.

In 1740 a Welsh historian drew attention to a rural custom of cutting labyrinthine designs in turf. The topic was taken up by nineteenth-century antiquaries – by P. Roberts in 1815, by someone using the pseudonym 'Idrison' in 1822, by W. H. Mounsey in 1858. Roberts spoke of the prevalence of the custom among the shepherds of the Welsh mountains, and gave a plan of their turf maze showing that it was the same as the Cretan spiral, enclosed by a semicircle on one side and by a straight line on the other. 'Idrison' noted the Cretan parallel. Mounsey testified that the custom survived in his own day with the herdsmen of Burgh and Rockcliffe near Carlisle, not indeed in Wales, but in country which long kept a Cymric character. All the authors agree on what the maze was called: the Walls, or Citadel, of Troy – in Welsh, *Caerdroia*.

With the shepherds and herdsmen the motive for cutting it is not stated. It may have been no more than a pastime, with any former meaning forgotten. Roberts refers to schoolboys challenging other schoolboys to draw it correctly, and to a tale that it was the plan of the defences of Troy, with seven walls and an intricate way through them. The general notion, at any rate, is not confined to the Cymry. There is a round turf maze answering to the Cretan

Ariadne's Dance

pattern near Brandsby in Yorkshire. Several times re-cut, it is twenty-odd feet across. This too is known as 'the Walls of Troy'. The same name, or 'Troy-town', is applied to several English turf mazes which do not follow the same course.

How did the Trojan motif find its way to Britain so long afterwards – and associated not only with mazes in general, but with mazes on the same septenary plan that is labelled as Trojan on the Etruscan vase? Edward Trollope, commenting on Mounsey's work in 1858, maintained that the name in Britain dated only from the classical fancies of Tudor times. On the other hand it is conceivable that the Britons learned the Game of Troy from their Roman conquerors. Some part may have been played by the Welsh legend, turned into pseudo-history by Geoffrey of Monmouth, which made out in Virgilian style that the Britons were descended from Trojans – to be specific, from a party of Trojans led by Brutus, a fictitious great-grandson of Aeneas.

Germany, Scandinavia and Finland have mazes somewhat resembling this. The northern ones are made with stones, and many are found on islands. They have a variety of names – the Ruins of Jerusalem, the Walls of Jericho, the Giant's Street, the Nun's Fence, the Maiden's Dance, the Troll's Castle. But it is noteworthy that in Norway and Sweden, variants of 'Troy' recur. We find *Trojin*, *Trojeburg*, *Trojenborg*, *Tröborg* and others. Trollope's theory of an English Tudor origin hardly fits here. The theme might have been picked up in Britain by Vikings.

No such speculation will account for three other specimens of the Cretan spiral. Two are in Cornwall. They are carved on a vertical outcrop in Rocky Valley, which runs down to a bay east of Tintagel. The work is bold and correct, with a continuous line representing the track. The third example is Irish, from Hollywood in County Wicklow. It was found by chance in 1911 during the pursuit of a weasel. A granite boulder was overturned, revealing a flat surface with the spiral carefully carved, about thirty inches across.

With these three mazes, the influence of Romans and the

Game of Troy is most improbable – the more so as Ireland was never Roman. There is no reliable way of dating them. The only clue is that they are near early Christian sites. Rocky Valley is just below the retreat of St Nectan. The Tintagel headland, an abode of Celtic monks, is only a mile or two away. The Hollywood boulder (now in the National Museum in Dublin) lay close to an upright stone with a cross carved on it, and to a lane leading to the pilgrims' road connecting the sixth-century hermitage of St Kevin with the monastery he founded at Glendalough.

Maze-spirals, though not this one, are to be seen in the pavements of medieval cathedrals – not only Chartres, already mentioned, but Amiens, Bayeux and Reims. Their purpose and symbolism are wholly uncertain. Any connection with the earlier carvings in Cornwall and Ireland would be the purest guesswork. It may be that these carvings mark holy places of the old order. The saints could have occupied the places with a view to their reconsecration. Some believe that the Tintagel carvings are pre-Christian by a thousand years or more.

Suppose we now take stock of all the instances of the spiral, including the last awkward three. No generalization springs to mind which carries conviction, or takes us further with the hypothetical maze on the Tor. One natural thing to try would be a two-way grouping. Some of the spirals which are on record follow the plan which fits the Tor, where the maze-threader turns first to the left. Others are the mirror-image where the first turn is to the right. The former group would comprise the Cretan coin designs, the Pompeian graffito, and the Rocky Valley and Brandsby mazes. The mirror-images are the Pylos tablet, the Etruscan vase diagram, the Naquane rock-carving, the Welsh *Caerdroia* as drawn by Roberts, and the Hollywood maze. Nothing emerges. It is all very unhelpful.

If the Tor maze exists, we cannot safely ascribe it to artistic or ritual influence from the Mediterranean. Rahtz's dating would make it earlier than any proved Mediterranean instance, even the Pylos one, and probably earlier than Daedalus and Theseus themselves, or whatever stage of Aegean society their legends may correspond to.

Ariadne's Dance

We might try to progress by way of parallelism, asking whether the Cretan spiral's significance corresponds at all to what we may have come to suspect at Glastonbury. The difficulty is that we do not know what the spiral's significance was. It has been argued that the ancient dance was a form of sympathetic magic, related to the movements of the sun in the sky. Circling into the maze and circling out again symbolized the turn of the seasons, into the darkness and constriction of winter, and out into the light and liberation of spring. It has also been argued that ancient mazes in general, and this one in particular, had to do with rites of death and rebirth. Something happened at the centre. The initiate entered a place of mystery, conquered some spiritual Minotaur, and emerged in triumph. The latter theory might accord with the Underworld theme, at Glastonbury or anywhere else, but does not add much to the little that can be said about it at Glastonbury.

With the Goddess aspect, there is some evidence of an equivocal kind. It relates wholly to the Cretan Labyrinth. The Minotaur himself was decidedly not feminine. However, his mother was Minos' wife Pasiphaë, whose name means 'she who shines for all', and who practised witchcraft; she may have had her beginning as a moon-goddess, or rather as the Great Goddess of Crete in lunar guise. The Cnossus Linear B tablet which mentions the Labyrinth designates some divine being as the 'Mistress' of it. But who was she? The Labyrinth spiral is akin to meanders of a simpler type, which occur on ritual objects from south-east Europe, and are associated with goddesses in the form of water-birds. The bird-goddess motif is said to show in the fact that the Labyrinth dance on Delos was called the Crane Dance. That may be so, but it does not seem to have much to do with Pasiphaë. No coherent thought takes shape. None of the arguments can be stretched to cover the instances of the spiral in the British Isles.

Lastly, in view of what Hecataeus says about the Britons and their Apollo-worship, it is fair to point out that where the spiral occurs, Apollo sometimes occurs also. The representation of the Labyrinth on the temple gate at Cumae, if it was real, very possibly took that form; and according to

Avalonian Quest

Virgil Daedalus flew there on the wings he had made, dedicated the wings to Apollo, and put up the temple for him. On the Cretan coin which gives the spiral most vividly, the god's profile is on the other side. Also, the tale of Theseus instituting the dance at Delos is meant to explain the fact that in classical times it had been danced there for untold centuries; and the dance circled round Apollo's altar beside a lake. Delos was his birthplace, and that suggests the presence of Leto as well, his mother. But once again, Hecataeus' British Apollo is only a Celtic god regarded as a form of the great Apollo. The latter's association with the Cretan spiral arises from other aspects of his larger, more complex nature. It has no certain relevance to the Tor or to what Hecataeus may seem to be suggesting about it.

What emerges from this survey is the kind of result that often does emerge from surveys of myths and symbols: a medley of linkages, coincidences, possibilities, which could support a certain view but are never decisive. The glaring absence is the absence of any instance of the spiral combining Goddess and Underworld aspects. Nothing short of that combination could make it really likely that we were getting usable clues to Glastonbury. Crete itself comes nearest, since it does supply a mysterious 'Mistress of the Labyrinth', and Theseus' exploit does probably have a ritual connotation of entry into the Underworld and death-and-rebirth. Neither feature survives at all clearly in the familiar literary version; both point to a very early meaning of the Labyrinth, long before 1000 BC, which might agree chronologically with a version of it on the Tor. It is worth adding that the most interesting involvement of Apollo is with the ancient dance-spiral at Delos rather than with the sophisticated Labyrinth of the literary story.

3

However, this is not the end. If we look far enough we do find this very spiral carrying both the Glastonbury motifs,

Ariadne's Dance

Goddess and Underworld in explicit unison. But we find it in a baffling place.

It is the chief sacred image of the Hopi of Arizona. The standard written exposition of it is in Frank Waters's *Book of the Hopi*. They call it the Mother Earth symbol. Or to be precise, their Mother Earth symbol has two forms, one square, one round, expressing different aspects of Hopi myth; and the round one is the Cretan spiral in mirror-image. A carving of it, five or six inches across, is on a rock just south of Oraibi. Another, about nine inches across, is on a rock south of Shipaulovi.

xii. Hopi Mother Earth symbol (round form)

Both forms of the symbol have several layers of meaning. Both stand for the womb of Mother Earth, the divine birth-giver. In the round form, the cross made by the line from the entrance and the line at right angles to it is an emblem of the Sun, the quickener. The single convoluted maze-track represents the road prescribed for a human being on the way through life. To follow this is to attain spiritual rebirth, through the eternal Mother.

Rebirth, moreover, is a re-enactment in the individual of a myth about the history of the human race, called the Emergence. This aspect is stressed more in the square form of the symbol, but the theme is present in both. In past ages, when most of humanity turned to evil, a creator-god set apart a chosen remnant. He sent them into a place of safety, where they remained while he destroyed the world and fashioned a new one. This has happened three times. The first and second times, the faithful remnant passed through a hollow hill built by the Ant People into an underground region, the womb of Earth. The third time they were hidden in hollow reeds. Each time, after the destruction and renewal, they 'emerged' into the new world to populate it. Our present world is the fourth. The round form of the symbol is said to be known to other American Indians, with a similar meaning. The Pimas speak of a spiral hole by which their ancestors 'emerged' from below, and say it was bored for them by the Spirit of the Placenta. The Cumas of Panama see the design as symbolizing the umbilical cord and the foetal membranes of the Earth Mother when she gave birth to her children.

Here, then, are the Goddess and Underworld motifs, both planted in a Cretan-type spiral. Of course it is the distance which makes this a problem. Imagine that we found the spiral, described as the Mother Earth symbol and endowed with its Hopi meaning, in early Gaul or Germany or somewhere else in the British Isles. In that case there could be no objection to pointing out the correspondences and inferring the logic of a Tor maze. It would make sense as the symbol itself, contrived around a hill with the Underworld inside and below it – a hill which is part of the body of the Goddess, if the landscape contours have any significance. The Tor is her breast, not her womb, but variations need not invalidate, and the nearby Chalice Hill supplies a womb if one is insisted on. In any case the spring

Ariadne's Dance

is close to the maze, below its entrance, and acceptably a Goddess spring if the maze has this meaning.

The double parallel is too good to dismiss, and everything fits... except the relative positions of Somerset and Arizona. Before asking whether the paradox can be resolved, I think it is proper to record a recent attempt to claim the Tor for the Mother by action rather than argument.

4

When I wrote *The Glastonbury Tor Maze*, I mentioned other cases of the spiral only in passing. However, I did glance at the Hopi Mother Earth symbol, and at the possibility that the Tor maze could have had something to do with a Goddess cult, presumably Neolithic. I closed on a point which struck me as interesting.

> Should the maze be generally accepted, this will have one notable result even if the background remains obscure. For the first time it will become feasible to reconstruct and re-live a Neolithic ritual, at least to some extent. We do not know what was actually done at Avebury or Stonehenge. But if people went to immense trouble to make a maze on the Tor, then we can be sure that whatever else they did, they threaded it. So can we.

Both hints were promptly taken up by the local Women's Group – 'Women's' in the feminist sense. Several of its members followed the work of the Matriarchy Study Group, a London-centred body which has published pamphlets on early worship of a Great Goddess, its suppression by 'patriarchal' religion, and the effects on the condition of women, past and present. This trend in thinking has had more impact in the United States, where the results have been called 'Women's Spirituality' and 'Goddess Consciousness'. It is another of the modern interests foreshadowed by Dion Fortune. I have felt, and still feel, a good deal of sympathy with some who express this point of view, which does not stand or fall with the dubious evidence which is too often cited.

The Glastonbury women fastened on the maze with some satisfaction, and claimed it for their Goddess by the method I had indicated: re-living the ritual. The guiding spirit was Kathy Jones, who practises psychic healing and kindred arts. Her maze-threading was booked for the night of the May full moon in 1980, which was in fact the night of 30 April. About forty maze-threaders, of both sexes, assembled on the Tor's lower slope when daylight was failing. They carried torches – hand-flares which, unlit, looked like bulrushes. The night was not ideal. The May full moon quickly vanished in clouds. Rain had made the hillside muddy and slippery. It was cold and, on the highest part of the Tor, windy (on the highest part of the Tor, it usually is). Of the forty starters, about ten followed the whole maze and climbed to the summit, taking three or four hours. Others, after a circuit or two, scrambled to the top by short cuts, there to wait staring down through the gloom for the file of torches to pass below at long intervals, circling clockwise and counter-clockwise.

Having business the next day, and not caring to go without sleep, I did not see this out myself. I learned afterwards that the end of the actual climbing was anti-climactic, but the sequel was spectacular. For an account of what happened I am indebted to the Swedish-born artist Monica Sjöö, herself prominent in the Goddess field, who came to join in. The following is an excerpt from her article 'Treading the Maze', which was published in two magazines, *Wood and Water* in England and *Womanspirit* in America.

> The original plan had been for all of us to spend the night on the Tor, by a bonfire, and then walk the maze down again at dawn. As it worked out instead, most people went off after a while, feeling cold and vaguely frustrated – feeling the lack of some form of celebration or ritual that the long walk seemed to have been leading up to. . . .
> Only a few of us remained on the Tor; four women and two men. We huddled into sleeping bags, close together,

Ariadne's Dance

and got some shelter from the wind at the foot of the tower. Everything was now in total darkness. I could after a while hear snores around me, but I was unable to go to sleep myself. Found myself trying to hang on to our covers with fists and teeth . . . heard strange sounds like rumblings, bells in the distance, etc. This is a place of high magic, and this was a powerful night of the year. I seemed to be waiting for something. . . . Through my closed eyes I seemed to see strange lights – and when I looked up I discovered the most wild and amazing lightnings constantly criss-crossing the sky. All the years I've been in Britain I have never seen anything like this!

Some of the others also woke up and someone said that she had heard stories of the lightning having been seen to strike the tower and spiral its way down to its base. We thought we might get fried alive if we remained where we were. We scrambled out of sleeping bags, stumbled half-awake away from the tower. Slithered, ran and fell the very long humpy road. . . Every few seconds we were as if in broad daylight while next in total darkness: on – off – on – off. . . . Figures illuminated against the sky . . . weird visual experiences. Total light but absolutely no sense of colours – like photographic negative/positive. This added to our sense of fantastic unreality. . . . We had a feeling of being actively driven off the Tor. This was now about three o'clock in the morning. When we arrived at Her base there came torrential rain.

On hearing of the storm, I remarked on its aptitude. According to Robert Graves, whose versions of myth are popular with Monica and her spiritual sisters, the Goddess's arch-enemy was the Thunder-God. Perhaps he was showing his disapproval of the respect being paid to her? Monica had no more to say about the maze, but it would be falsifying her reaction to leave out her final paragraphs.

We drove away, all of us wet and cold, cramped into the one available car. We arrived to a warm flat, with a fire and hot tea and food. Somehow we all felt an amazing energy despite it all – as if we had been storing the discharged energy/electricity of the storm within our bodies and psyches. At dawn a few of us drove back yet again to the Tor. We climbed up yet again, but this time taking the shortest path. The sun was not visible, and this time we found ourselves pelted by a hailstorm! Yet again we fled down the slopes and arrived back at the flat yet again wet through and through.

The strange thing about this night was not only the wild storm, but also what happened to some of us in the weeks following; the profound effect it seemed to have on us. One of the women went back home and had far-reaching discussions with her husband about their life together. Another woman ... found a few days later that while meditating she went into a trance that lasted many hours. She was unable to move or bring herself out of it. This had never happened to her before.

I myself found that I kept seeing images of the out-of-time-and-space distortions of the Tor that can clearly be seen and felt at certain points. . . . I am convinced that the ancients did these alterations of the mound deliberately so as to remove you into an experience of the otherworld – not being able to locate yourself in space, to give you a feeling of the fantastic and other reality; strange energies being summoned up in the landscape.

Monica's closing paragraph has a likeness to my own first impressions of Glastonbury, which I struggled to put in words in the opening section of *King Arthur's Avalon*, briefly quoted on page 132. Here an artist is speaking, and her comments carry more weight than mine. As for the Tor's 'profound effect', it seems to have spread beyond the ranks of the maze-walkers. Some months after that phenomenal night, a woman who did not live in Glastonbury told me that in a late stage of pregnancy, she had been irresistibly drawn to go there and climb the Tor. Soon afterwards she gave birth to a daughter. This did not strike her as remarkable till she heard that the same had happened to a friend of hers, with the same conclusion. Was there something about the Tor, she wondered, which had begun attracting pregnant women? I was able to add to the story, with variants. Three leading members of the Glastonbury Women's Group were all expecting children, and two of them had taken part in the maze-threading. In 1981 all three produced daughters. Well, if the ritual unleashed an *ewig-weibliche* energy, I cannot help it.

This feminist exploit had one further result. A few months after it, an American TV company happened to be making a programme called *In Search of the Holy Grail*. Learning of the Tor maze, and Russell's theory that maze-threading was ancestral to the Grail Quest, the producer came to Glastonbury with a helicopter. He assembled some of Kathy's maze-walkers and shot an aerial film of them filing along the terraces again. The original Grail having doubtless been a female symbol, they could allow it a place in the Goddess's sanctuary. They walked in daylight this time, carrying their torches, but not lighting them.

5

To revert to the problems of the maze. The truth is clear, yet bewildering. This pattern appears in only one place with a mythic content which is established and known in detail. When it does, the mythic content is essentially right. It tallies with the clues pointing to what was thought and done at pre-Christian Glastonbury. Yet the American location seems to rule out any argument from one to the other. They cannot be connected.

If it were a matter of design only, we might dispense with any idea of a connection. The identity might be merely an accident. Or it might be due to identical projection from the Jungian 'Collective Unconscious'. This was more or less Geoffrey Russell's opinion. The spiral could certainly be viewed as a specimen of the kind of pattern Jung called a mandala, which is said to symbolize the psyche, and to focus on a centre which is the true Self. I have suggested that this concept may explain the ability of some people – but only some – to see the Glastonbury Zodiac. Mazes in general plainly are mandalic. They can be construed as

Avalonian Quest

leading inward, through the convolutions of experience, to a goal which is self-knowledge, integration, fulfilment.

Jungian theory might credit the Cretan spiral with a special and heightened rightness. Mandalas, whether planned as sacred diagrams or spun out of patients' imaginations, supposedly tend to have a three-motif or a four-motif. Three and four are the key numbers in their symmetry. We keep finding triangles, crosses, squares. After a fashion, the Cretan spiral embodies both numbers. Its inward movement is in three phases, of which the first two are broken by a return outwards, and the third reaches the centre; while the lines forming the pattern end at four points. The latter feature, in the Hopi Mother Earth version, is emphasized by its expounders. They explain the four line-endings as standing for four directional landmarks in the journey of life.

Russell said the spiral first came to him in 1944 in a sort of vision, without previous conscious knowledge. He learned long afterwards about its other, more objective forms at Cnossus and elsewhere. He also learned that Dr C. A. Meier, who headed the Jung Institute at Zurich in succession to Jung himself, had recorded the case of a woman patient who drew the spiral unprompted, as a therapeutic mandala of her own. By that time Russell had come to suspect its presence on the Tor. In 1968 he discussed his theory with Dr Meier, who, understandably, took a Jungian view of the matter and remarked how 'thrilled' his late mentor would have been.

All that Jung says about mandalas may be correct, though not all the specimens in his published selection are convincing. Purely as a design, the Cretan spiral might find a niche with the rest of them, and look better than some. One interesting aspect of it has been pointed out by Dr Robert P. Thomas. If we number the paths, starting from the outermost, it becomes clear that a maze-threader's transitions from circuit to circuit form a neat series: three steps inwards from the perimeter to the third path, followed by one step outwards to the second, one step outwards to the first, and three steps in again to the fourth; then three steps in again, one out, one out, and three in to the centre. 3, 1, 1, 3; 3, 1, 1, 3. A maze track with the same number of circuits can be drawn in other ways, but in no other way, it seems, with such an exact rhythm and symmetry. We could imagine different devisers of sacred diagrams hitting on this one independently for aesthetic reasons.

But the known mythic and symbolic contents, however puzzling, show that this cannot be the whole answer. It is not a matter of design only. The Labyrinth motif and the Troy motif imply at least some transmission from locale to locale, and the Hopi-Glastonbury echoes, despite the huge spatial gap, are also a deterrent to the idea of independent invention. Those echoes oblige us to face a daunting question. Is there any way to conceive of the design being spread about with a Goddess and Underworld content (as the cross has been spread about with a Christian content), so as to reach both Somerset and Arizona?

It might be pictured as part of some religious 'package' at an unknown centre, a very long time ago. From there it was carried in three directions – to the British Isles, to North America, to the central and eastern Mediterranean. In Britain at first, and in part of America, it kept its symbolism. In the Mediterranean world the package became involved with other cults, other myths. To judge from Crete the main meanings may have been retained at an early stage, but with the passage of time they were altered or, at any rate, obscured.

If there is any ground for thinking that such a diffusion could have happened, we might be able to identify the starting-point. We might glimpse a context where a sacred design could have been ancestral to both the Tor maze and the Hopi Mother Earth symbol. Then these two instances of the same image, far apart as they are, could be placed in some sort of relationship. However tenuous such an argument is bound to look, the mystery justifies pursuing it; and even for such an outlandish notion, the clues exist. Simply as hints at matters which may one day be substantiated – that is the utmost – they are worth passing in review before returning to Glastonbury and trying to draw everything together.

CHAPTER TWELVE

A Point of Origin?

I

Hecataeus, in his account of the island and its temple, supplies the first of the hints. Oddly enough it is still a hint even if his reference to the Tor maze is illusory. He is writing about Britons, more especially devotees of the god he calls Apollo, and the god's mother. But his word for them is 'Hyperboreans'. It shows that he thinks of them in relation to a realm of belief outside Britain. To work out why he uses the word, and what he means by it, is – very gradually – to open a door.

People called Hyperboreans figure a number of times in Greek authors. They are defined by character and life-quality rather than geography. Their name is explained as meaning 'dwellers-at-the-back-of-the-north-wind'. Strictly it means 'dwellers-beyond-Boreas', which is not quite the same. The translation of 'Boreas' as 'the north wind' is a sophistication which came only with the invention of exact compass-points. Boreas was originally the strong cold wind which, in Greece, does normally blow from the north, but in some countries may be associated more with the north-east or the east. In the early times when Hyperboreans begin to be spoken of, their location 'beyond Boreas' is imprecise. All we can infer from it is that they were supposed to live on the far side of the place where the cold air started its journey. It implies a myth-image rather than a map-image.

One consequence of their living beyond Boreas was that they enjoyed a calm, kindly climate, untroubled by the bad wind and the weather accompanying it. That notion is present in Hecataeus. He says that their island 'is both fertile and productive of every crop, and since it has an

A Point of Origin?

unusually temperate climate it produces two harvests each year.' A Greek would hardly have said this of Britain, even though it may have been warmer when the report originated. But Hecataeus is not really describing, he is putting in a bit of Hyperborean legend. What is striking is that the same notion re-surfaces, with improvements, in Avalonian legend. Geoffrey of Monmouth's apple-island is 'fortunate' in much the same way. The romancer Chrétien de Troyes says that in the Ile de Voirre – Ynys-witrin – no storm ever strikes, no thunder is ever heard, the weather is always temperate. Tennyson's Arthur passes away to

>   the island-valley of Avilion
> Where falls not hail, or rain, or any snow,
> Nor ever wind blows loudly; but it lies
> Deep-meadow'd, happy, fair with orchard-lawns
> And bowery hollows crown'd with summer sea.

As Monica Sjöö discovered, the reality at Glastonbury can be rather different. Yet on a fine day it is easy to feel that it 'ought' to be more or less as Tennyson says, and really could have been when the water spread round about. Certainly in the mythic background, apart from any actual place, the Hyperborean motif suggests that we are in contact with something here. It remains to be seen what it is.

At the outset the motif explains why Hecataeus picks out, and stresses, the British god identified with Apollo. Wherever the Hyperboreans were imagined to be, they always had a special relationship with him. Apollo's principal home was at Delphi, which, according to the Greeks, was the 'navel' or centre of the earth. There he had his chief oracle. But he left Delphi for three months of every year to visit his Hyperborean friends, in a flying chariot drawn by swans. His practice of visiting them is another touch which occurs in Hecataeus, though the visits happen less often. At Delos, where Apollo was worshipped jointly with his sister Artemis, offerings wrapped in straw used to arrive regularly and were supposed to be of Hyperborean provenance. Close to Artemis' temple was a tomb where semi-divine honours were paid to two Hyperborean maidens who had come to Delos in the first days of its sacredness and died there.

As the belief about the offerings shows, the Greeks assumed, vaguely, that a Hyperborean nation did exist somewhere. It was peaceful, virtuous and happy. The members whom Apollo favoured and visited were a half-divine elite, a community who lived to be a thousand years old, and were beyond mortal access. In the words of the poet Pindar, 'Neither by ship nor on foot couldst thou find the wondrous way to the assembly of the Hyperboreans.' Since they could not be reached by land or water, it must be supposed that they were in the sky, this being the reason why Apollo flew when he paid his visits. The path he travelled by may have been the Milky Way. Northern folklore, in Lithuania for instance, tells of a 'road of birds' leading to the celestial regions. Some version of this idea may have attached itself to Apollo and inspired the imagery of the swan-drawn chariot.

Attempts were made to locate the Hyperboreans as a nation. They were located in different directions at different times, and not, originally, anywhere near Britain. When Hecataeus put them there it was the end of a long westward drift. Nor was this due purely to a change in geographical fancy. There was more to the Hyperborean saga than that.

It began to take shape with one of the most enterprising explorers in early Greek history. His name was Aristeas. He came from the island of Proconnesus, now Marmara, and was a priest of Apollo in the seventh century BC. Becoming interested in his god's link with the Hyperboreans, he set out, with fine practicality, to look for them himself: at least for those who might be encountered at ground level. He returned safely from his quest, and either wrote, or supplied the information for, a description of it in a poem entitled *Arimaspea* which was circulating between 670 and 600 BC. The text has long since vanished – a sad loss – but other authors quote or paraphrase portions of it. These show a knowledge of Asian peoples and folklore which suggest that Aristeas did make a very long journey, northwards and eastwards.

A Point of Origin?

He never reached the Hyperboreans. However, he did reach a place where he believed he was getting reports of them from the natives. These were the Issedonians. Beyond them, they said, were the Arimaspians. Beyond the Arimaspians was an area rich in gold, with griffins guarding it. In that land was a cave where Boreas lived. From it, presumably, the cold air-streams burst forth, pouring over Asia and veering down into Greece. Beyond the cave, just where they should be, lived the Hyperboreans.

Various clues indicate that Aristeas called a halt to his journey somewhere in the region of Lake Balkhash and the remoter approaches of the Altai mountains. He says things about the Scythian nomads in Russia which point to first-hand acquaintance. His story of griffins watching over deposits of gold sounds like pure fable. But there actually are gold deposits in the Altai country, and the name 'Altai' means 'golden'. The griffin story can be recognized, and supports Aristeas. It is a variant of a Mongolian legend which tells of colossal ants doing the same. This curious yarn spread widely, appearing in Chinese writings, in the Indian epic *Mahabharata*, and in the *History* of Herodotus. But these literary versions never give the monsters their correct location, whereas Aristeas does, more or less. He would seem to have heard it near the source. Boreas' cave is another persuasive touch. It is a piece of folklore heard to this day in the country towards the Altai. The terrific winds in the Dzungarian Gate east of Lake Balkhash are said to issue from a cave.

Aristeas' griffin region would be, roughly, the north angle of Sinkiang, extending up to the place where Russia, China and Mongolia meet. The Hyperborean territory would cover most of the Altai range and stretch beyond it, into Mongolia, and perhaps towards Lake Baikal. It has been suggested that Aristeas was hearing rumours of the Chinese, who, being civilized, might have sounded 'Hyperborean'. But the Chinese were surely too far away.

Indian legend, contemplating north-central Asia from a different angle, told of a people who dwelt happily among golden sands and fruitful orchards, and lived to an immense age. They were called the Northern Kurus. When

Greeks met Indians and heard of them, they took them to be Hyperboreans. As we shall see, the same information or quasi-information which reached Aristeas may also have reached India.

Another Greek who looks at the Hyperborean problem is Herodotus, in the fifth century BC. He gives a sketchy description of the Issedonians, placing them vaguely east of the Urals, and quotes Aristeas on the Arimaspians beyond and the Hyperboreans who 'extend to the sea'. The implication is that no other nation was reported between them and the Ocean which Greeks believed to encircle the world. He also quotes Aristeas as saying that the Arimaspians had only one eye. That detail is meant to cast doubt on his reliability. So are one or two hints that he was a dubious mystic and bogus wonder-worker. Herodotus' scepticism is sensible, but he is taking it unduly far. His own chief Hyperborean interest is in the offerings that came to Delos. He outlines the traditions underlying the custom, and explains that the offerings came via Scythia (here perhaps meaning Rumania) to the Adriatic, and thence to Greece. To judge from that route, wherever the alleged Hyperboreans were who sent the offerings, they were not as far east as the Altai mountains.

In spite of what Pindar says about the Hyperboreans' inaccessibility, the same poet tells us that Hercules visited their land in his third labour. No doubt he is thinking here of the mundane Hyperboreans at ground level. Hercules had to capture a golden-horned hind belonging to Artemis. It was one of five, and had escaped while she was harnessing the other four as a chariot-team. Hercules followed the animal for a whole year, evidently travelling a long way from Greece. He caught the hind in the Hyperboreans' country, where he met Artemis, who seemingly shared her brother's attachment to them. Pindar is obscure as to where Hercules went. Some of the material of the legend may have come from northern Europe, because the hind sounds like a reindeer. Within the Greek orbit there was no other species of deer with horned females, or a willingness to be harnessed for drawing vehicles. However, Pindar makes Hercules go to the Hyperborean land again, and bring back

A Point of Origin?

the wild olive. He also asserts that it lay among 'the shady sources of the Danube'. Whatever all these details imply, and however hard it is to make sense of them, they place the Hyperboreans in Europe rather than the remote recesses of Asia.

The puzzling allusion to the Danube can in fact be explained, and it is the key to what happened next. Early classical authors, including Pindar, thought it rose in the north-east rather than the north-west, probably because of a mistaken generalization about the rivers that empty into the Black Sea. Herodotus calls the Danube a 'Scythian' river after the tribes along its lower reaches, and the phrase shows how easily it could have been grouped with the Dnieper and the Don, also in Scythian country. Its headwaters were supposed to be in a range known as the Rhipaean mountains. A notion was current in the fifth century BC that the Hyperboreans lived among these mountains or just beyond them. Here then is what Pindar has in mind when he places the Hyperboreans at the Danube's sources: they must live there, because they live near the mountains where the sources are.

However, it was already becoming known that the Danube flowed from a different quarter. Despite his calling it a Scythian river, Herodotus says correctly that its source is in 'the country of the Celts', in the west of Europe. With this advance in knowledge the Rhipaean range had to move. The Hyperboreans moved with it, probably about 400 BC. They became confused in Greek minds with the Celts themselves, some of whom, as Herodotus knew, lived around the Danube's real source. A few decades after the Celtic sack of Rome in 390, we find an author supposing that the sackers were Hyperboreans. Posidonius, two centuries or so later again, equates the Rhipaean mountains with the Alps and places the Hyperboreans vaguely on the far side, thus involving them, again, in the Celtic world.

Hecataeus, however, had already taken a step of a more definite kind by shifting them to Britain. When we read the passage where he does so, we can see that he is following a trend. But he is also raising a new issue. No one could have imagined that the Danube rose in an island! The

Danube motif brings the Hyperboreans across continental Europe, but it cannot account for this leap over the Channel. What is Hecataeus thinking of? On the face of it, there must be a reason powerful enough to outweigh other indications of the Hyperboreans' whereabouts. None of them can be made to fit Britain, yet he puts the Hyperboreans there. The only place to look is in his own text. What can he have heard about Britain which led him to think it was their home?

His outstanding factual detail is that reference to the nineteen-year cycle. It points to Druid information. In Hecataeus we may have the earliest instance of a Greek notion which can be traced more clearly later – that in some sense the Druids, the Celtic priest-magicians, *were* Hyperboreans. It was rooted in the myth of the Hyperborean elite, Apollo's favoured community, and in a view which stressed religious rather than national character. After the long shift across the map, it was hard to give the Hyperboreans an identity as a settled people. But the idea that they were masters of a divinely-inspired northern wisdom, who might wander and spread and appear in various places, could be sustained.

It linked up with something else. Among the Greeks of the classical era, the chief body of wisdom, in that esoteric sense, was the Pythagorean. By his work in mathematics, and his conclusions on the importance of counting and measuring, Pythagoras laid the basis for exact science. However, he also invented numerology, and the school he founded had a mystical bias. His disciples believed in reincarnation and had dietary and other taboos. The sect (as it virtually became) had a special devotion to Apollo. The founder was said to have been a son of the god. Interest in Apollo promoted interest in his Hyperborean friends. Pythagoras may have been influenced by Aristeas' report.

A legend grew up about a Hyperborean sage named Abaris who had come to Greece. In earlier versions he carried a golden arrow. In later versions he rode through the air on it. Herodotus heard of the story, which, in his time, was already burgeoning, and quoted it in the same spirit as he quoted Aristeas: 'As for the tale of Abaris, who

5. Chalice Well, showing the lid designed by Frederick Bligh Bond.

6. Vertical aerial view of Glastonbury Tor. Owing to the angle at which the sun strikes it, the terraces show as lighter on the north side and darker on the

7. Course followed by the maze, reconstructed in keeping with Geoffrey Russell's theory. It is shown by the thick continuous line beginning at the left. Where this line is broken, erosion and other factors have made the course less clear. The asterisked lines show where 'ghost-terraces' run for an appreciable distance. The external dotted line marks the perimeter of the maze system (not the boundary hedge of the Tor property, which is left unmarked to avoid confusion). The distortion of the pattern is in no sense arbitrary. It corresponds to the shape of the hill. Maze-paths, or remnants of them, traverse every suitable part of it. Areas which they seem to avoid are simply areas which are too steep for them.

8. Distant view of Chalice Hill (left) and the Tor

A Point of Origin?

is said to have gone with his arrow all round the world without once eating, I shall pass it by in silence.' Some Pythagoreans, however, claimed that the arrow was a gift from Apollo which enabled its owner not only to fly but to cure diseases and make himself invisible. Abaris had presented it to Pythagoras, and Pythagoras, in return, had taught him philosophy. Nor was that the final step. Later it was asserted that Abaris taught Pythagoras. A Hyperborean sage had to be more than a pupil, however worthy. He had to be a master.

Besides transplanting the Hyperboreans into Celtic Europe, the Greeks discovered the Druids. A religious order like this, with its mysterious forest sanctuaries and its large claims about secret doctrine, was exciting to those of a similar turn of mind. Being Celtic, it was in the right milieu to be Hyperborean. That is why Druids began to blend with Hyperboreans and to be claimed as custodians of the northern wisdom. The opinion took hold slowly but strongly, especially among a Greek coterie in Alexandria. By now the old confidence in Greek superiority to barbarians had waned. The modish thing was to romanticize the noble savage, and the Druids were beneficiaries. They were not the only ones. Persian Magi and Hindu Brahmins were discussed with the same ill-informed reverence, and Pythagorean lore was ascribed to them. But in one respect the Druids outshone the rest. They taught, and Celts accepted, an emphatic doctrine of immortality. While Asian systems also affirmed it, in one way or another, the Druid version had a vividness and conviction which put it in a class by itself. A Celt could borrow on an IOU payable in the next world.

The doctrine of a full-blown afterlife was unfamiliar in the current thinking of Mediterranean peoples. Generally speaking, individuals survived only as bloodless and ineffectual shades. Pythagoreans were the most conspicuous of the few who did look to something more. In their case it was reincarnation. So the Druids were hailed (probably with only a very qualified accuracy) as believers in an afterlife on the same lines, and as good Pythagoreans, perhaps initiates of the school. They even had an advantage.

Avalonian Quest

Pythagoreans and Druids had drunk alike from the fount of Hyperborean Apollo, but the Druids had taught this particular piece of wisdom to a whole people. The hint that they were actually better than the Greeks bore fruit when Alexandrians began to turn Christian, and take a less lofty view of Pythagoras. Then the parallel was turned round. Fathers of the Church such as Clement and Cyril claimed that Pythagoras was a pupil of the Druids.

It was another version of the final glorification of Abaris. But it was, or could be, more specific. While there were Druids throughout the Celtic lands, they had their advanced colleges in Britain – so at least Julius Caesar heard. Hence an opinion recorded in all seriousness by Milton, in *Areopagitica*: 'Writers of good antiquity and ablest judgment have been perswaded that ev'n the school of Pythagoras, and the Persian wisdom took beginning from the old Philosophy of this Iland.'

To revert to Hecataeus, he is many years prior to acrobatics such as these. But his stress on religion shows that he thinks of the Hyperboreans in the semi-mystical way. He has heard about Britain's Celtic people and Druid priesthood with their astronomical lore. That is why he says the island is inhabited by Hyperboreans, and gives them and their country suitable attributes. He may have picked up the same piece of information Caesar did, making Britain the headquarters of Druid teaching: a place, therefore, not merely Hyperborean but pre-eminently so.

In all this strange history there is only one authentic first-hand investigator, the adventurous Aristeas at the very beginning. He alone gives the Hyperboreans a location which there is any reason to accept. So far as his account can be pieced together, he makes them the people of the Altaic region. After that the Hyperborean notion merely drifts, carried westward by rumours and guesses and geographical blunders, until it reappears in Britain in a new guise, referring to a northern wisdom more or less equated with Druidism . . . or with what some Greeks imagined Druidism to be. It is also involved with the Pythagorean system. The only way to accommodate all the data would be to suppose that some sort of 'Hyperborean' lore arose

A Point of Origin?

among the Altaic people, and was transmitted to Britain by Druidism, and to the Hellenic world via Apollo-worship and its Pythagorean outgrowth. I do not think any Greek takes such a comprehensive view as to say it, but the story as a whole implies it, so far as it implies anything coherent.

2

Wildly fanciful as all this appears, there was something in it. Those who built it up blundered their way collectively into a ghostly rightness. The fables and speculations are fables and speculations indeed. Yet they dimly reflect real happenings in the religious history of the Eurasian landmass ... or so it looks. The Hyperborean clue picks out a place of origin which was so in fact and not merely in fantasy. From there – approximately from there, at any rate – certain influences did spread to the British Isles and the Hellenic world. It can hardly escape notice that these are two of the three areas where the maze-pattern occurs. To argue on such lines sounds like myth-making in the true neo-Glastonian manner. But it remains strictly within the bounds of established scholarship.

The Mediterranean connection supplies more documentation than the British, and reveals the probable process more cogently. Professor W. K. C. Guthrie defined it in his discussion of the Apollo cult in *The Greeks and their Gods*. He pointed out that although Apollo rose to greatness in Greece, he entered it as a foreigner. Like other imported deities he was given a Greek birthplace, Delos, and a parentage to fit him into the Olympian family. But he was known very early in Asia Minor, and the legend about his Delphic oracle betrayed the truth, or part of it: he arrived at the holy place as an outsider, slew a resident dragon, and took possession.

He became very Greek. Yet much of his cult was alien, an affair of ecstasies and inspiration and oracular outpourings, with an un-Greek missionary zeal – this latter feature accounting for the strength of Apollo-worship in

Italy. His devotees, including Pythagoras himself, were credited with astral travelling, bilocation, magical healing and kindred feats. Another distinctive aspect was the prominence of women: not only Delphic priestesses, but women whom Pythagoras enrolled in his school on an equal basis with men.

Guthrie suggested – and his argument stands – that Apollo's Hyperborean link supplies the answer. All these un-Greek elements are characteristic of the native shamanistic religion of Siberia and Mongolia. The shaman is in essence a special kind of medicine-man. Or woman. It is likely that shamanesses were once the more important, though they have not been so in historical times. Guthrie's insight was reinforced by another scholar, E. R. Dodds, who traced many parallels in detail. It was approved from the other end (so to speak) by Mircea Eliade, the major authority on shamanism.

On this showing, Apollo made his annual Hyperborean journey to revisit his old home. He had begun as a god of shamans far off in Asia, borne to Greece by wandering priests, healers and soothsayers. Afterwards he became civilized, a patron of music, mathematics and other arts. But he never lost the traces of his primitive origin. When these were taken up and refurbished by the Pythagoreans, they became part of the stock-in-trade of a mystical system. This transmission of influence is the fact which was given legendary form in the tale of Abaris. As Professor Dodds put it, if Abaris existed, he may well have been a shaman. Even his golden arrow is an accurate touch. Arrows are symbols of the magical flight which shamans claim to perform; and they figure in rituals where they are pointed at those for whom prayers are said, and sometimes have pieces of gold bound to them.

Shamanism, as studied by anthropologists, may well be degenerate. Among the Mongols, the missionaries of Lamaistic Buddhism made strenuous efforts to suppress it, and it had to adapt to survive at all, crumbling and altering in the process. In Siberia, Russian rule in successive forms has ground it down. Long ago it may have been closer to the condition of a true 'wisdom'. But even the enfeebled

A Point of Origin?

remnant has points of deep interest, the more so because of their geography.

Aristeas' Hyperborean homeland – the only one, it must be repeated, which could be real – is around and beyond the Altai range. A loosely Altaic region in Siberia and Mongolia, stretching from the mountains towards Lake Baikal, is still the locale of a shamanism with distinguishing features. One of them is peculiarly apt and peculiarly intriguing. Shamanistic belief and practice always embody numerical factors with cosmic bearings. A shaman, for instance, may visit the gods by a trance-journey upwards through a fixed number of celestial stages, or downwards through a fixed number of infernal ones. He may express his magic number in some such device as a set of bells attached to his outfit. This in itself has a curious, far-off kinship with Pythagoras' numerology. But in Altaic shamanism, to an extent not found in other varieties, a favoured number is seven . . . and Apollo was a septenary god. He was born on the seventh day of a month; his festivals were on the seventh days of the months they occurred in; his emblem was a seven-stringed lyre; over the entrance of his temple at Delphi were inscribed the maxims of Seven Wise Men; one of his most notorious exploits was his massacre of the seven sons of Amphion, king of seven-gated Thebes. And it scarcely needs to be pointed out again that the maze-spiral has seven back-and-forth circlings, vividly depicted on the coin which has Apollo's head on the obverse.

It may be objected that seven is a universal magical number and the correspondence therefore means nothing. I explored this topic in a book called *The Ancient Wisdom*. It is too large a matter to discuss here, but the truth is that seven is far from universal in early periods; it appears strongly in some cultures but not in others. Enough for the moment to say that Apollo is the only septenary Greek god (except to the extent that his sister Artemis shares this quality), and that Altaic shamans are the only conspicuously septenary shamans.

With the British Isles and their Celtic paganism, documentation is more meagre but the impression is much the same. Anne Ross in *Pagan Celtic Britain* contends bluntly that the Druids were, in effect, shamans. Drawing on Irish sources, which preserve more of Celtic antiquity than British ones, she cites a description of the great Druid Mogh Ruith. He put on a 'dark grey hornless bull-hide' and a 'white-speckled bird headpiece with fluttering wings', and rose into the air – a typical picture of the appearance and supposed feats of powerful shamans in Asia. Other similar features of Druidism were the long initiatory training in wild places, and the claim to have direct contact with the spirit world and to converse with gods, all in association with magical healing techniques.

Professor Stuart Piggott sees more in Druidism than shamanism pure and simple. However, he allows that it absorbed elements, including shamanistic ones, which were much older and were in some cases derived from faraway sources. In the Mogh Ruith incident he discerns 'a fragment from a very archaic substrate of belief'. To quote at more length:

> The position of the Druids in European prehistory renders it improbable that their religion . . . did not draw on a long past of varied cultural traditions, not all necessarily Celtic nor even Indo-European. . . . There is a long prehistory behind the Druids. . . .
>
> [Shamanism] need not have been the whole content of Palaeolithic and Mesolithic religion but it could have been an important component, and one that could form a substrate in the ancient European tradition. . . .
>
> By the time of the historically documented Druids the background of possible religious tradition would then be roughly as follows. . . . There are three main antecedent phases. The first would be the traditions, predominantly Indo-European, going back to the second millennium BC and perhaps to its beginnings. Behind this again would be the wholly obscure religions of the Neolithic agriculturists. . . . Finally, underlying all, there would be the beliefs and rites of the hunting peoples of pre-agricultural Europe which might well have contained elements surviving in shamanism. It is a pedigree which could be a good 20,000 years in length.

A Point of Origin?

Folk-wanderings undoubtedly spread ancient concepts, ancient practices, ancient rituals, over an immense area. The Celts' ancestors drifted into central and western Europe from farther east. They had been in contact with peoples living farther east still, among them the Scythians, whose religion included shamanistic features. Piggott cites two items reaching out beyond, and implying 'a curious link with Central Asia'. One is a Celtic oath. An Irish chieftain's bodyguard swore to stand firm 'though the earth should split under us and the sky above on us'. The phrase might be thought a cliché, but in fact the only close parallel is in an inscription in the Turkic language, on the Orkhon River south of Lake Baikal: 'So long as the heaven above and the earth below have not opened, O Turkish people, who can destroy your rule?' Piggott's other item is archaeological. The Druids – or, at any rate, Celtic priests of the right period – made sacrificial offerings of the hides and bones of horses and oxen. Excavation shows that they favoured skulls and leg-bones. The same practice flourished in southern Russia from the third millennium BC onwards, and it has been noted in recent times as a custom of shamans, especially in the Altai.

We have a linkage then, not merely with Asia but with the same general region, the same people, even apparently the same Hyperboreans whom Aristeas located. Little can be proved as to the contents of the package that made its way westwards. But a hint that these were more than trivial appears in the Celtic legend of Merlin, who, in early versions, is an inspired madman prophesying in a forest and observing the stars – a kind of shaman, and also a kind of Druid.

What emerges is that the Cretan-type spiral could have reached two of the three areas where it is found, if it began as a magic symbol among Altaic shamans or their spiritual ancestors, a very long time ago. It could have reached the Aegean with votaries of Apollo, and the British Isles with the Druids, or rather with precursors from whom the Druids learned – precursors living far enough back to be plausible as the makers of the Tor maze. Perhaps, in the former diffusion, Apollo was not the chief element and only rose to prominence later. But if he rode on a shamanistic stream, the spiral's connection with him, however frail, takes on a new interest. Once again: the coin has his profile on it; the Labyrinth dance circled round his altar at his Delian 'birthplace'; the temple at Cumae, with the Labyrinth portrayed on its gate, belonged to him – so at least Virgil says. In the last case we do not know whether Virgil pictured the actual maze-design representing the Labyrinth, as it did at Pompeii. But he gives a full description of Apollo's Sibyl pouring out oracular sayings in a frenzy of divine inspiration, such as Guthrie and others regard as shamanistic.

Is anything like the maze-pattern known at or near the presumed source, in the Altaic country itself? Objects retrieved from a cave-burial at Mal'ta, fifty-five miles northwest of Irkutsk, include an oblong panel of mammoth ivory with lines of dots on it. These curl around, forming designs. In the dominant design the line goes spiralling out from the centre of the panel (or inwards to it, depending where you start), and it goes round seven times. This is a septenary spiral much older than any other. It might be an ancestor of more complex ones, and as Dr Thomas's analysis shows, once you start trying to complicate such a spiral

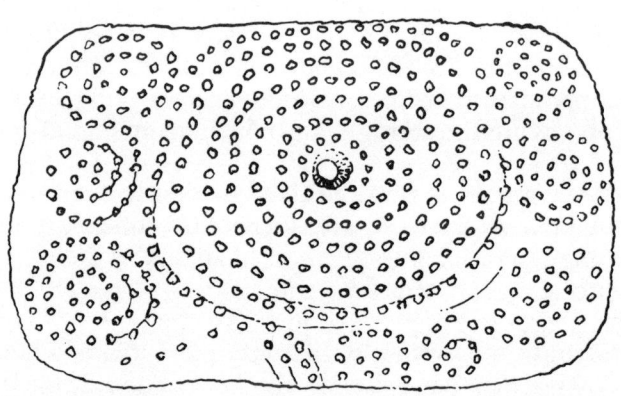

xiii. Spiral design on ivory panel from Mal'ta, Siberia

A Point of Origin?

at all, the peculiar elegance of the Cretan pattern makes it a likely result.

The Mal'ta objects include female figurines in a well-marked style. Similar figurines can be traced spreading westwards, but those are copies, and cruder. The Altai-Baikal region seems to have made the prototypes. While their meaning is open to debate, this area could have been the senior centre of a goddess cult. A septenary spiral, even a simple one, in that company is a datum not to be despised.

3

We come finally to the locale of the Hopi Mother Earth symbol. Two of the three diffusions can now be seen as possible. The third remains. Could a shamanistic package from the Altai-Baikal region have found its way to Arizona?

It could. The links here are very tenuous and doubtful. But an Asian centre, more or less as implied by the other lines of argument, would have been the only source from which a diffusion to the third area could ever have happened. The ancestors of the native American peoples crossed over from Siberia, via what is now the Bering Strait, and perhaps also along the chain of the Aleutians. There is no certainty as to when the migrations started. Archaeology has tended to push it back in time. It may have been under way thirty thousand years ago. It probably went on till the melting of the oversize polar ice-caps released masses of water, raised the sea-level, and broke previously-existing land bridges. The present degree of separation between the continents was reached towards 6000 BC. After that, further migration on a large scale is unlikely to have occurred, though minor movements by water could have gone on indefinitely.

Most of the descendants of the transplanted Asians ceased to be Asian, except in the sense of their remote ethnic kinship. The Eskimo of Alaska and northern Canada continued to resemble the Eskimo of Siberia, as they do

Avalonian Quest

still, but the Indians farther south created new cultures of their own. With these it is usual, and usually correct, to deny that any specific Asian elements survived. However, one thing does seem to have travelled to America; and this is the very thing which travelled in the other two directions as well – shamanism. The American shaman, with his ritual outfit, his trances and visions, his contact with spirits, his mystic affiliation to animals, is quite like the Asian shaman. Piggott is prepared to see the migration from Old World to New as underlying 'the recent distribution of shamanism, particularly in Siberia and America – among Tungas, Buriats, Altaians and Lapps, and from Eskimos through Chuckchees and Crees to Tierra del Fuego'.

One feature that reinforces the case is the antiquity and distribution of a religious reverence for bears. They have long been objects of awe right across northern Asia and far into America. Several reasons are apparent. Simply as an animal the bear has a character of its own. It combines fearful strength with a quasi-human quality, eating the same foods as human beings, taking up similar postures, standing on its hind legs. (The Apaches politely call the male bear 'the Old Man'.) Its life-style is symbolic: the winter sleep and spring waking suggest the seasonal cycle, the annual death-and-rebirth of nature. Understandably many peoples have had bear-myths and bear-rituals.

Finns, Lapps, the Ainu of Japan, all revere the bear. Some Siberian shamans dress in a bear's skin and are believed to turn into the animal, and in one Tartar dialect the word for a woman-shaman, *utygan*, actually means 'bear'. Medicine-men of the Sioux, Chippewa, Pueblo and Iroquois do much the same as the Siberians, invoking benign bear-gods with healing powers, and assuming their identity. Eskimo shamans receive visitations from the Great Spirit in polar-bear disguise. An American Indian spring ceremony is a 'grizzly bear dance' which mimes the creature's waking up, and the awakening of nature with it. Members of some tribes, until recently, would never kill a bear at all, or lay their hands on a dead one. Others have been willing to kill them for food, but apologize and arrange the remains in a pattern which assures that the bear passes

A Point of Origin?

into the spirit realm intact . . . and such magical laying-out is on record as a Lapp custom also.

The point of dwelling on this is not only that it connects Asian and American shamanism, but that it adds another strand to the Hellenic connection also. Apollo's sister Artemis was (among much else) a goddess of bears, even probably having an ursine guise of her own. Greek myth averred that the constellation Ursa Major, the Great Bear with its seven principal stars, was a companion of hers named Callisto who had been translated into the heavens. Callisto was really an aspect of Artemis rather than a distinct person. The Arcadians of southern Greece had a shrine of Artemis-Callisto. In the Attic festival of Artemis Brauronia, two young girls used to dance wearing dark yellow bear-skin robes. To turn from her worshippers to her brother's, Professor Dodds detects vestigial bear-myths among the Pythagorean legends, and notes a story that Pythagoras himself tamed one, an un-Hellenic feat.

America offers no clues pointing to a source-territory in Asia for its own shamanism. But the mythology of the Hopi, who preserve the maze as the Mother Earth symbol, has two features of special interest. First, it lays a great deal of stress on past migrations. The Hopi ancestors are said to have traversed vast tracts of country. While the tales have no useful geographic content, they suggest a stronger folk-memory of remote origins than most American Indians can show. Secondly, the Hopi have other sacred sevens besides the seven embodied in the maze-pattern. These are related to a creation myth. The primary god Taiowa brought into being another deity, Sotuknang, who then created nine universes. The first two were personal domains for Taiowa and himself. The universes of known life and visible beings number seven. From this reckoning, others follow. The Pleiades – a cluster of stars differently counted by different nations – are made out to be seven by the Hopi because they correspond to the seven universes. There are seven songs concerned with rain-making and other mysteries, which must be sung before the Pleiades dip below the horizon. In other words the Hopi have the

Avalonian Quest

same cosmic number which Altaic shamans have, and other shamans have not, at any rate with the same emphasis.*

In the outcome, the idea of this maze-spiral as a shamanistic symbol remains tenable. It is found in three areas to which shamanistic influence may have spread from an Altaic homeland, and nowhere else. If, at the point of origin, it had a Goddess-and-Underworld content, it could have kept this on two of its journeys, manifesting it at Glastonbury and among the Hopi. It could have lost it, if not perhaps at once, among the complexities of the south, being adopted there into rituals and legends with other meanings. One of those meanings, the Trojan, spread to Britain long after and re-interpreted the pattern, though not everywhere.

Goddess and Underworld motifs are found at the source. The Mal'ta spiral and female figurines *may* be associated. In modern shamanism, goddesses do not play a great part, but shamans are said to be on good terms with a Lady of the Waters and a Lady or Mother of the Animals. Moreover, quite apart from the figurines, there are good grounds for thinking that the female element in shamanism used to be more important, and that the Mother of the Animals (a being who recalls aspects of Artemis) may once have been a mighty goddess. As for the Underworld, that is important still, and in the Altaic scheme it is structured by the mystic seven. Shamans descend in their trances through seven levels to encounter Erlik Khan, lord of the dead, with his seven sons and seven daughters. An Altaic design could have combined the number with Goddess symbolism and Underworld symbolism. The motifs are all present now, and could have been at any time in the past.

It is possible, therefore, that the Tor maze (if real) shares a common origin with the Hopi Mother Earth symbol. The

---

* A correspondent, Mr Alan Plaister, tells me he has traced at least six parallels between Hopi and classical Greek religious practices. He mentions a ritual foot-race and women's ceremonies. Direct influence being ruled out, he favours a common source, which, on the present showing, would be Altaic. Intriguing as the theory is, it blurs the argument, because it implies that far more was transmitted from the source to Greece than the package with Apollo in it.

A Point of Origin?

pattern is the same, if in mirror-image. A symbolism of Goddess and Underworld, preserved by the Hopi to this day, could have reached Glastonbury with it and passed into the later mythology, where the two motifs still seem to appear, fragmented and transformed. To accept this, we would have to suppose that the maze-spiral is immensely ancient and that it began among Altaic shamans . . . or priests or priestesses ancestral to them. Obviously little can be proved except its actual distribution. However, in view of the many things which fit together, I think the Tor maze can at least be made intelligible as belonging to a network of facts in and out of Britain; that the network must be conceived as described, if it exists at all; and that if it does exist, the inescapable inference is that the maze is very old.

CHAPTER THIRTEEN

Sacred Mountains

I

In one respect, the maze as it seemingly occurs on the Tor is different from all other instances of it – in Britain and Ireland, in Italy and Greece and Crete, in Arizona. The others are flat. The one on the Tor is in three dimensions. It goes not merely in-and-out-and-in, but up-and-down-and-up. It is made by terracing a hill in septenary form. Given the Underworld association, that might appear a logical thing to do. Hollow hills are recognized points of entry. Nevertheless there is not, in fact, any other known case.

On this point Dion Fortune had another of her flashes of insight, crazily off-target, yet perceptive. After her reference to the Tor's 'terraced track', she goes on:

> It is well known that the ancients delighted to build their colonial cities upon the same plan as the mother city in the land of their race. Is it possible that our strange pyramidal hill, with its truncated top and its inland side as steep as earth will stand, may have been wrought to that likeness by human hands in memory of the sacred mountain of the mother continent?

The mother continent being, unfortunately, lost Atlantis. Since Atlantis is very thoroughly lost, it is no use hunting there for a prototype. But the guess is more acute than it looks. There actually have been sacred structures representing a sacred mountain. At least one hill has been artificially shaped as an image of it, a tourist attraction to this day in a populous land. As a last major question about the Tor, it is worth asking whether this may be a second way

Sacred Mountains

to relate it to external facts and thereby interpret it. Since the hill itself is not artificial, the question has to be whether its shaping could have reflected any concepts beyond whatever concepts are embodied in the maze as such.

Sacred mountains are widely spread over the world. So are mounds, pyramids and other temples that simulate them. Among the latter group the oldest that can be discussed with any assurance are the ziggurats of Mesopotamia. In their most primitive form these were mounds, heaped up in a land with no high country. Later they became structures. The building of them, by Sumerians and then Babylonians, can be traced from the fourth millennium BC, with advances in technique and developments in meaning.

By slow degrees a significant theme emerges. Mesopotamian temples have names like 'House of the Mountain' and 'Mountain of God'. The basic notion is that the temple is a magical model of a prototype mountain, made in the same spirit as a witch's image of a person which 'is' the person. In the early phases it is doubtful whether the prototype mountain was thought of as having a physical reality or location. It may have been vaguely imagined that it accounted for the night, because the sun retired behind it. But in essence it was a mythical centre of chthonic energy, the dwelling of a god who gave the land its strength and fertility.

Presently, religion moved into a more urbanized phase. The Sumerians' sacred capital Nippur was regarded as the world's centre, and its main temple-complex, the House of the Mountain, was the 'bond of heaven and earth'. A mystical shaft passed vertically through it, upwards and downwards, holding the universe together above and below, and the sky rotated around the top. Such a cosmic conception has been dubbed 'hierocentric'. It was taken over in the second millennium BC by the Babylonians, who made Babylon the world-centre, with a temple called the Mount of the Mountains of All Lands; and later by the Israelites, who located the centre at Zion, the ridge of Ophel which was the nucleus of Jerusalem, where the Lord's Temple stood. According to rabbinic tradition, this was the primal rock which God made first, building the rest of creation round it. Now it was his earthly home. The idea of Jerusalem as the centre of a flat earth passed into Christianity and can be seen persisting in medieval maps.

These sacred world-centres supply some more instances of seven as a sacred number. It may have been accidental that Nippur had seven gates. But there is no doubt about the great ziggurat of Babylon in its later glories, the Etemenanki, 'Temple of the Foundation of Heaven and Earth'. It was a kind of pyramid or cone 250 feet high. Ascent was by a ceremonial way spiralling round the outside seven times, from the base to the flat top where, in a shrine, the city's priest-king encountered gods and solemnized a ritual of divine marriage. (Geoffrey Russell noted the Etemenanki as a parallel to the Tor.) As for Jerusalem, the Lord's presence in the Temple was symbolized by the huge seven-branched lampstand, the Menorah.

There was, however, a difficulty in the idea of a capital city's temple as the cosmic centre. Of course it could be the centre of an earth which was flat, or, according to some, convex. But a shaft or axle going up from it vertically could not be the centre of the heavens. The starry dome did not revolve around the zenith. It revolved around the celestial pole. That point in the sky is roughly marked today by the Pole Star. Before about 500 BC it was in the constellation Draco. Wherever it was, inhabitants of the Middle East always saw the sky-centre as away to the north. Therefore, a new factor had to be added to the cosmic system, and the prototype mountain of mythology began to acquire a new role.

This, it should be said first, happened quite early. Scholars have argued that it was bound up with Babylonian astronomy and a scheme of seven planets, which achieved working order in the sixth century BC. Such an idea would have trouble with the septenary structure of some temples which were older. The first cosmic revision did involve the magic seven, but despite an inveterate delusion on this topic, the heptad concerned was not the heptad of planets but the seven-star constellation Ursa Major. (I believe I succeeded in proving this in *The Ancient Wisdom*.) Aware-

Sacred Mountains

ness of the constellation long preceded awareness of the planets. It was associated with the pole of the sky, which it circled and pointed to without ever setting, and it was believed to power the heavenly rotation, being analogous to a team of oxen turning a mill. Proof that the Sumerians related it to the sky-centre is that in the early astrological scheme, Nippur was matched with the Bear and the constellation was called the bond of heaven.

That phrase reflects the problem which the revised cosmology had to solve. If the 'bond of heaven and earth' in the central city did not sustain the sky-centre, what did? The ancient divine mountain, never banished from consciousness, now changed in character and function. It became the Mountain of Heaven and Earth, or World-Mountain, supporting the sky as a dome pivoted on its summit, dominated by Ursa Major. It towered above all other mountains, and was an abode of gods. On its heights was an earthly paradise. Below, the disc-world of humankind spread around, and the centre of that, as ever, was the temple in the capital city. This was mystically identified with the mountain and at one with it.

Astronomy required the mountain to be in the north, because the celestial pole was. The Sumerians may never have been very explicit on that point. The Babylonians were a little more so, to judge from the Old Testament. The prophet Isaiah denounces the king of Babylon (14:13), accusing him of impious pride: 'You said in your heart, "I will ascend to heaven; above the stars of God I will set my throne on high; I will sit on the mount of assembly in the far north."' The 'assembly' is the assembly of gods on the mountain, with whom the king aspires to be equal.

With Isaiah's fellow-Israelites, the editing of scripture, though efficient, did not quite blot out older beliefs. Zion is referred to once or twice in the Bible as Safon, and Safon was probably a Canaanite version of the world-mountain. Certainly the Canaanites regarded Safon as being in the north, and as having an earthly paradise on it. Seemingly Zion 'was' Safon. A more surprising text is Psalm 48, verses 1–2. This refers to God's 'holy mountain' as 'Mount Zion in the far north'. The 'far north' is the same quarter in which Isaiah places the Babylonians' divine 'mount of assembly'. Ezekiel, speaking of 'Eden, the garden of God', puts it on the 'holy mountain of God', and here too the mountain can hardly be the hill in Jerusalem, as the description shows (28:11-16). At the beginning of his visions the same prophet, being at the time in Babylonia, sees the Lord riding in his chariot out of the north (1:4). There, it must be inferred, the Lord has a home other than the Zion we know. The holy hill where he had his Temple was at some stage an *alter ego* of another Zion, another divine dwelling-place, the world-mountain in the north or something like it.

That impression is reinforced by a strange rabbinic teaching: that the Temple site in Jerusalem is the highest point of the earth. Obviously it is not, and no fanciful distortion of the earth's shape will make it so. If you approach Jerusalem by the uphill road from Jericho, the city is silhouetted against the sky; but when you are in it, Zion is plainly lower than the neighbouring hills. Again Zion seems to have undergone a mystical identification, and in this case, with a mountain conceived as the world's highest. The world-mountain was so conceived. In the Lord's eyes Zion is the same. Isaiah (2:2-3) prophesies that the hill with its Temple will become literally and visibly what it already is mystically.

> It shall come to pass in the latter days that the mountain of the house of the Lord shall be established as the highest of the mountains, and shall be raised above the hills; and all the nations shall flow to it, and many peoples shall come, and say: 'Come, let us go up to the mountain of the Lord, to the house of the God of Jacob.'

That was as far as Hebrew minds could carry the notion. Zion represented the cosmic mountain, or was a bilocated version of it, at present disguised but destined to be revealed for what it was. It could not be any more explicit. No Israelite would have dreamed of following in the ways of the Babylonians by making the hill, or the Temple, into a physical image. Israelite contempt for a structure such as the Etemenanki shows in the tale of the Tower of Babel, which was meant to reach up to heaven, and did not.

Traces of the same mode of thinking may appear in Greece. The Greeks knew nothing of the mountain as such. But they too claimed that the centre of the earth was in their own country, at Apollo's Delphi; and the awareness that there had to be a separate sky-centre, in the north, may have had something to do with Apollo's visits to the Hyperboreans by the aerial route. He was supplying a link between the centres in person.

The mountain figures in plain terms in Iranian legend, where the gods living on it are said to number seven. It is in India, however, that it grows to its most flamboyant stature. The Hindus had no capital city regarded as the earth's centre. If, as has been supposed, they adopted the mountain under Mesopotamian influence, they adopted it ready-made; and they placed it at the centre of earth as well as heaven, the mid-point of the cosmos. They gave it the famous name Meru.

Meru is far north of India, and made of gold. With its base at the centre of the flat earth, and its apex at the hub of the domed sky, it 'stands carrying the worlds above, below and transversely'. The source of the Ganges is here, though it does not become a visible above-ground river till it reaches India. In early descriptions the mountain has seven sides facing the earth's seven divisions. Others speak of seven levels rather than sides. Meru is frequented by gods and, more distinctively, by the Seven Rishis. These beings are divine seers and sages, concerned with the origins of life and knowledge in each cosmic cycle. They appear on earth at intervals to teach a fresh revelation. The Seven Rishis may be akin to other groups, such as seven Babylonian sages who are mentioned in the Epic of Gilgamesh, and the Seven Wise Men of Greece whose maxims were inscribed over the door of Apollo's temple. But in India the seven-starred Ursa Major enters decisively, because the Rishis are identified with the seven stars. The chief Hindu name for the constellation is Saptarshi, 'the Seven Rishis'.

In Buddhism, which began as a reform movement within

Hinduism, the world-mountain is Sumeru. Again it is at the earth's centre in a remote north and the cosmic axis runs through it. It has four sides, with a quadrangular city of the gods on top. Islamic legend adopts the mountain via Iran, but invents variants. One story makes it, still, the centre of a flat earth, with a bridge leading from its heights to heaven. Another describes its ascent as a purgatorial ordeal. Others stress the earthly paradise at its summit, and drop centrality, shifting it to Syria, Persia or India. Sometimes the mountain is identified with a real one, such as Adam's Peak in Sri Lanka. Sometimes a story reverts to the idea of its being the world's highest, with less commitment as to its whereabouts. However, Islam never quite loses the unity of the conception, and it is largely through Islamic transmission that the world-mountain appears again, reconstituted, in an amazing context – the *Divine Comedy*.

Dante's Mount of Purgatory is a Christian Meru. Knowing Earth to be a sphere, he still makes it central by placing it on an island at the antipodes of Jerusalem. In keeping with medieval geography, Jerusalem is the centre of the inhabited world, the land hemisphere. The Mount of Purgatory is the centre of the uninhabited world, the water hemisphere. It is incomparably higher than any other mountain. Souls, under the care of angels, are purged and prepared for bliss on a series of horizontal terraces encircling it, one above another, with connecting stairways. There are seven of these, one for each of the deadly sins.

At the top is the Earthly Paradise where Adam and Eve were placed by God, and would have lived always if they had not sinned. In cantos dealing with the approach to this blessed place, and with the place itself, Dante alludes twice to Ursa Major. He mentions Artemis' nymph who was enskied as the constellation, and calls her not Callisto but Helice, which means 'that which turns'. This is the name of the constellation rather than the nymph. When he describes a symbolic procession in the Earthly Paradise, he refers to seven candlesticks, standing for the gifts of the Holy Spirit headed by Wisdom, as 'the First Heaven's Septentrion'. 'Septentrion' is another name for the constellation, which guides the seafarer and never vanishes

Sacred Mountains

from the sky. While the heavenly spheres are not actually pivoted on the Mount, it gives access to them, and from the Earthly Paradise Beatrice leads the way upward among the planets and stars.

2

This world-mountain or cosmic mountain, joining earth to heaven, is the one which has truly been represented and modelled in the way Dion Fortune imagined. It may be questioned whether Mesopotamian temple-building ever imitated the mountain *qua* cosmic. But Hindu and Buddhist building did. Meru had its deputies, and Geoffrey Russell rightly directed attention to it in his theorizing about the Tor.

Hindu temple-designers represented the mountain by a sanctuary-tower (*vimana*) with a more or less circular upper structure in several stages. The Khmers of southeast Asia portrayed it in the shape of stepped pyramids. Sinhalese topes or shrines in Sri Lanka have a square stone in the centre which stands for the mountain. At Jalatunda in eastern Java, a sacred spring gushes from a hillside into a great stone tank, and a carved stone on a terrace symbolizes the top of Meru; the spring wells up through it and flows down into the tank by carefully planned channels.

Elsewhere in Java, Buddhism has left a more spectacular model. Twenty miles from Jogjakarta, the cultural capital of the island, is Borobudur. This is a huge Buddhist temple about twelve centuries old. The landscape round about marks a contrast which is frequent in this part of Indonesia. On one side is low-lying forest dotted with villages. On the other are mountains which rise abruptly. It is understandable that the Javanese, and their Balinese neighbours, are mountain-conscious.

Borobudur itself was made by taking a natural hill and building it over with dark grey stone encasing and hiding it. The hill was thereby structured as a model of the cosmic mountain – not of course a scale model, or an accurate copy,

Avalonian Quest

but an image in three dimensions with cosmic meanings. After long neglect due to the decline of Buddhism in Java, Borobudur was rediscovered in a tumbledown state because of erosion and water seepage. Recent repairs on a lavish scale have largely restored it. Today, souvenir and refreshment stalls cluster at the base. However, it still draws visitors with religious motives, who sometimes leave floral offerings.

The base is a great square platform. The next storey or layer is a square which is a good deal smaller, so that a wide terrace runs all round between it and the edge of the base-platform. All four sides of it are full of sculptured reliefs in trachyte, a pale volcanic rock, depicting scenes from the life of the Buddha for pilgrims walking on the terrace to contemplate. Above are further squares, rising one above another pyramid-wise. They diminish less sharply, so that the terraces round them are narrower than the first. Each has sculptures of its own. In all, the friezes comprise more than 1500 narrative panels.

On top of the highest square is a further storey which is circular and without sculpture, so that the last of the square terraces, surrounding it, is an artistic blank. The circle is surmounted by a smaller one, and that by another. There are no more friezes, but each of the final three terraces has stupas all round it. They are shrines made like a bell full of holes. Inside each stupa, visible through the holes, is a seated Buddha. One or two are broken and the figure can be seen more clearly. Surmounting the whole edifice is a much larger stupa, bell-shaped like the rest, but wider in proportion to height. This is solid, with no holes in it, and no image. On the topmost terrace you are walking round the rim of the bell. The spire at the apex rises to well over a hundred feet above ground.

Ascent is by steep staircases on each of the temple's four sides. The pilgrimage procedure is known, though the dilapidation and reconstruction have long prevented it from being properly carried out. Theoretically, pilgrims climb a staircase to the first terrace and walk round it, meditating on the mural reliefs. Back at the starting-point they climb to the next terrace and walk round that, and so

Sacred Mountains

on up and up, making shorter and shorter circuits. The route, in fact, is an inward-winding spiral adapted to the architecture. Since each terrace runs horizontally all round, and the route passes to the next above it by way of stairs, Borobudur is more like Dante's Mount of Purgatory than the Etemenanki.

The square terraces signify the realm of material being, and the meditative journey is a progress through it. Here the route is a series of straight lines and right-angle turns. Eventually it rises by way of the 'blank' level to the first of the round terraces above, and continues on these in circles. Here the pilgrim is in the spiritual realm, the realm of enlightenment, with stupas instead of sculptures. There are 32 stupas on the first spiritual terrace, 24 on the second, 16 on the topmost. With any of them it is an act of merit to reach in through one of the holes – diamond-shaped on the first two terraces, square on the third – and touch the hand of the Buddha inside. The pilgrimage ends at the giant stupa on top. It stands for the goal of the human quest, Nirvana, liberation, bliss.

When I visited Borobudur in September 1980, the restoration was still going on. Cranes were active, and a complete walk round the lower terraces was not allowed. Still the plan was easy to follow. At the summit, on the verge of Nirvana, I met with a breeze which took the edge off the heat, and also with four Californian tourists. The question which most concerned me was the number of terraces. Books which I had consulted contradicted each other. Did it or did it not agree with Meru and the Etemenanki . . . and Glastonbury Tor? After repeated checking (the count is curiously tricky) I established the answer. It does agree, in an unexpected and interesting way. The journey through the material realm passes along five terraces with sculptures beside them. The sixth terrace is the blank one, and transitional. A climber enters the spiritual realm on the seventh terrace. So the numerical character of the cosmic mountain is maintained. The upper, spiritual levels correspond to its summit-paradise.

In his television series *The Spirit of Asia,* David Attenborough filmed a Buddhist festival at Borobudur. A group of monks came from Sri Lanka for the occasion. They climbed the stairs, and held a ceremony at the base of the giant stupa. This event took place at the May full moon. At Glastonbury, Kathy Jones chose the May full moon for her ritual threading of the Tor maze. I am sure there was no influence in either direction. For some reason both parties saw the same point in the lunar calendar as correct.

3

In Java, besides other shrines such as Jalatunda, there is a popular lore in which the cosmic mountain persists. Despite official Islam the spirits of the departed are said to plunge into a volcano called Bromo, and pass from there to the paradise on Sumeru. In the island of Bali, however, just across the strait to the east, the case is different and the original notion has petered out. Its people are neither Buddhist nor nominally Muslim but Hindu. Balinese Hinduism is a living religion, but separation from India has given it a shape of its own. Its 'Mother Temple', Besakih, is a cluster of terraces and shrines approached by a broad uphill highway. Beyond the temple-complex rises Mount Agung, the highest mountain in the island, another volcano; and Agung itself is Bali's world-centre. The Besakih temple does not symbolize a cosmic mountain anywhere else. For the Balinese, Agung is enough. So far as the god-inhabited peak is part of their belief, they possess the thing itself, and its presence is powerful. When Agung last erupted, in 1963, they inferred that its resident deities were angry. Thousands prayed in the path of the lava till it stopped spreading.

This then is the end of the trail, and we must turn back to Borobudur. Given the terraces and spiral ascent, the notion of Glastonbury Tor as another model of the world-mountain does not look utterly irresponsible. The work would be far older, far cruder in execution. Yet it would also, in a sense, be more ingenious, using the maze-track

Sacred Mountains

to carry out the hill's septenary moulding, relating the convolutions of life to the central bond of the universe. Britain, however, is a long way from Java. The motif would probably have had to reach Somerset long before Buddhism even existed. *Pace* the Glastonbury Zodiac school, it did not come from the Sumerians. 'Somerset' is not derived from 'Sumer'. Nor (since Buddhism has been introduced) is it derived from 'Sumeru'.

There can in fact be no direct link with the countries in southern and south-east Asia where the world-mountain is known in myth, and represented by sacred structures. There might, however, be a link with some common source of inspiration. A fair question to ask is whether the myth anywhere has a real geographical reference, whether it has anywhere absorbed ideas about a real sacred mountain – an Agung of older and more influential potency. To identify such a mountain might suggest the whereabouts of the common source.

The recurrent 'north' in itself is hardly a clue. In the first place, the primary reason for it is astronomical and not geographical. In the second, 'north' is not the same for Palestine and Mesopotamia and India. It can be construed as meaning 'in a higher latitude than the place where the word is used', it cannot safely be pressed into meaning more. Nevertheless, a myth postulating a height central to the heavens might indeed have drawn in folklore from the real north. Lore of this kind is fairly widespread in Central Asia, telling of a mountain of the gods with a temple on top, the temple sometimes having a golden spire which dwellers below see as the Pole Star. Much of this may merely echo Indian beliefs about Meru, but not all of it necessarily does, and some may be related to cults of actual mountains among the Mongols and other peoples.

When we examine what Hindus say of Meru, we find what we do not in the Middle East, a serious geographical pointer. Near the end of the epic *Mahabharata*, the Pandava king and his brothers who are its heroes decide to quit the world. Together with the queen they walk round their kingdom, going to the east, then to the south, then to the west. Finally they head north.

Proceeding to the north, they saw Himavat [the Himalayas].... Crossing the Himavat, they saw a vast desert of sand. They then saw the powerful mountain Meru, the foremost of all high-peaked mountains.

(XVII.ii.1–2)

The story is condensed by the author's ignorance, or lack of interest. But his 'vast desert of sand', so un-Indian and un-Tibetan, is crucial. A traveller going north from the Himalayas does eventually reach one, Takla Makan in Sinkiang-Uighur. These verses embody hazy knowledge of some sort, though it gives out. The solid datum is that Meru is farther north than Takla Makan. Since the author has skipped the journey from the Himalayas to the desert, he may also be skipping the journey from the desert to Meru. If the Pandavas see the mountain immediately after crossing the desert, it has to be a mythification of the Tien Shan range or some peak in it, perhaps Khan Tengri ('Heaven-Lord' or 'Lord God'), a sacred mountain of the Mongols. Alternatively they could skirt the desert at its east end – a more probable action than crossing it – and continue through Dzungaria to the Altai. Any factual ingredient of Meru may have come from one of these ranges. Or the myth could have combined rumours of sacred mountains in both. Certainly nothing is relevant beyond the Altai, where the low-lying expanse of Siberia goes all the way to the Arctic Ocean.

Is Tien Shan the answer, or should we look farther north? The Altai would take us into country already considered for other reasons. Earlier in the *Mahabharata* is a description of Meru. As might be expected it is almost entirely fabulous, full of divine beings, gorgeous-plumed birds, and kindred marvels. But it does say that the mountain is made of gold, and, as observed before, 'Altai' means 'golden'. Another noteworthy passage concerns the nation of Northern Kurus. They live to the north of Meru in a place where the sands are golden and the trees bear wondrous fruits. They are always happy, always healthy, immensely long-lived. These mythicized folk are the ones whom Greeks heard about in India and equated with the

Sacred Mountains

similarly mythicized Hyperboreans, placed by Aristeas' report in the Altaic region.

These two passages (VI.vi and vii) form part of a discourse on world geography. It ought to be helpful but is not, being a medley of legends which cannot be fitted to a workable map. Still the clues suggest that Meru has touches of northern reality as well as cosmological myth. If the mountain's septenary aspect is taken into account as well, we are back with Altaic shamanism and its seven-mystique, and might wonder whether rumours from that source went into its making.

We must turn again to what shamans say and do, or are recorded to have said and done in historical times. None of this can be proof as to what their predecessors were saying and doing thousands of years ago. But anything in their lore which is like the Indian cosmic mountain must raise issues; and something like it does occur. An Altaic legend tells how, in the beginning, a great god sat on a golden mountain in the middle of the sky. Later he lowered it so that it rested on the earth. This naive version could be connected with the 'golden' Altai. A cosmic mountain is known more explicitly in the region as Sumer, Sumur or Sumbur. It has the 'navel' or centre of the sky above it, the Pole Star being attached to its summit. According to some tribes (admittedly not all) it has seven storeys.

Shamanistic lore includes not only the mountain but the idea of a substitute or representation. A recurrent feature of shamans' dreams and trances is a journey to the centre of the universe. Sometimes this takes the form of going to the mountain and climbing it. But sometimes, also, the shaman climbs a 'world-tree' which takes its place; and sometimes the symbol is humbler – a pole, even a tent-pole, imagined propping up the sky. The climb takes the shaman through the celestial levels, commonly seven, into the presence of the gods who live at the top. Altaic shamans are among several groups who keep actual symbolic trees and wooden posts, notched to represent the levels. Some climb up them literally and physically, while their spirits are climbing through the corresponding heavens.

The question of course is whether any of this is native

to the Altaic people, so that it could have influenced others far back in time, or whether it is merely a debased offshoot of Mesopotamian, Hindu or Buddhist concepts. Mircea Eliade, the principal authority on shamanism in general, takes the latter view.

> The conception of the seven heavens . . . goes back to Brahmanism, and probably represents the influence of Babylonian cosmology, which (though indirectly) left its mark on Altaic and Siberian cosmological conceptions too.

More explicitly, in the words of Giorgio de Santillana and Hertha von Dechend:

> The shaman climbing the 'stairs' or notches of his post or tree, pretending that his soul ascends at the same time to the highest sky, does the very same thing as the Mesopotamian priest did when mounting to the top of his seven-storied pyramid. . . .
> From the majestic temple at Borobudur in Java to the graceful *stupas* which dot the Indian landscape, stretches a schematized reminder of the seven heavens, the seven notches. Says Uno Holmberg: 'This pattern of seven levels can hardly be imagined as the invention of Turko-Tatar populations. To the investigator, the origin of the Gods ruling these various levels is no mystery, for they point clearly to the planetary gods of Babylon, which already in their far-away point of origin, ruled over seven superposed starry circles.'

If we ask an advocate of such views how these ideas reached the remote north, the answer may be that they were carried there by the lamas. And indeed the northern name of the mountain, Sumer or Sumur or Sumbur, is manifestly the Buddhist name for it, Sumeru.

Yet the case is not as strong as it looks. To begin with, the idea of 'the mountain at the centre of the universe' is found in North America. Specific mountains are thus regarded, one of them near Tucson in Arizona. The notion is naive and avoids astronomical problems, but there it is. It could have come from Asia with ancestral shamanism. It did not come from India.

Also, the argument about the seven-mystique is based on the dogma that this was derived from the seven planets and implies an advanced astronomy, whereas, as I have said, it is far older and derived almost certainly from the seven stars of Ursa Major. Shamans have never needed outside teaching in that respect. They pay divine homage to the Bear's seven stars. In a Mongol legend a divine being creates the constellation out of the heads of seven smiths. Smiths were regarded as wonder-workers with secret powers, closely akin to the shamans themselves. Written records dating from the fourteenth century show the Mongols have generally called the stars the Seven Old Men. They relate them to the Pole Star, the unmoving 'golden nail' of the sky. The Old Men recall the Seven Rishis with whom the stars are identified in India. In shamanism as influenced by the lamas, they are said to live on the top of Sumeru. But their concern is with primitive matters like increase and fertility; they are not sages, not imitation Rishis. Who knows which way the earliest influences travelled? Eliade himself slips in an odd little concession: 'It is probable that the shamanic ideology has played a part in the dissemination of the number 7.'

As for India and the Buddhist impact, manifestly 'Sumeru' did produce 'Sumer' with its variants. But the testimony of the Mongols themselves puts the matter in a different light. They are well aware of the Buddhist connection, but they regard Sumer as a Buddhist affair. Far senior to it is a network of real sacred mountains. One, Khan Tengri, we have noted already. Mountains are the abodes of spirits and deities, so awesome that Mongols do not ordinarily mention the mountains' names, but refer to them by polite epithets such as 'the holy', 'the beautiful', 'the high'. Important persons have been buried on the high places for thousands of years (this at least is attested by archaeology), and the powers which the dead draw from the mountain-spirits play a major part in ancestor-worship. Thirteen prominent mountains in the Altai are among those most revered; there is a prayer to the gods of Dzungaria which includes Altai Khan, Lord Altai.

Information on the special position accorded to this range was collected by Nicholas Roerich, the Russian artist and collaborator with Stravinsky. He came this way in the 1920s during a long expedition through Central Asia. His travel diary, published in 1930 under the title *Altai-Himalaya*, records much cryptic talk about the 'spiritual meaning of Altai', the 'general reverence for Altai', the 'coming of the Blessed Ones to Altai', the 'true significance of Altai'. Roerich is especially interested in the highest peak of the range, called Belukha by the Russians, which is near the point where Siberia, China and Mongolia meet. He gives its native name as Outch-Sure, said to mean 'Orion, dwelling of gods'. The 'wisdom of the shamans', he says, designates Orion as well as Ursa Major for worship. He even suggests that the mountain's name marks it as an indigenous counterpart of divine Sumeru.

In the upshot, then, the Altaic region supplies a cult of real sacred mountains which is undoubtedly ancient, plus ideas about the world-mountain, its septenary character and its representation, which very well may be. Belukha has perhaps been a special focus of divine power. If a shamanistic 'package' did travel westwards as proposed, carrying the maze symbol and forming a substrate of religion in Britain, it could have included the mountain and helped to inspire the conversion of the Tor into a sort of Borobudur. This may be a feeble and nebulous conclusion, giving only an incoherence. Nothing in the Asian mountain's scheme of ideas seems to have anything to do with Goddess and Underworld motifs. It can only be said that an artificial septenary ascent can be paralleled, and that if we explore the parallelism, the Pandavas' last journey points us towards an Altaic source of ideas which we have already been led to for other reasons. An area of overlap with those 'other reasons' might be the cult of Apollo. Besides much else that he did, he linked an earthly centre at Delphi with the Asian high place of the Hyperboreans. But at present there are far too many unknowns.

Sacred Mountains

4

That is not quite all. To reflect on an Altaic connection, far back, is to confront a relationship which is so unexpected and off-key as to have the air of a joke. It is the weirdest thing to emerge from this enquiry, and entirely in keeping with the rest of the data, but not in a way which ordinary reasoning can admit. I do not present it as an argument, only as a bizarrerie, a further instance of the trouble Glastonbury can cause.

Once when looking at a map, I was struck by the closeness of Belukha to the fiftieth parallel. Fifty degrees north of the equator is not far from one-seventh of the circumference of the globe (reckoned, that is, in degrees, without considering the flattening at the poles). One-seventh of 360°, worked out to the nearest minute, is 51° 26′. So here perhaps was the mystic seven again. Could this have been a motive for choosing a mountain of superlative sanctity: that it happened to be close to a magical latitude? Since thirteen peaks of the Altai are sacred, others might be closer yet. But Belukha, as the highest, seemed the proper one to consider. It is in fact 49° 46′ N. No method of finding latitude that was known before quite modern times would have shown with certainty that there was any error, any deviation from an exact one-seventh, the more so as it is most unlikely that observations would have been taken from the summit itself.

The natural retort is that there is no need to look for any reason beyond the mere superior height of Belukha, compared with any other mountains to be found for a long way. A normal view of the shamans' science would rule out anything more sophisticated. They could not have made the measurement. Indeed, they did not know the essential fact that the earth is round. This latitude figure could and should be dismissed, if it were not for another one. Glastonbury is in much the same latitude, 51° 9′ north of the equator – closer still to a true one-seventh. On an atlas-size map of the world, the difference in latitude between Glastonbury and Belukha is not easily visible. In terms of any

Avalonian Quest

but fairly modern technique (so far as is known) they are on the same parallel.

That too is not all. Belukha is 86° 40′ east of the Greenwich meridian. Glastonbury is 2° 43′ west of it. Added together giving 89° 23′, these figures show that if we measure along the parallel, Glastonbury is almost exactly one-quarter of the way round the world from Belukha, almost exactly 90°.

After finding so much about the possible meanings and relationship of the two, it is hard to come to terms with this crude spatial affinity. To allow that the Tor was chosen because it was the one eligible hill a quarter of the way round from a prototype, in the same approximate magical latitude, we would have to be very radical indeed. We would have to imagine people who knew the shape of the earth; who could measure latitude and (much more difficult) longitude; who could keep records through centuries of migration. If the Tor maze is as early as Rahtz suggests, or even as early as Hecataeus, it antedates any known people who could have fulfilled the requirements.

There is something even worse. As may be recalled, the ley-line enthusiasts have produced one line that really is quite impressive, the St Michael Line which begins at St Michael's Mount in Cornwall, traverses several churches dedicated to the same archangel, passes through the Tor with its ruined St Michael church, and goes on through Avebury. If that line was ever actually planned in antiquity, it would doubtless have been anchored on the two hills, St Michael's Mount and the Tor, with the other sites taking shape along it afterwards. (I have no idea how this would have been done, but those were the points incontestably supplied by nature; they could not have been contrived after the line was laid down.) Now if you draw the line through them, and carry it on till it cuts the *exact* parallel, 51° 26′, it does so at ... Avebury. Avebury is a precise one-seventh from the equator, 51° 26′ plus or minus a little, depending on where the measurement is taken – it covers a large area. It is as if Avebury's builders, dissatisfied with approximation, wanted a place that was exactly right, and picked it by relating it to the hills, one at least of which was already sacred.

Sacred Mountains

'As if' is the furthest this thought can go, and the idea that Avebury's builders could be so accurate is daunting indeed. The only point worth adding is that if the St Michael Line is interpreted thus, it is not favourable to the ley theory but adverse. It is a single-purpose line giving no grounds for suspecting that there are any others.

If, by the way, you step westward a further 90° from Glastonbury along the parallel, you arrive in north-west Ontario. If you then step a further 90°, you arrive, with only a slight swerve, at the volcanic island of Kiska in the Aleutians (52° N, 177° 30′ E). A last ninety-degree step brings you round to Belukha again. Neither of the two North American spots has any obvious significance. Yet it is curious that all four quarterings, with a north-south deviation from the mean of only a degree or so, give places which are on land. If you try it with any appreciably different starting-point, in this latitude or any other outside the polar regions, at least one of the steps will hit the sea.

5

Even that is not all. Another body of legend and belief points to the Altaic country. This too leads up to a statement about Glastonbury, which is in much the same order of bizarrerie as the spatial relationship, only more so. It cannot be given the status of serious evidence, nor can it be tossed aside.

Russia's expansion into Asia in the seventeenth century engendered a folk-myth about an eastern paradise, an elusive happy valley called Belovodye. This tale was popular in the sect of Old Believers, who dreamed of Belovodye as a refuge from persecution. It was searched for, and continued to be searched for into the twentieth century. Rumoured in various quarters, it was shifted farther and farther into the unknown; but at first it was in the Altai mountains. It sounds like the Land of the Hyperboreans as reported by Aristeas. But the Russians are unlikely to have owed anything to Greek authors. Almost certainly they were picking up a theme of Lamaistic Buddhism from the Kalmucks, a migrant Mongol people, which designated the same place in the Altai and called it Shambhala.

Lamaistic teaching in Tibet and Mongolia has had a good deal to say about it, much of it inconsistent. Shambhala probably belongs to pre-Buddhist tradition. Its full name is Chang Shambhala, North Shambhala. 'Shambhala' itself means 'quietude'. 'Chang Shambhala', the northern place of quietude, has much the same implications as 'Hyperborean', at-the-back-of-Boreas. Different fantasies have located it in different portions of the map. However, the word 'north' proves its true direction to have been north from Tibet. This is confirmed by a Tibetan legend in which four countries are contemplated as places of banishment for an offender, Shambhala, India, China and Persia. Plainly they represent north, south, east and west. Shambhala is sometimes associated with the constellation Orion, and this recalls the Altaic peak Belukha again, Outch-Sure, 'Orion, dwelling of gods'. Popular legends about Shambhala are – or used to be – more vigorous among the Mongols who are close to the Altai than among the Tibetans who are not.

Shambhalic lore is preserved in an esoteric system called Kalachakra, the Wheel of Time, which is supposed to have arisen in Shambhala itself. The mysterious place is variously described. The most detailed description makes it a secret valley in a mountain-cluster. It can be reached only by way of a cave or narrow defile, and even this is hard to approach because of a lake or dried-up lake-bed. Lamas declare that a profane traveller cannot find the path to Shambhala at all – one must be summoned. (Likewise, nobody can follow the 'wondrous way' to the Hyperboreans.) There is also an elaborate mythology about an Underworld, Agharti, which extends downwards from Shambhala and is part of its realm.

Mongolian lamas have taught that Shambhala has long been, and still is, a fountainhead of wisdom. Buddha himself went there to be initiated into its secrets and expounded Kalachakra before its king. Shambhala's kings are above

Sacred Mountains

normal humanity, as is the hidden population they rule, and one of them will emerge in a Messianic role. Between the First and Second World Wars this belief was a source of inspiration for Mongol nationalism. Japanese imperialists tried to exploit it. Some of the more mystical Nazis are said to have attempted to contact Shambhala, and enlist its occult forces.

Nicholas Roerich took the prophecies seriously, and seems to have thought that he could contact Shambhala. He drops many hints in his travel diary showing that he had his eye on the Altai. He heard a tradition that Buddha's supposed Shambhalic journey took him to 'the great Altai, where stands sacred Belukha'. But something happened during his expedition which remains puzzling. At the height of his expectations, in August 1927, he saw a celestial portent. A lama made it out to be a warning to turn away south. He did, and settled in India. His later writings show that the lamas, whatever their motives, succeeded in convincing him that Shambhala was somewhere else or was not an earthly location at all.

One of them, however, may have let a hint escape. Most startlingly he spoke of Shambhala as 'far beyond the ocean'. This was not purely diversionary. Another traveller, Alexandra David-Neel, quotes Mongols as saying it is 'an island somewhere in the north' – not any of the Russian islands, which are the only ones due north of that part of Asia. Both assertions are vague and the second, as it stands, is impossible. Yet the notion of another Shambhala in a remote island, another centre of wisdom, might be inferred. And so we come to the bizarrerie.

While Communist rule in Mongolia has almost destroyed Buddhism, as an organized religion, lamas survive as individual scholars. Some of them still expound the Kalachakra system, still connect it with Shambhala, and still say Buddha was a Shambhalic initiate. They have an English initiate of their own, Stephen Jenkins, who held a teaching post in Mongolia in 1970. He visited me some years ago and told me of a belief among the lamas that about 543 BC, towards the end of Buddha's life (to which they give an unusual dating), a European came to him to be taught the wisdom of Shambhala. This man, the lamas suspected, was a Celt. They believed that the Shambhalic 'presence' – it is hard to know how to express this – was transplanted to Britain.

Later, Stephen Jenkins published a book entitled *The Undiscovered Country*. In this he mentions Shambhala's connection with Orion, which seems to point to Belukha and the Altai if it points to anything earthly. But he also reaffirms the British idea.

> I was considerably taken aback when I began my instruction in the secret doctrines of the realm of Shambhala to be told by high-ranking Mongolian lamas deeply read in the subject that it had had a literal existence on the surface of the earth, and that it had lain far to the west. In the last 100 years discussion of the problem among them had narrowed down the possibilities, and opinion was now unanimous. The Kingdom of Shambhala had once been, they said, in the Island of Britain, the Celtic Britain of the last centuries before Christ.

Nothing shows in what sense Shambhala was established in Britain, or whether it ever ceased to be there, and if so, how and why it disappeared. In terms of history I suppose the notion would have to be that initiates of some kind carried Shambhalic lore westwards, and planted it in a British centre. This would still have been important at the time when Britain was the headquarters of Druid teaching, and Hecataeus wrote of the Hyperborean temple there. As it stands the story does not reach back as far as a plausible date for the Tor maze. But here, strangely and for no evident reason, we confront a shift or colonization exactly matching the movement of the Hyperboreans from the Altai to Britain, and to the real movement of ideas and images underlying it. In this case it is seen and mythicized from the other end.

The impression is that the lamas thought the British Shambhala (whatever it was) ceased to function a long time ago. This might only mean that, from their point of view, it did not count any more after the advent of Christianity. The 'island' Shambhala might be Celtic Britain itself . . . or, of course, it might be the Isle of Avalon.

CHAPTER FOURTEEN

Towards Sanity

I

In the final stocktaking, a clear line has to be drawn between the Tor maze itself and the hypotheses which it opens up. While proof could come only from archaeology, I conclude that the maze is more likely to be real than otherwise. Its plan is not invented *ad hoc* like the Glastonbury Zodiac. The essential design is one which occurs in a variety of contexts, some of them old. Although so complicated, it works, it can be adapted to the Tor. Moreover the apparent Tor maze is not selective: it uses all the terraces, and both the stones on the approach – perhaps also the one on the south side. This might be put down to chance if other hills showed the same possibility, but no hill has ever been pointed out which does. Even the possibility, here of all places and nowhere else, seems too far-fetched as a pure accident. The maze would resolve a recognized crux in the famous passage from Hecataeus, allowing his words to apply in a way which fits the Avalonian mythology; and for whatever reasons, the design has associations in other settings which also fit what is said and suspected of Glastonbury. A practical difficulty might be seen in the site's distance from early centres of population. But ideas on such matters tend to be fluid.

As to the rest – shamanism, sacred mountains, geographical oddities, the pronouncements of lamas – it is enough for the moment that facts and possibilities do exist. Combined, they support the belief that Glastonbury is rooted in very ancient realities. To cover everything, including the matter of latitude and longitude, we might have to imagine a sort of Ancient Wisdom: a migrant religious and scientific system, unknown to any accepted scheme of the past. The maze-design would be one of its symbols and a clue for tracking its diffusion. Such a thing cannot be affirmed on the evidence, yet it might be allowed to glimmer on the horizon. One by-product of this enquiry, the observation that Avebury is distanced from the equator by precisely one-seventh of the full circle, is intriguing in its hints both at the magic number and at accurate measurement.

However, there is no need to insist on an exotic origin for Glastonbury; only on an early one. Its likeliest beginning would have been as the sanctuary of a goddess, a pre-Celtic Mother localized here because of the female contours of the hill-cluster and because of the spring of tinted water. As in Crete and doubtless elsewhere, the goddess was Mistress of the Labyrinth. Inside the Tor – inside her body – was the Underworld. Ritual use of her maze went on in Celtic times, when she was Matrona with her son Maponus, the British Apollo. In the speech of the British Celts she became Modron. Later again, myth-makers turned her into Morgan, the enchantress and healer, who was remembered as divine even in the Middle Ages, and who had a home in the island of Avallach or Avalon. Glastonbury's island may or may not have become a burial-place as 'Melkin' says, and an abode of shades. At any rate it retained an awe which was kept alive by the hill-on-island topography and by Underworld folklore. That gave a mythic dimension to what would otherwise have been trivia, such as the notion that 'Glas' in 'Glastonbury' was 'glass'.

Nothing reveals whether any form of 'Avalon' was applied to the place as an early name, seriously used. Certainly Morgan's Elysian apple-island was not solely here. Geoffrey of Monmouth shows that it could bilocate and probably multilocate, and in the continental imagination of Chrétien de Troyes, Avalon and the Glass Island seem to have been different. Likewise, Glastonbury's contact with the Annwn-Underworld was not a monopoly. Annwn could be entered via Lundy and Grassholm, for instance. But the memory of Modron-Morgan, and the otherworldly aura, never quite faded. 'Avalon' was apt whenever it was bestowed.

Towards Sanity

On this point it is worth quoting Armitage Robinson. His *Two Glastonbury Legends* is habitually cited as the classic disproof of the coming of Joseph and the burial of Arthur. But it also contains a perceptive paragraph which is remembered less often, because it shows how, in one major respect, later exponents of the total-fabrication theory have taken his name in vain.

> We can hardly doubt that the monks searched for King Arthur's body in their cemetery because Glastonbury was already supposed by local tradition to be the Avalon to which the wounded hero had been brought. The great Tor, rising solitary and steep out of the watery moors, must needs have been an island of mystery from the prehistoric days when the lake-dwellers clustered round its base.... We may not unreasonably suppose that the name of Avalon was not first suggested by the inventiveness of the monks; that it represented some primitive tradition, and had clung to the spot in popular memory, in spite of the coming of Christianity and in spite of successive conquests of the land by Saxon and Norman invaders.

The maze, if it is real, and the myths and practices that relate to it, enable us to define Glastonbury's uniqueness. It was a great prehistoric sacred site, comparable to Avebury, Silbury, even Stonehenge. But unlike them it became a great Christian site. It was both. Christianization happened at many holy places, but not elsewhere in Britain with anything so vast, or with such a continuity or so immense a result. At Glastonbury a mighty pagan presence underlies Christianity. That is true today, quite apart from any theories about 'vibes' or forces. Once again: if people went to such trouble to make a maze on the Tor, then we can be sure that they threaded it. Their ritual is perpetuated in the shape of the hill. We can re-enact it, not with certainty as to what it meant, but with a confidence in the basic actions which cannot be felt at Avebury or other British sites.

It will be remembered that the *prima facie* reason for

scenting a continuity was the Marian dedication of the Old Church. Its un-typicality and its early date pointed to a goddess cult, not very long before. The maze and its associations now give support for this. The interval could have been surprisingly short. In the late Roman period, south-west Britain experienced a mild pagan revival, with new temples at Lydney, Brean Down, Maiden Castle in Dorset, perhaps Cadbury-Camelot. A renewal of ritual at the Tor would have been consistent with other developments. It is possible that the Roman oddments found in the Abbey – late third-century coins, for instance – indicate a nearby temple rather than a villa. A Christian community could have dedicated a church to the Virgin only a few decades later, when the Mother was recalled not merely as a legend, but as a living recipient of worship. A few priests or priestesses (Druids or Druidesses, if we care to call them so) could even have been tending the sanctuary still.

Celtic tolerance for the old mythology would doubtless have eased a transition from Matrona-with-her-son-Maponus to Mary-with-her-son-Jesus. That would have been in no way adverse to the lady's bardic conversion into Morgan. In that guise, perhaps, she retained a shadow of independence. None of this implies that the shift from paganism to Christianity was a mere evolution that blurred distinctions. The Celtic Christians' attitude to the old order never amounted to equivocation on basics. They could cling to pagan things poetically, not shunning them as utterly diabolic; but the Christian faith was truth and paganism was error, or, at best, error-foreshadowing-truth. The point at Glastonbury was that they had to reckon far more than usual with what was there already, unforgettable even in the landscape. Their actions, their modes of devotion, could not fail to be affected by it. Everything was transfigured, but not effaced, and after a while some of it could re-surface in legend.

Of Christian Glastonbury itself, enough has been said. Its legends of early foundation or frequentation seem to have drawn on factual tradition, though this may have had to do only with circumstances, not with persons. The continuity from paganism to Christianity may have been due to a deliberate decision to occupy and re-consecrate the great pagan site. It was followed in due course by the further continuity from Celt to Saxon.

With the story of Arthur's burial, several options are open. There was an old grave more or less as described, and the bones in it were conceivably his, interred or re-interred in the senior monastery of the West Country near Cadbury-Camelot. But light may now be shed by the indications that the 'real Arthur' was the High King who drops out of historical view in Burgundy. A confused memory that he went away in the direction of the Burgundian Avallon could have fostered a belief that his last earthly destination was the Elysian apple-island. This could then have led – roughly as Armitage Robinson proposed – to a more prosaic belief that it was the Somerset 'island' where Morgan, the lady of Avalon, had been living for ages. Clues like the spelling on the cross suggest that some such idea took shape well before the twelfth century, with or without help from an inscription, and that although the English did not preserve it, some Welshmen did.

As for the Grail, apart from Joseph, one is tempted to say that this is another case where there are too many unknowns. A few features of the Grail mythos might have Glastonian antecedents: the cauldron of Annwn, the feminine element, the Marian element. The last of these appears vividly in *Perlesvaus*, the romance written by a man who shows local knowledge, and professes to have used Abbey materials. Mary, it may be added, is figuratively identified with a Celtic cauldron of inspiration by the medieval Welsh poet Daffid Benfras, who plays on the word *pair*, cauldron, and *Mair*, Mary; while three German poets, saluting the Virgin, say 'Thou art the Grail' in plain terms. But this is getting a long way from Glastonbury.

Geoffrey Russell, of course, claimed a far closer connection, with his argument that maze-threading on the Tor was the basis of the quest. He suggested that early Christians actually annexed the maze, devising a rite of their own, the original Grail-seeing, to replace whatever it was that happened at the centre. In support for his theory, Russell could have invoked the signs of a Christian settle-

Avalonian Quest

ment on the Tor, near the entrance. But it fails to account for the first of the quest-romances, begun by Chrétien de Troyes, where the Grail is imperfectly Christian and lacks even an arguable Glastonian linkage. If the maze did play a part in the quest theme, it was a subtle, indirect one, a matter of conjecture.

2

Does any of this account for the 'great beginnings' which were surveyed in the second and third chapters?

What can surely be stressed is the combined effect of continuity and diversity. The pioneer Christians, it may now appear, settled at the last major holy place of the old Britain which was still in some degree active. Stonehenge and the rest, never having been used by the Celts, were long since dead. Glastonbury, however somnolent, was alive. If it had ceased to function it may not have ceased very long before, and the uncanny hill towered over all, with its ritual works and its Underworld folklore. The place was numinous and challenging, and the community may well have assembled there because it was. Glastonbury could have had the first of its great beginnings because of this Christian encounter with its paganism; because, for the new faith, leaving it alone would have been too much of a surrender. Further, once the community was formed, it would have been a worse surrender to go away again. The hermits remained, the church was built, the monastery grew.

That beginning led to the next. When the Saxons arrived, they acquired what they had never acquired anywhere else: a British centre of Christianity which, thanks to its position as well as its origins, was firmly-rooted and intact. The Old Church had already been there so long that nobody was sure who had built it. As Christian neophytes themselves – their king, Cenwalh, being a recent convert – the conquerors could not wreck Glastonbury or brush it aside. Here they found Celtic Christians whom they had to treat with respect. The Wessex kings, as its patrons, were almost forced into the novel experiment of an inter-racial community. Thus Glastonbury became a temple of reconciliation and the United Kingdom's symbolic birthplace.

Its character, plus geography again, helped it to survive during the Danish ravages. The Irish stayed on though few others did. When Dunstan's genius launched the revival of arts and learning, this was the community which he had to make his base. Again, in a different way, it stood alone. The special man and the special place found each other. Dunstan introduced another new factor, the Benedictine mode of life on the continental model. It helped to give his Abbey its outgoing, creative power.

Finally, owing to the meeting of peoples and influences, Glastonbury became the first spot in England where cultures blended and the Celtic Arthurian traditions found a footing. The advent of the Norman-French with their Breton associates brought in yet another new element. William of Malmesbury visited the Abbey, and unearthed its history and a little of Arthur's. Thereupon Caradoc of Llancarfan took up the tale, and Geoffrey of Monmouth set off the literary explosion. Geoffrey had no interest in Glastonbury himself, and romancers tended to lose sight of the place where the fuse was lit. But the Abbey's repatriation or adoption of Joseph and Arthur, feasible only because Glastonbury was what it was, gave it a continuing role.

Arguably then Glastonbury was the scene of such happenings partly because it carried on unbrokenly, partly because, at several junctures, its character produced a bringing-together which was unique as a stimulus. This may sound like de-mythologizing. I am not sure that it is. Advocates of the Unseen might refuse to accept that it could have occurred four times, in four different ways, by pure chance. They might urge that there are no complete answers on the level of normal history, normal psychology. We must resort to paranormal energies, good or evil or outside those categories; or we must think in terms of real, living Presences – gods, angels, spirits – active through the centuries to give Glastonbury a unique quality, if not by moulding its development, then at least by preventing other places from developing like it.

I feel bound to repeat that the impish multiple strangeness of the place – the recurrent just-*not*-working of explanations; the ambiguities and coincidences – will always leave an opening for such beliefs. Favourers of the Unseen have a title to respect, or anyhow to something better than ridicule. And I must suggest again that the 'strangeness' is a prime cause of the Glastonbury Madness, in the form in which it afflicts some scholars. They are thrown off balance by this place where the neat rational view always collides with facts which upset it, and, in doing so, encourage the romantics and mystics.

What about the romantics and mystics themselves, and what about the larger Madness? Behind it in its various versions there is always a tension, a disturbance, because at Glastonbury they too always find something that does not fit. Thus, many Christians have a special and powerful awareness of the place. But those who are committedly non-Catholic or anti-Catholic have to face the silent reproach of the ruins, the reminder that Glastonbury's great Christian establishment was always Catholic and never separated from Rome, and that it was killed by the very king who began the Reformation in England. The need to exorcize the spectre underlies the fantasies about Joseph or Jesus getting there first and founding a distinct British Church.

Christians who are not troubled in that way can still be unsettled, below the conscious threshold, by the feeling that Glastonbury is ... Other. The eerie Underworld notion is documented from St Collen through Weston's hill-climber in 1586, to the legends of chambers and tunnels in modern times. Moreover, the Arthurian revival since Tennyson has brought the Grail theme closer to Glastonbury than it was when the romances were written. In its offbeat, pagan-coloured Christianity the Something Else takes on a new life, and inspires unorthodox dreams, as John Cowper Powys's novel attests. Lastly, the weirdness of the landscape is palpable for those who have been conditioned by other landscapes. This may be the ultimate

Towards Sanity

secret of the spell, so far as it can be pinned down – the cause which enables everything else, however crazy, to work. But in relation to Christianity it can raise problems. The femininity of the hill-cluster is at odds with a male religion. Medieval Catholicism could neutralize the topographical factor, if it was felt then. It could retain the goddess while reducing her to Morgan, a mere chatelaine of the apple-island. More important, it could replace her worship with devotion to the Blessed Virgin, who, here as in many places, could assume the attributes of female divinities without ceasing to be herself. But the solution did not last. With the end of the Abbey the elements fell apart again.

Modern neo-mystics show the other side of the coin. They have been drawn by a convergence of causes: by the rebirth of interest in mythology and especially British mythology; by the ill-defined belief in a New Age, an Age of Aquarius; by a rejection of Christianity which is not the old atheism or humanism, but a search for an alternative spirituality, often with magical and occultish aspects. Here they can all catch glimpses of what they want. Glastonbury is a centre of British mythology. Its mythos includes the Grail, which is lost yet may be found, regenerating the Waste Land; and Arthur, the symbolic king who has gone, but will return and restore the golden age. Finally, because of the Grail and Celtic tradition, its Christianity can be regarded as different and perhaps not truly Christian at all, but an outgrowth from Druidism, the Zodiac cult, or other Mysteries of Britain.

For this group, nevertheless, the Christian element is a stumbling-block as the pagan element is for Christians. It is too tremendous to ignore altogether. They try to explain away Christianity in its orthodox form as a 'belief-system', with speculations betraying complete ignorance of it. They turn the Abbey into an exercise in sacred geometry related to megaliths. Above all they follow that intuition which may be prompted only by the spell-casting landscape, yet, in itself, is sound: they insist on Glastonbury being a pre-Christian sacred site. So indeed it appears to have been. However, too many of them are unable to handle the subject temperately or objectively. They feel such a need to prove the case, and cut down the Christian phase to an afterthought or even an error, that all things become acceptable – the Zodiac, ley-lines, fancies about Druids and Atlantis. It must be added (or rather reiterated) that some Glastonian zealots have it both ways, combining the Zodiac and the rest with fables about Joseph and a Christianity best described as Gnostic. The motive, I am afraid, is an eagerness to snatch at anything and everything if it will only minimize the Abbey.

Personally I believe in a rebirth. The Strong Magic is creative as well as demoralizing. If a rebirth is ever to happen, it cannot be forced. No one knows what form it should take, or (if we state the matter in terms of the Unseen) what it is that the presiding beings intend. Fay Weldon's warning holds. To try to exploit the energies is dangerous. The future must be allowed to unfold, and perhaps its logic will be plain without human effort. Recent years may have been witnessing a necessary negative prelude. The winds have blown away at least some of the nonsense, at least some of the delusion, at least some of the attempts of would-be gurus to domineer and dictate.

Neo-Druids, Goddess-worshippers and others are not all to be dismissed as serio-comic cranks. As I know, wise and well-disposed spirits are among them. Yet their outlook is surely partial. To be aware of Glastonbury with all it implies is to see an ampler prospect. The place has to be Christian – local instinct is right in that respect – but it could be the home of a more exploratory, adventurous, questing Christianity, nourished from many sources; a Christianity foreshadowed by the Celts and, in her own style, by Dion Fortune.

Today the road of Christian progress is widely assumed to lead in another direction. Theologians seek to demythologize, cutting out not only what is pre-Christian but a good deal of what is Christian too. The pruning process is meant to define a Highest Common Factor capable of uniting divided churches. To such a conception of the Faith, in the presence of the Tor and the Abbey, I can only reply: 'Not so, not so.' Part of the Avalonian destiny may be to remind the Church of a different way, a way of enrichment and development, acknowledging mystery, acclimatizing the mythic, absorbing wisdom from many traditions, interpreting Christian doctrines better in the light of them. That is how it often was in the Church's creative centuries. That is how it might be again. Better any number of quests, even if some are illusory, than the arid pretence that there is no quest at all.

APPENDIX

How to Thread the Tor Maze

These instructions are adapted from those in my booklet *The Glastonbury Tor Maze*, published in 1979 and re-issued with revisions in 1982. Some of the details must be regarded as provisional, because the National Trust carries out maintenance work and introduces improvements, which sometimes affect the way in which the course of the maze must be described. In 1980 the Trust's Tor Committee resolved that 'nothing should be done which would interfere with the maze features'. This amounted to a recognition that the theory should be taken seriously, though not, of course, to an endorsement of it. The resolution has been honoured. However, the 1979 booklet text has had to be modified here and there, not because I have seen any reason to reconsider the maze itself, but because a few of the landmarks have altered; and there can be no guarantee against further minor changes of the same kind.

The operation takes $2\frac{1}{2}$–3 hours, and is best attempted when the ground is reasonably dry.

Approach by Ascent Route A – that is, from the lower end of Well House Lane, just by its intersection with Chilkwell Street. As you come up via the field and stile to the bench, you will see terraces leading off on both sides. Note the marker stone with its smaller companion (a broken fragment?) immediately behind the bench. Go on up to the second marker stone, about seventy paces above. You are now on the level where you begin making circuits.

How to Thread the Tor Maze

Circuit (1)

Path III

Turn left at the upper stone, go over the little ridge and start along the path circling the Tor clockwise. Tend somewhat upwards, so that for a while you are walking close to the bank on your right, where the hillside rises above you more steeply. For the first few yards the terrace is indiscernible, but it soon appears as you come round the corner of the bank. The path can now be followed with adequate accuracy. Some way along, you need to go slightly downwards. Find the place by noting when you have a brown house on your left. Hereabouts a small trodden way should guide you obliquely leftward and forward, towards a place where the worn profile of your terrace just shows on the hillside in front of you. Head for it. Presently the terrace becomes well defined again, near a point where you can check your level by looking down to your left and seeing a large isolated bush on the terrace next below. Going along farther, you look down on a sapling enclosed in wire netting. Then, at the far end of the Tor, you reach Ascent Route B just below a manhole.

Now you are at the kink in the system, and must descend. Your terrace can be faintly seen beginning its downhill plunge beyond the manhole. For convenience you can go straight down and complete the crossing of Ascent Route B at the end of a wire fence among trees. Carry on diagonally downwards for another 15–20 yards, till you are aligned with the two gates of the field where people come up from the road. You are now on the correct terrace again, beyond its plunge. Swing round to the right and continue, with a bank dropping away on your left to the boundary hedge and fence.

Soon you pass just above a small wood. This wood has affected the configuration, and things are not perfectly clear. But the path turns slightly farther downwards (this is the other bend in the system), so that immediately after the wood you must descend a little way in order to proceed on the right terrace. You can check that you are on it by noting two broad and well-defined terraces farther down on your left. These are the two lowest, with Paths I and II on them, reappearing after their partial effacement among the trees and outside the boundary.

For some distance you are going along the stretch where Path III has its 'ghost-terraces' running parallel just above it. These *may* mark the course of early attempts at the same path, which were later replaced by the present one. Keep on round till you return to Ascent Route A, having circled the Tor once. You should now be a short distance above the upper marker stone, the point where you began the circuit.

Circuit (2)

Path II

Go down to the marker stone, and double back left along the terrace which is on a level with it (that is, the terrace immediately below the one you have just walked along). Circle the Tor counter-clockwise. There is now only one terrace below you on your right, a very wide one. As you get near the wood again, you pass close to the upper of two triangular enclosures. At the wood the terrace turns upwards and inwards. Human activity has confused the contours below the wood, but within it, while the effects of tree growth and erosion have wiped out the terrace, vestigial paths running up transversely still show roughly the course of the real path. Following these in whatever way is easiest, you will emerge at the upper fringe of the wood in a place where the terrace soon becomes clear again, in a patch of nettles. After that it runs along close to the boundary fence and, for a while, outside it. You can still see the terrace over the fence, but to avoid private property you must detour slightly by going along the inside.

You come to Ascent Route B at the wire fence mentioned

in circuit (1). To negotiate the kink, walk past it and climb a short way up. You can pick up the correct terrace again as the one immediately below III where you have already been; it runs four yards or so above the boundary hedge. You pass the sapling mentioned in circuit (1), being now on its level, and the isolated bush also mentioned. Presently there is a stretch where the path becomes indistinct in a weathered part of the hillside; it is not as easy to see when you are on it as it is from a distance. Bear somewhat to the left, and aim at the clearly visible point ahead where you are to go round the corner of the hill. A guiding landmark for this is the factory chimney in Street. Follow round and the terrace will become very well defined again. You return to Ascent Route A somewhat above the bench where the lower marker stone is, having circled the Tor twice.

Circuit (3)

Path I

Go down Ascent Route A past the bench, and double back to the right along the terrace leading off just below it. Circle the Tor clockwise. You are now on the lowest path, at the perimeter of the maze. It runs fairly near the hedge at the boundary and you can see the bank on your left dropping away to this. After a brief near-break where you should tend upwards, you come on to the outer edge of the wide strip of hillside on which Path II also runs, farther in. At the point where you are, the two terraces are not clearly distinguishable, but ahead you can see them separating again. Continue along the lower one, near the hedge, passing below the bush on II. When you approach Ascent Route B, a fence forces you inwards, off your terrace and on to II. Path I goes on into the fields and temporarily vanishes, or nearly so, having been worn away.

After crossing Ascent Route B at the steps, you are still compelled to detour, just inside the boundary fence and hedge, being on ground you have already covered going the opposite way. Over the hedge you can see a stretch of terrace in an orchard, which is the main width of II again. The terrace below that, which ideally you would be on, has almost disappeared owing to human activity. (Down in the fields and orchard, it is possible to pick out faint and uncertain traces of it, but they can hardly be detected from where you are.) Presently you get fully on to II, and then a vague contour of Path I, barely traceable with the eye, begins to reappear in the field below.

When you reach the wood you could get closest to Path I by scrambling down through it. However, it may be easier to keep on via the upper fringe of the wood and make your descent all at once after that, when you can end the enforced detour altogether. Towards the end of the wood you can look down and see Path I taking shape more clearly below in the field, its edge marked by a line of vegetation, which follows a very sharp apparent turn outwards and downwards. At the end of the wood, drop right down to the lowest terrace where it reappears fully, within the extended boundary. You are now back on Path I where you are meant to be, at the perimeter of the maze. Go between the triangular enclosures and past a cattle trough. Keep to the left, near the edge of the terrace, which is very wide. It brings you back to Ascent Route A close to the bench and lower marker stone. You have circled the Tor three times.

Circuit (4)

Path IV

Turn right and climb Ascent Route A, back to the upper marker stone. Go on upwards past it, ignoring the terrace on your right at its level, and the next one above; you have already been along both of them (beginning of II, end of III). Above the marker stone is a steep place, the end of the Tor's main ridge. Your next path leads off to the right of this. You can find it by following a way trodden in the grass, but care is needed because after the right-hand turn this gets on to a 'ghost' of III and would take you back on

How to Thread the Tor Maze

to it. So after going along it for about fifteen yards, leave it, forking left and slightly uphill. The true terrace is discernible. Go along circling the Tor counter-clockwise. Align yourself on the upper trees of the wood, which can be seen ahead. Presently you come to a steep and weathered area where the terrace vanishes. The path is reduced to a narrow and difficult ledge leading upwards, so that when you draw alongside the wood you are well above it. As you approach that point, your terrace reappears plainly. If you look ahead and down on your right, the next below is III, where you have already been. Following the terrace you are now on, you come round towards Ascent Route B with a bank rising on your left having a row of small trees along the top of it.

Here again is the kink. Go up transversely to the manhole on Ascent Route B. Continue along the terrace immediately above it. You will see two terraces below on your right; these, with the concealed one down by the hedge (which eventually comes into view also), are the three you have already been along. Your present path is not always distinct – like part of II, it is easier to see from a distance – but again you can align yourself on a point ahead: the top of the steep bank which you passed at the bottom on the first circuit of all.

When you draw alongside the brown house mentioned in the instructions for that first circuit, you are at the place where Path III goes slightly downwards. Here, IV nearly blends with it. More confusion may be caused by a short 'ghost-terrace' which seems to slant downwards from your left. It may be the result of an error during construction. Or it could be a later ramp joining terraces, if they were ever used agriculturally as happened in the 'Tor Linches' area (page 159). At any rate, incline left here. The contour of the bend can be faintly seen when the light is right. Work your way upwards to the top of the bank which is expanding ahead of you. Path IV is represented only vestigially along the brink, but soon the terrace takes shape again. Keep close to the edge and you will reach Ascent Route A near the top of the steep place above the upper marker stone. You have circled the Tor four times.

Circuit (5)

Path VII

You are now a little way below another bench, on the ridge, the higher part of Ascent Route A. Climb up to the bench and past it. Ten yards above it, halt and look upwards to your left. You will see the highest path of all, VII, running along the side of the ridge not far below the tower. Theoretically you should now go along this. If you walk up Ascent Route A a bit farther again, you can in fact start along it, and at first its terrace is well defined. But it peters out, because the highest stretch is weathered into virtual flatness. The hillside up there is steep, and difficult to traverse with no proper foothold.

You may prefer to avoid the difficulty by omitting VII on the north face and making a detour along the path next below it, VI, which can also be plainly seen from where you stand at the moment. You are at the correct level to get on to it. In the immediate neighbourhood of Ascent Route A on that side, Paths IV, V and VI are close together and barely distinguishable; individual terraces would be impracticable here because of the way the hill levels off. But they spread far apart as they go along the north face. If you decide to make the detour, turn left along VI and circle the Tor clockwise. As you go, you can look up to your right and see the terrace of VII running above you for some distance. You come round to Ascent Route B some yards above a bench, which is down a steep slope.

To revert, however, to VII's starting-point on Ascent Route A: if you prefer not to make the detour along VI, and would rather persevere with VII as you theoretically should, go up and along it. Beyond the place where its terrace peters out, faint traces of the path do seem to continue. The probability is that it leads very gradually downwards, converging with VI below and almost merging with it as you come to Ascent Route B.

How to Thread the Tor Maze

By whichever route you have reached this point, descend the steep slope to the bench, tending towards your right. This – somewhat conjecturally – is the kink for VII. Beside the bench, leading off clockwise, is a narrow but clear footpath which becomes recognizably VII again. Go along it as it winds upwards. Part of it is very steep, and steps have been made. These bring you to the top by the tower, the presumed centre of the maze. Formerly Path VII almost certainly climbed at a gentler angle and came round to Ascent Route A, lower down. At any rate you must not go to the centre yet. Continue to the left, to the last and topmost part of Ascent Route A, the final approach. You have circled the Tor five times.

Circuit (6)

Path VI

Turn left away from the tower, and go down Ascent Route A, keeping towards the left (south) side of the ridge and ignoring a better-trodden way on your right. You come to a short stretch where you descend more steeply. Go on down the next and more gradual descent till you are approaching the brink of another sharper slope. Double back left along the path at that level, and circle the Tor counter-clockwise. You can get your bearings from a large exposed area of rock and sandy soil which the path passes immediately above. The path is worn, but some of it is quite well defined, with traces of the terrace. As you approach Ascent Route B you pass above the line of trees mentioned in circuit (4).

Once more the kink. This is the most drastic instance of it. You should go up transversely to the neighbourhood of the bench. When you reach it, climb on up the steep bit above it, tending towards your right, till you get on to the terrace next above – which you may already have used as an expedient if you made the detour in the other direction in circuit (5). Whether you did or not, this is Path VI where you are now meant to be. Turn along it and continue. You return to Ascent Route A ten yards above the bench on the ridge, having circled the Tor six times.

Circuit (7)

Path V

Turn right, go down Ascent Route A till you are level with the bench, and double back to the right along the path which leads off there. At this point it is not clearly distinguishable from its neighbours, for the reason stated in circuit (5); but it can be seen on the hillside ahead where they spread apart, well below VI and VII, and above IV. Circle the Tor clockwise. You reach Ascent Route B near the bench, with your terrace bending down to the left of it.

Pass the bench, keeping it on your right, and go down. This is the kink again, here easily seen over a good deal of its length. The downward curve of your terrace carries you towards the terrace which has the row of trees on it. As stated (page 163), this runs too far to your left for a satisfactory junction, but the apparent overshooting may be later work: this is the area called 'Tor Linches' on the 1844 map. Path V can in fact be followed round fairly convincingly to a junction with its continuing terrace, towards the right-hand end of the row of trees. The terrace goes on clockwise, passing high above the wood, and then abruptly loses itself among nettles and bushes.

Pressing on a short distance, you come to a tree, a large round stone, and the bottom of the exposed area seen from above in circuit (6). This is the place discussed on pages 170–1, where it might be thought that the maze-spiral unexpectedly ends, and may once have turned inwards into a final subterranean passage, real or imaginary. Farther on is a steep incline with no visible way. Arguably the path resumes after a fashion, going round very doubtfully to the ridge and Ascent Route A again.

On present knowledge it is impossible to be certain what

How to Thread the Tor Maze

happens here. You may prefer to complete the maze-threading by clambering straight up through the exposed area. At the top of it, proceed to Ascent Route A where it runs on the highest part of the ridge. If you do attempt the dubious continuation of V, you will emerge on the ridge lower down. In either case you have circled the Tor seven times. Turn right and walk up along the ridge to the tower.

Notes

References are given here by short headings only. The full title of each work will be found in the Bibliography, under that heading. When two editions of a work are mentioned, the reference is to the more recent. When a heading only is given, without more exact specification by a page number or otherwise, the work is a general *passim* source for that topic.

Chapter One: The Extraordinary Place

Glastonbury in general: Ashe (4), art. 'Glastonbury', and (5); Ditmas (2); Greed; Mathias.
Fay Weldon: *Observer*, 17 February 1980.

Chapter Two: Beginnings in Half-Light

Early community and Old Church: Ashe (5), 35–6, 164–5; Dunning, 19; Finberg (1), 83–6, and (2), 346; Gildas, chapter 28; Stubbs, 6–7; Treharne, 25, 127; William of Malmesbury (1), 21–3.
Earlier Christian presence: Ashe (6), 41, 175–6; Dunning, 2 end; Gildas, chapters 7–8; Loomis (2), 250, 257; Scott, 25, 27; Treharne, 34–7, 128–9; William of Malmesbury (1), 21–3, and (2).
Lake-villages: Treharne, 13–21.
Tor and neighbourhood: Alcock, 251–2; Ashe (5), 279–80, and (8); Baring-Gould and Fisher, vol. 2, art. 'Collen'; *Central Somerset Gazette*, 21 August 1964; Ditmas (1); Fortune, 70; National Trust booklet; *Perlesvaus*, 204; Rahtz in Ashe (7), 111–22, and see also *Archaeological Journal*, vol. 127.
Arthurian question: Alcock, chapters 1–4; Ashe (1), and (6), 103–37; Morris, chapters 1–7.
Early Saxon phase: Ashe (6), 174–7; Robinson (1), 35.
Irish and cultural fusion: Chadwick, 174; Ekwall, art. 'Beckery'; Finberg (2); Loomis (2), 22; Mathias, 22–4, 34; Slover (1) and (2).

Avalonian Quest

Chapter Three: Beginnings in Daylight

Dunstan: Ashe (5), 152–62; Dunning, 19–20; Jerrold, 320; Knowles, 31–56; Robinson (2); Stubbs.

Arthurian Legend: Chambers, 16–19, 84–5; Geoffrey of Monmouth, 9–31 (Thorpe's Introduction); Loomis (1), chapters 1–11; Tatlock, 423.

Chapter Four: Joseph and Arthur

Legends and 'official' view of them: Dunning, 1–2; Gransden; Robinson (3); Scott; Treharne, chapters 6 and 7; William of Malmesbury (2).

Old Church's reinforcement: Robinson (3), 54.

Joseph: Lagorio, 213–17; Loomis (1), 254; Treharne, 98.

Gerald's demon anecdote: Chambers, 108.

Exhumation: Chambers, 112–14, 268–74; Treharne, 93–7.

Arthur's previous non-connection with Glastonbury: Treharne, 91–2, 106–7; his connection (Caradoc), Loomis (1), 18, 53.

Amesbury and Bamburgh: Ashe (4), arts. 'Amesbury', 'Bamburgh', 'Joyous Gard'; Morris, 100, 231.

No rival Avalon: Treharne, 9.

Contents of grave: Alcock, 76; Treharne, 102–3.

Modern work on site: Radford in Ashe (7), 97–110; *The Times* and *Central Somerset Gazette*, 16 August 1963.

Scholars' views on grave: Alcock, 75–6, 79–80; Markale, 69.

Cross and inscription: Alcock, 76–9; Dunning, 2; Treharne, 103–4, 112.

Latinization of 'Arthur': Alcock, 73; Chambers, 238–67.

Slaughter Bridge: Alcock, 164–5; Ashe (4), 187–91.

Fate of cross: Robinson (3), 59.

Chapter Five: The Saint, the Grail and the Thorn

Supposed annexation of Joseph by Glastonbury: Loomis (2), 258–9; Robinson (3), 39–40; Treharne, 98.

Grail and background: Cavendish, chapter 3; Graves (2), 105–8; Loomis (1), 15–16, and (2); Matthews, John; Rees, 42, 45; Williams, Charles, 78–9; Williamson, 54–7, 93.

Glastonbury indications in Grail matter: Cavendish, 178–83; Loomis (1), 285–6, and (2), 97–8, 251–2, 257, 276; *Perlesvaus*, 265; Slover (2), 272. With the Abbey of Glays, there is a

Notes

textual uncertainty, but nothing that gets rid of the significant 'Scotland'.
Origins of Joseph as hero, and possible historical antecedents: Ashe (5), 51, and (6), 31, 40–1; Cavendish, 153–4; Lagorio, 214–15, 230–1; Loomis (1), 287–90, and (2), 229–48; Mathias, 9; Robinson (3), 36; Treharne, 119–20.
Abbey's adaptation of legend and its implications: Jerrold, 428n; Lagorio, 217–30; Treharne, 114–18.
Melkin: Ashe (8); Loomis (2), 260–1; Matthews, John, 17–20, 92–4.
Thorn: Robinson (3), 45; Vickery.
Nanteos cup: Ashe (4), art. 'Nanteos'; *Pendragon*, 2.
Visit of Christ: Lewis, 80, 162–3, 167–8.

Chapter Six: Resurrection?

Abbey history and architecture: Ashe (5), chapters 6, 8, 9, 10; Radford (2).
Prophecy of rebirth: Ashe (5), 295; Mathias, 36–8. The prophecy is mentioned by Christopher Hollis in *Glastonbury and England*, but its source is obscure.
'Old British Church' theory: Jowett; Lewis.
Modern developments and projects: Mathias, 38, 40, 41–4; Nagel.
Bligh Bond: Bond; Fortune, 83–7; Mathias, 28, 39–41.
Rutland Boughton: Hurd; Mathias, 38–9.
Powys: *Observer*, 18 January 1981.

Chapter Seven: Way-Out

Theories in general: Roberts; Williams, Mary. For an individual one, see Gennaro.
Dion Fortune: Bromage; Fortune (the quotations from *Avalon of the Heart* are from pages 73, 107, 108–9); *Man, Myth and Magic*, art. 'Dion Fortune'.
Druids and oaks: Lewis, 30; Mathias, 36.
Chalice Well: *Chalice Well* booklet; Ekwall, first art. 'Chalk'; Fortune, 73–4; Mathias, 25–7; Roberts, 20–2.
Zodiac: Caine; *Central Somerset Gazette*, 28 April 1977; Crump; Jung; Maltwood; Mathias, 28–31, 39; Reiser, part 1; Roberts, 18, 36, 124–8; Williams, Mary, 8–12.

Avalonian Quest

Ley-lines: Devereux, chapters 1, 2 (Michael Line, 36–7); Hitching, 74–80; Roberts, 25, 173.
Sacred geometry: Mathias, 28; Michell; Williams, Mary, 31–5.
Friese-Greene: *Central Somerset Gazette*, 29 May 1964.

Chapter Eight: A Remoter Background

Possible pre-Christian site: Ashe (5), 22; Mathias, 25; Radford (2), 4–6.
Etymology: Chambers, 123; Ekwall, art. 'Glastonbury'; Finberg (1), 91–4; Slover (1), 148.
Ile de Voirre: Loomis (1), 67.
Collen: Baring-Gould and Fisher, vol. 2, art. 'Collen'; Ditmas (2), 5.
Weston: Ashe (5), 279–80.
Underground chambers: Roberts, 134–8.
Mary cultus in Old Church: Gildas, chapter 28; Souter, under *genetrix* and *mater*; Stubbs, 6–7.
Mary as successor of goddesses: James, 212–13.
Celtic water-deities: Ross, 84, 125, 245–8, 275, 279, 455.
Morgan and Avalon: Cavendish, 118–19; Chambers, 49, 121–2, 272, 273; Graves (2), 110; Loomis (1), 67, 163, and (2), 22, 24, 160–1; Treharne, 96.
Feminine aspects of Grail: Matthews, John, 14–17, 66.
Guinevere as mythic character: Rees, 284.

Chapter Nine: The Terraced Track

Maze theory: Ashe (3), and (5), 27; *Central Somerset Gazette*, 6 July 1973; Ditmas (1), 17–19; Fortune, 97; Glastonbury Conservation Society Newsletter, October 1980, January and April 1981; Mathias, 31–3; National Trust booklet, 6–7; Rahtz in Ashe (7), 114; Reiser, 47–51; Russell in Williams, Mary, 16–19; Saward, 24–5.
Caer Sidi, Caer Wydr: Graves (2), 90, 100, 108.
Background of theory: Hadingham, 98–103; Matthews, W. H., 44–6, 92–4, 157–60, 184; Purce, 111, 113; Saward, 19–20, 23.
Stones on Tor: Roberts, 25.

Chapter Ten: A Notable Temple

Underworld aspects of labyrinth: Ashe (2), 82–3, 90; Graves (1),

Notes

vol. 1, 318; *Man, Myth and Magic*, art. 'Maze'; Matthews, W. H., 23–8; Santillana, 290. Virgil's description of the Cumae temple is in *Aeneid* VI, lines 14–33.
Goddess figurines: Gimbutas, 124–31.
Hecataeus: Diodorus, vol. 2, 36–41; Hawkins, 164–7, 197; Piggott, 42, 80, 105; Rutherford, 133–4.
Apollo and British counterpart: Dodds, 161–2, n.36; Graves (1), vol. 1, 57; Ross, 270, 276–7, 293, 453–4, 458, 463–6.

Chapter Eleven: Ariadne's Dance

Tablets from Cnossus and Pylos: Gimbutas, 124–5, 131.
Labyrinth: Ashe (2), 85–8; Graves (1), vol. 1, 297–8, 339, 342–6; Hadingham, 100; Hitching, 154; Matthews, W. H., 6–23, 44–6, 52.
Significance of labyrinth and labyrinthine dance: Ashe (2), 87–8; Hooke, 41–2; *Man, Myth and Magic*, art. 'Dance', especially 595; Matthews, W. H., 66–9, 160–1.
Trojan connection: Graves (1), vol. 1, 297–8, 346; Hadingham, 100–1; Matthews, W. H., 52, 92–4, 150–1, 156–60.
Various instances of pattern: Gimbutas, 131; Graves (1), vol. 1, 346; Hadingham, 98–9, 101–3; Matthews, W. H., 92–4; Saward, 19, 23. Purce (98, fig. 8) gives an instance from an Indian manuscript. This is comparatively late and cannot be proved independent of British influence – a clear possibility in view of the British 'Troy' mazes.
Northern mazes: Matthews, W. H., 147–51.
Goddess and labyrinth: Gimbutas, 124–5; Graves (1), vol. 1, 297, 299–303.
Apollo and labyrinth: Graves (1), vol. 1, 342.
Maze in America: Matthews, W. H., 153–4; Waters, 29–31.
Maze-threading: Sjöö.
Psychological aspects: Jung; Russell in Williams, Mary, 16.

Chapter Twelve: A Point of Origin?

Boreas: Bolton, 115–16.
Hyperboreans, their character and location: Ashe (2), 99–102, 131–2, 145; Bolton, especially 2–4, 7, 8, 74–6, 93–6, 98–101, 114, 116, 118, 141; Graves (1), vol. 2, 110–12; Piggott, 79–81. The citations of Herodotus' *History* are from II.33, III.116, and IV.13–14, 26–7, 32–6 and 48–9.

Avalonian Quest

Apollo's Hyperborean connection: Dodds, 161–2, n.36; Guthrie, 74–80.

Greek philosophical connection: Ashe (2), 170; Bolton, 142–74; Piggott, 81–2, 86–7, 101–4.

Shamanism and background of Apollo, and magical character of seven: Ashe (2), 34, 80, 91; Dodds, 139–50; Eliade, 122, n.26, 152–3, 173, 200–1, 273–9, 388–9; Guthrie, 86n, 193–6, 204; Heissig, 36, 39, 45, 47; *Man, Myth and Magic*, art. 'Shaman'; Piggott, 82.

Shamanism and Druids: Eliade, 190–7; Piggott, 107–8, 159–64; Ross, 80, 83–4.

Mal'ta: Ashe (2), 147–8; James, 13–14; Purce, 100–1.

Shamanism in America, and bear cult: Ashe (2), 140–2, 146; Dodds, 166, n.61, 168, n.75; Eliade, chapter 9; Piggott, 160.

Hopi sevens: Waters, 3, 177, 183, 193.

Goddesses in shamanism: Ashe (2), 145–6; Eliade, 10, 42, 81; Heissig, 102.

Underworld in shamanism: Eliade, 172–3, 200–4, 259.

Chapter Thirteen: Sacred Mountains

Cosmic centre or sacred mountain and its representation: Ashe (2), 75–81, 94–7, 125; Eliade, 134, 264, 266–9, 492; Fortune, 97; Hooke, 66; Kramer, 139; *Man, Myth and Magic*, art. 'Mountain'; Santillana, 221; Wales, 7–10, 12, 88, 158–60, 170.

Astronomical heptad: Ashe (2), 103–26.

Meru: Ashe (2), 95–6, 125; *Central Somerset Gazette*, 6 July 1973; *Man, Myth and Magic*, art. 'Symbolism', see 2758; Santillana, 221, 301; Wales, 158–60, 170. The *Mahabharata* texts are VI.vi.10, 12, 20–31.

Mountain in Islam: Asin, 114–25; Hooke, 70. In Dante, see *Purgatorio* in general, and specifically XXV.131–2, XXVIII, XXX.1.

Java and Bali: Eliade, 267; Wales, 123, 127–8.

Northern cult of sky-centre, sacred mountains especially Altai, and the number seven: Ashe (2), 144; Bolton, 97–100; Eliade, 9, 169, 260–1, 266, 273–9, 406; Heissig, 48–9, 102–10; Roerich (1), 35, 37–8, 112, 289, 306, 314, 349, and (3), 45, 140; Santillana, 123–4. The *Mahabharata* texts are VI.vi.10, VI.vii. 2–14, 26–8, and XVII.ii.1–2.

Ursa Major: Heissig, 46, 81–4; Roerich (1), 41, 303–4, and (3), 140; Santillana, 128, 383–4.

Notes

Shambhala: Ashe (2), 151–5; Hitching, 239–41; Jenkins, 39–40, 158; Roerich (1), 15, 35, 37–8, 49, 110–11, 143, 256, 337–8, 353–4, 359–62, 372, 396, 406, (2), 13, 21, 28, 50–1, 71, 73, 78–9, 81–7, 104, 108–10, 118–23, and (3), 2, 12, 45, 294; Tomas.

Chapter Fourteen: Towards Sanity

Avalon quotation: Robinson (3), 16–17.
'Mary' in Grail mythos: Matthews, John, 14–17.

Bibliography

Alcock, Leslie, *Arthur's Britain* (Allen Lane, The Penguin Press, 1971).
Ashe, Geoffrey:
  (1) 'A Certain Very Ancient Book', *Speculum*, April 1981, p. 301–23 (The Medieval Academy of America, Cambridge, Massachusetts).
  (2) *The Ancient Wisdom* (Macmillan, 1977; Abacus, 1979 – page references are to the latter).
  (3) *The Glastonbury Tor Maze* (Glastonbury, 1979; revised edition, Gothic Image, Glastonbury, 1982).
  (4) *A Guidebook to Arthurian Britain* (Longman, 1980).
  (5) *King Arthur's Avalon* (Collins, 1957; Fontana, 1973 – page references are to the latter).
  (6) *Kings and Queens of Early Britain* (Methuen, 1982).
  (7) ed., *The Quest for Arthur's Britain* (Pall Mall, 1968; Paladin, 1971 – page references are to the latter).
  (8) 'The Unknown Holy Place', *Torc*, Autumn 1974 and March 1975 (privately published magazine, Glastonbury).
Asin, Miguel, *Islam and the Divine Comedy*, translated by Harold Sunderland (John Murray, 1926).
Baring-Gould, S., and Fisher, John, *The Lives of the British Saints*, 4 vols. (Cymmrodorion Society, London, 1907, etc.).
Bolton, J. D. P., *Aristeas of Proconnesus* (Oxford, Clarendon Press, 1962).
Bond, Frederick Bligh, *The Gate of Remembrance* (1918; re-issue, Thorsons, Wellingborough, 1978).
Bromage, Bernard, 'Dion Fortune', *Light*, Spring 1960 (College of Psychic Science, London).
Caine, Mary, *The Glastonbury Zodiac* (Grael Communications, Torquay, 1978).
Cavendish, Richard, *King Arthur and the Grail* (Weidenfeld and Nicolson, 1978).
Central Somerset Gazette, Wells: issues dated 16 August 1963 (Radford's excavations), 29 May 1964 (Friese-Greene's univer-

Bibliography

sity plan), 21 August 1964 (queries regarding Tor), 6 July 1973 (Russell and maze), 28 April 1977 (correspondence regarding Zodiac theory).

Chadwick, N. K., *Early Brittany* (University of Wales Press, Cardiff, 1969).

Chalice Well (introductory booklet: Chalice Well Trust, Glastonbury; revised edition, 1972).

Chambers, E. K., *Arthur of Britain* (Sidgwick and Jackson, 1972; reissue, 1966).

Crump, Barbara, *The Round Table of the Gods* (privately published, n.d.).

Devereux, Paul, and Thomson, Ian, *The Ley Hunter's Companion* (Thames and Hudson, 1979).

Diodorus Siculus, *The Library*, translated by C. H. Oldfather and others, 10 vols. (Loeb Classical Library, London, 1933, etc.).

Ditmas, E. M. R.:
(1) *Glastonbury Tor: Fact and Legend*, West Country Folklore Series No. 16 (Toucan Press, Guernsey, 1981).
(2) *Traditions and Legends of Glastonbury*, West Country Folklore Series No. 14 (Toucan Press, Guernsey, 1979).

Dodds, E. R., *The Greeks and the Irrational* (University of California Press, 1953).

Dunning, Robert W., ed., *Christianity in Somerset* (Somerset County Council, 1976).

Ekwall, Eilert, *The Concise Oxford Dictionary of English Place-Names* (Oxford University Press, 1936; revised edition, 1959).

Eliade, Mircea, *Shamanism* (Routledge and Kegan Paul, 1964).

Finberg, H. P. R.:
(1) *Lucerna* (Macmillan, 1964).
(2) 'St Patrick at Glastonbury', *Irish Ecclesiastical Record*, June 1967.

Fortune, Dion, *Avalon of the Heart* (1934; reissue, Aquarian Press, 1971).

Gennaro, Gino, *The Phenomena of Avalon* (Cronos, 1979).

Geoffrey of Monmouth, *The History of the Kings of Britain*, translated by Lewis Thorpe (Penguin, 1966).

Gildas, edited and translated under the title *The Ruin of Britain* by Michael Winterbottom, in *History from the Sources*, vol. 7 (Phillimore, Chichester, 1978).

Gimbutas, Marija, *The Gods and Goddesses of Old Europe* (Thames and Hudson, 1974).

Glastonbury Conservation Society Newsletter, October 1980, January and April 1981.
Gransden, Antonia, 'The Growth of the Glastonbury Traditions and Legends in the Twelfth Century', *Journal of Ecclesiastical History*, October 1976, pp. 337–58.
Graves, Robert:
  (1) *The Greek Myths*, 2 vols. (revised edition, Penguin, 1960).
  (2) *The White Goddess* (amended and enlarged edition, Faber, 1952).
Greed, John A., *Glastonbury Tales* (St Trillo, Bristol, 1975).
Guthrie, W. K. C., *The Greeks and their Gods* (Methuen, 1950).
Hadingham, Evan, *Ancient Carvings in Britain: a Mystery* (Garnstone, 1974).
Hawkins, Gerald S., *Stonehenge Decoded* (Fontana/Collins, 1970).
Heissig, Walter, *The Religions of Mongolia*, translated by Geoffrey Samuel (Routledge and Kegan Paul, 1980).
Hitching, Francis, *The World Atlas of Mysteries* (Collins, 1978; Pan Books, 1979).
Hooke, S. H., ed., *The Labyrinth* (SPCK, 1935).
Hurd, Michael, *Immortal Hour* (Routledge and Kegan Paul, 1962).
James, E. O., *The Cult of the Mother-Goddess* (Thames and Hudson, 1959).
Jenkins, Stephen, *The Undiscovered Country* (Neville Spearman, 1977).
Jerrold, Douglas, *An Introduction to the History of England* (Collins, 1949).
Jowett, George F., *The Drama of the Lost Disciples* (Covenant, 1961).
Jung, C. G., 'Concerning Mandala Symbolism', in *Collected Works*, vol. 9, part 1, translated by R. F. C. Hull (Routledge and Kegan Paul, 1971).
Knowles, David, *The Monastic Order in England* (Cambridge University Press, 1950).
Kramer, S. N., *History Begins at Sumer* (Thames and Hudson, 1958).
Lagorio, Valerie M., 'The Evolving Legend of St Joseph of Glastonbury', *Speculum*, April 1971, pp. 209–31 (The Medieval Academy of America, Cambridge, Massachusetts).
Lewis, Lionel Smithett, *St Joseph of Arimathea at Glastonbury* (1922; revised edition, James Clarke, Cambridge, 1976).

Bibliography

Loomis, Roger Sherman:
(1) ed., *Arthurian Literature in the Middle Ages* (Oxford, Clarendon Press, 1959; reprint with corrections, 1979).
(2) *The Grail: from Celtic Myth to Christian Symbol* (University of Wales Press, Cardiff, 1963).
Maltwood, K. E., *A Guide to Glastonbury's Temple of the Stars* (1935; reissue, James Clarke, Cambridge, 1964).
Man, Myth and Magic, ed., Richard Cavendish, 7 vols. (BPC Publishing Ltd, 1970–2).
Markale, Jean, *King Arthur: King of Kings*, translated by Christine Hauch (Gordon and Cremonesi, 1977).
Mathias, Michael, and Hector, Derek, *Glastonbury* (David and Charles, Newton Abbot, 1979).
Matthews, John, *The Grail: Quest for the Eternal* (Thames and Hudson, 1981).
Matthews, W. H., *Mazes and Labyrinths* (1922; reissue, Dover, New York, 1970).
Michell, John, *City of Revelation* (Garnstone, 1972).
Morris, John, *The Age of Arthur* (Weidenfeld and Nicolson, 1973).
Nagel, Jim, *Toward a New Abbey of Glastonbury* (Green Trust, Glastonbury, n.d.).
National Trust, *Glastonbury Tor* (booklet, n.d.).
Observer, issues of 17 February 1980 (interview with Fay Weldon) and 18 January 1981 (Naomi Lewis on John Cowper Powys).
Pendragon, Summer 1981 (Pendragon Society, Bristol).
Perlesvaus, translated by Nigel Bryant (D. S. Brewer, Cambridge, 1978). Also known in Sebastian Evans's version as *The High History of the Holy Graal* (Dent, 1910; reissue, James Clarke, Cambridge, 1969).
Piggott, Stuart, *The Druids* (Thames and Hudson, 1968; Penguin, 1974 – page references are to the latter).
Purce, Jill, *The Mystic Spiral* (Thames and Hudson, 1974).
Radford, C. A. Ralegh:
(1) 'Glastonbury Abbey', in Ashe (7), q.v.
(2) *Glastonbury Abbey: the Isle of Avalon* (Pitkin, 1976).
Rahtz, Philip, 'Glastonbury Tor', in Ashe (7), q.v.
Rees, Alwyn and Brinley, *Celtic Heritage* (Thames and Hudson, 1961).
Reiser, Oliver L., *This Holyest Erthe* (Perennial Books, 1974).
Roberts, Anthony, ed., *Glastonbury: Ancient Avalon, New*

Jerusalem (Zodiac House, 1977; revised edition, Rider, 1978).
Robinson, Joseph Armitage:
   (1) *Somerset Historical Essays* (British Academy, 1921).
   (2) *The Times of St Dunstan* (Oxford, Clarendon Press, 1923).
   (3) *Two Glastonbury Legends* (Cambridge University Press, 1926).
Roerich, Nicholas:
   (1) *Altai-Himalaya* (Jarrolds, 1930).
   (2) *Himalayas, Abode of Light* (David Marlowe, 1947).
   (3) *Shambhala* (Nicholas Roerich Museum, New York, 1978).
Ross, Anne, *Pagan Celtic Britain* (Routledge and Kegan Paul, 1967; Cardinal, 1974 – page references are to the latter).
Russell, Geoffrey, 'The Secret of the Grail', in Williams, Mary, q.v. See also *Central Somerset Gazette*, 6 July 1973.
Rutherford, Ward, *The Druids and their Heritage* (Gordon and Cremonesi, 1978).
Santillana, Giorgio de, and von Dechend, Hertha, *Hamlet's Mill* (Macmillan, 1970).
Saward, Jeff, *Caer Sidi* (privately published, 1979).
Scott, John, *The Early History of Glastonbury* (Boydell, Woodbridge, Suffolk, 1981: an analysis of William of Malmesbury's *De Antiquitate*).
Sjöö, Monica, 'Treading the Maze', *Wood and Water*, Candlemas 1981 (Swindon).
Slover, Clark H.:
   (1) 'Glastonbury Abbey and the Fusing of English Literary Culture', *Speculum*, April 1935, pp. 147–60 (The Medieval Academy of America, Cambridge, Massachusetts).
   (2) 'William of Malmesbury and the Irish', *Speculum*, July 1927, pp. 268–83 (as preceding).
Souter, Alexander, *A Glossary of Later Latin to 600 A.D.* (Oxford, Clarendon Press, 1949).
Stubbs, W., *Memorials of St Dunstan* (Rolls Series vol. 63, 1874).
Tatlock, J. S. P., *The Legendary History of Britain* (University of California Press, 1950).
Times, The, 16 August 1963 (Radford's excavations).
Tomas, Andrew, *Shambhala: Oasis of Light* (Sphere Books, 1977).
Treharne, R. F., *The Glastonbury Legends* (Cresset, 1967).
Vickery, A. R., *The Holy Thorn of Glastonbury*, West Country Folklore Series No. 12 (Toucan Press, Guernsey, 1979).

Bibliography

Wales, H. G. Quaritch, *The Mountain of God* (Bernard Quaritch, 1953).
Waters, Frank, *Book of the Hopi* (Ballantine, 1969).
William of Malmesbury:
  (1) *The Acts of the Kings of the English*, translated as *William of Malmesbury's Chronicle* by John Sharpe, revised by J. A. Giles (Bohn, 1847).
  (2) *De Antiquitate Glastoniensis Ecclesiae*, translated by Frank Lomax as *The Antiquities of Glastonbury* (Talbot, 1980). See also Scott.
Williams, Charles, *Arthurian Torso*, a fragment edited with discussion by C. S. Lewis (Oxford University Press, 1948).
Williams, Mary, ed., *Glastonbury, a Study in Patterns* (Research into Lost Knowledge Organization, London, 1969).
Williamson, Hugh Ross, *The Arrow and the Sword* (Faber, 1947).

Index

Abaris, 208–10, 212
Abbey, Glastonbury, see Glastonbury
Abbey Barn, 99, 129, 140
Acts of Pilate, 55, 77, 79
Adamski, George, 127
Adomnan, 72
Aethelwold, 46
Alchemy, 86
Alcock, Leslie, 35, 66, 69
Alfred the Great, 43
Altai, 205, 210–11, 213, 215, 216, 220, 234–9, 241–4
Ambrosius, 35–6, 47–8, 64
Amesbury, 64
Anchor Inn, 32, 105, 113, 117
Anglican Church, 14, 100, 104, 106, 108, 118
Anglo-Saxons, 21–2, 28, 33, 35, 37–9, 49, 63
Annales Cambriae, 36, 37, 73
Annwn, 78, 85, 138, 139, 148, 149, 156, 246
Anthemius, 35
Apollo, 172, 174, 175–8, 191–2, 203–4, 208, 209, 211–13, 215–16, 227, 238
Aquarian Age (New Age), 15, 127–8, 253
Ariadne, 183–4
Aristeas, 204–6, 210, 213, 235, 241
Artemis, 144, 176, 203, 206, 213, 219, 220, 228
Arthur: and Grail quest, 15, 78, 80, 103; his reputed grave, 15, 18, 31, 47, 58–75, 82, 88, 97, 133, 147, 247, 249; origins of his legend, 33–7, 46–53, 251; his name, 34, 71–2; prophecy of his return, 37, 47–8, 61–2, 109–10; modern Arthurian literature, 110–11; various mentions, 20, 30, 100, 107, 139, 142, 143, 146, 171, 203
Arthur of Argyll, 72
Arviragus, 84, 90, 103, 133
Assembly Rooms, Glastonbury, 107, 129
Athelstan, 43
Atlantis, 115, 119, 222, 254
Attenborough, David, 231–2
Avallach, 51, 146–7, 176, 177, 246
Avallon (Burgundy), 51, 73, 249
Avalon: as equivalent to Glastonbury, 14, 30, 58, 70–3, 79, 81, 82, 85, 116, 132, 136, 137, 147, 244, 246–7; as mythical or doubtful location, 15, 49, 51, 58, 65, 137, 146, 148, 176, 203, 246
Avebury, 118, 126, 156, 195, 240–1, 246, 247

Babylon, 223–5, 236
Badon, 36, 49
Bali, 232
Bamburgh, 64
Bear cults, 218–19
Beckery, 40, 60
Bede, 25, 47
Bedivere, 31, 49
Beecham, Sir Thomas, 107
Belukha, 238–44
Benedict, St, church of (formerly Benignus), 13, 40

Index

Benedictines and Benedictine Order, 44–6, 98, 105, 109, 146, 251
Benignus, St, 40
Beon, 39–40
Bere, Richard, 102
Blake, William, 15, 96
Blome, John, 86
Bond, Frederick Bligh, 106–7, 113, 117
Borobudur, 229–31, 236
Bosworth Psalter, 46
Boudicca (Boadicea), 25, 57, 83–4
Boughton, Rutland, 107–9, 114, 128
Brandsby, 181, 188–9, 190
Brigit, St, 40, 42, 145
Buckton, Alice, 117
Burrows, Ray, 19–20

Cadbury Castle ('Camelot'), 35, 52–3, 63, 74, 84, 90, 110–11, 132, 248, 249
Caerdroia, 181, 188, 190
Caer Sidi, 156
Caer Wydr, 156
Caine, Mary, 119–20
Cam, River, 74
Camden, William, 68–9, 71
Camel, River, 49, 74
Camelot, 35, 52, 53; see also Cadbury Castle
Camlann, 36, 51, 74, 147
Canterbury, 44, 46, 64
Caradoc of Llancarfan, 48, 50, 63, 133, 136, 137, 142, 148–9, 251
Caratacus, 87
Carew, Sir Peter, 100
Carley, James P., 86
Catholic Church, 104, 105, 108–9, 114–15, 252, 253
Celtic Christianity, 41–2, 78, 115, 147, 248
Cenwalh, 33, 38, 250
Ceridwen, 148
Chalice Hill, 13, 31, 32, 86, 99, 116, 139, 145, 159, 160, 194

Chalice Orchard, 31, 33, 113, 116
Chalice Well and earlier spring, 31, 32, 116–19, 127, 133, 135, 145–6, 168–9, 178, 194–5
Chancellor, Matthew, 117
Chesterton, G. K., 128
Chrétien de Troyes, 78, 137, 203, 246, 250
Christ, Jesus, 25, 54, 58, 76, 78–80, 85, 90, 96, 127, 141, 248, 252
Christianity: origins in Britain, 21–7; attitudes of modern neomystics, 112, 118, 128, 253
Church of England, see Anglican Church
Collen, St, 30, 138–9, 149, 157, 168–9, 171, 252
Columba, St, 40, 72
Conservation Society, Glastonbury, 129, 159
Constans, 29
Constantine the Great, 21
Constantine, pretender, 29
Constantine of Dumnonia, 132–3
Cretan spiral, 155, 161, 165–7, 171, 178, 180, 182, 190–3, 200–1, 215; see also Maze
Crump, Barbara, 119
Cumae, 170, 178, 187, 191, 216
Cunobelinus (Cymbeline), 90

Daedalus, 170, 182–6, 190, 192
Dances, 184–6, 191, 216
Danes, 43
Dante, 80, 148, 228, 231
David, St, 85, 141–2
David-Neel, Alexandra, 243
De Antiquitate Glastoniensis Ecclesiae (interpolated work by William of Malmesbury, q.v.), 24, 55–8, 76, 84, 87, 89, 91, 141
Dee, John, 100–1, 122–3
Delos, 184, 192, 203, 211, 216
Delphi, 203, 211, 213, 227, 238
Deruvianus, 57
Devereux, Paul, 125
Din Guayrdi, 64

282

Index

Diodorus Siculus, 172–3, 183
Dodds, E. R., 212, 219
Drayton, Michael, 101
Druids and modern Druid revivalists, 115–16, 118, 130, 153, 173–4, 185, 208–11, 214–15, 244, 248, 254; Druid oaks, 116
Dugdale, William, 153
Dunning, Robert, 26
Dunstan, St, 23, 44–6, 65, 67, 72, 101, 143, 251

Edmund, 44
Edward I, 60, 62
Edward III, 62
Edward VI, 100
Edward VII, 106
Eleutherius, Pope, 25
Elgar, Sir Edward, 107
Eliade, Mircea, 212, 236, 237
Elizabeth I, 100
Estoire del Saint Graal, 76–7, 79–80, 81, 83, 87
Etemenanki, 224, 226–7, 231
Etruscans, 180, 186–7, 190
Eyston, Charles, 93

Faganus, 57
Festivals, Glastonbury, 107–8, 127
Fielding, Henry, 14
Finberg, H. P. R., 29, 137
Findhorn community, 128
Fortune, Dion, 113–15, 116, 118, 119, 124–5, 128–9, 154, 166, 195, 222, 229, 254
Freeman, E. A., 131
Friese-Greene, Graham, 127

Galahad, 80, 148
Gandhi, 109–10
Gawain, 49
Geoffrey of Monmouth, 48–51, 58, 64, 70, 71, 74, 90, 146–7, 189, 203, 246, 251
George and Pilgrims Hotel, 99, 140

Gerald de Barri (Giraldus Cambrensis), 58–9, 68, 70, 71, 72, 74, 147
Gildas, 25, 28, 35, 46, 47, 48, 63, 142–3
Giraldus Cambrensis, see Gerald de Barri
Glastonbury: town, 13–20, 107, 117, 129; Abbey, origins and history, 13, 14, 15, 21–33, 43–6, 81, 82, 95, 98–102, 105–6, 108, 112, 126, 132, 140, 179, 248, 250, 253, 254; names, 14, 136–7, 246; lake-villages, 26–7, 66, 90, 132; Saxons' adoption of early community, 38–9, 250; Irish at, 39–42, 44, 72–3, 83, 251; role in cultural fusion, 38, 41; role in Arthurian legends, 46–8, 52–3, 58–75, 107–8, 133; role in Joseph legend, 54–8, 76–97; pre-Christian aspects, 86–7, 135–49, 156, 168, 247, 248, 250 (see also Maze); expectation of rebirth, 102, 109–10, 126, 129, 254; latitude and longitude, 239–40
Goddess-worship and goddesses, 15, 144–9, 169, 171–2, 177–8, 191–9, 217, 220–1, 246, 254
Godney, 27
Grail, 15, 30, 52, 57–8, 60, 76–88, 94–6, 103–4, 118, 130, 146, 148, 156, 199, 249–50, 252
Graves, Robert, 169, 197
Graves, Tom, 17
Guinevere, 48, 49, 59, 63, 68–9, 82, 148–9
Guthrie, W. K. C., 211–12, 216
Gwyn ap Nudd, 138–9

Hawkins, Gerald S., 173
Hecataeus, 172–8, 183, 191, 192, 202–4, 207–8, 240, 244, 245
Hengist, 33, 49
Henry II, 59, 61, 63, 64, 71
Henry VII, 110
Henry VIII, 35, 95, 99, 101, 138

283

Index

Hercules, 206
Herodotus, 205–9
High History of the Holy Graal, see *Perlesvaus*
Hollywood (Co. Wicklow), 181, 189–90
Homer, 176, 183–4
Hopi, 193–5, 200, 201, 217, 219–20
Hopkins, Gerard Manley, 104
Horner, John, 100
Horsa, 33, 49
Housman, Laurence, 108
Hughes, Chancellor, 75
Hume, Cardinal, 109
Hyperboreans, 172–3, 202–13, 215, 227, 235, 238, 241, 242, 244

Ine, 24, 38, 44
Isaiah, 225–6

Jackson, Kenneth, 70
James I, 93
James II, 123
James, Roger, 100
Janes, Kenneth, 108
Jardine, Ernest, 105–6
Java, 229, 232
Jenkins, Stephen, 243–4
Jerusalem, 79, 83, 88, 223–6
John the Baptist, St, church of, 13, 94
John of Glastonbury, 85, 96
Jones, Kathy, 196, 199, 232
Joseph of Arimathea, 14–15, 20, 21, 54–8, 76–97, 104–5, 118, 132–3, 141, 249, 251, 252, 254
Joseph, husband of the Virgin Mary, 94
Josephus, 88
Joyous Gard, 64
Jung, C. G., 113, 123–4, 157, 199–200
Juvenal, 84, 133

Kay, 49
Kennion, Bishop, 105–6
Knowles, David, 28, 46

Kurus, Northern, 205–6, 234–5

Labyrinth, 155, 169–70, 178, 180, 182–7, 191–2, 201, 216, 246; in Egypt, 183; see also Maze
Lady Chapel, 22, 67, 99, 140
Lagorio, Valerie, 87, 91
Lancelot, 30–2, 64, 80, 82, 116
Langport, 81
Lawrence, Derek J., 159
Lazarus, 92
Leland, John, 35, 52–3, 68, 71
Leto, 172, 176, 177
Levin, Bernard, 127
Lewis, L. S., 104–5, 108, 118
Ley-lines, 124–6, 127, 130, 133, 179, 240–1, 254
Llancarfan, 37, 48, 53, 70
London, 22, 122–3
Loomis, R. S., 64, 76–7, 79–80, 81–2, 88, 132
Lucian, 184
Lucius, 25, 57

Mahabharata, 205, 233–4
Mahoney, Derek, 75n
Malory, Sir Thomas, 31–2, 64
Mal'ta, 216–17, 220
Maltwood, Katharine, 119, 122, 135
Maponus (Maponos, Mabon), 177–8, 246, 248
Martin of Tours, St, 29
Mary, the Virgin, 23, 56, 60, 85, 91, 94, 96, 115, 141–5, 148, 248–9, 253
Mary Magdalene, 92
Mary (Queen), 100
Mathias, Michael, 129
Matriarchy Study Group, 195
Matrona, 148, 171, 177–8, 246; see also Modron
Matthews, John, 86
Maze on Tor, 154–7, 160–7, 170–1, 175, 195–9, 215, 222, 240, 244, 245, 249–50, 256–65; mazes elsewhere, 154–5, 169–72, 179–95

Index

Meare, 27, 39, 90, 99; Meare Pool, 14, 45
Meier, C. A., 200
Melkin, 85–7, 136, 246
Melor, St, 64
Melwas, 48, 133, 148
Merlin, 48, 49, 118, 146, 215
Meru, 227–9, 233–5
Meton, 174
Michael, St, 107, 139; church of, 14, 32, 126, 139, 240
Michell, John, 124, 126, 179
Milton, John, 210
Modred, 49
Modron, 148, 172, 177–8, 246, 248; see also Matrona
Monmouth, Duke of, 14, 123, 133
Morgan le Fay, 146–8, 177–8, 246, 249, 253
Morgan, R. W., 104
Mounsey, W. H., 188–9
Mountains, sacred, 222–9, 232–8
Murray, Muz, 127

Nanteos cup, 95–6
Naquane, 188, 190
National Trust, 14, 159, 162, 256
Nennius, 36–7, 51, 71, 73, 143
New Age, see Aquarian Age
Nichols, Ross, 116
Nostradamus, 122–3, 133

Old Church, 22–7, 29, 39, 44, 54, 61, 63, 76, 86, 89, 91, 133, 139, 141–5, 148, 248, 250
Ovid, 185–6

Parker, Archbishop, 104
Parzival, 80
Patrick, St, 22, 39, 40, 46, 57, 72, 89, 92, 101–2
Patrick Senior, 40, 46, 74
Paul, St, 55, 87, 104
Paulinus, 54
Perlesvaus (*The High History of the Holy Graal*), 30–1, 80, 81, 82, 116, 119, 122, 136, 148, 249
Peter, St, 55, 104
Philip, St, 25, 56–7, 91
Piggott, Stuart, 214–15, 218
Pilgrimages, 108–9
Pindar, 204, 206
Plaister, Alan, 220n
Plutarch, 184
Pole, Wellesley Tudor, 117
Pomparles Bridge, 60
Pompeii, 180, 182, 190
Pomponius Mela, 147
Ponter's Ball, 135–6
Powell family (Nanteos), 95
Powys, John Cowper, 108, 113, 117, 145, 252
Priddy, 96
Pylos, 180, 186, 190
Pythagoras, 208–13, 219

Radford, C. A. Ralegh, 66–8, 69, 107, 135, 145
Rahtz, Philip, 29–30, 40, 117, 156, 168, 175, 190, 240
Ralph of Coggeshall, 71, 74
Reid, R. D., 159
Reiser, Oliver L., 157
Rice, Edith, 19
Richard I, 15, 61, 62
Ringwode, Austin, 102, 109
Riothamus, 34–6, 50–1, 73, 249
Rishis, the Seven, 227, 237
Robert de Boron, 79, 81–2, 87, 148
Roberts, Anthony, 113
Robinson, J. Armitage, 33, 38, 55, 60, 106, 247, 249
Roerich, Nicholas, 238, 243
Ross, Anne, 213–14
Rousseau, J. J., 109
Russell, Geoffrey, 85, 154–8, 170, 199–200, 224, 229, 249–50
Rutherford, Ward, 173

Sacred geometry, 106, 126, 133, 179, 253

Index

St Michael's Mount, 126, 240
Santillana, Giorgio de, 236
Saxons, see Anglo-Saxons
Shamanism, 212–21, 235–8
Shambhala, 242–4
Shaw, George Bernard, 107
Silbury, 145, 156, 247
Sjöö, Monica, 196–8, 203
Slaughter Bridge, 74
Somerset, Duke of, 100
Spenser, Edmund, 110
Stonehenge, 118, 122, 123, 126, 156, 173, 176, 195, 247, 250
Strata Florida, 95
Sumerians, 119, 135, 185, 223–5, 233
Sumeru, 228, 232, 233, 236, 237

Taliesin, 146
Tancred, 62
Tasciovanus, 90
Tennyson, Alfred, 31, 94–5, 103–4, 203, 252
Tertullian, 25
Theseus, 182–4, 186, 190, 192
Thomas, Robert P., 200–1, 216
Thorn, Glastonbury, 93–4, 133
Thorne, John, 100
Tintagel, 49, 181, 189–90
Tor, Glastonbury: appearance and formation, 13–14, 131, 145, 198; 'aura' and psychological impact, 17, 18, 112, 127; early settlement, 29–32, 39, 118; Dion Fortune's views on, 115, 154, 222; neo-Druid ceremonies, 116; pre-Christian significance and 'hollow hill' motif, 135, 138–40, 149, 170, 242, 246, 250; terraces and maze, 153–71, 245, 256–65; Goddess motif, 194–9; as model of sacred mountain, 222–3, 238; various mentions, 86, 105, 179, 231, 240
Torc, 87n, 127
Treharne, R. F., 21, 26, 60–2, 65, 66, 68, 70, 76, 81, 89, 92

Trevelyan, Sir George, 128
Tribunal, 99
Trollope, Edward, 189
Troy, 186, 201; game, 180, 187–8; 'walls' or 'town', maze design, 181, 188–9, 220
Twelve Hides, 38, 98

UFOs, 15, 120, 125, 127
Underworld, 78, 138–40, 149, 169–71, 178, 185, 191, 194, 220–1, 246, 250, 252
Ursa Major, 219, 224–5, 227, 228, 237, 238

Vespasian, 79, 83, 88
Virgil, 170, 178, 187, 192, 216
Vortigern, 33, 47, 49

Walter, Archdeacon, 50
Waters, Frank, 193
Watkin, Fr Aelred, 17
Watkins, Alfred, 124–5
Wearyall Hill, 13, 26, 31, 40, 60, 89, 93, 94, 119, 145
Weldon, Fay, 18, 130, 134, 145, 254
Weston, Fr William, 32–3, 118, 139–40, 168, 252
White, T. H., 31, 110
Whiting, Richard, 100
William of Malmesbury, 23–6, 28, 39, 44, 47–8, 50, 54, 59, 63, 70, 71, 74, 86, 88, 133, 137, 141, 142, 251; *De Antiquitate Glastoniensis Ecclesiae* (interpolated text), 24, 55–8, 76, 84, 87, 89, 91, 141
Williams, Mary, 112
Wilson, Angus, 108
Wilson, Colin, 108
Windmill Hill, 13, 99
Wirral Hill, see Wearyall Hill
Wood, Sir Henry, 107
Worgret, 28
Wrekin Trust, 128, 157

Index

Xenophon, 173

Ynys-witrin, 14, 28, 56, 57, 136–7, 156, 203

Zodiac, Glastonbury, 119–24, 125, 127, 130, 133, 155, 178–9, 199, 245, 254